THE EXECUTION OF SHERLOCK HOLMES

Jaico Sherlock Holmes Series

THE EXECUTION OF SHERLOCK HOLMES

Jaico Sherlock Holmes Series

DONALD THOMAS

JAICO PUBLISHING HOUSE

Ahmedabad Bangalore Bhopal Chennai
Delhi Hyderabad Kolkata Lucknow Mumbai

Published by Jaico Publishing House
A-2 Jash Chambers, 7-A Sir Phirozshah Mehta Road
Fort, Mumbai - 400 001
jaicopub@jaicobooks.com
www.jaicobooks.com

Published in arrangement with
Pegasus Books LLC
80 Broad Street, 5th Floor
New York, NY 10004

To be sold only in India, Bangladesh, Bhutan,
Pakistan, Nepal, Sri Lanka and the Maldives.

THE EXECUTION OF SHERLOCK HOLMES
ISBN 978-81-8495-436-4

First Jaico Impression: 2013
Third Jaico Impression: 2014

Printed by
Trinity Academy For Corporate Training Limited, Mumbai

For my parents

JUSTIN MELVILLE GWYN THOMAS 1900–92

DORIS KATHLEEN THOMAS, *née* SERRELL, 1906–55

ACKNOWLEDGMENTS

I am most grateful for information kindly provided on Johann Ludwig Casper and Carl Liman by Ms. Helen D'Artillac Brill of the University of Cardiff and on respirators of World War I by Mr. Martin Boswell of the Imperial War Museum, London.

CONTENTS

1

THE EXECUTION OF SHERLOCK HOLMES

A PROLOGUE BY JOHN H. WATSON, M.D.

BEFORE SETTING OUT on my story, I must say something of the late Charles Augustus Milverton of Appledore Towers, Hampstead. Those of my readers who have read the story of that title may recall a little of what follows. Though dead for three years, the ghost of this scoundrel threatened greater harm to Sherlock Holmes than Professor Moriarty himself had done.

Charles Augustus Milverton! My friend called him the worst man in London, more repulsive than fifty murderers with whom we had dealings. A reptile, said Holmes, a slithery, gliding venomous creature with deadly eyes and an evil, flattened face. This king of blackmailers lived in luxury by bribing treacherous valets or the maidservants of men and women in a high position. The most virtuous soul need only be guilty of a trivial error of conduct, no more than a mere indiscretion. Once in Milverton's hands, a single thoughtless letter or even a note of two lines had been enough to ruin a noble family.

Once or twice his fame as a poisoner of reputations reached the columns of the sporting magazines. I recall Sherlock Holmes pointing out to me a couplet in *Turf Life in London.*

A viper bit Milverton—what was his plight?
The viper, not Milverton, died of the bite.

Such was our enemy. As Holmes remarked, that round smiling face concealed a heart of marble. Milverton squeezed his victims little by little, by holding a threat over them and a false promise before them.

One or two more payments and the poor wretches thought they would be safe. They never were. Only when no more was to be got, or in two cases when the victim retired to his dressing room carrying a revolver loaded with a single bullet, did this villain's prisoners gain their release.

Milverton's last extortion was to be £7,000 from Lady Eva Brackwell, shortly before her marriage to the Earl of Dovercourt. This was the price asked for several imprudent letters written by the young woman a year before. These were addressed to a country squire, ending a fond childhood friendship which had briefly blossomed into romance. Unfortunately for her, it was an easy matter to cut off or otherwise alter the date on some of these notes. The "warm friendship" was thus represented as continuing secretly long after her betrothal to Lord Dovercourt. A dishonest servant of the squire's, amply rewarded, placed the papers in Milverton's hands. Unless young Lady Eva paid the price, Milverton swore the Earl of Dovercourt would receive this correspondence a week before the wedding. He insisted to her ladyship that he always carried out his threats. To weaken would destroy his reputation and profession.

To any decent mind, the conduct of such a villain is so monstrous that there is a temptation to think it cannot be true of any man. From the evidence of my own eyes and ears, I know it to be true. I was present at our Baker Street rooms in January 1899, when Milverton adjusted his cravat with a plump little hand and said to Holmes in a voice like soft but rancid butter, "You may be assured, my dear sir, that if the money is not paid promptly by the fourteenth, there will certainly be no marriage on the eighteenth."

How supple and skillful a blackmailer is! How knowing in his choice of victims! Many a bridegroom might forgive a past flirtation, and Holmes suggested as much to our visitor. But Milverton was accustomed to choose his prey with care and to infuse his own peculiar venom into the falsehood and rumour that attended the cancellation of an engagement in high society. A year earlier Captain Alexander Dorking had defied him over jewellers' receipts and hotel bills relating to a long-dead liaison with a fast woman. Two days before the captain's wedding to the Honourable Miss Clementina Miles, an announcement in the *Morning Post* informed the world that the marriage would not, after all, take place. The bride's forgiveness of the groom was not enough to repair the damage caused by the incriminating documents. Milverton had also insinuated a tainted gossip into the clubs of Pall Mall so that it might reach the ears of the young lady's family and society in general. This hinted at a loathsome disease, contracted by the captain ten years earlier in an act of undergraduate folly. In January 1899, Lady Eva well knew the sort of tales that would circulate if she called Milverton's bluff. There could be no marriage to any man after that.

Sherlock Holmes had reluctantly agreed to act as intermediary on the young woman's behalf, offering the scoundrel her little fortune of £2,000. Milverton laughed in his face and would take nothing less than the £7,000 demanded. He suggested that her ladyship might easily raise an extra £5,000 by taking the family jewels inherited from her grandmother and exchanging them for imitations done in paste. Even had she done so, Holmes warned her that the reptile would return for more. So long as a penny remained in the victim's purse, there was never an end to blackmail. This was one of few occasions when Holmes and I resolved to do wrong in order that right should prevail. There could be no compromise. A viper's nest can be cleared in only one way.

A week later we set out for Hampstead on a blustery winter's night, carrying what Holmes called his "up-to-date burgling kit with every modern improvement which the march of civilization demands." We judged that Milverton would be in bed by the time we made our way through the laurel bushes of the extensive garden. It took only a few minutes to find the weak point in the defences. Holmes's diamond-tipped glass cutter silently removed a circle from a pane in the conservatory door. By turning a key on the inside we passed into the drawing room, our identities concealed by black velvet masks, like a pair of Limehouse footpads. Ahead of us, the study was sufficiently illuminated by a well-banked fire for Holmes to work on the tall green safe without turning on the electric light.

He would leave no trace, no scratches on the steel mirrors of the lock. With the skill and accuracy of a surgeon he used his instruments upon the somewhat antiquated Milner device. His strong yet delicate hands showed the quiet competence of a trained mechanic. After twenty minutes, the lock clicked. He drew the door of the safe half open to reveal a score of packets, each labeled and tied with pink tape, like a lawyer's brief. At that moment a door slammed somewhere deeper in the house and we heard footsteps approaching us. Holmes closed the safe, though without locking it, and we drew back behind the long velvet curtains drawn across the windows. The door to the inner room opened and the snick of an electric switch filled the air with a harsh brilliance.

He was visible through a crack in the curtains! Not a shadow of suspicion touched his features as Milverton in his claret-colored smoking jacket sat down in a red leather chair with a cigar in one hand, a document in the other, and began to read. The back of his broad grizzled head with its patch of baldness was towards us. My fingers tingled at the thought of how easily a blow to the skull from Holmes's jemmy might rid the world of this genteel blackguard. But that would not serve our purpose. How long we might be trapped behind the velvet drapery was therefore impossible to guess. I noticed, however, that our unwitting host looked at his watch with growing frequency and impatience. He was clearly expecting something—or someone. Presently there was a footfall on the veranda and we heard a gentle tapping. He got up, crossed the room, and went out to open the door.

I heard little of the conversation at that distance beyond recognizing his quiet visitor as a woman. As they turned to come in, I heard him say, "Half an hour late!" and "Made me lose a good night's sleep!" Then a little more clearly, "If the countess is a hard mistress, this must be your chance to get even with her. Five letters which compromise the Countess d'Albert? You want to sell and I want to buy. It only remains to agree on the price."

They were both in the study now, she a tall, slim, dark woman with a veil over her face and a mantle under her chin. Milverton was saying, "I should want to inspect the letters, of course." She had her back to us, but presently I could see her making the gestures of raising her veil and dropping the mantle from her chin. He turned to her and looked startled at first; then he seemed about to laugh. There was no hint of fear in his voice. "Great heavens, it is you!"

"The woman whose life you have ruined!" she said without the least tremor in her voice. "The wife whose husband broke his gallant heart and died by his own hand!"

"You were so obstinate," he said softly, wheedling her almost as if offering a caress to console her. "I put the price well within your means. Yet you would not pay." Then his face changed, as if he had seen something concealed from us. "I warn you that I have only to raise my voice, call my servants, and have you arrested!"

She turned a little and I caught the suggestion of a smile on her thin lips. There was a crack, no louder than the snapping of dry wood. He stared at her, as if turned to stone, but did not fall. The sharp sound cracked again; her arm was stretched out and now the muzzle of a small silver revolver was not two inches from his shirt front. A third and fourth time she fired. He remained motionless for a moment longer, as if the shots might have been blanks. Then he fell forward, coughing and scrabbling among the papers on the table. "You've done me!" he gasped and at once lay still.

The woman dropped the gun and hurried into the darkness of the veranda. Holmes strode from behind the curtain and turned the key in the door that connected us with the rest of the house. There were now several voices and sounds of movement. Without a word he flung open the safe door. In two or three armfuls he carried the packets of papers across the room and dropped them onto the banked coals of the fire, which blazed up in sudden brightness as it consumed them. Finally he scooped up the silver revolver and said, "This may be useful, Watson. I rather think there are two shots left."

With that we raced for the brick wall dividing the garden from its surrounding heathland. Even as we sprinted across the lawn, we were illuminated, for shafts of white electric light shone suddenly from every uncurtained window of the house. Several pursuers were almost at our heels. They so nearly caught us that one of them snatched and held my ankle as I went over the top of the wall. He might have brought me back into their grasp but Holmes chose this moment to fire over their heads the two last shots from the little gun. They flung themselves down, and a run of two miles in the darkness across Hampstead Heath took us clear.

The beautiful assassin, though still unknown to me, was picked out by Holmes a few days later from an Oxford Street photographer's display of the beauties and celebrities of the previous London season. As for the silver revolver, I never saw it again. When I asked him what had become of it, he said, "I tossed it away, just after we cleared the wall. It was empty."

"It may be found!" I protested.

"I do hope so, my dear fellow. Do you not see? The lady who rid the world of that reptile stood in danger. In her confusion, she dropped the weapon on his carpet and that might have been her undoing. It was plainly the gun that had killed him and, if it were traced to her, might have put her life in peril from the law or from the criminal underworld. Now she is safe, and so she deserves to be after suffering so much at his hands. They will hardly think she was one of the pair who scrambled over a six-foot wall and sprinted across the heath."

"The villains may trace the gun to you instead."

"I hope they may," he said, lighting his pipe from a long spill. "They will find me well prepared for them."

Such chivalry was characteristic of my friend, but, as you shall see, he was to pay dearly for it.

THE DISAPPEARANCE

THREE YEARS HAD PASSED since that windy January night on Hampstead Heath, and I had long ago assured myself that we and the world had heard the last of Charles Augustus Milverton. How mistaken I was!

There are few greater horrors in life than when a constant companion, a husband, wife, or child, sets out from home in the most usual way and never returns. It is surely worst of all when there is no message, no report of a death, injury, derangement, or desertion. I had not even seen Sherlock Holmes set out from our Baker Street rooms on a spring morning in 1902, though the sound of his feet on the stairs and his shout to Mrs. Hudson told me he was going.

He did not return that evening. I was used to his mysterious absences for several days when he had an important investigation in hand. We had recently been occupied in "The Case of the Naked Bicyclists," which led to the bizarre circumstances of the Moat Farm Murder.* Yet there was nothing in this investigation to take Holmes away so unaccountably.

*For an account of this adventure see "The Case of the Naked Bicyclists" in Donald Thomas, *Sherlock Holmes and the Voice from the Crypt*, Carroll & Graf, 2002.

All the same, I waited. After a few days longer, I began each morning by running my finger down the small "wants" and "offers" in the personal column of the *Morning Post.* This was our regular means of communication in such emergencies. The codes we used were known only to each other and might be seen in the press by millions of readers who would be none the wiser. Each of these little announcements was prefaced by the two letters NB for "nota bene." To the uninitiated, they appeared to be mere puffs for well-known products or services, unusual in a column of this kind but without being exceptional. NB marked them out.

The signal that invariably opened our communication was "Rowlands Antimacassar Oil." Since one example saves many words, let me suppose that Holmes had gone suddenly to a secret address in London and wished me to join him. After the antimacassar oil advertisement, the next NB would name a city or county. In this case it might be "'London Pride' Pipe Tobacco. Threepence an ounce." So much for that day's column, which gave me "London." Next day NB might add "Grand Atlantic Hotel, Weston-super-Mare. Preferential Rates Available." Knowing already that he was in London, I would merely count the letters of this second message and make a total of 60. From our folders of London maps I would draw sheet number 60 of the Ordnance Survey's invaluable microcosm of the capital. As those who use it will know, sheet 60 covers the Paddington area from Hyde Park in the south to the Regents Park canal in the north and from Chepstow Place, Bayswater, in the west to Seymour Place in Marylebone. Further down the column might be a second NB announcement. "Bisto Makes Tasty Soups." That would be all. Counting the letters in each word I would find 5 + 5 + 5 + 5.

We had divided the vertical and horizontal edges on our maps into 100 equal lengths. Therefore 5 + 5 and 5 + 5 would stand for 55 by 55. On this basis I would take sheet 60 and measure 55 from the east, along the bottom of the map, and 55 from the north, down its left-hand side. Using a ruler, I would discover that the two lines from these points would intersect on the west side of Spring Street, almost within the shadow of the great railway terminus at Paddington station. The invaluable Ordnance Survey marks each dwelling house, though no more than a millimeter in size. For whatever reason, in this example Holmes would be found at 8, Spring Street, Paddington, to which I must make my way.

It was rarely indeed that we had recourse to such secret and unbreakable codings, which covered not only locations but a variety of necessary information. By this time, I had been Holmes's companion and colleague for more than a dozen years. You may imagine that we had planned for most contingencies. Yet no one outside an insane asylum could have anticipated the horrors which beset us in the spring of this fateful year. The days passed and the *Morning Post* personal column bore no messages.

A week went by, ten days, a fortnight. I inquired after those "found drowned," after victims of road accidents, the subjects of inquests from murder to suicide. I visited mortuaries in Lambeth, St. Pancras, and Chelsea. It was to no avail. I put aside my aversion to my friend's addictions, and gained entry to dockside lofts and cellars frequented by the opium smokers of Limehouse and Shadwell. I half mentioned my fears to our friends at Scotland Yard, saying that Holmes had gone off I knew not where. Lestrade and Gregson pulled wry faces, chuckled, and suspected that Mr. Holmes was "up to his old tricks." After all, what could they do with such information as I had to offer them? I did not think he was up to any tricks.

If you have read my account of his final encounter with Professor Moriarty in 1891, the dreadful struggle on the brink of the falls of Reichenbach, the plunge into the swirling waters, you may recall that this was preceded by weeks—perhaps months—of anticipation. Holmes would close the shutters on entering a room, as if against an assassin's bullet, saying, "It is stupidity rather than courage to ignore the danger when it is close upon you." This was so unlike his usual self-assurance that I worried, all those years ago, if he was well. He looked even paler and thinner than usual.

Then, on a single day in the course of that year, there had been three attempts on his life. In the morning, as he walked the short distance from our rooms to the corner of Bentinck Street and Welbeck Street, a two-horse van was driven straight at him, full-pelt. He sprang for the footpath and saved himself by a fraction of a second as the van disappeared. Within the hour, walking down Vere Street, he escaped death by an even smaller margin when a large brick from one of the house roofs shattered at his feet. The police were summoned but concluded that the two-horse van was driven by a madcap and that the wind had blown the brick from a pile of materials waiting to be used in repairing the upper storey of the house. That very evening there was a direct attempt against him in a dark street, when a ruffian with a bludgeon tried to knock his brains out. The fellow found to his cost that he was knocked cold instead by his intended victim and given in charge to the police.

By contrast, there had been nothing of this sort in the present case. Just then my friend was still engrossed in the matter of the Moat Farm murder. Nothing in that afforded a reason for attempted assassination! Yet at the time of the earlier threats—and often since then—Holmes had talked of the great criminal conspiracies underlying crimes that might appear separate and unconnected. He called it "some deep, organizing power which for ever stands in the way of law, and throws its shield over the wrongdoer." The men who wielded such power would surely give all they possessed to eliminate Sherlock Holmes. He claimed that he had felt their presence even when the mystery of a case had been solved—and in other cases in which he was not personally consulted. When Professor Moriarty had been unmasked, Holmes thought at first that he had beheaded the monster of criminal conspiracy. Instead, like the Hydra, it had lost one head only to grow many more.

Moriarty was dead, there were no two ways about that. Yet I now began to speculate on the names of men who had particular cause to wish the destruction of Sherlock Holmes or, as was often the case, had paid with their lives but had left behind others who might be no less passionate for his downfall. In the recent past he had been the means of sending to prison for fifteen years Herr Hugo Oberstein, the international agent in the case of the secret Bruce Partington submarine plans. He had protected and exonerated those who rid the world of Giuseppe Giorgiano of the Red Circle, a fiend who had earned the nickname of Death in southern Italy. Oberstein was behind bars and Giorgiano was dead, but the one had a foreign government loyal to him and the other a gang of cutthroats sworn to vengeance. I confess that, at this stage, the name of Charles Augustus Milverton had not so much as crossed my mind.

After three weeks there was one person whose assistance I had not sought and to whom I must confide my fears. Mycroft Holmes, of Pall Mall and the Diogenes Club, was now the government's chief interdepartmental adviser. He must be told of his younger brother's disappearance. "Not only is he an adviser to the British government," Sherlock Holmes had once said to me, "on occasion he *is* the British government." All the same, I did not see what Brother Mycroft could do now. It was a terrible thing to admit to myself, but after a few weeks instinct assured me that I should never more see him whom I have always known to be the best and wisest of men.

If you have the patience to read what follows, you will find that I was wrong, though in what condition I saw him was another matter. By then Sherlock Holmes appeared as a man who has the shadow of the hangman's rope upon him. You will also understand why this narrative could not have been made public at an earlier date. Even now, I have wondered from time to time whether it would not be best to burn all the notes and the evidence, to let the tale die with me. It was never one that we discussed often in the future. Yet I hear that voice again in my mind. "If you are an honest man, Watson, you will set this record against my successes." It may be that, in this case, posterity will judge that Sherlock Holmes succeeded to an extent he never equaled, either before or since.

THE TRIBUNAL

WILLIAM SHERLOCK SCOTT HOLMES! You stand charged that you, with other persons not in custody, did willfully murder Charles Augustus Milverton, at Hampstead in the County of Middlesex, upon the sixth day of January in the year 1899. How say you? Are you guilty or not guilty of the charge wherewith you have been indicted?"

Holmes had known from the first that they meant to murder him, come what might. The semblance of a trial continued during the evenings of three days, but these preliminaries to his execution had been devised solely to make his death more gratifying to them. When the ritual was over, the memory of the proceedings haunted his sleep every night in the time they allowed him before he was to be hanged. Every night, in that well-ordered mind, the nightmare took a precise form.

"The dream," as he afterwards called it, began invariably with a jolt, like a great heartbeat of warning or fright, which brought him from the depths of unconsciousness to the mists of a drugged hyoscine sleep. Then there began the calling of his names and the indictment.

In his dream, he struggled to repudiate the two self-appointed judges who sat beyond a sunburst of arc light. Except for the brief moments when they seated themselves or left their places, he had seen them only as an actor sees the rows of an audience through a haze of limelight. In the nightmare of light, his mouth moved but his throat remained silent and impotent to answer. During his waking ordeal, a week previously, he had said simply and clearly, "It is a matter of fact that I killed Charles Augustus Milverton. I did so to rid the world of a noxious villain. I did it alone. I would do it again and think my own life not too great a price to pay."

"Your gallantry in protecting your friend Dr. Watson is commendable," the voice said sardonically. "It is wasted, however. It will not prevent him from standing where you stand now. You fled in his company and were seen to do so. The matter of a young woman on the premises is also under our investigation."

"You are in error. Charles Augustus Milverton died by my hand and I required no assistance."

"Guilty or not guilty!" the voice rapped out. "Make your plea!"

"A man does not plead to gangsters and impostors."

"Then you shall be entered mute of malice, as if pleading not guilty," said the voice behind the arc light, "and your trial shall proceed at once."

He could have sworn he recognised the voice of this presiding "judge." Yet it had belonged to that man whom he had seen most efficiently shot dead at Appledore Towers, Hampstead, by a young woman's silver revolver three years earlier. Indeed, we had read the report of the inquest on Charles Augustus Milverton in the *Times* with its verdict of "murder by person or persons unknown."

Two dimly defined figures faced him from behind a broad oak table. Beyond them stood a man in a prison warder's uniform of some kind, a person whom they addressed as Master-at-Arms. He was to guard and, if necessary, subdue the handcuffed prisoner. Holmes, seated on an upright wooden chair, had been weakened by the hypnotic that had kept him unconscious for many hours. He might have been a lone prisoner at the far end of the earth for all that he could tell.

As the voice behind the light talked on, in its mockery of the judicial process, he strove to calculate how long he had been kept in a drug-induced coma. The opening of his "trial" was the first day of full consciousness. Even then, his coldly rational intellect was at work behind the fuddled eyes. Holmes had no memory of how he came to be there, apart from recalling a taste in his mouth. Yet that taste was everything to him just now. It had been sweetish, partially disguising something salt and harsh. That was his first clue. He knew that the sweetness was merely sugar of milk, universally employed to make medicine palatable. The harshness that it veiled was surely hyoscine hydrobromide, an hypnotic that can wipe from the patient's mind all memory of events heard, seen, or felt during the period of its operation.

Sherlock Holmes the analytical chemist, with his extensive apparatus in our Baker Street rooms, had tested hyoscine once or twice with a fingertip taste. The memory of it was as securely catalogued in that invincible mind as if it had been entered in the files of St. Mary's Hospital or the Radcliffe Laboratories. He knew better than any man how powerful a weapon the narcotic might be in the hands of the criminal world. Those who had drugged him evidently knew no more than that it would erase the memory of subsequent events and had made the mistake of believing that the memory of tasting and taking it would be lost as well. Meanwhile, Holmes confronted them behind their shield of light. He must first discover who these enemies were, where he was, and how they had brought him there.

In the course of his "trial," he understood that it was not their plan to kill him at once. Others who sought revenge upon him had been invited to watch him die. In the meantime the men who sat in judgment would break his spirit, so that the witnesses of his death might see him kneel for mercy and plead for his life as he was dragged to a beam from which the heavy rope of the gallows dangled. The story of Sherlock Holmes as a coward and a weakling in the end would do more to exhilarate and encourage this criminal brotherhood than any other coup.

Every night they gave him a choice as he lay on the wooden bed in his condemned cell. He might either drink the contents of the medicine glass, which would render him unconscious until morning, or be held down while a hypodermic syringe sedated him. He drank from the glass, if only to determine the drug they used. One touch on the tongue was enough.

His captors took no chances with him. A steel anklet and a light, five-foot steel chain locked him to a ring and a wall plate, whose four screws were deeply set into the stonework of the cell wall. This chain was just long enough for him to reach a small alcove with a basin and a drain behind the head of the wooden bed and too short for him to reach the guard who watched him while he was waking or sleeping. The anklet, almost tight to the skin, scraped flesh and bone whenever he moved.

As for his surroundings, the door from the cell to the passageway and the door to the exercise yard outside were both locked and barred. In the corridor sat two more guards who would enter immediately to their colleague's assistance at the first sound of a disturbance and who, meantime, scrutinized the length of the cell through a glass spy hole every ten or fifteen minutes. For good measure, there was a bell within the guard's reach. If pressed, it would bring immediate assistance from the men who sat outside.

It seemed useless for a man to fight against the effects of a nightly potion of hyoscine. Holmes knew this well enough. Yet after the first dose he knew something more. A sweet vegetable taste on his tongue suggested that hyoscine had been reduced and mingled with another drug. In order that it should have a more powerful effect, they had fortified it with an opiate. It was precisely in making doubly sure he was in their power that they gave Sherlock Holmes his first hope of defeating them.

I believe I was the only man on earth who knew of my friend's pernicious addiction to narcotics at times of idleness, a secret compulsion that is now common knowledge to those who have read of him. So long as he was alive this was never revealed to another living soul. Much has since been made of his use of cocaine and the hypodermic syringe, somewhat less of his use of opium. It was opium which took him to those dens of Wapping or Shadwell, of which I have already written elsewhere. Medical men will know, if others do not, that the use of opiates habituates a man to them. It is notorious that the greater the use, the less potent the effects. It would have been absurd to suppose that, even then, he could have fought off the effects of such a dose as they administered each night. Yet even before his "trial" ended, by an effort of subconscious will and as the hours of the night wore on, he was able to rouse himself to the level of "twilight sleep," the effect of hyoscine alone.

My friend confessed to me that the labour of this partial awakening was atrocious. Each time that he attempted to rise from the drugged depths of consciousness, he went through a period of delusion. It seemed that he was manacled to a monstrous engine of some kind, whose wheels or piston rods he was forced to turn with more pain and effort than he had ever known. At last he overcame the resistance of the mechanism and gained a momentum through which he floated free of his labour. Then, with a thump of the heart, his dream would begin again.

As in the repeated showing of a film or the constant rehearsal of a play, his accusers took their seats in his dream. A curiosity of his twilight sleep was that Holmes began to see details hidden from him in conscious reality. It seemed that the effects of the narcotics forced upon him had dulled part of his waking brain during his trial. Only in this hyoscine sleep did he identify his "judges" from the shadows beyond the arc-light brilliance. As these accusers took their seats on the previous evening, Holmes now recalled that he had made out a smooth-shaven moon face, the features veiled from further identification by the brilliance of light. In the world of a waking dream, his subconscious mind endowed this blank moon with a fixed smile that conveyed malign cruelty. Imagination added hard gray eyes behind gold-rimmed glasses; memory recalled spite in a voice that was smooth and suave. Among the wraiths of semiconsciousness he heard the man address him. Holmes could not tell at first whether the words were an invention of his own fancy or whether he had heard them in the drugged torpor of his ordeal.

"You think us impostors, Mr. Holmes. Yet no men alive have a better right to demand the forfeit of your life. Charles Augustus Milverton, whom you murdered, was my elder brother. I am Henry Caius Milverton, and you might have verified my existence had you chosen to do so. Do not deny your crime, I beg you. The silver revolver, caliber .22, was found. It was child's play to compare the fingerprints upon it with those upon several objects obligingly but unwittingly handled by you."

Holmes strove after the reality of the voice. Was he merely deducing the identity of Henry Caius Milverton from a dream? He knew instinctively that the words were real, spoken to him and blotted out by the next onset of hyoscine. In his mind he turned a little from the glare of light, trying obliquely to see beyond it. The voice continued, introducing a second judge.

"My colleague Captain James Calhoun, denounced by you as the head of a murder gang in Georgia, was not lost at sea, as you supposed. Because the sternpost of his ship's boat was found floating in mid-ocean after a severe gale, you thought him drowned. Had you been as clever as you would have the world believe, you would have seen at once that the debris was deliberately set adrift where it would be found. The *Lone Star,* for whom your minions waited at Savannah, entered Bahia three weeks later, unremarked, as the *Alcantara.* A lick of paint, Mr. Holmes, was sufficient to defeat you."

"You have the conceit of clever men, Holmes"—the well-fed drawl was Calhoun—"but you were watched as soon as you accepted the case against me, even when you were reading ships' registers and insurance files at Lloyd's of London."

Henry Milverton chuckled at the colonel's pleasantry and resumed.

"Somewhere beyond these walls," the voice continued, "is Colonel James Moriarty, who is detained for the time being over matters relating to a family heirloom. Unusually, he bears the same first name as his brother, the professor whom you sent to his death at the falls of Reichenbach eleven years ago. It is a long time, is it not? And yet no doubt, Mr. Holmes, you are familiar with the old Italian proverb. Revenge is a dish which persons of taste prefer to eat cold. Before the melancholy conclusion of your history, Colonel Moriarty will demand certain satisfactions for his brother's death—satisfactions which you will be in no position to deny him."

The voice uttered a rich chuckle, as if in appreciation of its own consummate wit, and then proceeded.

"Consider the matter of the Greek interpreter. On the basis of a newspaper cutting, you believed Harold Latimer and Wilson Kemp, whom you sought for murder, had stabbed one another to death in a railway carriage near Budapest. You should not, Mr. Holmes, believe all you read in the papers. These gentlemen and others will be invited to watch you dance your last half hour in the noose."

"Mr. Latimer is a knave," said Holmes mildly, "one who tortured and murdered the brother of the girl he had promised to marry, in order to extract from him the family fortune."

"So you say, Mr. Holmes."

Sherlock Holmes endured this banter in the world of a dream, but his mind was elsewhere. Scrutinizing the architecture of his "courtroom," drawing out the half-remembered details with an effort that approached physical pain. Despite the central glare of light, he had seen that it was not a room but a vaulted space, the meeting of four massively built and stone-flagged passageways. Each was faced by a gothic arch. Nothing in the shadowy perspectives told him whether he was in England or in Europe, in a remote fastness or at the centre of a great city. Piece by piece, he reassembled the image of it. He woke next morning with the central enigma unraveled in his mind. The key to it had been a name, Henry Caius Milverton. He repeated that name over to himself silently, as if fearing that another sleep would wipe it from his mind.

During several days, whenever the "court" was not in session, he was to remain in the cell, his last refuge until they led him out to the gallows. It was a bare whitewashed room with a slightly arched brick roof supported on iron girders and tunnel-like in shape. At one end, behind the head of his bed, was the small, open alcove with its basin, a gutter, and running water. He was watched day and night by one or other of Milverton's "warders."

His furniture consisted of the solid wooden bedstead about nine inches in height from the floor, with a thin mattress and a single blanket. There was a table and a wooden upright chair by the bed and another table and chair at the farther end of the cell for the use of the warder. The table and chair by the bed were removed at night, as if for fear he might make some use of them to escape. The cell was lit on its long outer wall by two iron-grated windows with small panes of opaque fluted glass. Its floor was laid with red polished tiles. His food was already cut up and brought to him on a white tin plate, without cutlery. No doubt they feared he would cheat them by using a knife to escape or to make away with himself before the appointed date.

Holmes had taken measurements with a sure eye. The cell was almost nineteen feet long by eight feet wide and seven feet tall at the lowest point, where the roof and walls met. The long wall adjoining the corridor was blank, apart from the plate to which the anklet and chain were attached and a double gas bracket for illumination after dark. The narrow wall at the far end, facing the bed, had a door leading at right angles to the corridor. On the other long wall were the two narrowly barred windows and a door to a yard. This wall was also lit from a double gas bracket. The narrow wooden bed with its rough prison-issue blanket and a canvas pillow stood along the wall adjoining the corridor at the far end from the door.

The light anklet chain, when stretched at full length, allowed him to reach the basin in the alcove behind him. In the opposite direction, he could stretch to a point almost halfway down the length of the cell. It stopped short of the door to the yard and the wooden chair with its table where the guard sat. As well as the guards in the corridor, two men took it in turns to watch him within the cell. With the chain on his ankle he could not have reached them, even if an attack would have made escape possible. Such food as he was brought was put on a plate just within his reach and then the guard drew back. It was made plain to him that he would never leave this cell, except for sittings of the "court," until the morning when they took him out to the gallows shed in the yard. It was equally plain to them that no one could save him, least of all Holmes himself. This belief he considered to be their greatest weakness.

Even at night as he slept his drugged sleep, there was a guard in his cell, as well as the others in the corridor outside, within easy call. Yet night and his dreams offered him hope. Though he was required to drink the glass of hyoscine hydrobromide, it must have seemed to his guards a superfluous precaution. He could scarcely move from the bed. Both doors were beyond his reach, and though he might stretch out an arm to touch the nearer barred window with his fingertips, he would be seen and heard at once.

With such precautions, it mattered little to his guardians whether he swallowed the hyoscine hydrobromide or not. All the same, they were instinctively obedient to Milverton and would make him do it. Holmes understood that he had been given the sedative merely so that he should not be troublesome in the hours of darkness by arguing or pleading. He was careful to give no trouble. After a couple of nights they took less interest, and the man who brought the glass sometimes glanced away if distracted by sound or movement. It was possible for Holmes to tip a little from his glass so that it fell upon the woolen socks covering his feet while he sat crossed-legged. The man who came to take the empty glass away would lean toward him, perhaps to smell the sweetness on his breath. It was always there, and this seemed to satisfy them that they had reduced their captive to obedience. They would not risk giving him an overdose without Milverton's authority, and it seemed that Milverton was usually elsewhere.

After he had spent several nights battling against the drug's effects, the upper level of what he called his twilight sleep became easier to attain. In this state, Holmes knew that he had once heard the rumble of a man's breath. With their prisoner helpless, the guards usually spent the night sleeping on the wooden chair. This item of intelligence began to form the basis of their captive's plan. A night or two later, lying half-conscious, he heard something more. It would have meant little to most men, but to Sherlock Holmes it made clear a large part of the mystery of his abduction.

At first he was not quite sure, in the fog-like vapours of hyoscine, that he had truly heard it. Yet he knew that if it were real, it must come again. It seemed like the boom of the dreadful engine to which he was attached as he struggled to consciousness. He now heard it again, four times in quick succession. It was no engine, but a large clock. If it had struck four, he would wait until five to judge its direction. Yet, to his surprise, the four booms came again in much less than a minute. This time it had a deeper tone and, almost at once, he heard it four times more in a note higher than either of the other two. Holmes, the musician, composer, and author of a critique on the motets of Orlando Lassus, enjoyed the gift of perfect pitch. He had only to hear a sound in order to pick out its equivalent on a keyboard.

That night he had heard E natural four times, B flat in the octave below, and then G natural in the octave higher. No man ever knew the streets of London and their great buildings as he did. In campanology, those three bells and those intervals between them occur only in the striking of St. Sepulchre's, St. Paul's Cathedral, and the descant of St. Martin's-le-Grand. He woke next morning with the exultation of a child at Christmas. What might have been inaudible in the remote "courtroom" or when the streets were crowded could be heard in the silent hours between the last drunkards shouting their way homeward and the carts at dawn making their way to market. He knew, as surely as if he had drawn lines of triangulation on a map, that he was in the grim and disused limbo of Newgate prison. The vaulted space forming the "courtroom" was at the meeting of the four great passageways, like aisles and transepts under a cathedral tower.

Until a few months before, as my readers may recall, Newgate had been the most feared and fearful gaol in England's history, filled with many of the worst specimens of mankind. It was a detentional prison where they were held during their trials. Those condemned to death or corporal punishments remained until the dates of their executions or whatever form of penalty had been ordered. A corridor with fifteen death cells and the execution shed in the yard outside had a simple motto on its archway: "Abandon hope, all ye who enter here." Holmes now had not the least doubt that it was in one of these cells that he was held prisoner. No one in the world outside would think of searching for him in this disused fortress of despair.

His enemies had timed their revenge with devilish precision. Parliament and the City of London had resolved to pull down the ancient prison in Newgate Street and build the court of the Old Bailey on its site. The last man in the condemned cells had been hanged in 1901, as had last woman, Ada Chard the baby-farmer. Other prisoners were transferred to nearby gaols. The building and its contents passed from the prison board to the city corporation. For several months, prior to demolition, it stood empty, "in the hands of the contractors." A supply of gas to the lamps was maintained and the unused gallows of the execution shed still remained in working order.

How easy it must have been for the contractors to pass the custody of the empty building to subcontractors in those last weeks. Henry Milverton and his accomplices had devised a poetic extermination for Sherlock Holmes, a warning to others who might interfere with the workings of a mighty criminal empire. Yet Holmes was not naive enough to believe that all this had been done merely to destroy him, when they might as easily have run him down in the street or dropped a boulder on his head. His death delighted these men, but it was a mere pastime that coincided with some greater plan. Behind the charade of a court and a Newgate hanging lay a criminal enterprise that might shake the entire world. It was something that perhaps only he had the power to prevent. Whatever the plot might be, it depended on a criminal gang having possession of the prison for some weeks or months. What the objective might be, Holmes could not at the moment deduce. But he swore to himself that he would find out.

The most curious aspect of his plight was that when sentence was pronounced upon him on the following day, he felt lighter in his heart than he had done since the nightmare began. It came as no shock to him, not even a surprise, to hear the ritual words in Henry Milverton's oily tones. "You are to be taken back to the place whence you came and from thence to a place of lawful execution. And there you shall be hanged by the neck until you be dead." Any other man chained to the wall of the condemned cell, with guards outside and within, far from help and with the gallows waiting in the yard, must surely have given up hope. Yet Holmes put his faith in one indisputable fact. The power of his mind, the strength of his reason, the observing and analytical machine that he became at such times, were stronger than all his captors put together.

The man whom they called the master-at-arms, a burly and grizzled fellow, led him away in handcuffs from the last act of the trial. This time he was not immediately returned to his cell, but taken in an opposite direction. The prisoner and his escort came to an iron-faced door topped by steel spikes. The master-at-arms produced a heavy key and opened the largest Bramah lock that Holmes had ever seen, drawing back its bronze bolt with a massive rumbling. They crossed the paved floor of a somber high-roofed lodge, from which it was possible to hear the sound of traffic in the street, and passed through a doorway leading to what had evidently been the prison governor's office. The walls were still hung with notices by the Court of Aldermen forbidding liquors to be brought into the prison or setting out rules for clerks and attorneys who were visiting their clients.

In a well-lit anteroom, where descriptions of prisoners were taken, an open cupboard displayed the irons worn by the notorious burglar, highwayman, and prison-breaker of a century before, Jack Shepherd—iron bars an inch and a half thick and fifteen inches long. Holmes noticed irons for the legs, about an inch in diameter and clasped with strong rivets. On the wall of the office there still hung two old paintings of the penal colony at Botany Bay. Yet his attention was held by three rows of faces arranged along the top of a low cupboard. They were the death masks of men and women who had been hanged at the prison for a hundred years past.

Henry Milverton was behind him now, pointing out a prize specimen among the masks. "There, Mr. Holmes, is Courvoisier, publicly hanged more than sixty years ago for the murder of Lord William Russell. You will see that the brow is low, the lower part of the face sensual. The upper lip, like that of most of the group, is abnormally thick. As your lip will be, Mr. Holmes, for it is congestion caused by the process of hanging—or rather of strangling. You will observe that some, like Courvoisier, have died with their eyes open and some with them shut. Those whose necks are broken by the drop have their eyes closed, those who drop short and choke to death have them open, as yours will be, Mr. Holmes."

Holmes said nothing, but he noticed for the first time a weighing machine in one corner of the room.

"You will oblige us," said Milverton, "by standing upon the scales. Your weight is of importance to the master-at-arms, so that the end may be as we wish it to be. Many people, Mr. Holmes, have looked forward to this spectacle and it would never do for your final appearance to be too brief. You must expect us to have some sport with you after you have put us to so much trouble. A short drop and a long dance for you, I fear, Mr. Sherlock Holmes."

Holmes stood upon the metal plate of the machine but still said nothing. The grizzled brute, whom they called the master-at-arms, fiddled with the bronze disks of the weights—first he added one, then replaced it with a smaller one—until the metal arm of the balance oscillated slightly and was still. Milverton pretended to busy himself with some papers but as soon as the weighing was over he looked up.

"Good-bye, Mr. Holmes. We shall not meet again until the morning of the great occasion. It is the custom, is it not, to allow a man three clear Sundays before his execution? That we cannot do. However, it will be a week or more before some of our friends are here, so you may make whatever peace you can in that time with whatever gods you think may spare you their attention. There will come a point, however, when you will wake each morning not knowing whether this is—or is not—to be your last. A morning when you are merely allowed one more day to live will make you think yourself the luckiest man alive. Fancy that, Mr. Holmes! At such times, as your despair becomes unendurable, you will consider us as your dearest benefactors for allowing you one more brief day! You have no idea how well we shall get on!"

Holmes fixed the man with his sharp but steady gaze. Milverton held his eyes for a moment, then smirked and looked down at his papers.

The way back to the condemned cells was not by the route they had come. It led down an ill-lit corridor and over a covered bridge. There was a glimpse of four galleries of cells under a glass roof, all deserted and silent. Holmes and his escorts passed through an iron gate and along a small passage, paved with slate, beside an exercising ground that he calculated must border on Newgate Street. There was not an inch of that short journey that was not catalogued in his mind. I daresay he could have told you the number of paving slabs they had crossed, how many were chipped, and where the cracks were.

He noticed, a little beyond the bridge and the glass roof, a side opening with several sets of clothes or uniforms hanging upon wall-hooks. Next to it was a recess with a sink, three razors and brushes, a hand-mirror face-down upon a stone surface. At such moments, I had often observed, he became an invincible brain without a heart or the tremor of a nerve or a pang of affection. Perhaps it was as well for him that this should be so. As they came out under a covered arch he saw for the first time what lay beyond his opaque cell windows. It was a yard beyond reach of the sun with the cell block on one side. Its walls rose sleek as marble to what Wilde, the prisoner-poet, had called "that little tent of blue which prisoners call the sky."

Abandon hope. . . . The builders had chosen an apt text for the condemned block. Even a man who could free himself from the chain at his ankle, render himself invisible to the guard in his cell, open the prison locks on the outer door, spirit himself from the cell into the yard, might just as well have surrendered to the hangman. The smooth expanse of the great walls was almost unbroken. In the north-west corner, half-way from the ground to the summit was an old water tank, neglected since the days when it had provided the first water supply to the buildings below. Above it, just below the top of each wall ran a stout wooden axle set with sharpened steel wire. A man who attempted it would find that he could scarcely hang by as much as a finger without encountering the savage metal.

Holmes walked slowly between his guards, as if it were a great effort to move his legs in time with theirs. They did not hurry him. There was surely a satisfaction in showing him the hopelessness of his situation. He could only guess what part such men had played as common criminals before they put on the livery of Milverton's prison officers.

Along one wall of the yard, the paving had been dislodged by the sinking of the ground. There were single letters engraved on the stone at intervals, a G, an L, and an M and another G. Holmes did not need to be told that he was walking over the graveyard of men and women who had been hanged at the prison and whose bodies, mouldering and rotting in quicklime, caused this subsidence in the ground. If his escorts smiled as they passed, it was with amusement at the famous Sherlock Holmes now walking over his own grave. At one end of the yard he noticed a shed, like a small stable. Through its open doors he glimpsed a black platform on wheels. Thirteen steps led up to its top, which was large enough for several men to stand upon. Though no rope was coiled on the beam above it, this was plainly to be the means of his death. Holmes glanced at it and knew what the way ahead must be.

While he sat on the bed in his cell, one of the escorts locked the anklet to the links that chained him to the wall, removed his handcuffs, and left him to his own contemplations. There was no mirror in the cell. Holmes knew only by touch that a beard had begun to establish itself on his face and that his hair was unkempt. Such things mattered nothing to him just then. As he sat on the edge of the narrow wooden bed, his thoughts were far away. His formidable intelligence was tuned only to victory over his adversaries. Without intending it, they had now shown him a path to freedom. It was not a certain path, but it was the only one. Even before he could begin upon it, there was a battle to be won.

He took up his usual position, sitting cross-legged and silent at the head of the bed, his gaze concentrated upon whichever guard sat at the table in the far end of the cell. The man who kept watch was beyond the range of Holmes' capable and efficient fists but never beyond the reach of those unblinking and penetrating eyes.

THE CORPORAL OF HORSE

THERE WERE TWO MEN who took it in turns to watch him as he woke or slept. They had divided their duty so that each kept vigil for two days and then two nights alternately. At night they slept in the wooden chair, beyond the range of the chain that held his anklet.

Holmes gathered that the name of the first man was Crellin. He was tall with a lantern jaw, dark hair piled on his head like an old-fashioned courtier's wig, and a look of brutalised cunning. A movement of his mouth seemed at first to promise a skeptical smile. It was no more than a misalignment of the lips. Crellin might laugh, but he never smiled.

The other man was more slightly built, his complexion so deeply reddened by the sun, the skin so tight and shiny on the bones of his face, that he looked as if he had been boiled. Holmes heard him referred to as Mac. At a glance, this smaller man seemed the less pugnacious of the two. Holmes decided to put the matter to the test. It was not necessary that he should defeat all his captors. One might be enough.

He had once remarked that from a single drop of water the logician could infer the existence of the Niagara Falls or the Atlantic Ocean without ever having seen either. It now seemed that by knowing the nickname of one jailer Sherlock Holmes proposed to find a path to freedom from the condemned cell of the most closely guarded prison in the world. The thing was so utterly impossible that not even Henry Milverton would feel that he needed to protect himself against it.

From the moment the warder who was his daytime keeper entered until the man left at dark, Holmes was the hawk-faced, cross-legged idol whose eyes drilled into the guard's mind and thoughts, scattering them like ninepins. I had seen him confront a practised trickster or a hardened scoundrel and with this same unblinking stare fix the unfortunate wretch for perhaps thirty seconds. None of them ever endured it longer. Some, like Professor Moriarty, tried to turn it to laughter, but the flame scorched them. To be burnt like an insect by such unblinking and brilliant fire for an entire day would beggar description! On the first occasion, Crellin glared back at the steady glitter of those eyes. He growled a threat, as if that settled the matter, and looked away. The eyes gave him no rest. Chained as he was, Sherlock Holmes pursued the sullen bully into the dark shadows of his mean soul.

Yet it was a waste of time. Crellin might squirm, but he would not squeal. He had taken Milverton's shilling and must do as he was told. After an hour he growled threats of coming to do for Holmes with his heavy fists, but he never dared to set foot within reach of the prisoner's chain.

Mac was a different case. The line of the mouth was far more sullen, but it was the self-doubting sullenness of the uneasy child. Perhaps, when he took the same shilling, he had not bargained on being the instrument that would prepare an innocent man for the hangman's noose. Not that Mac would compromise his own safety or risk his own skin to save him, but he squirmed far more readily than Crellin. The cross-legged inquisitor gave him not a moment's rest from the steady eyes. At first Mac pretended not to notice, but in the confined dimensions of the cell he could not help it. He got up and stood at the opaque window glass, for all the world as if he could see through it and admire the view. He turned his chair and sat sideways to the man he was guarding. He pretended to read. He clasped his hands behind his back and with head lowered paced an absurd eight-foot sentry-go across the cell and back, as if in deep thought. And then he turned to Holmes and shouted,

"Look somewhere else, will you? Look somewhere else, blast your eyes!"

But the man whom he must help to kill spoke not a word from Mac's entry at morning until his departure at evening. After his first two days it was plain that Mac dreaded the cell. Holmes had found a weakness in their scheme, not in chains or locks, or in hyoscine. It existed in the man they called Mac. The man's flaw was a tender conscience, and the poor devil dreaded that any of the others should detect it. Holmes could tell this by the way he loudly and unevenly, with his fellow jailers before entering the cell, laughed for Holmes to hear him and know that he cared nothing. Once inside, before the keen-eyed inquisitor, it was a different story.

Sherlock Holmes, for all his fame, was a mortal man. Neither I nor any other living soul was ever to know what terrors he may have felt in these long hours. Yet not by a word or the blink of an eyelid did he betray them. There are those who will scoff and tell you that all this was the bravado of a schoolbook hero. It was nothing of the kind but, rather, his inner concentration on the nub of a plan formed in a mind that was hard as a diamond and by thoughts clear as perfect crystal. He must judge to the minute when the silence was to be broken. There would be one chance and one chance only. The moment came on the fourth day, in the middle of a long afternoon. His words were spoken loudly but not too loudly. The tone, however, was sharp as the crack of a circus whip and Mac jumped at the sound of them.

"Listen to me, McIver!"

Perhaps it was the sound of his own name, spoken by a man who could never have heard it used, that broke the fellow's composure. Cross-legged and still, Sherlock Holmes spoke again. His voice was too soft to be heard beyond the cell, and it now seemed intended to comfort the man who had been set to keep watch on him.

"I think, Corporal McIver of the 21st Lancers, that it is time for you and I to exchange a few words."

The reddened skin grew tight as a mask on the cheek-bone, and the elongated eyes looked straight at Holmes, stilled by fear, like a rat before a basilisk.

"I understand entirely," Holmes continued. "The first thought in your mind is that Mr. Milverton—or by whatever name your master calls himself—will cut your throat once he knows that you have revealed your identity to me. You are, or rather were, Corporal McIver of the 21st Lancers, a veteran of the cavalry charge against the Sudanese rebels at the Battle of Omdurman, lately discharged from the Army as the victim of a distressing medical complaint—Egyptian ophthalmia. All you wish now is to marry your childhood sweetheart. But that is not easy, is it?"

Holmes had softened him up carefully over many hours. Now the mesmerised incomprehension in McIver's eyes turned to outright fear.

"You cannot have set eyes upon me until you saw me in this place," he said in a stage whisper, fearful of being heard by those outside the cell, "and I know nothing of you. You cannot tell me who I am."

"Quite so," said Holmes soothingly. "However, let me assure you I know enough—if not all—about you. The 21st Lancers, the Battle of Omdurman, your discharge from the Army on medical grounds. The woman you had hoped to marry. I know more than enough to have left a hidden message already, scratched somewhere and somehow—in the plaster of a wall perhaps. When this building is dismantled, as it soon will be, such a message including your name would lead the police straight to you. It has even been known for a prisoner in this very gaol—Benson was his name—to leave a dampened paper message on the floor where one of the guards would tread on it unwittingly and just as unwittingly lose it on the dry pavement outside these walls. Have no fear. I am sure you have been warned against such tricks. There are far better ones than that, believe me."

"Mr. Milverton knows of all your tricks," said McIver hastily.

"Not quite all of them, I think," said Holmes amiably. "What Mr. Milverton does know, however, is that once in the hands of the police, you would betray him and his entire conspiracy. And you know perfectly well, Corporal McIver, that were I to say as much to him as I am saying to you now, you would be dead before this evening's sun had set."

"What can you tell?"

"Enough to end your life even before mine. If your master knew that I had identified you and had already taken measures to pass on that knowledge, you would not live the hour. He would not dare allow it. Whether I inform him or not is a matter for you."

The eyes that had fled from Holmes's scrutiny before could not bear now to leave his face. In a sudden flood of panic, the discharged soldier had fallen victim completely to Holmes's precept that "What you can do in this world is a matter of no consequence. The question is what can you make people believe that you have done." He had not half finished with the wretch, while McIver struggled to imagine how a total stranger could have known so much about him.

"When you were invalided home from Egypt," Holmes continued, "and discharged from your regiment, you were thrown upon your own resources. Had you held the rank of sergeant, a pension might have been procured for you. Yet a sergeant is, shall we say, *rara avis in terra*—a rare bird. If I am not mistaken, a cavalry troop consists of some sixty troopers plus six corporals and one sergeant. You were not he. It is not to be wondered at that you have failed to find regular employment since your return. Your malady sits plainly upon you."

As Holmes was talking, McIver's face showed the contending emotions of a man who feels himself ever more securely snared and yet hopes that the snare may break and set him free.

"You may guess, Mr. Sherlock Holmes," he said, mingling scorn with trepidation, "but you cannot know. Mr. Milverton would see your tale for what it is."

"I do not guess." said Holmes mildly, "I never guess. Mr. Milverton knows that to his cost. You appear to forget that while you have watched me in the past few days, I have also watched you. You are a mere prison guard, but it is my profession to observe. Your name was easy to discover. Indeed, at my arrival I heard distinctly one of your accomplices call you Mac."

McIver got up from his chair and stood as if he might advance upon his prisoner. "That is nothing!"

"In itself. . . . " There was something like steel in Holmes's voice that made the man sit down again. "In itself it is nothing. However, I have had ample opportunity of observing you, even when you were out of earshot. I had a distinct view on the second day, as I was led back down the corridor. The man I believe you call Crellin stood behind you and spoke. You turned to him. He had spoken a name—or a word—to make you turn. I assumed it was your name and, of course, lip-reading is necessary in my walk of life. Indeed, I have written a little monograph on the production of sound from labial distortion. From the chuckle to the scream."

McIver was staring at him now, as if he dared not miss a word.

"Well, now," Holmes went on, "I had no doubt that the first syllable of the word spoken by Crellin was 'Mac.' I would expect that anyway, for I had heard you called by it. Try forming it for yourself. There is a characteristic compression of the lips followed by a sideways opening of the mouth. Crellin's lips then made the shape of an 'i.' This is easily read, being the letter which opens the mouth higher and narrower than any other. Quite unmistakable. Then his upper teeth touched his lower lip harder than they would make an 'f.' Therefore, the sound could only be a 'v.' Finally, the lips protruded in a flute-like way and the skin on his throat was strained a little tighter. To the trained eye, this could only be 'er.' It was not difficult."

"Very clever!" The man was shaken but still scornful.

"And then there are your boots," said Holmes.

"What of 'em?"

"Army boots," Holmes said, "still worn by you after your discharge."

"Any man could buy boots like these. Workmen's boots, more like than army ones."

"Indeed," said Holmes indulgently. "However, such boots are made of black pimpled leather and are worn as such by civilian workmen. Yet consider this. Any man who has been a soldier knows that the first command to the unfortunate recruit is to take a hot iron and to iron out the pimples of the toe caps so that they are perfectly smooth. They can then be polished for the parade ground until, if you will forgive the cliché, the poor recruit can see his face in them. Your boots are not those bought by a civilian worker. Rather, they are boots worn by a man who has lately been a soldier and can afford no others."

For some reason, the revelation about his boots shook McIver more thoroughly than the discovery of his name.

"Why are you not afraid?" he asked Holmes suddenly. "I do not understand it."

Holmes smiled at him, the lips thin and hard.

"If I were afraid, not you or any man should know it. For fear merely begets fear, and that would never do. Allow me to proceed. Boots of that kind are not worn by a sergeant, whose footwear gleams all over and is of an easier type. Therefore, you could only be a corporal or a private trooper. Oh, do not ask me how I knew you were a horseman. Merely watch the way you walk, when next you pass a plate-glass window. You have recently done some years of foreign service. Your complexion tells one at a glance. I deduce that you went with Lord Kitchener's expedition to reconquer the Sudan six years ago. A soldier who suffers, as you do, from Egyptian ophthalmia can scarcely dispute that. All the other mounted regiments of that force were Egyptian levees. Any man who reads his morning newspaper knows that the 21st Lancers were drafted in to lead the charge at Omdurman and that they were the only British mounted regiment sent for that purpose."

It was with some gratification that Holmes saw the man bow his head and stare at the floor of the cell to hide his confusion.

"Solar discoloration of the epidermis is a phenomenon essential to the work of the criminal expert," Holmes assured him quietly. "In your case, the effects of the Egyptian sun have been prolonged and have hardly begun to fade. The inner surfaces of your wrists remain white, as does a thin margin along the hairline of your forehead, which was covered by your helmet. There is a marked degree of permanency in the burning elsewhere. I judge that this would not have been acquired in less than five or six years, which approximates to the departure of the 21st Lancers for service in the Sudan campaign. You are evidently a man of some capability, and such a man does not usually serve in a single posting for six years without rising to the rank of corporal or, at any rate, of acting corporal. There are significant losses among a regiment overseas for six years, more from sickness than from battle, and significant vacancies for promotion. In either rank you would be referred to as Corporal McIver. Your modest advancement suggests to me a satisfactory character as a soldier and that you have lately turned to crime from particular necessity and not from mere viciousness."

The unhappy wretch looked up at him again, desperate now to prove his tormentor mistaken on any point at all. If he could knock down one of Holmes's deductions, perhaps the rest would follow like skittles.

"You cannot tell why I came home. You are no doctor."

"Indeed not," said Holmes in the same quiet and sympathetic voice. "Yet you bear unmistakable marks of a disorder upon the lids and rims of your eyes. For many years the contagion known as Egyptian ophthalmia has been brought back by soldiers who have served in that country and have had the misfortune—or imprudence—to mix there with certain forms of low company. Moreover, I have observed that when your duty is to guard me at night, you take a white tablet from each of two bottles, evening and morning. They are plainly homeopathic powders, which are customarily compressed into tablets for convenience. My eyesight is not deficient, and in passing I have read the labels on the bottles."

By looking at McIver now, it was evident the fight had gone from him.

"*Argentum nitricum* and *Hepar sulphuris*," said Holmes, "are each admirable treatments for a number of complaints but are seldom combined, as the good Dr. Ruddock tell us in his 'Vade Mecum,' except in the treatment of this ophthalmic condition or of an ulcerated throat. It seems obvious that you do not suffer from the latter, and therefore it follows, from simple observation, that you are a prey to the former. Soldiering has been taken from you as a result of your complaint and you have been returned to your native country."

He paused and McIver said nothing. Holmes continued his explanation.

"For some reason you have felt obliged to turn to villainy, a profession to which it seems you have proved to be singularly ill-suited. It cannot be from destitution, for you showed a good character as a soldier and your indisposition is not such as to preclude you from all employment. What is the thing that most often makes a man of your age and condition act, contrary to character, in return for the promise of a substantial sum of money? Why, surely, the most common reason is to provide for a future with a woman whom you love. You have not long returned and have had little time to find a partner for life. This suggests that you knew one another before you sailed to Egypt and that she has waited faithfully for you during your absence. Now, how long do you suppose she would be safe if Milverton settled accounts with you?"

That last thrust went home. There was silence for a full minute. Holmes had said all that he proposed to say and did not break it. At last McIver looked up.

"What will you do?" he asked, and his voice shook. He no longer doubted that if Holmes spoke to Crellin or Milverton, he would most certainly be dead before sunset, perhaps after such retribution as should make that death itself a blessing. Holmes was in no hurry to reply. He waited a moment longer. The cross-legged graven image sitting at the head of the bed lacked only the curled pipe that he used to smoke in this posture in our Baker Street rooms.

"No," said Holmes at length, "I believe the question is, Corporal McIver, what will you do?"

The man had stumbled into a quicksand of panic and knew not how to get out.

"I cannot save you, Mr. Holmes. How can I? I am searched every time I leave and enter. For days I am not allowed to leave at all."

"I do not suggest you should save me. In any case, I do not fear my death. Yet I might ask for those dignities and comforts that are the right of any man, even one under sentence."

He told me that there was no mistaking the relief on McIver's face. The man was far more weak than wicked and now saw that he might escape, whatever the fate of his prisoner.

"What comforts?" he asked, suddenly eager to know the price.

"Water," said Holmes, "a glass of water that is free from any drug, a glass which stands upon your table and which you will bring me to drink from when I require it."

"You shall have that, by all means. You might have had that anyway, by merely asking."

"And then," said Holmes thoughtfully, "confined as I am, held by a chain and deprived of movement, I feel it a toll on my physical well-being."

"I cannot free you from that chain, Mr. Holmes!"

"I would not ask it. So far as you are my friend, I am yours, and I do not willingly put my friends in danger."

At this, he half thought McIver might kneel and say, "Bless you, Mr. Holmes," or some other stage nonsense.

"I feel a dreadful lethargy," he explained. "Food sits on my stomach, kills my appetite, and I sense a great lassitude."

McIver was far out of his depth as he stared back.

"What is it that you want, sir?"

"More than anything," said Holmes slowly, "I should like the most ordinary remedy in the world. I have no means of escape and you cannot set me free. Yet for as long as I am permitted to live, I should like a packet of charcoal biscuits every day. You may obtain them at any pharmacy or any druggist. I believe they would do me great good."

After what had passed between them, this request appeared so trivial that McIver seemed to doubt his good fortune. How could a condemned man who nonetheless held the corporal at his mercy ask for so little?

"Is that all?" he said hesitantly.

"For the moment." said Holmes. "There may be other little things. Rest assured, I shall not put you in danger. What should I gain by that?""

McIver almost laughed with relief as he spoke.

"Of course I shall bring a store of charcoal biscuits, a supply for a week or two. That is nothing. I can bring them as if they were for my own use. You shall have water whenever you want it."

Then his face darkened a little.

"How do I know you will say nothing of what you have discovered?"

"You have my word," Holmes said icily. "I have never broken it yet, for good or evil, not even to Professor Moriarty and his kind. Besides which, to betray you would not save me. So long as you are obedient in these little matters, you shall be safe."

That night, before he left, McIver brought the glass of water, unseen by the others. Crellin, knowing nothing of this, followed a few minutes later with the hyoscine solution. Holmes took that glass in his hand while the bully moved the bedside chair and table from his reach. Then Crellin turned and, standing over his prisoner, watched him drink down the glass. No one who had seen Holmes's sleight-of-hand with far more difficult objects could doubt that the contents of the glass he had drunk was water. The hyoscine, no more than half a glass, had been disposed of under cover of the blanket.

That night, after the gas had guttered and the glow of the mantel had dwindled like a dying sun, it was Crellin who slept, the man's bulk against the table, while the oil lamp spluttered and faded. Almost silently in the darkness, Holmes felt for the seams and the threads of the cheap mattress. Before dawn, with teeth and nails, he had made an opening no more than a few inches long and well concealed in the fold of the canvas beading. Even had they found it, the rent he had made in the material might have seemed like wear and tear. Yet they never searched. He had begun to depend upon this. After all, he was a prisoner whom they saw chained to the wall, drugged by night, with the eyes of his guards constantly upon him, in a cell that was locked, inside and out, by keys always beyond his reach. Nothing was passed to him but food and drink. Even the food was first cut into pieces so that he need not be allowed the use of a knife or a fork. What could he have that would be worth searching for?

When the work was done, Sherlock Holmes lay back and thought of the mountain he must climb. To escape from the cell was only a beginning. There was no way out through the prison building with the first guards a few feet outside the cell door and many more beyond them. The sixty feet of smooth granite that rose from the yard were his only hope. His enemies knew much of Sherlock Holmes the public man, but his private life was as secret as only he could make it. His adversaries knew little of Sherlock Holmes and his chemical researches and nothing whatever of Sherlock Holmes the disciple of Paganini and scholar of polyphonic music. Nor did they know of him as a mountaineer who had attempted the so-called Widow-Maker glacier of the Matterhorn. He had yet to conquer it, but he was one of few who had come back alive from the attempt.

It was not in any of these accomplishments that he now placed his hope, but in another area of expertise. No man in the world was as well-informed in the minutiae of sensational and criminal literature as Sherlock Holmes. His extensive library, shelved on the walls of our Baker Street rooms, would have been so much dry reading to those who sought his destruction. Yet he knew and could recall every page that was of interest to him.

Somewhere in all those pages were two or three devoted to Henry Williams, a childhood chimney sweep and an adult burglar, sixty years ago. Holmes had read of him and visited the old man on his deathbed. There it was that Henry Williams, whose adventures grace the twentieth chapter of the *Newgate Chronicles*, imparted to my friend the secrets of his craft. For Henry Williams, all those years ago, had lain in the death cell of this same great prison when burglary was still a hanging matter. And Henry Williams had escaped the gallows by becoming the one man who had scaled those fearful walls of Newgate Gaol.

QUIET AS THE GRAVE

IT WAS ONLY THE MORAL INSANITY of Milverton and his accomplices that had allowed Sherlock Holmes a lease on life until the "witnesses" of his murder should arrive to enjoy a gallows tableau of vengeance. Brief though the time left to him might be, and however urgent the necessary action, he knew that he must wait until the conditions were exactly right for what he intended. Once again, he would have one chance—and one chance only. He required a night when Crellin was the warder in his cell after McIver had carried out his evening duties and withdrawn. Holmes wished the corporal of horse no harm. McIver had been essential to him, the one man over whom he could exercise command. Whatever this ex-trooper suspected, he dared not report it to Crellin or Milverton, for fear of the story that Holmes had to tell. Captive and captor were indissolubly bound by their pact.

Two days later a half-caught murmur from one of the guards in their purloined prison board uniforms suggested to Holmes that Henry Milverton himself was in Newgate that night. If Milverton was there, the master-at-arms and the execution shed might have been prepared for the next morning. Holmes knew that this night was the only one on which he could count. He would be free or he would die in his own way. If death was the choice, he would take with him Milverton and as many of his accessories as possible. Nine years earlier he had faced Professor Moriarty with the same resolve at the falls of Reichenbach. He remarked then that his own life was an easy price to pay for the destruction of such evil.

McIver had done his duty in the cell by day and was to be one of the two men to keep watch in the corridor that night, sleeping by turns but ready to assist Crellin in the cell if need be. Just before the change of guards, the corporal brought a glass of the sweet and oily hypnotic.

"The water, if you please," said Holmes quietly. "I find the taste of this draft quite as abominable as its effects."

The man's nerve withered in his presence. He could not meet the dark and penetrating gaze, perhaps knowing that murder was intended in the morning. He turned away to fill the water glass. For the benefit of anyone else who might chance to see him, Holmes raised the glass of hyoscine to his lips, then threw back his head as if to swallow the contents and be done with it. Before McIver could turn, in one flowing downward movement of his arm to suggest exhaustion, he had tipped the eggcupful of fluid between the wall and the bed. The sickly mixture had merely wet his lips to give off its sour-treacle odour. McIver brought the glass of water. Whether he suspected what had become of the drug, Holmes never knew. Yet, with the prisoner chained and watched in a locked cell, what did the sleeping draught matter? It was intended to prevent a condemned man from giving trouble. Holmes had been careful never to give trouble.

"My time is short and I think we may not speak again," he said softly to the corporal, handing back the glass. "You are a weak and foolish man but not, I think, a wicked one. From now on you must follow your conscience. I daresay I shall never be in a position to help you, but, should it happen, you may depend upon it that I will do my best to set you free."

McIver's eyes betrayed his helplessness and he murmured even more softly in his turn.

"You must not speak to me now, sir. You must not, if you wish me well."

Holmes smiled. It was the second time that McIver had called him "sir," the instinctive deference of the old soldier to his commander. Given a few more days, he might have turned this jailer into an ally.

"One more thing." he said quietly. "On no account enter this cell tomorrow morning before others have done so. Mind you see to that."

It was as much as he could do for the frightened corporal of horse. Perhaps it was because they had heard something about the hour of his death that the others seemed a little more careless with him that night. It must have seemed to them that they had only to keep an unconscious man safely in his cell for another eight or nine hours. Perhaps soon after dawn, in the presence of Milverton and his criminal associates, three warders and the master-at-arms would drag their half-conscious captive to the execution shed twenty yards away across the exercise yard.

Crellin entered to find Holmes already lying on his side with the upper blanket drawn over him. The man locked the door with his bunch of keys, returned it to his belt, and made a perfunctory search of the prisoner. An oily sweetness of the drug hung in the close air and the jailer's nostrils could detect it. Neither man spoke. For his part, Holmes sensed the customary odour of drink on this ruffian's breath. Crellin inspected the manacle on the left ankle of his prisoner and pulled hard against the fastening on the wall to check its strength. He crossed the room to the wooden chair on which he had sat during every night of his vigil, in profile, with his back to the wall, his right arm resting on the bare wooden table beside him.

Sherlock Holmes had calculated his reach as a matter of simple mathematics. It was too short to touch Crellin. The chain allowed him five feet, enough to reach the little alcove behind him with its washing basin and drain. In the other direction, by lying flat, he could add a further six feet and at least two feet more for his extended arms. Measuring the paving tiles beside his bed by rule of thumb and allowing for the width of the floor, he had calculated that he would be almost two feet short of the chair on which Crellin sat. Henry Milverton did not make the mistake of underestimating his captive. The jailers would always be beyond his range.

Crellin lit his warder's night lamp, which Holmes had identified at first sight as the "Hesperus" model made by Jones & Willis of Birmingham. It was lit or extinguished without any need to remove the glass chimney. The reservoir when full might last for several hours, but on previous nights it had guttered and faded after no more than two. As on all those other nights, Crellin now came closer and shone the lamp on the sleeping figure of the prisoner. Satisfied by what he saw and sure that it was safe to sleep, he went back and set the lamp down on the tiles beside his chair. Before sitting down, he went through the usual ritual of crossing the cell and pulling down the draw chain beside the gaslight on the opposite wall. Behind the three glass fish-tails of its shade, the double flame dwindled to a dying glow. Without a glance at the sleeping figure under the blanket, he went back and stood by his chair to extinguish the second double gas lamp above him. He turned down the wick on the Hesperus oil lamp and positioned it beside his chair again, perhaps eight inches away. The cell was in shadow, no better lit now than by the gentlest nursery night-light.

Sherlock Holmes lay motionless, waiting impatiently rather than fearfully to begin his work. Unless he could extinguish the low flame of the conical burner, his hopes were at an end. Twice in the next hour one of the men outside shone a lantern through the spy hole of the cell. The path of light missed Crellin, nodding on his chair, but illuminated the prisoner's bed and the upper half of the little alcove behind it. There was no sound from the passage, and during the half hour that followed, the light did not appear again. If ever a man possessed his soul in patience, it was Sherlock Holmes in the depth of that night. Twice more, far beyond the prison walls, the bell of St. Sepulchre's tolled and the deeper notes of the great cathedral followed it.

He knew to the inch and to the minute what must be done. Like all drunkards, Crellin would fall at first into a deep sleep that would leave him insensible for half the night. Then he would become restless and, finally, would wake suddenly and without warning. During the first of these phases the plan must be carried out. As Holmes listened, he heard the breathing grow slower and deeper, almost dwindling into silence. The man's head remained pillowed on his arm, which in turn still rested on the table beside him.

During his first hours in the cell Holmes had reckoned its dimensions as nineteen feet long, by eight feet wide and seven feet high. One thousand and sixty-four cubic feet. Some of that capacity was taken up by furnishings and fittings, notably a solid three-foot-square stone table at the far end and the wooden bed. The total space remaining was about a thousand and fifty cubic feet. He had even estimated the capacity of the wooden chair, now removed beyond his reach for the night. It seemed designed for the death cell, its joints being carefully dovetailed, without a single nail that might be used as a key or the condemned man's means of self-destruction.

As for the fittings, the four fish-tail gaslights, a pair on each of the long walls, were of the common type with a Sugg-Letherby's No. 1 burner. Each of the four would be fed by ten cubic feet of gas an hour. A slight odour of spirit as they were lit had assured Sherlock Holmes that they were fed by that cheaper type of fuel known as water-gas, commonly used in public buildings. If released unlit, its high concentration of carbon monoxide would be enough to poison almost all the air in the cell by the end of sixty minutes. Those who breathed it might not be dead at the end of the hour, but they would never regain consciousness unaided. Yet even had his enemies thought Holmes capable of reaching the draw chains of the burners, they knew that he must be the first to die.

Among the volumes frequently taken down from his Baker Street bookshelves by my friend were the varied works of Dr. Daniel Haldane of Edinburgh, including *Haldane on Poisons*. Newgate prison, like most such institutions, tendered for the cheapest sources of fuel. These included this old-fashioned water-gas piped from a mains supply. It had once been produced by the decomposition of water, now often replaced by the use of petroleum as its origin, which gave it that spirituous odour on lighting. Its economic brightness was caused by the high concentration of carbon monoxide. Its use was more easily and carefully regulated in old and ill-ventilated public buildings than in private homes. It was seldom supplied to private citizens because of a greater danger of explosion if it should be misused.

It was the duty of the two guards in the corridor to shine a lamp through the spy hole of the cell door from time to time to make sure that all was well within. Holmes had noticed in the past night or two that they did this every half hour or so to begin with and then, as they took their chance to sleep, they seemed content to shine the beam on the prisoner's bed at intervals of an hour or more. He waited until one of the men outside had shone the lamp through the spy hole. It was past midnight and he judged that it would be the best part of an hour before they did that again.

No man ever moved as silently and with such economy of movement as Sherlock Holmes. With no more sound than a shadow he stripped off his shirt and held it in one hand. In the other hand he carried the light steel ankle chain clear of the floor so that it made no more noise than a silk rope. At the limit of the chain he stared down at Crellin, several feet away. The man, now palefaced from drink, was sleeping so deeply that his breathing was scarcely audible. There was a sickly perspiration on his forehead and his mouth sagged open. Holmes knelt silently and then measured his length across the cold paving of the tiled floor, reaching his arms at full stretch toward the Hesperus lamp by Crellin's chair. The bully heard no more sound than if a bird had glided overhead.

My friend's calculations were correct. The lamp stood about a foot beyond the tips of his fingers. Using the buttons of the shirt cuffs to link the arms together as a lasso, he held the garment by its tails and cast it like a frail noose. It hit the glass chimney silently but slithered down without effect. For the first time the measured and controlled beat of Sherlock Holmes's heart began to quicken. He cast again and this time saw the cotton arms snag on the top of the lamp's glass chimney. Controlling his breath, as if for fear of waking the guard, he shook and worked the loop of cloth gently until he saw it slide down the far side of the glass to encircle the lamp at its base.

His remarkable hearing was tuned to every nuance in Crellin's breathing. He knew that he must now draw the lamp toward him without rousing the sleeping warder. The Hesperus lamp had been constructed so that the oil and the wick sat in a smooth metal bowl that formed its base. Yet to drag smooth metal roughly toward him would cause a rasping on the tiled floor that might wake the sleeper.

Crellin gulped air into his throat and Holmes stopped at once. He waited until the sound of the man's breathing was regular again and then tilted the lamp a little by pulling on the cotton noose. Only the smooth and rounded edge of its metal base now touched the tiles as it ran in a series of three brief crescents, as if on the rim of a wheel. It made no more sound than the feet of a rat hurrying across the dark yard outside. Once only in the next ten minutes did Crellin shift against the table with another heaving breath.

Holmes eased the lamp quietly toward him and still there was no further movement from his guard. Presently his fingers touched the warm metal of the lamp base. As he drew back to the darkness of his bed, he held in his hands a treasure greater than the wealth of kings.

Without hesitation he carried the lamp silently into the little alcove with its basin and drain, where he turned down the wick as low as he dared without extinguishing the flame. Then he heard the movement of the metal cover on the spy hole and had just time to slip back and draw the blanket over him on the bed before a tunnel of watery light illuminated the cell. He thought that he had little more to fear from this hourly inspection. Two men in the corridor guarded the cell door that night. One was McIver. The other was either the brutal master-at-arms or one of his assistants. When two men performed such a duty, it was the weaker who was given the chore of an hourly inspection while the other slept. He had no doubt, in this case, that the weaker was McIver.

In the faint light that illuminated the cell from the alcove, he moved toward the draw chain controlling the supply of gas to the fish-tails on the far wall, just on the near side of Crellin's chair. The chains were closer to him than the lamp had been, but higher on the wall. The ankle chain was too short for his purpose, but by turning his body sideways he could reach a point a foot from the wall and a foot short of the metal pull. With a quiet breath he flicked the cotton noose of the shirt at its full length until he caught the chain and started it swinging like a pendulum against the wall. Keeping the metal links free of the wall, he flicked it harder, so that it swung further away from him and came further back.

The extent of its nearer swing was eight inches short of his stretched fingers, as he measured it by sight, then six inches as he flicked it again, then four. Four inches would doom him as surely as four miles. Then the thin metal links brushed his fingertips, but he lost them again. And then, as it came swinging back, he snatched with all the energy of his being and just held it. Now he had only to draw gently on the thin chain. A moment later, he heard the first whisper of escaping gas issuing from the double jet above Crellin's head as he slept.

The two fish tails on the nearer wall were more easily within his range, but it had been necessary to make sure of the more distant ones first. With a single flick of the cotton shirt he caught the swinging links. Silently he pulled at this chain controlling the burners behind the fish-tails. The whisper of water-gas became a rush. Much was still in the hands of fate but now only one path lay ahead of him, for better or for worse. Stripping the rough canvas cover from the prison pillow, he arranged the under-blanket and the pillow to give some semblance of a sleeping figure beneath the thin upper layer. Enough to satisfy McIver. Then he groped in the thin mattress for the packets of medicinal charcoal that the corporal had brought him.

Lighter than air, the whispering gas was filling the upper layers of the cell and time was beginning to run against him. The length of the chain at his ankle allowed him to move into the alcove with its basin and drain, where the flame of the oil lamp still wavered. In a few moments he must extinguish it. Holmes knelt down where the waste pipe ran into a gully that led to the grating of the drain outside. However faint and tainted, it was the one supply of air. Using the canvas pillow cover, he worked quickly to form a hood that might be worn like a surgeon's mask, tied by its tapes behind his head. It was common knowledge from his own experiments that charcoal was the best air filter, absorbing the poisonous compounds of gas. How much it would absorb or with what effect, only the next hour would tell. As he was making his preparations the bell of St. Sepulchre's tolled three times, as if hurrying on the dawn.

Now I must break a confidence that is no longer of great matter. Sherlock Holmes contributed much to chemistry and science in general but did not care to do so under his own name. He intended that his enemies should have no idea of these interests. The world did not know that under the name of the chemist Hunter he had contributed a paper, "On the Effects of Pressure on the Absorption of Gases by Charcoal," to the *Journal of the Chemical Society* in 1871, where the world may still read it. In his study of history he had been much taken by the startling proposal of Lord Cochrane in 1812 to defeat Napoleon three years before Waterloo by an invasion of France under cover of "sulphur ships." To effect this, however, the attackers must be protected by a mask of some kind—and there was none. However, my friend had corresponded with the late Dr. John Tyndall in 1878, following that great man's invention of a respirator. This enabled firemen to breathe for thirty minutes or more in smoke that would otherwise have killed them, and allowed coal miners to survive who must otherwise have been suffocated by gas.

Dr. Tyndall's respirator consisted of a hood attached to a metal cylinder or pipe, packed with charcoal, surrounded by a layer of cotton wool, moistened with glycerine, and fitted with a piece of wire gauze at the end to hold the pad and the charcoal in place. Holmes turned down the wick and took the extinguished Hesperus lamp. He removed its glass lantern. Working with the deft fingers of a craftsman, he found the two buttons of the screw heads that tightened the metal wick holder to the base and shielded the reservoir of fuel. He undid them and carefully drew the metal sheath from its base. It tapered to a hole at the top, round which he could just measure forefinger and thumb. It was enough. Further down was a slot that admitted air to the base of the wick.

Though time was short, Holmes worked characteristically, always with haste but never in a hurry. Within the metal cylinder of the wick holder he formed a lining of loosened woolen padding from the mattress. Though he had no pure glycerine, it was a principal ingredient of the soft soap allowed him. He used the soap and a palmful of water to moisten the cotton waste at the open end of the metal cone and the lower air slot, sufficient to catch grosser particles of carbon in the air. The broken biscuits of Mostyn's Absorbant Medical Charcoal, like small pebbles, then filled the metal cone through which he must draw breath.

Using the water jug again, he moistened the canvas pillow cover and formed it into a hood about his head. His mouth and nostrils were enclosed in the larger end of the conical wick holder, the wet canvas about his head forming a crude seal against contaminated air. Then he lay on the chill stone of the tiles, the tapered end of the metal wick holder directed to the waste-pipe hole at the end of the gutter that ran from the basin. Whatever air reached him from the yard outside would lose some of its impurities in his makeshift filter. So would the gas that began to fill the cell. He held fast to the hope that the floor of that alcove was almost the last area that the silent and swirling deadliness of the carbon monoxide would reach.

If it were my purpose to make a fine hero of Sherlock Holmes, I might say that he lay on the cold tiles, breathing steadily but economically through the device he had fashioned, and that he prayed. Yet one had only to be in his company for five minutes to recognise in him the most perfect reasoning and observing machine the world has ever seen. He was not devoid of faith or human warmth, but at that moment, if ever, only cold reason and critical observation would save him.

Once he had told me that logic alone would lead a man to the deep truths of religion. Then, again, he asked what is the meaning of this circle of misery, violence, and fear in which we live? It must tend to some end, or else our universe is ruled by chance, which is unthinkable. But to what end? There, he said, is the great outstanding perennial problem to which human reason is as far from an answer as ever.

How long he lay there, the cold striking like a steel blade to his bones, I never knew. He heard St. Sepulchre's deep notes twice more, at least, and the cathedral bell that followed. He saw a flickering reflection beyond the alcove, a lantern shining through the spy hole. But he had calculated the risks with his customary inhuman precision. Whoever looked through the spy hole would see a shape under the blankets and, knowing that Crellin was keeping guard, would also know that the shape must be that of the prisoner. Had there been no guard in the cell, they would have looked him over thoroughly at short intervals.

In the iron chill of that night Holmes waited for the pale yellow lantern light to play again on the wall by the alcove. But he had seen it for the last time. He waited and listened. As he did so, if he is to be believed, Sherlock Holmes soothed his nerves by rehearsing in his mind a book that had shaped much of his character since he first read it at the age of ten. It was no fairy story of giants or goblins but the

Prior Analytics of Aristotle. "A syllogism is a form of words in which, when certain assumptions are made, something other than what has been assumed necessarily follows from the fact that the assumptions are such. . . ."

Cold reason told him that the plan must work, but reason may fly away or be flawed in the lonely dark hours of such a night. An undetected current of air might draw the gas astray from Crellin and toward the alcove. Holmes had calculated, as surely as any hangman, the direction in which his victim's body would fall. When the muscles no longer held the frame, Crellin would slide from the chair. He could not fall to his right, because the table would stop him. If he fell to the left, his body lying on the floor with the keys at its belt would surely be within the prisoner's reach. It was most likely that Crellin would do neither but would fall forward. In that case, if the fall was forward and slightly to the left, Sherlock Holmes might be saved. If it was somewhat to the right, he was certainly destroyed. In the gas-filled cell, he would have become his own executioner. It was not a matter of cold reason, after all, but the spin of a gambler's wheel.

Such precision of thought would have been preposterous in any other man who lay perspiring on the cold tiles with a fear that at any moment he might scent the faint rotting smell of water-gas seeping through the suffocating wad of charcoal. If Crellin had not fallen by then, Holmes was as good as dead. Yet Holmes was not any other man. He was surely the only one alive who might have escaped from such captivity. St. Sepulchre's tolled again and then he heard a thud, easily audible in the alcove but not in the corridor beyond the thick walls and stout door of the cell. At that moment, he who had breathed so economically in the past hours stopped altogether and held his breath as he waited for the louder clatter of the chair. But there was no clatter. Crellin alone had fallen. After lying immobile for so long, Holmes moved with the speed of a cloud crossing the moon.

Only the reflection of the night sky through the uncurtained window glass lit the cell. He took the deepest breath of air his lungs would hold and crossed the threshold. Through the swirling spirit odour of gas, he saw the dark shape of Crellin's body. The man might still be alive or already dead. Had he fallen toward the table, the keys on his belt would be far out of reach. Then there was nothing but the hope that prisoner and jailer might die together in a blast that would shake Newgate Street. The odds were finely balanced. Yet on this occasion, Fortune and mathematics had favored the brave. Crellin's body had toppled away from the table to the left, toward Holmes, head and shoulders within reach of the ankle chain and the extended arms.

With aching lungs Holmes held his breath and drew the heavy burden of the body further toward him until he could reach the half-dozen keys on the ring at Crellin's belt. The keys to the corridor and the yard outside would surely be there. Unless the game was to be lost, the key to the metal cuff round the prisoner's ankle must be with them.

With his throat compressed and veins swelling, logic and probability fighting the weight of fear, Holmes touched the keys in the darkness and knew that three of them were too big to fit the steel anklet. The image of a fox gnawing through its leg to escape the trap flashed like fire behind his eyes. He tried the first of the other three keys and felt it jam in the lock of the leg iron. While fighting against the beating in his skull and the pain at his breastbone, he slowly and judiciously eased it clear. The second was far too loose a fit. That left only one more.

But in the darkness he had started at the wrong end of the row of keys and now, as he tried the last of all, the lock moved. For the first time since his arrival in that place, the steel fell away and his leg was free of the anklet. The first of the three larger keys failed in the lock of the door to the yard. The next turned the lock, and he took the handle in a strong but noiseless sweep. To his dismay, the unlocked door stuck fast and, in his bursting chest, he felt a chill of incomprehension. A bubble burst from his throat; he took in a mouthful of poisoned air, and he forced it out again by naked willpower. As his throat closed, choking, a part of his mind that seemed far removed from the agony told him that he had not yet drawn the door bolts free. Holmes snatched for them, drew them carefully and silently back, gently freed the door, and stumbled into the cold night air of the yard, muffling the convulsions of his throat in the pad made from the canvas pillow cover. Yet this was not his escape. It was a mere chance of escape, a chance that most men would have contemplated—and despaired.

HENRY WILLIAMS'S LEGACY

How long he lay outside the yard door he did not know, nor whether the jailer who had fallen from his chair was alive or dead. When he opened his eyes, the door to the cell had swung shut under its own weight. Sherlock Holmes pulled himself up and tried the handle. The lock had not closed again. He covered his mouth and nostrils with the wet canvas of the pillow cover and went into the darkness. With the door open, the air began to clear. A first predawn lightness was in the sky, enough to make out the lineaments of furniture and other objects.

The shape of Crellin was lying facedown by the chair in the place where Holmes had left him. It seemed evident in an oblong of reflected moonlight that the guard must be dead. His head lolled stupidly to one side, the eyelids half open and half shut. Dixon Mann's *Forensic Toxicology* was as familiar to Sherlock Holmes as the English dictionary was to others. From what he could see in faint light from the yard, Crellin's cheeks were a healthy cherry pink. The lips were moist, no doubt from a froth that had dispersed when breathing ceased. The eyes, as he raised the lids, were wide and staring. He did not need to look for a pulse in order to know that carbon monoxide poisoning had killed Milverton's bully stone dead long before the prisoner had made his escape into the yard.

Though the open door had cleared the air immediately around it, the water-gas floated sluggishly in the rest of the long cell. It had saturated the air and the fabric. Holmes stepped out into the yard, drew a hard breath, and closed his smarting throat. Back in the cell, he dragged the body across to the bed. It took all his strength to lug Crellin onto the hard surface and cover him with the blanket. Then he went back through the door to the yard, closed it, and locked it from the outside. In the cell the gas still bubbled from the four unlit jets. Having warned McIver to let the others enter first, Holmes was prepared to let them take their chance. They had carried out their inspection every morning before it was fully light, lamps in hand. There was so little daylight in the deep well of the prison yard that the cell needed light long after sunrise. The blast from a gas explosion, touched off by the flame of their lamps, might make the body on the bed and those of the intruders conveniently unrecognisable. His enemies would not know whether he was one of the victims. Nor could he be certain at once which of them might have perished. As a final touch, he had locked the anklet round the leg of Crellin's corpse. An inspection lamp shining through the spy-hole of the door would show them a figure lying under a blanket with a crown of dark hair visible and the chain in place.

Presently Sherlock Holmes stood in the cold mist of the morning by the locked outer door of the cell. If he got no further than this, then despite all his ingenuity he would be caught and killed before the sun lit the great cathedral cross half a mile away. In his white shirt, dark trousers, and socks, his shoes tied together by their laces round his neck, he prepared to test the truth of Henry Williams's story.

This was the moment of pre-dawn greyness, half an hour before the watery gold in the east and the first long shadows of the early spring sky. In a far corner of the yard he could make out the low elongated shed with its beam above the gallows drop. On three sides, Newgate's walls rose above him, high and sheer, smooth and deadly with a patch of a pale cloud far overhead, still touched by late moonlight. The fourth side of the yard contained the condemned cells with three rows of barred windows above them. The roof of this structure was a dozen feet lower than the tops of the walls on the other three sides, but Holmes turned his back on it. At roof level, a thin metal canopy extended a dozen feet along its entire length. It was designed to trap a climber beneath it, being too frail to take a man's weight. The wall face, as Henry Williams had promised him, was the only way.

He glanced up at the polish of a blank wall, laying his hand on it and touching an icy smoothness. It was useless to look for crevices that might bear the pressure of a foot or the grip of fingers. The weight of stone blocks pressed them so tightly together that even a gap in the mortar would scarcely have given lodging to a fingernail.

Holmes was better versed in prison lore than any other man. His copy of the *Newgate Chronicles* commemorated a number of felons whose time had come and who tried in their last hours to climb these walls by studs or hessian on their shoes. One or two had started well, only to fall back into the yard. They were supported on the trap and hanged on time.

The old iron tank was high above him on a bracket in the angle of two walls. A rusty stain of water down the stonework below showed where it had overflowed from time to time. Above the metal cover of the tank and a little to one side of it, the wooden axle set with sharpened wire ran round the three walls that enclosed the cell block. It was this device which would throw the climber downwards, if his fingers lost their grip on the steel wire.

When they brought him back from his tribunal, Holmes had made a passing and surreptitious study of this device. The prison authorities had not supposed that any prisoner could gain such a height or that, if he did, he would keep a grip on such a vicious deterrent as the axle. At the best, he might hope to dangle there if he chose, at a dizzy height above the paving of the yard unable to climb up or down. Milverton's men had not prevented my friend from studying such defences. Nothing would have pleased them more than to watch him calculating the hopelessness of an escape and breaking down from weariness, Sherlock Holmes pleading for his life at the end.

If he sometimes showed little mercy to others, it was certain that he now showed none to himself. He would not fear to go where the humble chimney-sweep had gone before. Crossing to the angle of the wall in which the now disused iron tank had been installed, high overhead, he touched the surface of the stone again. It was beyond reason that they could have raised an object of such weight and bulk as a metal tank to so great a height, and fixed it there, without using scaffolding and thereby defacing the masonry in that angle. There were certainly no convenient crevices for the hands or feet, but Henry Williams had described to him how the broken face of the stone might prevent a hand or foot from slipping if the pressure of the climber's body could hold him in place. Like a sweep's boy or an acrobat, Sherlock Holmes now stood barefoot in the cold morning and prepared himself for an assault on the towering wall. Williams had never mastered the art of the chimney-sweep or the prison fugitive more surely than Holmes, his last apprentice.

It was, the old man had told him, a matter of lodging in the corner and working your hands behind you "like a crab," braced by the feet where the two walls came narrowly together. The dying sweep boasted of having worked to the top inside a great factory chimney. "And keep yer boots and stockings orf," he added. "That's what does for most that tries it." Immediately after this conversation, my friend had been intrigued enough to try the method and found that with practise, it could be made to work. Without that practise, it is doubtful that even Holmes could have accomplished such a climb. In the angle behind him, however, he could feel that the stonework was "rusticated," as builders call it, that is to say broken and ridged from the devices of the water engineers. With his back to the icy wall, he now prepared to put the old man's wisdom to its final test.

As yet there were no sounds from the gaunt prison building. A guard who shone a light through the spy-hole of the cell door would still see a dark-haired figure asleep under the blanket and would have no reason to enter. Crellin's chair was to one side of the spies' field of vision. They would assume that he was still sitting there. Where else should he be?

Putting the danger of pursuit from his mind, Sherlock Holmes took up his position. It required both hands against the surface behind him and one foot across the narrow meeting of the walls to brace himself. Yet it was a trick that a thousand sweeps' boys learnt before their childhood was over. He drew up the other foot and used it as a lever across the angle. The soles of his feet felt the slight contours of the stone and for a moment he clung motionless, clear of the ground.

The art was to move the hands, as the old man had told him, like the claws of a crab. Wedged in the angle, the purchase of his feet holding him, his palms and fingers now worked alternately upwards. It was a game that children might play to the height of a few feet. It could also carry a man like Henry Williams to sixty feet, if his nerve was strong. He glanced up as a thin drift of river cloud darkened the early dawn.

With a patience that he showed only in extreme peril, Holmes moved himself cautiously, an inch at a time, as the early mist became a faint grey light. He held his body in the angle, feeling skilfully for the furrows of the surface that gave purchase to palms and fingers. As if through instinct, he did not put a hand or a foot wrong, though the urgency of escape quickened his blood as full daylight began to penetrate somewhere beyond the yard. His hands pressed the broken surface until it tore at his skin, yet he breathed long and slowly, as though with the inhuman indifference of a machine.

Sometimes it was difficult to find a corrugated patch of stone behind him. Once he lost his hold and his hand slipped, though he saved himself on the chipped corner of a block an inch or two lower down. Then he stopped and breathed slowly, never looking down at the death that waited in the yard below if he were to fall from the height he had now reached. From time to time, he turned the palm of one hand a little, just sufficiently to wipe sweat or blood on his shirt or trousers.

At length the flat and rusted underside of the tank was close above him. Sherlock Holmes used to say, modestly, that he was stronger than most men, but the truth was that he was not strong in a conventional way. It was in his sinewy arms and legs that he had such power. I had seen him not merely bend a poker into a semi-circle but straighten out one which had been recently bent by a threatening visitor. Had all else failed him, I daresay my friend could have made his living as Hercules at a fairground. Such power served him well in moments like these.

Two hundred feet from the little shops housing map-makers and ships' chandlers, he fought for his life on the prison wall. Where the iron angle supporting the tank was fixed, the stone had been coarsened by damage and he found a better hold. He reached and caught the metal strut. The purchase of his feet against the wall levered him. Praying to whatever gods might be that the bracket was not rusted through, he snatched again and hung by both hands, his feet dangling as if from the summit of a church tower.

The long reach of his arms and legs proved to be his salvation. He swung until he could kick out with both feet and find leverage across the angle of the walls once more. With one hand gripping the bracket, he stretched upwards and sideways with the other, found a metal bar for one foot and hoisted himself, face-down on the cover of the tank.

The worst of the climb was over, and the ordeal of the sharpened wire lay ahead.

The length of a long wall separated him from the rooftop that led the way to freedom. Yet with the self-confidence which irritated so many of his rivals, Sherlock Holmes never doubted that what he had just done, he could do again. Now he had only to stand upright and stretch to one side, in order to touch the wooden axle with its sharp metal wire where it ran along the wall. It was the only link to the first rooftop above the street.

His shirt or whatever cloth he might wrap round his hands to protect them from the sharpened wire would weaken the sureness of his grip on the wooden axle. "The blades may hurt you," Henry Williams had said, "but they won't kill you. Not unless you let 'em. What you must do is make up your mind, tell yourself there's a hundred feet to get past. P'raps it ain't so many. Then you hang on for dear life and count. After ten, there's only ninety to go, after forty there's only sixty. You'll do thirty and you're more than half-way to fifty, so you mustn't give up. You do fifty-one, and you've got less to go than you've done already, having come through so much. You're nearer the finish than the start. So you ain't going to give up and drop now, are you? Not having come through all that and with less to go! That's common sense."

For a brief moment, Holmes stood on the metal surface high above the yard and smiled at the old man's wisdom. He said aloud to himself for the second time that morning, "Fortune favours the brave." Though he never boasted of it, he knew as he prepared for his ordeal that to fail now would very probably make my own life forfeit to Henry Milverton and, possibly, that of the young woman whose silver revolver rid the world of the villain's elder brother.

Each change of hand-hold would bring him six inches closer to his goal. At every change, as his weight hung from the axle, he might shed blood from his hands. Whatever the pain, it was not an eternity. Perhaps no more than a few minutes. Closing his mind, as if all this was happening to another man in another world, he gave his concentration to counting the changes of grip, measuring what must still be endured, and seeing in his mind the dwindling numbers ahead. When he passed fifty, he heard the old man's voice again, "So you ain't going to give up and drop now, are you? That's common sense."

Working hand over hand along the axle, he thought only of the roof he must reach. Far from the pain in his hands he continued to count the growing number of wounds that were past and the dwindling number to be endured. At last he hung above the abandoned cell block, the flat roof a dozen feet below him. There was nothing for it but to release his grip on the end of the wooden axle. Most of those who met him found Sherlock Holmes physically languid rather than agile. Only when circumstances required did he exercise his phenomenal dexterity. He had the suppleness of a cat, and nothing less would have enabled him to drop so accurately and without injury to the rooftop below. He landed squarely on the flat lead of its surface. It was the first prison block, whose roof led towards the street.

He knelt for a moment, then pulled himself upright and listened. There was no light in the yard below. The voices which he could hear at a distance were surely those of market porters setting out their street-stalls, nothing more than the men talking as they walked to and fro with baskets on their heads.

By keeping below the parapet of the roof, he would be hidden from the street. It would not do to come this far and then be taken for a rooftop burglar, seized and delivered to the prison gate by hopeful reward-hunters. The flat roofs of the prison and the street lay ahead of him in succession, with several alleyways below. It was now that he took the greatest care. Somewhere, the old sweep had told him, there was a low brick wall belonging to a bookbinder. It marked the first rooftop beyond the prison. Two men who had followed Williams in his attempt to escape the gallows had made the mistake of coming down before they reached this wall. They had found themselves trapped in the old press yard behind the prison wall, where reluctant suspects had once upon a time been pressed to death, if necessary, with increasing iron weights on their chests to make them give evidence.

The voices below him, whoever they had come from, were now silent. He crawled forward, close to the parapet with his head well down, taking cover in the angle of deeper shadow which the early sun had not as yet dispersed. Time might be against him, but Holmes was a man of exceptionally acute hearing and he still heard no sound of alarm or pursuit. Instead, he looked up a few minutes later and saw, across the flat roof, a dividing wall no higher than his waist. It was painted with white letters, "Bindery."

He made his way to the roof-hatch, put on his shoes, and slipped quickly and unnoticed through the bookbinder's premises. Assuming the purposeful air of a journeyman, he crossed the street below and was lost among the sooty tenements of the city. Just then, in the yellow light of the new day, there was a brief lightning flash behind him, reflected in the sky ahead. The cold air and even the paving under foot shook with a monstrous roll of thunder, rattling the glass of the shopfronts. A deep and resonant roar sounded across the rooftops, as if the sound had taken a second or two to catch up with the tremor of a blast. Then all around there was a pattering like hail, as fragments of stone rattled down from the sky. From somewhere else came a clatter of glass broken by the force of the detonation. The carters and the costermongers at their stalls looked up, as if waiting for a sequel and a gathering of storm clouds. But the single shuddering roar fell to a rumble and faded. There was silence, a caustic stench of burnt fabric, and then the unmistakable flickering and lapping sounds of flame.

As the ill-clad figure of the fugitive made his painful way, slow and stooping among the market traders in the shabby streets, he calculated that the lantern flames of the execution party had ignited more than a thousand cubic feet of water-gas with a detonation like a howitzer shell.

BROTHER MYCROFT

HAVING GIVEN you the account of Sherlock Holmes's ordeal, as I later heard it from his own lips, I must now return to the circumstances of my own life during his curious disappearance.

To most of those who recall that spring of 1902, it was a time of celebration. A little more than a year earlier Victoria, the great Queen Empress, had gone to her reward, after sixty-four years on the British throne. Few people had ever known what it was to be alive except when she reigned over them. That New Year had been a time of solemn pomp, a great funeral, and commemoration. Now the flags flew in the bright spring air among the preparations that went forward for the coronation of her eldest son as Edward VII in August.

Such public jollity made my own despondency all the deeper. The columns of the *Morning Post* had brought me nothing, and in the circumstances, I cared very little for flags and bunting, for crowned heads and fireworks.

A further week or so passed, after I had spoken to our friends at Scotland Yard about the strange disappearance, and still I heard nothing of Holmes. Even if I went back to Lestrade or Gregson and told them that he was still missing, what could they do? Worst of all, I now faced the disagreeable task of informing Mycroft Holmes that some accident or villainy had surely overtaken his younger brother. By the middle of April, the matter could no longer be put off. We were to lunch together at his club, the Diogenes, in Pall Mall. All that I knew—or rather did not know—must be put before him. Yet what he or the entire government could make of it was beyond me.

During this time, I had gathered no positive evidence of being spied upon—and yet I felt sure it must be so. If Holmes was right in believing that a wide criminal conspiracy was at work in London, my enemies would arrange matters so that I should never see the same shadow twice as they followed me about. There would be enough of them for one to watch me for a mile or an hour at a time and then be replaced by another. For this reason, I gave up hansom cabs and had taken to traveling by the new electric underground railway. A man may be followed easily in a cab, but I had mastered the art of getting on a train as it pulled in and getting out at the last minute to see if any other passenger did the same, thus forcing my follower to reveal himself. Sometimes I was quick enough to do this and still board again if the coast remained clear. At other times I waited alone on the platform for the next train or the one after. Yet another of my shadows might be waiting at a station further on and I should be none the wiser.

Sometimes I would come up into the daylight from the underground station and perhaps notice that a man who had been reading his newspaper by a lamppost now folded it and walked in the direction that I had taken. Of course, it was a hundred to one that he was an honest fellow who had stopped to check the price of gilt-edged stock or the odds offered on the favorite in the 2:30 at Epsom races. How, in any case, could a spy know that I would leave the train at this place? Yet there are only six stations on the line from Baker Street to Waterloo, and they could set a dozen men after me, if they chose, so that one waited at each stop of the train. If Holmes was right in describing the extent of such a criminal conspiracy—and if it mattered enough to them—they could watch me day and night, even from other premises in Baker Street.

I had lived like this for a few weeks, trusting no one and looking everywhere about me. At first I took it for granted that those who shadowed me would be men. Then one day I had the thought—what if one or more of them was a woman? I had been entirely unprepared for that. I wondered whether I should challenge them when there was a policeman standing by to see fair play. Once I saw a fellow coming after me as I left the street door in Baker Street. My blood was up. I turned to confront him and damn the consequences. Moreover, I had a vague recollection of seeing that face and figure before! At the last moment I recognised him as Fothergill, a medical student at Cambridge and Barts Hospital, who had been scrum-half for Harlequins half a dozen times when I played rugby football for Blackheath.

In the end I knew this would not do. I must assume that they were always watching—and make the best of it. On an April morning I left the train at Trafalgar Square to keep my appointment with Mycroft Holmes. I went up the steps and into the open sunlit space with Admiral Nelson on his column far above the chestnut trees in bud.

Pall Mall is surely the home of the gentleman's club. I left the square by Cockspur Street and passed the Regency grandeur of the Royal United Service Club with its full-dress portraits of Crimean generals seen through long Georgian windows. I passed the intellectual elegance of the Athenaeum with its philosophers and men of letters, the Travellers Club, and last of all the Reform with its air of literary periodicals and Liberal statesmen. Yet our times have changed and not much for the better, as it seems to me. The air of the wide avenue from Cockspur Street to St. James's Palace was raucous to a point that would have shocked Sir Robert Peel or Lord Palmerston. An organ-grinder, of all things, was rolling out the favorite of the music halls, "Rosy, you are my posy. . . . You are my heart's bouquet." Worse than that, a uniformed constable was standing by amiably and listening, as if giving the performance his blessing.

Three times, in that promenade of taste and decorum, I was accosted by beggars. One thrust himself in my way, the smell of beer upon his clothes, and complained of a wife and three little ones to find a living for. I dismissed him with the injunction to find work at the dockside hiring yard in Wapping or Shadwell. The second complained of needing a sub until Saturday, which was as good as to say he had drunk his week's wages already and had a tidy sum due for payment on the slate at some tavern in Lambeth or Clerkenwell.

Finally, there was a one-armed beggar sitting against the wall between the Reform Club and the Diogenes. I am not a medical man for nothing, and I could see plainly that his second good arm was carefully concealed by his coat. He rattled a tin cup and complained of being an "old sojer wot lorst a limb" at Maiwand in the Afghan campaign. If you know anything about me, you will know that Maiwand was the battle in which I sustained a wound which ended my career as an army surgeon. If this fellow had ever been nearer to Maiwand, or Afghanistan, or India, than Clapham Junction, I would eat my hat.

I do not as a rule see red, but I did so now. How could I not, when I thought of fallen comrades exploited by this mean cheating? I thundered at him that he was a disgrace to the nation, a wretch who sullied the name of honours won in that campaign—and that I should do such things—I knew not what they were, but they should be the terror of such as he! At this point, in his sly and insinuating manner, he said, "You'll have to speak close, guv. I don't hear so well as I used."

It was almost more than flesh and blood could stand. I leant into the unwashed odour of him, the ginger hair and slobbered beard, the crafty gaze of those eyes, the nose that scented easy money.

"I shall certainly . . ."

Before I could add what it was I would certainly do, he spoke softly.

"As you value both our lives, Watson, give me in charge to that policeman just beyond you. The fellow standing opposite us at the St. James's Square turning has had me in his sight for the past half hour. Let the club porter do it for you."

How I kept my composure after all that had happened, I cannot tell you. Yet to hear his voice was to know that every word was in earnest. I straightened up and said loudly, "You are no soldier but a common scoundrel. Bread and water is too good for you!"

I strode up the steps of the Diogenes Club and gave my instructions to the hall porter. He looked from the doorway and saw at a glance the scene I had described. The policeman was still listening to the barrel organ. The "old sojer" from Maiwand was still sitting disconsolately against the wall of the Reform Club, holding out his enamel cup to passersby. Opposite the St. James's Square turning, a man in a long coat that was too heavy for the spring warmth was pacing slowly and glancing at his watch from time to time, to give the impression of one who was kept waiting at a rendezvous.

The porter crossed Pall Mall and began to walk towards the policeman. Behind me, the voice of Mycroft Holmes said, "My dear Dr. Watson! Why do you come alone? Is not Sherlock with you?"

Curiously, both children had been given the first name of William, which was why neither used it. William Mycroft Holmes was tall and portly, in so many respects the antithesis of his younger brother. In the matter of clothing, he must have been the despair of Savile Row. The suit that a careful tailor had made for him looked as if it had been wrapped round a miscellaneous bundle rather than a measured body. The face was round, while his brother's was aquiline. Yet the gray eyes had that same penetrating gaze, and the forehead, unusually wide, was crowned by the flat and short-cut hair of a schoolboy. If the body was absurd, the head, without being in the least handsome, spoke of double-firsts in mathematics at Cambridge or in classical languages at Oxford—or both. He was, I had heard from Sherlock Holmes, a Fellow of All Souls and traveled to Oxford every week to dine at that college among the nation's intellectual elite. Mycroft had won his fellowship by a brilliant contribution to classical grammar in a competitive essay on "The Resolution of Enclitic δε." Yet to the nation, he was virtually unknown. Sometimes fun had been poked at him, but you may be sure he never saw the point of it. Sherlock Holmes assured me that this paragon, as a Balliol undergraduate, had been the target of satire in the famous book of college rhymes.

My name is William Mycroft Holmes,
A giant among little gnomes.
You've lost your Greek optative verb?
I'm thinking, kindly don't disturb.

"Where is Sherlock?"

There was no time for explanations. I led him to the window of the Diogenes Club. The barrel organ had fallen silent and we were just in time to see the constable crossing Pall Mall. He stooped and spoke to the derelict who looked up from his sitting place.

"I do not understand," said Mycroft Holmes simply, as the constable took the beggar's arm and encouraged him to his feet. They began to walk away towards Vine Street police station.

"That is your brother." I noticed that the loiterer near St. James's Square gave one more look at his watch, for the sake of verisimilitude no doubt, and then walked away in the other direction.

"My brother? Sherlock? That beggar?"

I nodded. The shock of the past ten minutes after weeks of terrible anxiety had drawn the energy from me.

"That is your brother."

"Masquerading as a beggar in Pall Mall? But why? Does he not see how he might embarrass me?"

"You shall hear everything, so far as I know it."

Mycroft Holmes was not mollified by this. He looked down at me from his considerable height. There was a mixture of incomprehension and reproof in his expression, which now gave him something of a sulky air. He shook his head slowly.

"I have tolerated his frolics and farces, goodness knows," he said plaintively, "but this is quite beyond everything. On my way here I stopped and heard the story of his dreadful injury. I was so taken by it that I gave the fellow half a sovereign. I do call that the limit!"

THE HOMECOMING

1

IT WAS ENOUGH for the time being that I had seen him alive. I still could not say he was safe if the stranger who stood across the street from the Diogenes Club was what I suspected. Yet I knew that if Holmes were to survive, he must be left to his own devices. When the mysterious beggar was led away by a police constable, the watcher on the opposite pavement ended his vigil, and I believed Holmes had won the first hand in the game. Had I embraced the vagrant as my friend, we might both be floating in the river with our throats cut by now.

Communication between us appeared to be impossible. How easy it would be for our opponents to intercept a letter addressed to me by bribing a dishonest postal sorter or, more likely, by planting their own man to work at the sorting office by means of a forged reference. A message scrawled on the morning newspaper pushed through our letter box, or slipped inside its pages, would also be read.

My thoughts ran upon a message added to a newspaper or a letter. No doubt the thoughts of our enemies followed the same path. Only one who knew the workings of that indomitable intelligence would understand that Holmes might transmit the most detailed and vital messages invisibly, by means of what was missing rather than by what was added. I recalled the mysterious incident of what the dog did in the nighttime. But the dog did nothing in the nighttime, I protested. Precisely, said Holmes, that was the mystery.

The morning after the Pall Mall encounter, I unfolded the newspaper which awaited me on the breakfast table and saw that there had been a mistake. It was not the *Morning Post* but the *Times*, and it was dated the day before yesterday. Looking at the front page, it was distinctly marked in pencil "221b Baker Street." It had frequently happened that the wrong paper was delivered by a careless newsboy. That it should be two days out of date was no mere error.

Those who have read our Lauriston Gardens mystery in *A Study in Scarlet* or *The Sign of Four,* may recall the "unofficial force" always at the disposal of Sherlock Holmes, his Baker Street Irregulars. He need only send Mrs. Hudson's Billy for them. Ten minutes later, accompanied by a wail of dismay from our landlady, naked feet would patter on the stairs as with a loud clatter of voices a dozen dirty and ragged little street arabs burst in on us. Yet in the presence of Sherlock Holmes they were as smart and obedient to command as they had just been ragged and disrespectful.

These young scamps had often been our eyes and ears, once showing themselves better able to keep a log of Thames river traffic than any division of Scotland Yard. How easily might one of them insinuate himself into Baker Street newspaper delivery. How easily might a villain who tracked Sherlock Holmes be tracked in turn by twenty pairs of eyes following every movement and manoeuvre. It is a truth that the most consummate villain, or the most widespread yet tightly controlled criminal conspiracy, is helpless against one thing—the will of the people. In our case it was not only the prospect of half a sovereign for work well done that attracted these little brigands but the adventure of working with the most famous detective in London.

I opened the paper again, no longer wondering who had sent it or how it had got here. But there was no message, nothing written on any page except the address of our rooms on the first. I stood up and shook the pages, one by one. Nothing fell out. I sat down again, went through it more carefully, and noticed that there was a page missing. It would scarcely have been noticed by anyone checking to see if a message had been written in the margin or hidden between the pages. Nowadays a single page of newsprint is sometimes added to supplement the folded double pages and this was how the mutilated one appeared.

Without stopping to finish my breakfast or even my coffee, I called a cab from the rank at Regents Park and went straight to my club—the East India in St. James's Square. The East India takes in every morning and evening paper from the capital with quite a few of the better-class provincials. I turned to the missing page of yesterday's *Times*. The major item, a continuation of Home News under the Cricket columns, was not in doubt.

THE ELECTRIC STORM

Another Electric Explosion in the City

> Fresh details have emerged from the City of London concerning the electric explosion which occurred early in the morning of Thursday last. It is the latest in a series of such accidents to the electric supply affecting the Newgate Street area. On the last occasion, our readers will recall from our report of 6 January, a series of the electric conduit boxes opposite St. Sepulchre's and in Newgate Street itself were seen to issue smoke and shortly afterwards exploded with a burst of flame. In the present case, it is reported that a far larger explosion occurred within the disused buildings of Newgate prison.
>
> Contrary to first reports, there was no injury or loss of life. We are grateful to know that this misunderstanding has been clarified. The contractors' men had not yet arrived for their day's work. It is thanks to this, rather than to any vigilance on the part of the electric supply company, that serious injuries, indeed fatalities, were avoided. Several windows in Newgate Street were cracked by the blast and one win-

dow display in the direct path was wrecked. A column of smoke was seen to rise above the high walls of the exercise yard of the deserted prison. Any person at the centre of the explosion, where happily there were none at this hour, must infallibly have perished.

It had been supposed that the supply of electricity, an amenity which reached only certain wards of the prison, had been disconnected some time ago. This was evidently not the case. A supply of commercial water-gas was also continued by the Aldgate Coal and Coke Company. An electric spark appears to have been the cause of the explosion. Disconnection of their supply has now been undertaken by the Charing Cross and City Electric Light Company from the company's Newgate Street conduit box.

It is stated on behalf of agents to the subcontractors that no serious damage was sustained beyond a small area within the prison which had in any event been prepared for demolition in a few weeks' time. A small fire which had begun was brought quickly under control without requiring the attendance of the London Brigade. There is nonetheless a cause of severe misgiving as to the safety of the Charing Cross Electric Light Company's mode of supply and the wisdom of allowing a flow of highly volatile water-gas to continue in such ancient and ill-ventilated premises as these. A report of the Cripplegate Ward Fire Committee is to be presented to the next meeting of the ratepayers. The matter is also to be debated next week at the monthly meeting of the Court of Common Council to be held at the Guildhall on Wednesday.

Only when I heard the complete story of my friend's escape did I understand that he was coming down to freedom from the roofs of Newgate Street as the lighted lantern flames touched off the gas filling the condemned cell. The whole truth, to which the newspapers did not have access, was that the door and windows of the condemned cell had been blown clean out into the exercise yard, along with several feet of its wall. Even as I read the newspaper report, it told me a hundred times more than it might have conveyed to any other reader. As a medical man with some experience of injuries from explosion in battle, I could not believe that anyone in that cell itself—or many of those in close proximity—would have survived the ferocity of a blast that did such damage.

As I sat on the library sofa before the log fire, I knew this was a veiled account of how Sherlock Holmes had escaped from the tightest corner he was ever in. Had all his enemies been destroyed? It seemed at least one might still be tracking him, to judge by the incidents in Pall Mall. Could they tell whether Holmes had perished in the blast or not? Knowing the man they were dealing with, they would not be fools enough to take the explosion for an accident. Had my friend thought his time had run out and had he striven to take them all with him—only to make a lucky escape?

I flatter myself I came close to the truth, even before hearing his account. As a medical man, I knew an eruption of highly explosive water gas would leave human debris in the ruins. Whether any belonged to their captive would be hard to say. I did not yet know my friend had taken the precaution of locking the metal cuff round the ankle of his dead guard. There was a chance that Crellin might pass as the body of Sherlock Holmes burnt beyond recognition.

I could only make my way back to Baker Street and await further communications. The next morning brought another copy of the *Times*. It was two days old, but there was not a page missing.

Clearing aside the breakfast things, I spread the paper on the table and began to go through it minutely. There was no item of news that could be of the least relevance. I was reduced to running my finger down the first of the Deaths columns and when I reached the foot of it, I felt as if my heart took a final leap and stopped. The corner of the page was torn away. To a casual glance, it might seem that this was damage inflicted by the sharp edge of the letter box or by carelessness. The complete copy of the paper in the club library told me otherwise.

> Milverton. Suddenly at Claremont, Cape Town, on the 14th inst., Henry Caius Milverton of The Borders, Windlesham, Surrey. The interment of ashes and a memorial service will be held at St. George's Church, Windlesham, on a date to be announced.

In all our dealings with the criminal underworld, there were perhaps half a dozen names never to be forgotten. Milverton was one of them, though which Milverton this might be I had as yet no idea. However, as I read the announcement, the message from my friend could not have been plainer. One other thing I knew from it, whoever Henry Caius Milverton was, he had died a good deal nearer to home than the Cape Province of South Africa! The announcement was clearly intended to appease the curiosity of those who would otherwise wonder how their acquaintance had—more literally than they would guess!—vanished into thin air. Of course, I could not even begin to prove it, but I felt to a certainty that Henry Caius Milverton had been blown to smithereens in that Newgate explosion.

Next evening I had an unexpected visit after dinner from Mycroft Holmes. His mood was partly one of annoyance at the game his brother seemed to be playing with us all and partly a real concern for the safety of that brother's life.

"I had it out with Inspector Lestrade this afternoon," he said aggressively, throwing off his coat and sitting down by the fire. "He and his people are subordinate to us in the hierarchy of government, which is sometimes rather useful. All the same, in my position it does me no good, you know, to have Sherlock playing the fool all over London."

He was plainly very agitated and got up at once. Pacing round the room, he paused to wave a hand at the chemical table, sadly unused in recent weeks.

"Why can he not settle to something worthwhile? What does he see in all this trumpery? You will find one day these escapades will land us all in chancery."

"I wish he was here so that I could ask him what he sees in it," I said sadly.

This seemed to mollify him. He poured himself whisky from the decanter, added a dash of seltzer, and sat down again.

"I came tonight, Watson, because Lestrade told me something this afternoon. It sounds to me like a tale from a schoolboy's magazine, but you ought to hear it."

"I should like to."

"Very well. Lestrade spoke of some business a few years ago. Three men were killed in England, all from the same family. Name of Openshaw."

"The case of the five orange pips."

He pulled a face.

"Call it what you like. Rumour says, according to Lestrade, that each of them received an envelope containing five orange pips. This was to tell him he had been chosen for assassination. A boys' magazine story, pure and simple!"

"But what of it?"

"A criminal gang came from the United States, from the state of Georgia. Its members belonged to what is called the Ku Klux Klan and its leader was Captain James Calhoun."

"Quite correct," I said helpfully. "Calhoun escaped from England after the murders, but his ship, the *Lone Star*, went down in an Atlantic gale that autumn. The sternpost was found floating, all that remained of the vessel."

"No!" He slapped his knee.

"I fear you must explain that," I said cautiously.

"According to Lestrade, that was what the world was meant to think. Captain James Calhoun was not dead then—but he is now."

"I don't understand that."

Mycroft Holmes sighed, as if despairing of me.

"Lestrade has it on the authority of an American treasury agent with whom he has had professional dealings. Whatever you and my brother may think, the U.S. Treasury never believed Calhoun was lost at sea. A sternpost! The whole thing was only too easy to arrange. Calhoun has operated since then under assumed names, closely protected by his criminal organization. A treasury man working incognito was able to attend a grand council, or whatever it may be, of this Ku Klux Klan. He identified Calhoun as being present."

"But Calhoun is dead now?"

Mycroft Holmes stretched his feet toward the fire, a mannerism he shared with his brother.

"He is dead now, quite recently. But the curious thing, according to Lestrade's information, is that he is said to have died in England."

I seemed to hear the voice of Sherlock Holmes cautioning silence and said only, "An odd story."

Mycroft Holmes laughed, a thing he seldom did. Then he poked the fire irritably.

"Odder than you suppose. According to Lestrade's story, Calhoun was killed in London—murdered, presumably—and yet there is no body."

There is no body! I thought of Henry Caius Milverton, for whom there was also no body, merely a jar of ashes. Once again I kept this to myself. However, I offered a lame explanation.

"Your brother merely presumed that Calhoun had gone down with his ship. He did not regard it as proven fact."

Mycroft Holmes raised his flourishing eyebrows.

"Merely presumed, did he? It is not like Sherlock merely to presume. He is so damnably sure of himself as to be insufferable. When you see him, you had better pass on the information. Tell me, Doctor, are you sure that you know nothing of my brother's whereabouts?"

"Quite sure," I said humbly.

He lumbered to his feet.

"It really won't do to have him acting the goat all over London as he seems to do at present. A one-armed beggar! You can tell him; it seems he listens to you. He will damage reputations other than his own. What's more, it doesn't do for him to be always hobnobbing with men further down the hierarchy, Lestrade and the like. Tell him when you see him."

"You may be sure I will."

With that, he plodded down the stairs to the cab, whose horse and driver had waited patiently throughout his visit. And so Brother Mycroft began his stately progress back to that little world of his own, where the sun rises each morning over the Palace of Whitehall and sets every evening behind St. James's Street. Beyond that, for him, lies outer darkness.

If two such men as Henry Caius Milverton and James Calhoun had died without a body between them, there was surely much more to the story of Newgate. On the following morning there was no copy of the *Times*. The *Morning Post* appeared as usual. I read it over my coffee and toast, folded, it and laid it down. Only then did I notice that where the penciled address "221b Baker Street" should have been, someone had written "23 Denmark Square, EC."

From my days as a medical student I knew Denmark Square, just off the City Road where it runs down toward Finsbury Pavement. It is not the most salubrious part of London—shabby terraces with a dusty patch of grass and a few stunted trees at its centre. I took sheet 53 of the Ordnance Survey map of London from the shelf and confirmed that 23 Denmark Square was the southernmost house of the terrace forming the eastern side of the square. On the reverse of the sheet are lists of those businesses that occupy premises on the map. At 23 Denmark Square, on the ground floor, was James Pocock & Son, pianoforte action makers and repairers of musical instruments.

It seemed I now knew where I might find Sherlock Holmes. But was he hiding there, held captive, or merely awaiting my arrival? Surely it was better to go at once than to delay and find that I had come too late. An hour later, I took the Metropolitan Line from Baker Street to Liverpool Street, through smoky tunnels and in such crowds that I could not tell if I was being followed or not. The carriages rattled along a deep canyon with embankments of brick on either side. Above us were blocks of warehouses, a gasworks with tall chimneys like minarets. The fiery mouth of an open retort glowed like the crater of a volcano.

The City Road is lined with dirty unpainted buildings and choked by heavy drays and baggage carts. Ramshackle oyster bars and little drinking shops with grimy uncurtained windows were well patronized by early morning. I turned into Denmark Square. The decaying houses were tall enough to have accommodated at first the prosperous families of a lawyer, a bill broker, a merchant of India rubber or Norwegian timber. Now the handsome terraces were sooty tenements with a different family in every room above the ground-floor workshops.

At the centre of the square was an area of grass worn brown by the crisscrossing of footsteps and two chestnut trees not yet come into leaf and looking as if they never might. I took my seat on a bench at the centre of this dusty isolation. I had not seen anyone following me—but then I did not suppose that I should.

I took out a paper and began to read. The rumble of carts, cabs, and twopenny buses from City Road was constant. Scales and arpeggios rose from the premises of the piano action manufacturer. Repairing violins is a considerable part of such trades, and a craftsman began to tune and play, simply at first and then with flowing confidence.

As I sat there, I lost interest in my newspaper, my thoughts filled by the nobility of such sounds in a place as desolate as this. But what was the music? I would guess the composer was Bach. A theme wove and interwove a rich tapestry of sound that became an advancing wall of sublime melody in counterpoint. I had no doubt who was playing that gimcrack violin, and I thanked heaven Holmes kept his musical accomplishments secret from enemies and allies alike. This was not his beloved Stradivarius, but Holmes could conjure celestial harmonies from a tinker's fiddle. The performance was not intended to ease my mind or lift my spirits. When my friend was engaged upon an inquiry, everything pointed to one end.

A simple theme had begun this majestic fugue. Now, as it wove in and out of the music, I half recognized it. I almost snatched hold of it, only to feel it slip away. I knew it, I could swear I did, but I am not knowledgeable enough to tell one of Bach's fugues from the other. Perhaps I had heard it in company with Holmes at a St. James's Hall recital.

The great tapestry of sound mellowed and softened, gathering for the grandeur of its conclusion, sunset clouds weaving together, dissolving and combining in sonorous triumph, a minor key moving into position for a final sublime chord in the major. Very softly the elusive theme was stated alone and I knew what it was. Indeed, I sang it softly to myself as I listened.

Half a pound of tuppeny rice, half a pound of treacle,
That's the way the money goes, pop goes the weasel!

Who but Holmes could make something so splendid out of material so simple? But there was more, to remind me of the second verse of the old nursery rhyme.

Up and down the City Road, in and out the Eagle . . .

The Eagle! That famous tavern in the City Road was close to where I sat. As a medical student at Bart's, the oldest hospital in the City of London, I had known the promenade bar with its music hall, garden orchestra, magic mirrors, French ropedancers, and infant prodigies! The nursery rhyme figured in our boisterous singsongs. I had often reminisced to Holmes about those days.

I got up, as if I had been merely sitting to pass the time, and took a roundabout route to Shepherdess Walk and the tavern, all yellow London brick above and gold paint on black at eye level with handsome plate-glass windows. The tiled entrance lobby and the pale green marble pillars led to long bars and ample space. There were customers at the tables, but not one who might be Sherlock Holmes. Just then, someone stood up and walked away from a table where he had sat alone.

He was a stout, florid-faced man, his red hair somewhat darkened by age. I did not recognize him as he passed me, and for that I give thanks! I should surely have greeted him instinctively and given the game away. He was some years older than when I had last seen him, and it was something in his eyes rather than in his face that prompted my recollection. Mr. Jabez Wilson!

In the scrapbooks of our investigations, which I have compiled over the years, Mr. Jabez Wilson brought us one of our first cases, the affair of the Reheaded League. That league proved to be a cover for the most ingenious and ruthless gang of bank robbers. Sherlock Holmes had saved Jabez Wilson from being unwittingly implicated in the crime and had earned him a modest reward from the bank's insurers. Mr. Wilson had professed eternal indebtedness to his benefactor. It was not the least surprising if he had given shelter to Sherlock Holmes at 23 Denmark Square in his present hour of need.

We passed as if we were strangers. I sat with my glass of ale and listened to the barroom piano playing "Daisy, Daisy, give me your answer do." On the buttoned leather of the seat beside me lay a discarded copy of the *Racing Times*. I glanced at it without picking it up. It had been folded open at a page on which someone had underlined a horse for the 3:30 at Cheltenham. The horse was Noli Me Tangere and I had no doubt that the underlining was Mr. Wilson's.

Noli me tangere: "Do not touch me," or in the famous regimental motto, "Do not come near me." Thus I received my instructions. I finished my glass of ale, drew out my watch to check the time, and walked down the City Road with the air of a man who has an appointment to keep. Presently I came to a doorway. Its brass plate promised an oculist. In the waiting room I inquired whether a member of the practice might be free to give my eyes an examination. Half an hour later and a guinea the poorer, I came out into the street again.

As I walked past the steps of Wesley's Chapel with its statue of the great founder himself, I noticed an orphan flower girl with the last of her day's offerings laid out on the cold stone, violets and wallflowers, roses and carnations, forced in hothouses for early sale. Her dark print dress was plain but not torn, and her shoes had seen better days. I judged she was about fifteen, and the barefoot child who hung about her, no doubt her sister, about eleven. Such children often share a single room with two or more other families in the Drury Lane tenements. The elder came forward, towards me, crying out, "Flowers! Pretty flowers! Here's spring to a certainty! Twopence for a buttonhole! And it shall be twopence for my night's lodging, not a dram of gin!"

I did not doubt her, but she was upon me before I could reply, touching my face.

"Feel my hand, how cold it is."

Without more ado, she began to pin a white carnation in the buttonhole of my lapel.

"Only be careful how you undo it," she said, almost laughing now.

"Take this, my poor girl."

I drew my hand from my pocket and pressed a sovereign into her outstretched palm. She stared at it and cried, "The heavens be your honour's resting place," then turned to her young sister. With such treasure, they could shut up shop, certain of a warm meal and bed.

Only be careful how you undo it! Most of the Baker Street Irregulars had sisters or female cousins as destitute as they. If this was not one of them, I thought, may I be shot.

I reached Baker Street and, despite my impatience, walked up the stairs from the sooty air and blackened brick of the railway as if I had all the time in the world. No one followed me, but one pair of eyes would surely be trained on our front door as I walked toward Regent's Park. Once inside our sitting room, I closed the curtains, put up the gas, and drew the white carnation from my buttonhole. The stem was protected by a twist of silver foil. When I unwound it, the foil was lined by a slip of paper. On this, in diminutive letters, was a message. It was the first direct news of Holmes since his disappearance.

> My dear Watson, I write this with gratitude to our redheaded friend. The events of my captivity and escape are such as you may now guess. Henry Milverton and James Calhoun perished at the hour they had chosen for my own death. Two underlings have survived. Beware the disgraced Petty Officer Alker, Master-at-Arms, a naval hangman. Most important, kindly address to me by first collection tomorrow a shoe box wrapped in brown paper, tied with blue string, and sealed with wax. "Poste restante, City Road Office, London ECI' will find me. Make no secret that you are sending it to me. Our lives remain in danger. Noli Me Tangere.

2

I slept little that night as I pondered how to send a parcel by mail to ensure that our enemies saw the address upon it but without letting them know that I wished them to see it. At such moments I missed the presence of my friend beside me. What if the spies had found me unproductive and had ceased to spy upon me? I might have reassured myself. Until Sherlock Holmes was in their grasp again, I was the most likely person to lead them to him.

There was a warm summer wind and a scent of blossom as I set off down Baker Street with a wrapped shoe box under my arm on the following morning. I had as yet attached no label to the parcel. The coronation of our new king, Edward VII, was to be the spectacle of the season. Every window of the stationers and trinket shops offered mass-produced cards for sale, looking like the largest and most splendid playing cards you ever saw. Each displayed a crowned figure in full coronation robes of crimson or royal blue braided with gold, be it King Edward or Queen Alexandra, the Prince or Princess of Wales. A coronation ode by Dr. Benson of Eton College set to music by Sir Edward Elgar, was thumping out from the regimental bandstand in the Regent's Park, and was soon to be taken up by massed choirs the length and breadth of the land.

Land of hope and glory
Mother of the free . . .

In the post office I took a gummed label from a packet and wrote in large capitals the poste restante address my friend had given me. I was at one of the wooden tables provided, and before I could finish the final line, a fellow pushing through the crowd jogged my elbow suddenly and—I could almost swear—deliberately. My pen flew across what I had just written. I swung round on him. He was a stout, florid-faced man, his red hair somewhat darkened by age. Mr. Jabez Wilson of the Redheaded League treated me as a total stranger once more. Raising his hat, he said, "I do beg your pardon, sir, indeed I do. Entirely my fault. I really am so sorry."

He went on his way, struggling through the crowd. I saw that Holmes had opened a door for me, and I knew exactly what to do.

Muttering to myself, I screwed up the label, made a great display of irritation, and tossed the crumpled paper into the wire container of the basket in the corner of the room. I took a fresh label, and at length I handed the package to the clerk. I turned to the door and made my way out onto the steps.

Sunlight over the eastern rooftops was turning the day from spring to summer, warming the walls and terraces. I stood there for a moment, as if I had forgotten something. Turning abruptly, I made my way back to the counter. There I bought a dozen cream-laid envelopes embossed with a blue stamp and asked loudly, as if to reassure myself, whether a parcel handed in at 9:30 that morning would reach the City Road post office before the end of the afternoon. I was promised that it would. Then, as if finding the easiest way out through the crowd, I edged round past the wire basket into which I had thrown the first crumpled label. At such an early hour the basket had contained only that label, two folded sheets of paper that someone had discarded previously, and a messenger boy's apple core. The folded sheets and the apple core were still there. The crumpled label with Holmes's address upon it, which had been resting on top of them, was gone.

Dressed in a country suit and hat with a pair of optician's horn-rimmed spectacles containing plain glass, I passed an hour after the postal delivery ruining my digestion with cups of coffee at the refreshment stall that fronts the corner of the City Road and Denmark Square. On that corner stands the City Road post office, also in line of sight from 23 Denmark Square, across its dusty central lawn.

Customers pushed their way in by the door marked "push" and came out through the door marked "pull." I did not look for customers, however; I watched for the shoe-box parcel tied with blue string. Whoever carried that was my man or, indeed, woman. Mr. Jabez Wilson was surely the most likely, unless Alker or one of our opponents tried to pass himself off as the recipient and collect the item from the counter.

I waited in vain until almost five o'clock. Then, to my dismay, I saw Sherlock Holmes striding confidently from Denmark Square towards the post office door. He wore a dark suit and hat, as if to advertise his presence. Why, after such careful concealment, had he now given himself away so completely and defiantly? I did not approach him, for that would have made matters worse.

I sat at the small metal table under the tin canopy of the stall, where I was hidden by the crowd of drinkers standing or sitting around me. Presently, Holmes reappeared with his parcel. He did not return to Denmark Square, but began walking down the City Road in the direction of the Metropolitan underground railway at Moorgate. It was that time of day when the commercial streets of the City begin to fill with shopworkers and office clerks pushing their way homeward.

I stood up, but even before I could step out from the canopy I saw the man who, I swear, was the master-at-arms. He did not look precisely like the fellow who had kept vigil in Pall Mall when Holmes was playing at being a military beggar. Yet there was enough about him to suggest that he was the same. Now I observed him in more detail. There was a broad face with the look of a smile at the mouth until you reached the eyes and saw that he was not smiling at all. He was heavily built, though not tall, and the strength in the arms suggested how easily he had pinioned those poor wretches who had struggled to gulp down a few moments more of breath and life. If his reputation is to be believed, he had adjusted the noose round the throats of seven murderers and three mutineers of the Pacific Squadron, as well as innumerable Chinese and Indian rebels. Though the afternoon was still mild, he was wearing a dark overcoat with the collar turned up.

My attention was briefly caught by a red-faced and bandy-legged little lounger who got up from a table near me. He, however, went off in another direction and was evidently not involved in the matter. Nothing in that bustling street of trade and traffic can have suggested to Holmes that he was now being followed. He did not so much as glance in Alker's direction. My friend seemed in mortal danger, and yet I knew by instinct that I must not frighten off his pursuer. I had my revolver in my pocket, but it would have been impossible to fire it in such a place as this without the danger of hitting an innocent bystander. On the other hand, how easily might Alker, in the growing pressure of the crowd, draw level and slip a knife between the ribs of Sherlock Holmes.

Thanks to the jostling crowd, I was able to take up my position about ten feet behind Alker and follow him as he was following Holmes. Even had he caught sight of me, he might not have recognized me; but, in any case, the master-at-arms had eyes only for his quarry. As we crossed between the lumbering wheels of carts and wagons, towards the station, I became certain that he had come on his own.

Alker was not much more than a brute, but he had something of a brute's simple cunning. He positioned himself so that in the press of passengers towards the train he was able to push his way into the carriage next to the one that Sherlock Holmes had entered. From time to time Holmes had made a movement at the last minute, as a matter of precaution, but never dextrously enough to outwit the patient hatred of his unseen adversary.

I had not the least idea what my friend's destination might be. On these occasions one can only take a ticket for the longest journey and alight at whatever station may be necessary. As Alker sat in one carriage next to that of Holmes, I sat, or rather stood, in the carriage beyond it. By now I was as determined that Holmes should not see me and give the game away as I was that I should outwit Alker.

If our destination was Baker Street, we had surely taken the longest and slowest route, by way of Tower Hill, Westminster, Kensington, the bleak suburbs of West London, Paddington, and Marylebone. I consoled myself by believing that Holmes knew what he was doing and that he could scarcely come to harm on the train with Alker in a different carriage. At every station I moved to a point where I could see who got off the train. It was at Kensington that I saw the tall, gaunt figure of Sherlock Holmes step down to the platform and walk slowly away. Kensington, it seemed to me, had no connection with the case at all. Perhaps it was a blind, as they say. He did not even look round as Alker went cautiously after him. I let several passengers precede me and then took up the pursuit. The whole business had an element of farce, and yet, as events were about to show, it had death at its heart.

It was not difficult to keep track of Holmes and his shadow, by using the rounded bulk of the Albert Hall and the Albert Memorial. Then Holmes, unaware of how close danger and death had come, made the worst mistake of all. With the sun below the horizon and dusk setting, he turned through Alexandra Gate into the vast unlit territory of Hyde Park. By the time that we reached the far side and the streets that led home, the trees, bushes, and grassland would be in darkness, the perfect terrain for an assassin.

Already the parkland seemed deserted. A photographer was wheeling out his black canvas booth through the gate; ribboned children and their governess were carrying off the toy yacht they had been sailing on the Round Pond of Kensington Gardens. Alker continued to shadow Holmes with consummate ease among so many trees and the bushes of laurel or rhododendron. The way led parallel with Kensington Gore for a while. Then Holmes turned, as if to cross Rotten Row and leave all safety behind him. He walked unhurriedly, without once looking back, still carrying his parcel and deep in thought. He was offering himself for the kill.

I drew the revolver from my pocket, but kept it concealed. Beyond the tops of the furthest trees, where the great Park Lane terraces show their upper floors, there were lights in several windows. It would soon be too dark to shoot. There was nothing for it but to attack or accost Alker. He was in the open some forty yards behind Holmes and I was about as far behind him again. We had reached the wide earthen carriageway of Rotten Row, lined by chestnut trees on either side, where "pretty little horse-breakers" of the 1860s broke more hearts than horses. Even now the Sunday morning "church parade" of open carriages, with drivers and grooms in livery and silk hats, makes it the parade of gallantry, no less than the mounted regiments galloping in the weekday dust.

What followed was so rapid and so unreal that I can still scarcely believe I was a witness. Holmes turned suddenly and shouted in a tone of anger, "Watson! You had really better leave all this to me!"

As if that were a signal, there was a drumming like a boxer's gloves on a canvas training bag. A fine bay horse with its head down, pulling against the bit, came pounding over the bare earth of the Row as it gathered speed. I stood still, stricken by astonishment. These is no other phrase for it; the whole thing was like an apparition. On the horse's back was a figure in regimental uniform of some kind. It was growing dark, but not too dark to make out a scarlet jacket, brass buttons, and a cavalry trooper's cap on his head.

Alker stopped as well, for he had been about to cross the hardened earth of Rotten Row in pursuit of Holmes. Now he was prevented from doing so by the approach of the horse. The trooper was riding as if a pack of hellhounds might be after him, and even from where I stood I could hear the snorting breath of his mount.

Alker took a step or two backwards, as if to keep clear of the galloping horse whose hooves were now showering earth to either side. I could see that the rider was leaning forward, his chest along the horse's neck. He appeared to be performing some trick in which he would whisk something from the ground as he sped by. Then I saw that what he held in his hand was a cavalry saber. Suddenly he held it out sideways. It did not flash, for there was too little light, but I could swear that I saw a pale gleam. It cut the air with no more than a whisper and then there was a sudden whistling sound as the air left Alker's body through his severed neck while his head bumped along the dried earth.

I was unable to move from the spot in my terror and fascination—even though this might have been some madman who intended to kill us all. I saw that Alker's headless body remained upright for several seconds before it crumpled to the ground, as if some lingering message from the missing brain was still controlling the dying limbs. I had heard of such grisly wonders in cavalry engagements.

I need not have worried about the rider's intentions. He looked neither to right nor to left, never slackening his speed. The hoofbeats grew gentler until dusk veiled the identity of the man whom I was to hear of as the corporal of horse.

Sherlock Holmes appeared to be unmoved.

"A weak man, perhaps, but not a wicked one," he said calmly. "Now he may live without fear. I shall not betray him to our friends at Scotland Yard if you do not. If I calculate correctly, he is the only one remaining of those with whom I had dealings during the weeks of my captivity. Others were to have been there but were prevented for one reason or another. I fear it is not impossible that we may yet hear from them. However, let us be thankful that we have purged the world of the majority."

I did not reply. The shock of what had happened deprived me of the power of motion for a few minutes, but I did not sleep all that night and I was physically incapable of speech until late on the following day. Whether the corporal of horse contrived on his own to rid the world of the one conspirator who might kill him, or whether he and Holmes planned the whole thing together, I do not know. I may say, however, that my friend did not betray him and nor did I.

3

The papers were full for many days of the "Headless Man" mystery in Rotten Row. Yet the nine-days' wonder passed. Before it was over, we received a visit from our friend Inspector Lestrade, to whom we told nothing of what we knew. Scotland Yard had concluded that the murder was done with a cavalry saber, but they had concluded little more. Alker was known to them as a man of fifty-five who had ended his naval career at forty and then found a place among such dealers in female flesh as Henry Caius Milverton. It must have cost our Scotland Yard a good deal to say, "We should value your views upon the case, Mr. Holmes."

But Sherlock Holmes was capable of seeing nothing in a case as easily as he could see a great deal. He listened to what our visitor had to say of the evidence in the murder and then sighed. "I fear, Lestrade, that I cannot make bricks without straw."

My friend felt that he owed Corporal McIver a debt of honour and that the debt had been paid. When we were alone, he put the entire adventure from his mind.

He sat quietly for a moment and then with a new eagerness changed the subject of our conversation.

"You will recall my little composition, an improvised prelude and fugue for the violin upon the nursery rhyme 'Pop Goes the Weasel'? You heard it while I was concealed in the house of Mr. Jabez Wilson in Denmark Square."

"I recall it. I thought it very clever."

I was about to add that it seemed clever as a pastiche, but happily he cut in ahead of me.

"I have never before thought of setting down my compositions on manuscript paper and offering them to a music publisher. I am tempted to make an exception in this case. I propose to solicit the attention of either Peters in Leipzig or Messrs. Augener, who have once or twice inquired of me whether something of mine might be available to them."

"But you cannot become Sherlock Holmes the composer! The world knows you as Sherlock Holmes the consulting detective. Would it not cause confusion?"

He took the pipe from his mouth and contemplated the plaster ceiling rose of the electrolier.

"True. I should have to assume a nom de plume of some kind, to compose, as the French say, *sous le manteau*—and that would belittle the composition. I might suggest instead that it is a discovered fragment from the past, by one who was a master of counterpoint. I could not masquerade as Johann Sebastian Bach; that would be absurdly overweening. I think, though, I may fairly lay claim to one of the great man's sons. I believe that would meet the case. I shall perhaps be Carl Philipp Emanuel Bach. Yes, I think so. That would not be excessive in this instance."

"You cannot possibly do that, Holmes! All the world knows 'Pop Goes the Weasel.'"

"You underestimate the cultural *snobisme* of the age, my dear old friend. They will know it, to be sure. But will they dare to admit to one another that their minds run upon such lowly things as they sit in the Wigmore Hall or some other recital room?"

He put down his pipe and stood up. He opened the case, drawing out his Stradivarius and bow. Protest was useless. There would be no stopping him now.

2

THE CASE OF THE GREEK KEY

1

If Sherlock Holmes devoted all his energies to defending the honour of a humble chambermaid on Monday, he was as likely as not to be engaged in saving a peer of the realm from disgrace on Tuesday. He had a voracious appetite for humanity, its foibles and its failings. Indeed, he often put me in mind of that Latin tag that I had been made to learn at school. "*Homo sum, humani nihil a me alienum puto*": "I am a man and nothing human is alien to me." I once quoted this to him, in part to see his reaction, adding that it was one of the wisest comments of the great Roman orator, Cicero. Holmes stared at me, drew upon his pipe, and then said, "I believe you will find, Watson, that Cicero said no such thing. The comment, if you wish to attribute it, comes from a very tedious Roman playwright. Should you care to verify it, you will find that he lived two centuries later than your great orator."

Yet my judgment of Sherlock Holmes was not in error. After his death it was my duty as the executor of his will to list the rough copies of his correspondence still lying in his old tin trunk, which remained in the Baker Street attic. There were many letters or notes to the poor and the desperate for whom he had worked without fee, rather as great defenders in the criminal courts will take poor persons' defences without recompense of any kind. When he was once asked why he did this, he replied that he believed—as Francis Bacon had done—that every man is a debtor to his profession and must make some return.

Yet there was another extreme in his work. Among his posthumous papers were three rough drafts, much revised, of letters that began with a formal but imposing phrase, "Mr. Holmes, with his humble duty to Your Majesty. . . ." What follows is an account of how one of these came to be written. The paper on which it is set out appears a little yellowed and brittle with the passage of time. Those who now read the circumstances of the case will understand at once that an earlier disclosure of the events might have put the very safety of the nation in peril.

To begin the story, I must go back to an October morning in 1908. It was not long after dawn, and the scene was an area of sloping downland above the cliffs of St. Alban's Head in Dorset. Several groups of figures, some of them in the topcoats and uniforms of senior naval officers and others in formal dress beneath their winter coats, stood looking out to sea. Though a morning mist still veiled the further distances of the English Channel, a thin sunlight already touched the pale green waves.

By his own choice, Sherlock Holmes and I stood at a little distance from the others, as if to show that we were there as guests and not as of right. In his close-fitting cloth cap and gray travelling cloak, he stood apart in more senses than one. Behind us, more than a mile inland, the little lanes and paths that ran from the village of Worth Matravers were closed and guarded by parties of Royal Marines. They had orders to let no one through under any pretext for the next hour. You would have looked in vain for a naval attaché from the great European embassies in Belgravia or Eaton Place. Not one had been invited.

As we stood silently, a throb of powerful engines sounded across the calm water, growing presently to a heavy beat of turbines in the stillness, like the drums of an ancient war god. A newly built leviathan was coming in from the Western Approaches to the start of a measured mile, returning to Portsmouth Dockyard after sea trials in the Atlantic. The main trials had been held in the remoter areas of the ocean. The performance on this October morning was as much as the illustrious spectators were allowed to see. Presently and quickly the ship materialised from the sparkle of October mist, the brightness of veiled sky shining on her flanks of pale grey steel. From the groups of senior officers and Whitehall dignitaries came the murmuring of a single word: "*Dreadnought*!"

Sweeping past us through the gentle tide, the length of the most powerful and best-armoured battleship the world had known sliced the water with the grace of a cruiser. Even Sherlock Holmes stood in silence, admiring the clean lines of her hull. The decks were clear of the conventional clutter of a capital ship. Before and aft of the two modern funnels, the deck areas held a series of gun platforms able for the first time to sweep through arcs of fire not much less than 360 degrees. A tripod mast gave a commanding view to the control platform and its gunnery officers. The mighty gun barrels themselves were ten and twelve inch, enough to destroy any other ship afloat at a distance of six miles or more and to riddle the thickest armour plate at three miles.

I witnessed this speed trial thanks to the friendship between Holmes and Admiral Sir John Fisher, First Sea Lord and architect of the new Royal Navy. Fisher was known for his maxim "Hit first, hit hard, and keep on hitting." A close friend of King Edward, he was rumoured to have urged the sovereign to "Copenhagen" the Germans at Kiel, as Nelson had done the French, by striking at them first and without any declaration of hostilities while England still held the naval advantage. The king was horrified, the cabinet outraged, and Fisher lamented to his friends that the country no longer had the leadership of a William Pitt—or even a Bismarck.

Holmes and Fisher had been friends since the assistance that was given to the First Sea Lord in the case of "The Naval Treaty." Since then, Holmes would never hear a word spoken against Sir John, whom he described as having "not an inch of pose about him" and to whom he gave the motto "Sworn to no party—of no sect am I. I can't be silent and I will not lie."

As we looked on, *Dreadnought* seemed to turn on her heel at the end of the measured mile—18,000 tons moving with the precision of a torpedo boat—gathering speed again towards Portsmouth Dockyard. I just made out the wake washing away behind her stern, until the mist hid her once more. The distinguished spectators stood in silence. Here and there a pair of field glasses was buttoned into its case once more. Yet there was no cheering and no jubilation at the sight of such power, merely a sense of awe. Beside me, Holmes quoted Rudyard Kipling in a soft but ominous tone.

A-down the stricken capes no flare—
Nor mark on spit or bar,—
Girdled and desperate we dare
The blindfold game of war.

"Mark my words, Watson, the blindfold game of espionage must be played first. Grand Admiral von Tirpitz and his Ministry of Marine in Berlin will see to it."

We turned away to the carriages that had brought us from the railway.

"All the same," I said, trying to cheer him, "Jackie Fisher has got Tirpitz snookered. There are five of these monsters building in yards on the Clyde and the Tyne. Tirpitz has not one. If he had one, he could not use it without deepening and widening the Kiel Canal to get from the North Sea to the Baltic, and dredging the approach to every dockyard. If he deepened those sea-lanes, our thirty-three battleships could sail in and bombard him at close range."

Holmes stamped impatiently over the downland.

"It will not end there," he said firmly, "mark my words."

In this, he was right. Kaiser Wilhelm and his Grand Admiral spent many millions of pounds deepening and widening the Kiel Canal for the new High Seas Fleet, as well as dredging the sea routes to naval bases on the North Sea. The keels of their first Dreadnoughts were laid: A submarine fleet was under construction. Fisher's battleship had bought him time but not victory in the race. A new advantage must be sought but, for the present, the matter rested there. I heard no more from Holmes than the venomous insults exchanged between the First Sea Lord and Admiral von Tirpitz.

Tirpitz began putting about a story that Sir John Fisher had deliberately engineered a German naval scare in England in order to get increased naval estimates passed by Parliament. Indeed, Tirpitz claimed that Fisher had admitted this to the German naval attaché in London. On hearing this, Fisher sought out the attaché at an evening party, at which both were guests, and told him, "Tell Tirpitz—using the immortal words of Dr. Johnson—'You lie, sir, and you know it.'" Not another word was spoken. Such was the unhappy state of relations between the two great naval powers.

I now move forward to the point where these powers became antagonists in a period of preparation for a great European war. How tragic it seemed to those of us who remembered England and Germany as close allies during the reign of our great Queen Empress, Victoria. At her deathbed, King Edward and Kaiser Wilhelm had knelt in prayer together, as they were soon to walk behind her coffin, the one her son and the other her grandson. All this was put aside as the war hounds of Europe growled ever more menacingly across the narrow seas.

2

IT WAS AN AFTERNOON of early autumn, when the trees in the park had lost very little of their summer green. The air of Baker Street was as warm as June and the shops still had their striped awnings pulled out above greengrocers' baskets and booksellers' tables. By instinct, Holmes and I could now tell when a cab or a carriage slowed to a halt outside the door of our lodgings. On the present occasion, however, I rose from my chair with a feeling that this vehicle lacked the cheerful harness rattle of the cabs that usually brought our visitors.

Through the net curtains I saw a twopenny bus on its way to Marble Arch, the sides placarded with advertisements for Old Gold Virginia Tobacco, Van Houten's Cocoa, and a new production of *The Rivals* at the Haymarket Theatre. On the far side of the street, hidden from view until the bus had passed, was a closed carriage. Its black coachwork gleamed, its brass lamps were immaculately polished, and a horse fit for the Ascot Gold Cup stood patiently between its shafts. A liveried coachman held open its door. Two men stepped down and prepared to cross the street. My attention was caught by a small discreet gold crown emblazoned on the black gloss of the carriage door panel.

There was no mistaking the first man as he came across the street. He had taken the precaution of wearing mufti, but even without his uniform Sir John Fisher was known to thousands from his photograph in the picture papers and his caricature in *Vanity Fair*. It was an open, honest face with a dour humour in the lines of the mouth and a quiet merriment in the pale eyes. The dark hair was short and neat, the complexion sallow, for he had been born in Ceylon. His enemies murmured that his mother had been a Cingalese princess—hence his wicked cunning and duplicity.

When I saw the man behind him, I understood the gold crown on the door panel. These two men had been friends for more than twenty years, since Viscount Esher supported Fisher in demanding a modern Royal Navy for a modern world and in reforming the Committee for Imperial Defence. It was believed that no two public men in England held such power. Twelve years earlier, Lord Esher had been appointed by the prime minister, Mr. Balfour, as permanent secretary to the

Board of Works. Behind this banal title lay the reality of such influence behind the scenes as only a gray eminence can exert. Lord Esher's task was to superintend and maintain the homes, comforts, and ritual of the royal family. He had the ear of the monarch to an extent that most prime ministers would envy. He had installed the lift at Windsor Castle for the ailing Queen Victoria and had pushed her bath chair when she expressed a wish to see once more her childhood home at Kensington Palace. In 1897 he had staged the dazzling imperial pageant of her Diamond Jubilee, and persuaded his "Dear and Honoured Lady" to extend the route of her procession south of the River Thames, so that she might be seen and applauded by her poorer subjects. Small wonder that in the new reign, Esher remained the intimate of her son, Edward VII.

"Hello," said Holmes, standing behind me. "It seems they mean business. I suppose Jackie Fisher or Reggie Esher alone might suggest a pleasant social visit. Two of them together can only mean trouble of some kind."

Presently there was a knock at the door and Mrs. Hudson, more flustered than was customary, ushered in our two distinguished visitors. There was a cordial babble of greetings, in the course of which I was introduced to Lord Esher, whom I had already recognised from his photograph in the *Illustrated London News* of the previous week. Then, from the depths of the armchair in which my friend had installed him, Fisher said: "My dear Holmes, I must come to the point of our visit with somewhat indecent haste. In a moment you will understand why. So far, the full details of this matter are known only to Esher and myself—and to one other person whose identity you will readily guess."

"Not Mr. Asquith, I think," Holmes interrupted sardonically.

Esher shook his head.

"No, gentlemen. Not even the prime minister is privy to the entire story. We are here with the knowledge and approval of King Edward himself. It seems that he reposes a good deal of confidence in the name of Sherlock Holmes."

I thought that Holmes sounded a little too suave in his reply.

"I was able to render His Majesty a small service some years ago in the so-called Baccarat Scandal. A most disagreeable affair of an officer and gentleman cheating at cards in his presence. It came, in the end, to a trial for libel. The Prince of Wales, as His Majesty then was, had been required to give evidence."

Fisher turned a little and stared at him directly.

"Cast your mind back to certain other cases that came your way at the time. The affair of the Naval Treaty, the blackmail of a crowned head by Miss Irene Adler, and, perhaps especially, the disappearance of the secret plans for the Bruce Partington submarine."

"Naturally I still have the papers relating to every case."

Fisher's impatience was a driving force of his character. He turned to Holmes.

"Never mind the papers. Did you—then or at any other time—acquire information relating to the ciphers of the German High Seas Fleet?"

"Or any German system of codes, come to that," added Lord Esher quietly.

Holmes looked at them for a moment as if he suspected a trick. He had filled his pipe but, perhaps out of deference to our guests, had not yet lit it.

"The Imperial German Navy has had nothing to do with any case of mine," he said presently, waving a match to extinguish it. "So far as I am aware."

There was no mistaking the disappointment in the faces of our two visitors.

"However," he continued, "a practical working knowledge of coded messages is certainly necessary in my profession. I have deciphered the hieroglyphics of the Dancing Men and the riddle of the Musgrave Ritual. As you are no doubt aware, my solution in the Musgrave case led to the recovery of the ancient crown of the kings of England, lost by the Royal Stuarts after the execution of Charles I. You may also care to take away with you a small monograph of mine on the use of secret communications in the war of Greece against Persia during the fifth century BC. Despatches from Athens to Sparta were sent as meaningless strings of letters on a strip of cloth. When the strip was wound round a particular wooden baton, in a spiral and at precisely the angle known only to the sender and the recipient, the random letters formed themselves into words."

"Very interesting, Mr. Holmes," said Lord Esher, who looked as though he did not find this story interesting in the least. "The question is whether, from your experience or your researches, you can break the German naval code—and do it within the next fortnight."

"If it is to be done, by all means let it be done quickly," Holmes replied with that languid air of self-assurance that so irritated both his adversaries and Scotland Yard. "I daresay any fool could do it, given time. A fortnight sounds like a generous allowance for a man of moderate intelligence."

"I have to tell you," Fisher interposed, "that our best cryptographers at the Admiralty have tried for two months without success."

"That does not surprise me in the least. Pray tell me what, if anything, is known about these most interesting ciphers. What are they used for?"

The First Sea Lord and Viscount Esher looked at one another and, by the slightest change of expression, seemed to agree silently that they must reveal more than they had intended.

"Our instructions . . ." Fisher began.

"From His Majesty, I presume?"

"Our instructions are to tell you all that you may need to know in order to accomplish this. You will also understand why it must be done. It seems that we have a spy at the very heart of Admiralty intelligence. He has apparent access to warship design, speed, gunnery performance, and the devil knows what else. Let us not be self-righteous about it. I may tell you in strictest confidence that we have our own man in Berlin. He makes his reports to our naval attaché at the embassy."

"I should have been surprised had it not been so," said Holmes equably.

"According to this source, information is being passed by the traitor in our ranks to an enemy agent in this country. The encrypted messages are then transmitted by Morse code over a relatively short distance. We must assume that they are picked up by a German naval vessel in international waters, perhaps no more than five or ten miles from Dover or Harwich. The coded transcript then goes to the Ministry of Marine in Berlin, to the Wilhelmstrasse. Our man there has no official access to decoded messages and has seen only two, at considerable risk. Both related to Royal Navy gunnery signals. He has seen a number of transcripts, still encoded, and provided us with sequences of letters. These match certain sequences in Morse transmissions that our monitors have intercepted. It has been impossible to decipher more than a few words in all. Even that is mere luck. It seems plain that the code not only differs in every transmission; it differs from word to word in a single message."

"His Majesty is determined," added Esher, "that the turncoat in our service shall be hunted out and put behind bars in the shortest possible time. He regrets only that in time of peace the scoundrel cannot be hanged or shot."

Holmes raised his eyebrows. "Have a care, my lord! With my humble duty to His Majesty, he must do no such thing as hunt the rascal out and expose him to the world. Do you not see? In this game, the turncoat is your most valuable piece upon the board. If you can pick him out and leave him be, all may yet be well. If he is clapped behind bars, Tirpitz will close down the entire business and you will have lost the only thread that guides you through the maze. Let well alone."

I do not think Lord Esher, to judge from the expression on his face, relished returning to his royal master and telling him that Sherlock Holmes thought his instructions mistaken.

"If time is at a premium," said Holmes enthusiastically, "may we have sight of these unusual documents?"

Sir John Fisher cast his eyes round the room. The disagreeable truth was that there was no surface large enough to display the transcripts except the worktable of Sherlock Holmes. This disreputable piece of furniture was stained by overzealous chemical experiments, while a medical scalpel lay in a butter dish, near a dismantled Eley revolver and a blood-stained nightstick peeping from its newspaper wrapping. Unabashed by this, Holmes all but swept the contents of the table to the floor in his eagerness to have the coded messages before him.

We arranged four chairs round the table. Admiral Fisher opened his briefcase. A folder containing fifty or sixty transcriptions of intercepted transmissions was laid before us. If I describe the first, it will do for all the rest. There were no words, merely blocks of fourteen letters at a time. The first line may suffice.

WTRYILJGDVJNLS DDPYUGSHMKRWEX CNBJJUSDTINCRL

How on earth such drivel could contain details of warship design, gunnery trials, speed at full steam, diesel consumption, and armored plating was beyond me. Fisher looked up at us.

"You may save yourselves the trouble of trying to substitute one letter of the alphabet for another. Our cipher clerks have run the entire gamut in the past few months."

"I should not dream of such a thing." Holmes stood and walked across to the window in easy strides. He turned and came back towards us. "The message may elude us at the moment. The nature of the code can scarcely be in doubt."

"Can it not?" asked Esher skeptically. He was in no mood to let Holmes play the prima donna at such a time as this.

Holmes sat down again. "If your information is correct, it is quite plainly a looking-glass code."

"Perhaps you had better explain that," said the First Sea Lord uneasily.

Holmes looked from Sir John to Esher.

"As sender and recipient, you would each have a copy of the same piece of plain text. It would probably be a page from a book, a novel, or the Holy Bible perhaps. That would be the key to the cipher. Let us suppose that you wish to send Lord Nelson's famous signal at Trafalgar, 'England expects.' Let us also imagine that the first words of the cipher key in the hands of each of you are 'In the beginning.' Now, line up the two phrases. Your signaller will not want to transmit for longer than necessary. Therefore, for speed and convenience, you may construct a grid of the alphabet beforehand, running *A* to *Z* across the page and *A* to *Z* down the left-hand margin." Sherlock Holmes's long bony fingers worked deftly with pencil and ruler on a plain sheet of paper.

CIPHER KEY: IN THE BEGINNING

SIGNAL: ENGLAND EXPECTS

A B C D E F G H I J K L M N O P Q R S T U V W X Y Z

B C D E F G H I J K L M N O P Q R S T U V W X Y Z A

C D E F G H I J K L M N O P Q R S T U V W X Y Z A B

D E F G H I J K L M N O P Q R S T U V W X Y Z A B C

E F G H I J K L M N O P Q R S T U V W X Y Z A B C D

F G H I J K L M N O P Q R S T U V W X Y Z A B C D E

G H I J K L M N O P Q R S T U V W X Y Z A B C D E F

H I J K L M N O P Q R S T U V W X Y Z A B C D E F G

I J K L M N O P Q R S T U V W X Y Z A B C D E F G H

J K L M N O P Q R S T U V W X Y Z A B C D E F G H I

K L M N O P Q R S T U V W X Y Z A B C D E F G H I J

L M N O P Q R S T U V W X Y Z A B C D E F G H I J K

M N O P Q R S T U V W X Y Z A B C D E F G H I J K L

N O P Q R S T U V W X Y Z A B C D E F G H I J K L M

O P Q R S T U V W X Y Z A B C D E F G H I J K L M N

P Q R S T U V W X Y Z A B C D E F G H I J K L M N O

Q R S T U V W X Y Z A B C D E F G H I J K L M N O P

R S T U V W X Y Z A B C D E F G H I J K L M N O P Q

S T U V W X Y Z A B C D E F G H I J K L M N O P Q R

T U V W X Y Z A B C D E F G H I J K L M N O P Q R S

U V W X Y Z A B C D E F G H I J K L M N O P Q R S T

V W X Y Z A B C D E F G H I J K L M N O P Q R S T U

W X Y Z A B C D E F G H I J K L M N O P Q R S T U V

X Y Z A B C D E F G H I J K L M N O P Q R S T U V W

Y Z A B C D E F G H I J K L M N O P Q R S T U V W X

Z A B C D E F G H I J K L M N O P Q R S T U V W X Y

He worked with such intensity that I swear, for the moment, he had forgotten any of us was there. Then he looked up.

"I do not find such a grid essential, but few people are trained to encode messages in their heads. Very well, then, gentlemen. 'England expects' and 'In the beginning.' Take the first letter of each. If you will follow my pencil tip, you will see that a downward line from E on the top horizontal line and an inward line from I in the left-hand vertical column will meet at M. The first letter of our encoded signal is therefore M. Following the same process with the second letter of the signal and the cipher, N and N meet at A. Perhaps you will take it from me that if you follow the remaining letters and note where their lines meet on the grid, ENGLAND EXPECTS is encoded as MAZSEOH KFCRKGY."

It seemed to me, as the saying goes, that our two guests were trying to hang on to his coattails. Holmes remained composed and self-assured.

"You will understand the simple advantages of this system at once. The message is transmitted as MAZSEOH KFCRKGY. The normal tools of decoding are useless. It will not do for your Admiralty cryptographers or their unseen adversaries to puzzle which letters stand for A, B, C, and so forth. Nor will it help you to look for the frequency with which letters appear, assuming that the most common letter in almost any language is E, the next most common T, followed by A. In my example, our original message contained the letter E three times. When encrypted as a looking-glass cipher, however, the first E appears as M, the second as K, and the third as R. As for frequency, the only encoded letter which appears more than once is K, which stands for E on the first occasion and C on the second. T never appears and A only once."

There was a profound silence, broken at last by Lord Esher.

"Put as you put it, Mr. Holmes, the whole thing sounds quite ghastly."

"In other words," said Fisher quickly, "you tell us that the code cannot be broken."

"I did not say that. It is necessary to know or deduce what text is being used as the key."

"But if that text may lie anywhere, in thousands of books and millions of pages, in dozens of languages, the code cannot be broken. Surely that is what it amounts to? Our own people are only able to say that the same groups of letters are sometimes repeated. As you describe it, these may be repetitions of the same words or differing words that appear in the same letters by chance."

Holmes shrugged.

"A code may be broken in only two ways," he said patiently. "It may be possible to penetrate it a little, at least sufficiently to deduce the principle of its construction by internal evidence. More likely, it must be a matter of trial and error. The code-breakers of His Majesty's Admiralty have tried and it seems they have erred. It remains to be seen whether I shall do better. I have the advantage, at least, of recognising what sort of code it appears to be."

It need hardly be said that as I sat there I felt increasingly uncomfortable in the final stages of this encounter. Once or twice I caught the exasperation in glances between Admiral Fisher and Lord Esher. Yet, as in his dealings with Scotland Yard, Sherlock Holmes hardly bothered to disguise his belief that incompetence at the Admiralty had caused the predicament our visitors now found themselves in. This was to put a considerable strain on his friendship with the First Sea Lord. Yet Sir John Fisher was realist enough to know that Holmes was the one man in England who might help him. The transcripts of the intercepted signals must remain where they were—on the shabby worktable in our Baker Street rooms.

For three days Sherlock Holmes scarcely moved from that stained table on which the transcripts were laid. He worked in his purple dressing gown and, for all I know, his pajamas underneath. From first to last he went at his task in a silence that almost forbade anyone in the room to move or breathe. His efforts were broken only by the sound of another sheet of crumpled foolscap hitting or missing the wicker of the wastepaper basket. He looked up, without expression but with evident reproof, every time I tried to turn a page of the *Morning Post* without rustling the paper. I was so obviously a hindrance that I thought it best to leave him to himself. I went for walks nearby in Regent's Park, where the first yellowed leaves blew and scuffled about the broad avenues of trees. I lunched at my club each day, where at least I could be sure of conversation. Finally I dined there, alone.

Coming back to our rooms as the evening mist of an October night began to gather, I found no welcome fire dancing in the grate. Mrs. Hudson's timid housemaid had been told not to interrupt "the gentleman" by laying one. No meals were set out on our dining table. Holmes picked at the food like a gypsy from a tray beside his writing pad. He took little nourishment, unless shag tobacco could be counted as such.

On the first day he went to bed very late. On the second, as I came into the unaired room at breakfast time, it was plain that he had not moved from his writing chair all night. By any description, he looked white and haggard, like a man who has lost a stone in weight.

"This really will not do, old fellow," I said gently. "You will crock yourself up. That will be the end of it. What good will that do?"

He glowered and said nothing. I ate my bacon and eggs, trying not to clink the cutlery. The rustle of butter or marmalade being spread on toast seemed unthinkable. All that day he might as well have been in a trance for what I could get out of him. He sat at the blotter with a few books at his side and covered page after page with scrawled figures, letters, calculations, variations of words in half a dozen languages. Once again, only the light crunch of discarded paper aimed at the basket broke his absolute concentration. He glared at the work before him.

It was just as I was going to bed that I noticed a sudden brightening in his face, shattered though he looked. He glanced up from the folio page before him.

"Before you turn in, Watson, have the goodness to hand me the third book on the right from the second shelf down."

I took down a slim red volume, lettered in gilt, its cover tarnished somewhat by frequent reading or reference. My only interest was in going to bed and I did not bother to read the title. I noticed, as he opened it, that the flyleaf bore a neat but faded inscription. "To Mr. Sherlock Holmes with the author's best wishes and sincere thanks." I thought nothing of this. There were a few dozen volumes on our shelves presented to him by their grateful authors, whom he had helped out of one fix or another. He peered into its pages, his sharp features contracted in a frown. There was no sound now but the hiss of the white gas lamp that illuminated the table.

At last I said quietly, "I beg you to put away these things until tomorrow and get some sleep. This cannot go on without detriment to your health or your concentration and ruin to your eyesight."

"Yes, yes," he said impatiently, "good night." After that I might as well not have been in the room.

Though I had taken no part in his day's labours, I fell asleep at once. The next thing I knew, my shoulder was being tugged violently. I sensed that this had been going on for some time in an effort to rouse me.

"Watson!" I saw that his features were alive with excitement; even the sleepless pallor had gone. "Get up! I need your immediate assistance. I believe I have it, but you must help me."

"Holmes, it is pitch dark. What time is it?"

"A little before four o'clock. I must have your help in this, old fellow. I need you to listen and tell me whether I am right."

From the comfortable darkness of my bed I moved slowly downstairs to the tobacco-fogged gaslight of the sitting room. I could not see how on earth he had broken such a code as he described. As I entered the room, Holmes threw down on his table the book I had handed him before going to bed. I picked it up and glanced at the title. *Through the Looking-Glass and what Alice found there.*

"I deserve to be shot," he said triumphantly. "Where else should the answer to a looking-glass code be, except in Alice?"

By his chair lay the graph-paper grid of the alphabet that he had drawn up for our visitors. Beside it was a sheet of paper with a single line of writing at the top. He handed it to me with the grid, so that I could follow him. He was as close to exultation as I had ever known him.

"Put these two together, my dear fellow, and that is the answer. At least in this case."

I looked at the grid. It was, after all, nothing but the letters of the alphabet written horizontally across the top and vertically down the right-hand side, the squares filled in accordingly. Then I studied the first line of the coded message he had been working on. It was in the familiar blocks of fourteen letters each.

PRPMUQAKENUJQR BNAVQPNVABTLLZ TQSLLAMCZSLKWG JPSOOSLBYPYVCK WGJHXHYABCDHSF

I could make absolutely nothing of this gibberish, nor could I see what help was required. In short, I was not a little irritated at having been woken from sleep to be confronted by it.

"You may see something in it," I said wearily, "but I do not. There is a sequence of A, B, C, D toward the end, and that is about all."

He took up the children's storybook and read aloud the first lines.

"One thing was certain, that the *white* kitten had had nothing to do with it—it was the black kitten's fault entirely."

"Holmes! It is past four in the morning. Whatever this nonsense about kittens may be, tell me and let us have done with it. I should like to go back to bed!"

He pushed another sheet of paper across the table. In this case, he had written three entries across it, one beneath the other, seventy letters in each case.

1) WHAT IS THE KEY? *One thing was certain, that the white kitten had nothing to do with it—it was the black k*
2) WHAT IS THE ENCRYPTION OF THE SIGNAL? *prpmuqakenujqr bnavqpnvabtllz tqsllamczslkwg jpsooslbypyvck wgjhxhyabcdhsf*
3) WHAT IS THE MESSAGE CONTAINED IN IT? *Belt nine inch; Main six inch; Upper amidships six inch, five inch, four inch; Forward fiv(e)*

As I reached the third of these questions, I knew at once that there would no more sleep for either of us that night.

"I deserve to be shot," he repeated happily. "Where else should one find the key to a looking-glass code but in that supreme authority—the work of the Reverend Charles Lutwidge Dodgson, known to the world as Lewis Carroll? I was prepared to try the beginning of every paragraph against every signal in these transcriptions. It is not a long book, little more than a hundred pages, but it would have taken us a week or more. Yet sooner or later there is always a stroke of luck in these matters. One does not count upon it, yet one expects it. The key to the cipher in the fifth signal was in the opening lines of the story! How crass I have been! Yet it is all the fault of these Admiralty people and their invariable knack of missing the point."

"And the message? What is being measured?"

"I have got a little further than the line you have seen." He picked up the paper on which he had been working, and began to read once more. "Belt, nine inches main; six inches upper. Amidships, six inches, five inches, and four inches. Forward, five inches and four inches. Aft, extending sixteen feet above and three feet six inches below the load waterline. Bulkheads four inches, forward and aft. Barbettes, that is to say gun turrets, nine inches and eight inches. Gun shields, nine inches. Conning tower, ten inches forward, two inches aft. Communication tube, four inches and three inches forward. Four-inch battery, three inches. Before I woke you, I was able to identify references to light protective plating of a mere inch over the ammunition magazines."

"But what does it amount to?"

"It amounts, my dear friend, to a complete inventory of the armour plating on our latest Dreadnought battle cruiser, faster than yet as powerful as any battleship, but sacrificing armor for speed. Twenty-eight knots, to be precise. Unless I am much mistaken, this is the top-secret legend of particulars for HMS *Tiger*. All her strengths and weaknesses are here. Von Tirpitz would sell his ears and whiskers for such information. Were I an enemy captain or submarine commander, I should now know where a lucky shot just below the waterline or aft of the funnels and abreast of the magazines would blow a battle cruiser of twenty-eight thousand tons to Kingdom Come."

If this were true, the Royal Navy had been dealt a near-mortal blow and did not even know it. No longer in a mood to sleep, I sat down in my chair. This secret, revealed to the walls of our curtained sitting room in the small hours of a foggy autumn morning, was surely the most momentous that had ever been uttered there. In the hands of a future enemy, it could lose us a major naval battle in the North Sea or the Atlantic. It might well cost us a war.

3

"The blindfold game of war," said Holmes quietly. "All Europe seems to be at peace under sunny autumn skies. Yet the four of us are now engaged by the enemy as surely as if ultimatums had expired and ambassadors had been withdrawn. The battle of smoke and mirrors begins."

A warm morning light filled the sitting room, from which the last odours of a heartily eaten fried breakfast had not quite faded. Holmes had sent his wire to Fisher with strict orders that the First Sea Lord was to travel in mufti and by hansom cab. Fisher from Whitehall and Lord Esher from Windsor had arrived simultaneously, suggesting that they had convened a hasty conference before meeting us. Esher looked relatively composed at what he now heard, but Sir John Fisher's complexion was drained and white as candle wax.

"What is to be our first step?" His question was directed at Esher, but it was Holmes who intervened.

"Do nothing, Sir John. Allow the traitor continued access to secret documents and to think himself secure. Let the transmissions continue. Only see to it that the most vulnerable documents are replaced by copies that contain as much false information as possible. Give away only what you think the enemy may know already and what he might gather from public information. Apart from that, feed him falsehoods, if you can. Tirpitz has no reason, presumably, to know that your man in Berlin has discovered what is going on. Here is your chance to lead the grand admiral a dance. It is all you can do. Follow that one gleam of light. A single arrest will leave you in darkness."

This time it was Sir John Fisher who got up and crossed to the window. With one hand in the palm of the other behind his back, he gazed down at a file of children being brought home from play in the park.

"We cannot change course," he said at length. "So long as we had five or six of the Dreadnought class of battleship and Tirpitz had none, we were ahead. If I had had my way, we should have followed Lord Nelson's example and Copenhagened the High Seas Fleet and the Kiel Canal, with fifteen thousand Royal Marines ashore, but the king would not have it. Now Tirpitz has his Dreadnoughts—and his submarines. Make no mistake, my dear Holmes, the game has changed. We can outdo him only by faster ships carrying the same armament. That, gentlemen, is the rationale of the Dreadnought battle cruiser, of which we have a dozen and he has none. Speed rather than armor plate is its protection. Last month, two ships of the class, *Inflexible* and *Invincible*, were steamed at full speed, seven thousand miles to the Falklands. There was not the slightest hitch in their water tube boilers or their turbine machinery. They would be upon the enemy before he could know it. But an enemy who had the secrets of their design, particularly areas less endowed with protective armour, would know exactly where to put a torpedo or a shell through these weaker points."

The First Sea Lord turned from the window.

"You must not intervene," Holmes insisted in the same calm voice. "Information must continue to flow. The Morse code signals must be allowed to go out as usual. The best you can do for the moment is to let them carry falsified legends of ships' particulars or misleading figures of turbine and boiler performance."

Fisher pulled a face.

"It will be difficult. We may cause confusion in our own ranks."

"Nevertheless, it must be done," said Holmes patiently. "There is no other way."

A dozen times in the next few weeks a plain envelope arrived "by hand of messenger," usually a young Royal Navy staff officer in mufti bearing details of the intercepted signals. Once again Sherlock Holmes worked day and night. This time not a sentence, not a phrase, in *Through the Looking Glass and what Alice found there* matched the garbled blocks of fourteen letters. Perhaps, as a matter of routine, our enemies had switched to another text as their key. Holmes grew more gloomy as the October days drew in and November took its turn.

"They cannot suspect anything amiss," I said, trying to reassure him. "After all, their signals are still being sent out."

He did not seem to be much reassured beyond sighing and saying, "It means we are left with trial and error, Watson. Brother Mycroft and the advanced mathematicians are apt to refer to certain numbers so vast that they are 'beyond computation.' Such are the odds against us now."

He sat one afternoon with a dozen transcripts before him. Jackie Fisher was at him every day, insisting that until one more signal was deciphered there was no way of knowing whether our spy had been deceived by the falsified documents.

Presently, Mrs. Hudson brought a tray of tea things and set the silver teapot down beside him on the table. As the good lady went out again, Holmes turned to me and said, "This is all wrong. It cannot be done."

I was shaken by his remark, for it was the only occasion on which I had heard him use such words. Then he paused and corrected himself.

"It cannot be done in the way that we are doing it now. The key may be in any book in the world or in a single word used over and over. We are being led by a ring in our noses. Our mistake, Watson, is that we are beginning at the beginning, when we should be beginning at the end."

"How can we begin at the end? We need the key first to decipher the message."

He shook his head.

"We shall never fathom the key. That is what they count upon. At a guess, it would take a length of time approximately equal to the present age of the universe. Let us ignore the key and, instead, try to guess correctly even a small part of the signal sent. We shall try to work backwards from the letters of the encrypted signal to the letters of the code. Once we have part of the code, we may work forward to the rest."

Having no better suggestion, I let him have his way.

"However elusive the key to the code, my dear Watson, we may be sure of certain words in the messages sent. Remove their disguise and you have part of the key."

"Such as?"

"Given the events of the recent past, it is inconceivable that '*Dreadnought*' should not be among the words in the signals. May I be shot if one block of fourteen letters does not contain that name. The secrets of that class of ship is the prize they seek."

"Dreadnought is eleven letters, not fourteen," I said cautiously.

"Very well. Let us allow for Teutonic formality. 'HMS DREADNOUGHT' will give us fourteen letters."

He gathered up the transcripts and we prepared to work through the night. It was a little after two in the morning when we were working on a recent signal. The fourteen grouped letters were still gibberish—KQSUDIMUUCFSLL.

"Once again," said Holmes patiently, "suppose that these letters signal 'HMS *Dreadnought*,' what will the cipher key be?"

Carefully, he began to trace the sequence back. We had tested hundreds of these groups against the reading "HMS DREADNOUGHT" in the hope each time that this was their message—but without success. One by one he followed the present string of letters to see whether they might yield a key. Two minutes later we stared at the result. It was a key and a message in one.

"DEAR ME, MR HOLMES"

I felt the shock like a blow to the chest. The thing was impossible, and yet, as we had worked through the night, it now seemed as if our distant and invisible enemies had been thinking our very thoughts for us. We got up and went in silence to our usual arm chairs. After so much work, my despair was all the greater.

"Well, that is the end of it," I said miserably "How the devil could they know?"

Holmes knocked his pipe out against the fireplace and refilled it. For a moment he said nothing. Then he lit his pipe and turned to me.

"I believe they could not know. Therefore, they did not know. If I am right, this is in every sense a lucky shot, a shot in a thousand. It has a ring of heavy Germanic facetiousness. You will recall that several of my adventures, such as they are, lie in the hands of the public, thanks to your gift for romanticized narratives. I should find it remarkable if they were not read by such men as these. This was a phrase of the late Professor Moriarty's and has circulated widely. We must proceed on the assumption that it is pleasantry among our adversaries and no more."

"Can we do that?"

He seemed remarkably unruffled.

"You will observe that several signals were sent after the date of this one. That surely would not have happened had they thought the hunters were on their trail. You will also recall that when our visitors have come here, I have surveyed the street from time to time. I do not think that they were followed or watched. All the same, it may come to that. I think it is as well that we should hold future discussions with Sir John and Lord Esher away from public scrutiny."

I was far from reassured. On the following afternoon a private room of the Diogenes Club was secured for us by Mycroft Holmes. We had thrown off any pursuers by taking a twopenny bus from Baker Street to Oxford Circus, alighting, then getting on again after the waiting passengers had done so. Anyone following us would have had to get off and on as well. None did.

Furthermore, Sir John Fisher assured us that the Morse code transmissions had continued. Two signals were intercepted in the previous week. Had the signallers believed that their codes had been deciphered and that they themselves were in danger, they would have fled before then. It seemed as if the use of "Sherlock Holmes" in their key was, after all, merely a joke among those who thought themselves superior even to the famous detective.

Yet my relief was short-lived, as Sir John spread before us the latest transcripts. I expected the usual groups of fourteen letters. What I saw was quite different.

72-48-03-61-74 | 82-30-42-13-06-53 | 29-71-46-22 | 38-72-49-17 |

The First Sea Lord looked up at us.

"They have abandoned Morse for a two-digit code. Our monitors now hear two series of short pulses from one to ten. A pause. Two more. Then a long pulse, no doubt to signal the end of a word. It is something entirely new. At any rate, our people have never come across the like of it. What do you say to it now?"

Holmes stretched out his long legs and touched his fingertips together.

"Never fear, Sir John. I believe you are wrong in supposing this device to be new. Something tells me that it goes back many centuries. Moreover, the fact that the signals are still going out confirms, as you say, that their reference to me was mere whimsy inspired by Watson's turn for romantic fiction. In that, as so often in such matters, it seems I have been proved correct."

4

Further precautions were taken. There was no more post "by hand of officer." Intercepted signals were to be relayed direct to us from the rooftop mast of Admiralty Arch. Pride of place on his worktable went to an "ink-writer" devised by Holmes some years earlier. From a wire aerial it could take down messages in Morse. Rescued from the attic, this contraption worked on an accumulator battery. I saw only a square glass jar filled with sulphuric acid and distilled water. By means I did not comprehend, an endless strip of white paper moved slowly above the inkwell as a message was received. A stylus attached to the mechanism kept pace with the signals of each transmission, drawing dashes or dots in time with it. Holmes assured me that it required only an electric current from the battery to pass through a magnet. A lever would then lift a small ink wheel into contact with the paper.

"The length of an ink mark depends upon how long the current flows," he said, not for the first time. "Dots or dashes are determined by the duration of the current. By this means, our friends at Admiralty Arch can transmit to us in Morse code. In the case of the new code, however, they will transmit dashes for digits of ten and dots for single numerals, making up the pairs of numbers that our adversaries now appear to prefer."

"Black magic!" I said uneasily.

He laughed and shook his head.

"Not in the least, my dear Watson. Have you noticed, by the way, that each pair of numbers in the ciphers appears to stand for something like a letter or a syllable? Taken together, they must certainly equate to an alphabet in some form. In every one of the ciphers the double digits run from one—with a nought before it—to eighty-seven. Now consider this. That is far too few for a system like the Chinese, where each ideogram stands for a word and many thousands of symbols are required. At the same time, it is rather too many for a purely alphabetical system as we know it. Our alphabet has only twenty-six letters, after all, and the Greek has only twenty-four."

"Very well, then eighty-seven symbols cannot be an alphabet."

He chuckled.

"Not as you or I think of it, Watson. However, I would bet a good deal that what we are looking at is a code written in syllables rather than letters, though based upon an alphabet. That should narrow down our hunt considerably."

"I wish I could see how. As yet we do not even know which alphabet it may be. This is worse than your looking-glass nonsense."

Before he could reply, there was a knock at the door and Mrs. Hudson came in.

"Mr. Lestrade and a lady to see Mr. Holmes, supposing it might be convenient."

I would have suggested it was anything but convenient. Holmes beamed at her.

"By all means, Mrs. Hudson. It will be a sad day when we are too busy to see Inspector Lestrade."

Our landlady withdrew, and after several measured steps upon the staircase her place in the doorway was taken by Lestrade, our small but wiry bulldog as I thought of him. The lady in his company seemed not the least remarkable. She looked very much what she proved to be, a widow of sixty obliged to take in lodgers, dressed on this occasion in a dark red hat, a brown travelling-cloak and a fox fur of uncertain quality about her neck.

"Good morning, gentlemen," said our Scotland Yard friend. "Allow me to introduce you to Mrs. Annie Constantine of Nile Street, Sheerness."

Holmes bowed as if before a duchess.

"My dear lady, my dear Lestrade, you are both most welcome. Please take the chairs by the mantelpiece and tell us to what we owe the honour of this visit. I confess I have been expecting something of the sort for two or three hours."

Lestrade did not look best pleased by this. When Mrs. Constantine had been arranged in a chair by the fireside and fresh tea had been ordered, he sat down opposite Holmes and said: "Expecting what exactly, Mr. Holmes?" His eyes widened and he looked more than a trifle put out. "I do not see how you can have been expecting something you knew nothing about."

Holmes laughed merrily but there was no merriment behind his eyes.

"Allow me to explain. Several days ago it was arranged that Superintendent Melville of the Criminal Investigation Department at Scotland Yard should be informed by his inspectors of any unusual entry by beat constables of the London area in their station Occurrence Book. Not crimes, you understand, but anything out of the ordinary that was reported—the results were to be conveyed to me. Special attention was to be given to the Thames estuary."

"Ah, then you were not being so very clever just now, were you, Mr. Holmes?"

My friend ignored this snub.

"I said to myself at the time, if there is anything worthy of note, it will be an officer with the capacity and shrewdness of Inspector Lestrade who recognizes it and acts at once."

There was a pause while the morning tea tray was set down and then Holmes began to pour.

"Perhaps I had better hear what this good lady has to tell us," he said genially, handing her a cup.

Mrs. Constantine looked at Lestrade, as if for permission to speak, then turned to Holmes.

"As you mayn't have heard, Mr. Holmes, I keep a lodger. Usually a young single gentleman that has the first floor back. I breakfast him, but otherwise he does for himself. Last year Mr. Henshaw came to me, Mr. Charles Henshaw, a very genteel young man. He teaches French, not at school but to professional young men with examinations to pass. They come to the house and he has the use of the downstairs drawing room to give them lessons. Otherwise, the upstairs is his domain."

"Really?" said Holmes indifferently, though for reasons I could not see he was missing neither a word nor an inflection of her voice. "A nice young man?"

"Ever so nice. Regular at the Congregational chapel on Sundays. And I don't mind telling you that if I'd known there was to be so much trouble as this, I'd have acted otherwise on Monday morning."

"What trouble precisely, madam?"

"Well, Mr. Holmes, it was the middle of this last Monday morning and everything in the street was as quiet as you could wish. Nothing but Mr. Lethbridge the constable, that lives two roads away, coming down on his beat. Then it happened."

She sat back and folded her arms, as if the matter was at an end.

"What happened, Mrs. Constantine?"

"The bang, Mr. Holmes. I was at the back, where the maid was taking out the clothes from the washhouse to dry on the line. I was just tipping out ashes from the grate of the copper. Then there was a flash that lit up the window of the upstairs back room—Mr. Henshaw's study—brighter than day and a bang that rattled every windowpane in the street. My first thought was the gas fire had gone up. Seeing Mr. Lethbridge patrolling the street, I rushed out and called him. He ran back and went up the stairs first and I went up behind him. I half expected to find poor Mr. Henshaw stone-cold dead. But there he was, sitting on a chair, just looking a bit shocked. And the strange thing was—after such a bang that might have wrecked the entire house, not a thing in the room seemed harmed."

"Curious," said Holmes gently.

"It was curious all right. Ever so sorry, he was. Went to light the gas fire and it somehow blew back. Only thing is, Mr. Holmes, there was no match that had been struck, the fire wasn't lit, and there was no smell of gas. But there was a horrible smell of something else. Till that moment I never really thought about it, but I think I smelt it up there before, from time to time, only not so strong. Anyway, that was the end of it. Mr. Lethbridge went back to his beat and I suppose Mr. Henshaw went back to reading French. Then, last night, there was a knock at the door and I'm told I'm wanted at Scotland Yard today."

If my friend felt any excitement at this, he concealed it admirably under an appearance of casual interest.

"Tell me about the flash, Mrs. Constantine. Did it at all resemble the bright flash you see when the metal poles of a tramcar cross a connexion?"

"Now you mention it, sir, it was just like it. That hadn't occurred to me."

Holmes stood up and walked past the worktable to a jumble of books, papers, bottles, and implements on an old sideboard. He came back with a small six-sided clear-glass bottle and drew the stopper from it.

"Will you tell me, Mrs. Constantine, whether the smell that you say was not like gas was anything like this? You need not get too close to it, just enough to be able to smell. Just smell and do not inhale."

He held it at a little distance and waited until the fumes drifted across to her. Mrs. Constantine gave a slight cough, screwed her face up, and exclaimed, "Ugh! Nasty, beastly stuff! What he wanted with it I do not know. But that's it, sir." She took a long sip from her cup of tea.

"Perhaps, Mr. Holmes," said Lestrade, "you might let us into your little secret."

"I have no secret, Lestrade. What Mrs. Constantine could smell was sulphuric acid."

"What's he doing with sulphuric acid?" the inspector asked suspiciously.

"What's he doing short-circuiting a battery, Lestrade, and a fully charged battery at that, on a Monday morning? Tell me, Mrs. Constantine, does your Congregational chapel have electric light?"

"I think its Sunday school hall does. That was only built three or four years back."

"Then I daresay that is how he charges his accumulator battery—and why it was fully charged on Monday morning. Tell me a little about this nice young lodger of yours. Does he travel much, for example? Abroad, perhaps?"

She laughed at him.

"Lord bless you, Mr. Holmes, I shouldn't say he'd been further abroad than the end of Margate pier. No. He does go to Oxford every week or two, on a Saturday, to buy books for his French."

"Rather odd, is it not, that he should not buy them in London, so much closer?"

"Well, you see, Mr. Holmes, I was given to understand that he has a friend he meets in Oxford. They take tea together."

"Ah," said Holmes, "that must be it. One more question, dear lady. From what part of the country does he come?"

Mrs. Constantine looked troubled and then replied,

"I don't know that I could say, Mr. Holmes. Not from round our way, I should think. He talks quite like a gentleman, that's all."

"Very good." My friend looked thoroughly satisfied. "One more word, Mrs. Constantine. I am quite sure you have nothing to fear from the young gentleman. The police are merely looking for unusual occurrences over a very wide area—is that not so, Lestrade?—and that is the sole reason you have been troubled. This is clearly nothing more than a trivial domestic mishap. You will continue to allow him to lodge with you, shall we say for the next six months? He seems, after all, an admirable tenant in every other way."

"I can't say as I know about that," she said with a slight coloring of indignation.

"I do not believe you will have further cause for complaint, but I must have your promise upon this. Nor must you say a word to him or anyone else about our conversation. I must have your solemn promise upon that, too."

She hesitated and I intervened.

"Perhaps you have a sister or a friend with whom you might care to stay for a few weeks, until the upset of this has worn off. Provided the maid could look after Mr. Henshaw."

"I might, sir. However it may be, you shall have my promise for the next six months. As to what has passed between us here, mum's the word."

To meet Mrs. Constantine was to know that the promise would be kept. She was the type to sweep Napoleon and his invaders out of England with a broom and a bucket. As our visitors left, it was only Lestrade who seemed in a fit of the sulks, piqued that he was not to be let further into the secret.

Holmes was jubilant. He was not a man much given to wine, but that evening we shared a bottle of Dom Perignon, one of six dozen presented to him several years before by a client and as yet untasted.

The next morning there was no sign of him. He was not an early riser, and until I inquired of our landlady's maid-of-all-work, I had supposed he was still sleeping. His room was empty and my day passed idly but agreeably, a day chiefly remarkable for the autumn's first flurry of snow. At six o'clock I heard his shout to Mrs. Hudson on the stairs. He was back.

"I thought you had gone missing," I said, half joking.

He flung down his hat and stick on the chair; his cloak followed.

"My dear Watson, I have spent the day in that most admirable of institutions, Somerset House. In painted halls and palatial apartments, enjoying unrivalled views of the river steamers on the Thames, one may study the records of births, marriages, and deaths to one's heart's content."

"Whose birth, marriage, or death?"

"No one's. There is a far smaller section where those who have changed their names by deed poll are obliged to register the fact. I confess that the name Charles Henshaw sounded to me like—what shall we call it?—a light adaptation of something else. I was not entirely surprised to find that at Chatham Registry Office—not a million miles from Sheerness—it was adopted several years ago by Karl Henschel."

"A German?"

"I confess, I should have thought so. In this case, when he changed his name, he was already an Englishman, or rather a German who had become a naturalised Englishman on a visit to Australia. You could hardly bury a secret much deeper than that."

"But Mrs. Constantine has not the least doubt that he is English, through and through."

"He is a linguist, my dear chap. A German linguist, particularly, will often speak more correct English than an Englishman born and bred. As for teaching French to English youths—or English to French youths—what better cover could there be? You might suspect him, perhaps, of being French by birth or sympathies. If he were German, you might say, the last thing he would do is to teach French in England."

"And his Saturday visits to Oxford, what about those?"

"We shall be at Paddington tomorrow for the early train. On my way home, I paid a brief visit to Scotland Yard. Whitehall and the Embankment looked quite charming in the snow, quite like a Camille Pissarro sketch in oils. Superintendent Melville has deputed Inspector Tobias Gregson to shadow Herr Henschel, as we had better call him now. Gregson is one of the best men at the game. Even were Henschel to suspect that he was being followed, he would see that Gregson had slipped away from him in London. At Paddington I shall look for Gregson on the platform for the Oxford trains. He will tip us the wink, as they say, and identify Henschel. I have our man's photograph this afternoon, taken without his knowledge yesterday. Then, my dear Watson, Gregson will be on his way and the game will be in our court again."

5

"You may as well pack your razor and a clean collar," said Holmes at breakfast. "I have wired ahead to engage rooms at the Mitre Hotel. I daresay it may prove an unnecessary precaution, but it is as well to be prepared. Your army revolver you may bring if you please. I cannot suppose it will be necessary on this occasion."

Saturday morning had dawned bright and cloudless as midsummer, giving the lie to "drear November." Under his travelling cloak, Holmes wore a dark suit with a gold watch-chain over the waistcoat. This formal attire was scarcely what a lounger would choose for a weekend. As our cab rattled along the Marylebone Road toward Paddington station, I could not help wondering what our spy might look like. Would Karl Henschel be the bearded agent of romance or merely a young man who might be mistaken for an insurance clerk? One thing seemed certain, he could not be the traitor in the Admiralty. Sir John Fisher had assured us that there was no Charles Henshaw on their records.

At Paddington the concourse of the great railway station was bustling with weekend travelers crowding about the bookstall, the flower-sellers, and the cab ranks. Columns of smoke rose to the high curve of the glass roof from several green-liveried engines of the Great Western Railway waiting to depart. There was no train at the platform for Oxford and only a handful of passengers waiting by the leather trunks and wicker hampers, neatly piled for the luggage van.

It was hardly twenty minutes later when I recognized Gregson in his pale gray topcoat and bowler hat, keeping well back from his quarry. He scarcely needed to "tip us the wink." From where we stood it was quite plain to see who his quarry was. I should have taken the young language teacher for an army subaltern on weekend leave, neatly turned out in a belted Norfolk jacket and twill trousers, a black leather bag at his side. Slightly built, clean-shaven and with short-cropped hair, he had an air of peremptoriness about him.

The young man's back was to us as Holmes looked Gregson in the eyes at a distance of several yards and inclined his head an inch or so. Our Scotland Yard friend in his gray topcoat walked past us as though we had been strangers and disappeared on the far side of the bookstall. We made our way to the further end of the platform, which would bring us close to the exit when the train reached Oxford.

It did not seem that Henschel was accustomed to spend the night in Oxford but would return to Sheerness by a train that would leave for London in the late afternoon or early evening. At our destination, however, we had already arranged for a hotel porter to take our travelling bags from us and carry them to the Mitre Inn.

There was no difficulty in finding a compartment to ourselves on the journey. A dreary hour of West London was followed by enchanting views of the Thames valley running among the winter woods of the hills with flooded water-meadows to either side. It was not yet midday when we saw from the railway line the spires and towers of the ancient city.

The station approach at Oxford was lined by luggage wagons and cabs, but Henschel crossed the road and began making his way toward the centre of the town on foot. We kept well back, walking separately, until he turned up the wide thoroughfare of Beaumont Street with its plain but handsome houses. The creeper-covered windows and archway of one of the colleges faced us from the far end. I was as sure as I could be that our man had no idea he was being followed. He did not once look back or make any manoeuvre to suggest that he was trying to throw off a shadow. Our only risk was that an accomplice lay further back, trailing us in turn. Yet there was no sign of such a man, and he would have been astute indeed if he had been able to shadow Sherlock Holmes unobserved!

I was conscious that every stretch of open street or pavement increased the danger of Henschel spotting us. I need not have worried. At the top of Beaumont Street he turned into the wide courtyard of the Ashmolean, the university museum, which was raised on a plinth with its Grecian portico, pillars, and statues, a sculptured goddess sitting high above a classical frieze. As the corner concealed us briefly, I drew level with Holmes and said, "For all we can tell, he may have come like any other tripper to see the collections. It seems more than likely."

We separated again, two visitors dutifully and individually making our tour of the exhibits. The museum was admirably laid out for the purposes of tracking our suspect. Tall display cases running across the galleries make admirable cover for the hunter, yet one step beyond them gives a wide view ahead and behind. To begin with, from our concealment among the displays of classical sculpture on the ground floor, we watched Henschel go up the grand staircase leading to the galleries above.

Holmes waited until the young man had turned the corner to the second flight of steps and then walked slowly after him. I saw my friend pause and begin studying a dark van Eyck landscape on the half-landing. He had his back to the flight of stairs up which Henschel had gone to the floor above. Yet as Holmes stood there, I could see that in the palm of one hand he held a small round pocket mirror, reflecting the stairs behind him and the gallery above.

I followed cautiously up the staircase, well lit by its roof lights, to the wide and airy exhibition hall of the first floor. Before me lay a vista of Italian Renaissance art, to which we and our quarry were the only visitors just then, except for two ladies talking quietly together and a middle-aged gentleman on his own. There were display cases ranked in the center of the gallery and paintings along the walls to either side. I am no expert in such matters, but the small brass plates on each frame identified for me two Botticelli sketches of nymphs in woodland and a dimly lit papal portrait by Fra Lippo Lippi. How such things could be connected with espionage and naval codes defied explanation.

Holmes had disappeared from view. However, I became aware that Henschel was paying very little attention either to the paintings or to the Florentine ceramics and silverware that filled the glass display cases between them. He walked to the far end of the gallery and there helped himself to one of the small green canvas stools that filled a metal rack. These stools are commonly supplied in the great museums and art galleries for those amateurs who choose to spend a day sketching or copying some work by a master. The Ashmolean is next door to Mr. Ruskin's School of Drawing and Fine Art, which provides an ample supply of pupils. You will see such students busy every day in the galleries, as if they might be in the Louvre or the Uffizi.

Yet Henschel did not sit down to sketch any of the paintings. He held the folded green canvas of the stool in one hand and his black bag in the other as he walked through a side turning into a set of smaller exhibition rooms. This area was devoted to archaeological displays and, once more, the tall glass cases afforded ample cover. Each of them was layered with shelves on which were set out fragments of pots, amphorae or pithoi, small votive objects, here and there what appeared to be a rusted blade or implement.

Karl Henschel passed "Mesopotamia," "Ancient Egypt," "Anatolia," "Ancient Cyprus," and stopped at a display of cases along the far wall marked "Ancient Crete and the Aegean." There he opened out his little stool of green canvas and sat down. From his leather bag he took a small copying board to which was clipped a pad of paper.

I believe he had not the least idea that anyone else was there and probably he did not care. Why should he? He got up and walked away, into another room. He must have opened his pocketknife, for I heard him sharpening a pencil into a basket that had evidently been provided. The polished boards of the wooden floors acted as an excellent soundboard and I knew I should hear him coming back the moment he moved. While the coast was clear, I strolled past the case where his stool was parked and paused like a casual visitor to see which display meant so much to him that he had come from Sheerness to make a sketch of it.

I would not have crossed the road to copy what I now saw before me. Imagine, if you will, a few dozen scraps of old clay tile. Most were the colour of slate, a few looked like dark terra cotta, rather the colour of burnt sealing wax. Some were roughly square and a smaller number were oblong but sandy-colored and tapering at one end. None of them was more than five inches square. There was also a small ornament that I noticed was labelled as a seal ring.

This entire collection was described on its plaque as "Linear B" tablets, most from the ruins of the Minoan palace at Knossos on the island of Crete. I remembered, from my schooldays, that this was the location of the labyrinth where Theseus slew the Minotaur in the famous legend. A small printed card informed the visitor that these clay tablets dated from a time before the Trojan War, probably about 1500 B.C. They had been found during the past ten years by Sir Arthur Evans, in his excavations of the site.

There were marks upon these baked clay tablets. A few were single downward strokes, which looked like some method of counting. For the rest, imagine tiny representations of an axe head, a five-barred gate, a wigwam, a fish, a star, and so forth. Such was the writing of Linear B. A further display card attempted to describe the pronunciation of certain words. I learnt that "at-ku-ta-to" signified ten working oxen and "at-ku-do-nia" fifty of the same beasts. Then I heard a movement in the next room and walked quietly but quickly away, behind the screen of another case. I took a glance presently and saw that Henschel was now sitting before this curious display and making small neat sketches of the tablets.

For the next three hours, taking turns, we kept up our scrutiny. It was not difficult since we had Henschel bottled up in the set of smaller exhibition rooms. He could not come out except by returning through the displays of antiquities and then down the avenue of Renaissance paintings to the grand staircase. From where he sat, he could hardly be aware that we were, at varying levels, always within sight of that exit route.

Holmes even equipped himself with one of the canvas stools and chose the portrait of an amiable Venetian courtesan by Carpaccio, before which he became the model of concentration. He sat with his notebook and pencil as other visitors came and went. Presently, a thin elderly man with pince-nez, walking stick, a rather rusty frock coat, and a neat gray beard took a stool from the rack and sat before a Piranesi sketch of the Coliseum. He paid no attention to anyone but, after almost an hour of noting and sketching, he stood up, polished his pince-nez with a blue silk handkerchief, dabbed his watery eyes, and returned his canvas stool to the rack. Holmes sketched angles and features, lost to the world in Carpaccio's portrait, until the old man had shuffled past him on his way out.

At the instant that the tapping of the old scholar's walking stick reached the half-landing of the staircase, Holmes sprang up and approached the rack of stools in a dozen quiet strides. I followed him as he added his folded stool to the rest. His eyes scanned the metal frame rapidly and came to rest on the four metal tubes that were its corner posts.

"As I thought!" he breathed sharply. His forefinger entered the nearest of these upright supports and screwed out a coiled piece of paper, no more than a single sheet of manuscript. As he unrolled it, I had just time to see:

57-09-83-62-15 || 19-80-05 . . .

His finger was to his lips as he returned it to its hiding place. Though his voice rose no higher than a whisper, its urgency was never in doubt.

"After him, Watson! He is not agile enough to have got far!"

"Henschel?" I gasped.

"Leave him. It is best that he should not see us again."

He strode to the staircase and went down it, two at a time, closing on the hobbling frock-coated gentleman with his stick, who was just going out into the museum courtyard. Then my friend slackened his pace and sauntered a dozen yards behind him, like a casual visitor once more. We took up our vantage point behind one of the stone pedestals and watched the old man walking across Beaumont Street and turning down it the way we had come. Then, to my surprise, he suddenly drew a key from his pocket, slid it into the latch of a white-painted door beside him, and disappeared into one of the handsome plain-fronted houses.

Sherlock Holmes was triumphant.

"And that, Watson, is how they do it! Now let us have no more of this until Monday morning. We have done all that is required of us for the time being."

It seemed to me that we had done nothing of the kind. However, Holmes was in no mood to listen to argument. He insisted that we should not hurry back to London at once, or indeed the next day. Monday would be time enough. That evening we dined in the lamplit parlour of the Mitre with its low beams and memories of the coaching inn it had been until half a century before. Holmes pronounced the food and wine excellent. He talked of archaeology and the stupendous discoveries at Mycenae by the great German Heinrich Schliemann. How three gold-masked figures, warriors of the Trojan War, had been unearthed and how, when the masks were removed, their perfectly preserved faces had been recognizable for some minutes before they crumbled into dust.

"'Today I have looked upon the face of Agamemnon,'" he recited with a chuckle. "No wonder Herr Schliemann sent that telegram to the King of Greece. Now, one pipe before my bed, my dear fellow. Sufficient unto the day is the evil thereof."

We retired to the sitting room that he had reserved for our use, while the groups of tall-hatted undergraduates began returning to their colleges before lock-up and the life of the university passed by in the lamplit street below us. Great Tom began to toll his hundred strokes from Christ Church tower, at the end of which time the porters would shoot the iron bolts across to close the main gates and those who were not inside their colleges must face the justice of the dean or the proctors on Monday morning. Only now were we solitary enough to discuss the afternoon's events.

"That old man was not our Admiralty spy," I said incredulously. "He cannot be!"

Holmes laughed and lit his cherrywood pipe from the fire.

"No, my dear fellow. The game is played in three moves, not in two.

There is the spy who passes information. There is the old man who encodes it. Then there is Henschel who transmits it. Perhaps Henschel is also useful in formulating the language of the code."

"A language that no one has used for more than three thousand years?"

"Precisely. In the present case, its rarity is what makes it unique. Almost nothing was known about Linear B until Sir Arthur Evans discovered the first tablets at Knossos. The meaning of the language is virtually unknown today. A string of meaningless ciphers. What better code could there be? It is not necessary to know its ancient meaning in order to give it a new one for purposes of espionage. It is the last thing in the world that anyone would think of!"

"But the code is written in numbers."

"Quite right, Watson. On Monday morning I propose to put that difficulty to someone who can answer with rather more authority than either the Admiralty or Scotland Yard."

On Sunday he was content with a riverside stroll round the circuit of Addison's Walk, where that famous essayist of the *Spectator* used to take his constitutional as an undergraduate at Magdalen. I noticed, however, that after breakfast he had withdrawn to the hotel writing room and penned a note. As he handed it to the page boy I was able to read the address: "J. L. Strachan-Davidson, Esquire, The Master's Lodging, Balliol College." On our return, as the river mists began to halo the lamps of the street, Holmes inquired of the concierge and was handed a small neatly written envelope in reply.

On Monday morning we set out to walk a few hundred yards down "The Turl" in search of our adviser. I knew little of the Master, as I must now call him, except as a younger man, "the lean, unbuttoned cigaretted dean." He was a tall and angular Scot of luxuriant eyebrows and formidable reputation, an authority on Cicero and Roman criminal law. Holmes assured me that I should find all I needed to know of him as a tutor in one of the famous college rhymes.

Take a pretty strong solution
Of the Roman constitution,
Cigarettes not less than three
And mix them up with boiling tea.
Then a mighty work you've done,
For you've made Strachan-Davidson.

"I was once able to do the Master a small service concerning a scrape that one of his undergraduates was in—a nasty but petty blackmail. As you know, I do not expect favor returned for favor. However, he is good enough to write to me that he welcomes the opportunity to renew our rather slight acquaintance."

Once inside the lodgings on the college's Broad Street front, we were shown up immediately to the Master's sitting room. The door stood open and from within came the sounds of a tutorial in progress. Two young men were sitting in arm chairs and Strachan-Davidson, his back to the fireplace and his arms stretched out at either side along the mantelpiece, was in full flow on the subject of Sparta's invasion of Athens during the Peloponnesian War.

"Do come in!" he said enthusiastically. "Lord Wroughton and Mr. Sampson are just construing for us book four of Thucydides. Find chairs, if you can."

We found them among the comfortable disorder of the room, books piled here and there, papers gathered untidily.

"Now, my lord, if you please."

Lord Wroughton was a dark-haired and fresh-faced young man with the embarrassed look of one who had spent the previous evening dining not wisely but too well, when he should have had Thucydides as his sole companion.

"*Tou de-pe-gig-no-menou therou,*" he muttered, "*Peri sitou ek-boleen* . . . 'In the following summer, when the corn was in full ear.'"

"Yes, yes," said the Master with Scots impatience, "and when was that?"

"It was . . . that is to say, Master, I believe. . . ."

Sherlock Holmes took pity on the unfortunate young nobleman and intervened.

"I believe, Master, that we are safe in dating the expedition of the Syracusans against Messina as 1 June 425 B.C."

The Master's eyebrows rose.

"Really, Mr. Holmes? After two and a half thousand years in which even the season has been a matter of debate, you are able to tell us the precise day?"

"It is really very simple, Master. Climate and season of every kind are necessary subjects upon which the criminal investigator must be informed. In this case, given the dates of ripening corn in Attica lying between 20 May and 10 June, the corn in full ear would scarcely be before the end of May. No reference is made to harvest, however, which suggests that the date of sailing was well before the end of the first week in June. Though I would allow a little latitude, I believe you will find that the tides necessary for embarking and landing the invading force would give very little alternative to 1 June. The coastline is not an easy one for shallow draft."

"Dear me," said our host genially. "Well, if Thucydides is to become a matter of criminal investigation, perhaps we had better leave him there. Lord Wroughton and Mr. Sampson, I shall be pleased to receive you both at the same time next week, in the hope that the first five chapters of book four will be firmly in your minds by then. Good morning to you."

As the two young men excused themselves deferentially to Holmes and myself, the Master shut the door and turned to us.

"My dear Mr. Holmes,"—only now did he shake our hands—"though it is a great pleasure to make your acquaintance again, I confess I have been puzzling what use Linear B could have for you. One moment and I will put the kettle on."

Holmes stretched his dark-suited legs before him.

"Every possible use, Master. The matter is in strict confidence, of course."

"Of course. I imagine you would not be here otherwise."

"You are a collector of seal rings and coins from the ancient world, I believe."

Strachan-Davidson turned round with the kettle in his hand, beaming at us.

"You have heard of my winter journeys to the Middle East, I imagine. A numismatist in a dahabeeah, as my young men call me here, a coin collector in an Egyptian sailing boat. I have one or two seal rings. You may still pick them up from market stalls in Cairo and in western Crete, you know."

"And Linear B?"

"I have followed the work of Sir Arthur Evans with great interest. A good many of the texts were published lately in his book *Scripta Minoa*. Unfortunately he is still in Crete, so you cannot very well consult him."

Holmes nodded.

"The question is a simple one, Master. Could Linear B be used as the basis of a code? I beg you to consider the question most carefully."

The Master's ample eyebrows rose once more.

"Oh yes, indeed. Linear B *is* a code, Mr. Holmes. Nothing else. It is a code so remarkable that no one has yet resolved it. A few decipherments here and there but very few and amounting to very little. Much of the rest of our understanding is guesswork. A school of thought, to which I am inclined to belong, believes these symbols to be early forms of classical Greek. From that there has been an attempt to evolve pronunciation. There is far to go."

"Deciphered or not, its structure might form a modern naval or military code?"

The Master handed us tea in silence.

"The subject matter is the palace of Knossos, particularly its ships and arsenal. However, to draw each pictogram would be laborious. Nor could you print them, for no printer's type would be available."

"How do scholars make texts available to each other? I imagine that must often happen."

"Indeed, Mr. Holmes. The problem has been solved by certain scholars in Etruscan and Babylonian by reducing ancient symbols to modern numerals. Each symbol is given a number, as a kind of shorthand."

"Could each Linear B symbol be a letter of an alphabet expressed as a number?"

The Master shook his head.

"No, Mr. Holmes. It is early days but, it seems, each symbol is a syllable rather than a single letter."

Sherlock Holmes let out the long sigh of a man who is vindicated after all.

"Thus," Strachan-Davidson continued, "a modern message in Linear B would consist of several double digit numbers in groups, each double digit representing a syllable or whatever unit the code-maker chose and each group making up a word. It could serve for whatever message you wished to send. You would not have to decipher Linear B to use its signs as such a form of communication, though you might choose to do so."

Holmes was in his familiar attitude, listening with eyes closed and fingertips pressed together.

"One further point, Master," he said, now looking up. "What advantage would this system have to distinguish it from any other form of code?"

Strachan-Davidson looked surprised.

"Only one, Mr. Holmes. Every other form of code, in letters or numbers, is adapted from something commonly understood in its uncoded form. It may be a word, a book, a numerical formula. However disguised or distorted, common knowledge lies behind it. In the case of Linear B, very little is known. Even that little knowledge is shared by only a handful of men throughout the world. The rest of mankind is excluded from the game, so to speak."

"Precisely," said Holmes quietly, "how many of that handful live in Oxford?"

The Master thought for a moment.

"Sir Arthur Evans, but he is in Crete. There are two of his assistants, but they are with him. There is the keeper of antiquities at the Ashmolean."

"And no others?"

"Dr. Gross is not a member of the university. He was deputy keeper in the department of antiquities at the Royal Museum in Berlin. He retired and has lived in Oxford for a year or two."

"An elderly man with pince-nez who lives in Beaumont Street, I believe?" Holmes inquired innocently.

"Then you are familiar with him?"

"A passing acquaintance."

Yet those who knew Sherlock Holmes well, medical men above all, would have detected a quickening beat at the temples accompanying such a lucky shot in the dark. We took our leave presently. Holmes did not ask the Master for a pledge of confidentiality. Anyone who had been in the presence of Strachan-Davidson for any length of time would know that such a request was quite unnecessary.

6

BY THAT EVENING, we were before our own fireside again in Baker Street, though not before Holmes had insisted upon a detour to the St. James's Library, of which he was a member and from which he carried off that imposing volume which bears upon it the name of Sir Arthur Evans and the cryptic title *Scripta Minoa.*

We had just finished our supper of "cold fowl and cigars, pickled onions in jars," as the poet has it, when Holmes filled his pipe again with the familiar black shag tobacco and crossed to his worktable. He laid a pile of blank paper and the intercepted signals on one side of his wooden chair and placed the *Scripta Minoa* on the other. He selected a fresh nib from the box for his Waverley pen, then sat down with a cushion behind him, as if for a prolonged study of the puzzle.

There would be no more conversation that night. I made the best of a bad job, selecting a volume of Sir Walter Scott from the shelf and retiring to my own quarters. I do not know at what hour, if at all, he went to bed that night. He was sitting at the table next morning, the air once again as thick with smoke as a "London particular" fog, *Scripta Minoa* at his side. There was no weariness about him but the exhilaration of the hunter at the chase.

"We have them by the tail, Watson," he said triumphantly. "In the past hours, I am convinced I have learnt Minoan arithmetic from Arthur Evans's drawings. A single vertical stroke is a one. A short horizontal dash is ten. A circle is a hundred. A dotted circle is a thousand. A circle with a horizontal bar is ten thousand. There are eighty-seven known syllabic signs in Linear B, but the double digits of the good Dr. Gross number ninety-two. There can be no doubt that those five extra double digits represent the means of counting."

For the next two days and a good part of their nights he worked his way through intercepted signals that had previously been meaningless strings of double digits. Most of them remained so. Yet here and there he swore he was able to decipher numbers in the messages. Our sitting room bristled with his gasps of frustration and self-reproach as he failed to reclaim anything more. Elsewhere, sets of numerals were repeated, but it was not yet clear what they meant. It was on the afternoon of the second day that he thumped the table with his fist and uttered a loud cry.

"Eureka! I believe we have it!"

Even now he could not decode the alphabet or syllables represented by the double digits of Dr. Gross's cipher. Yet on the previous day he had identified five separate double digits as the Mycenean system of counting. That was all he needed. In the scanning of the present document he had decoded sequences of such numbers, though the letters of the alphabet and all its words still eluded him. The numbers he had decoded began with the sequence, 685, 3335, 5660, 120 . . . Even though the adjacent words remained a mystery, these numbers struck a chord in the formidable memory of Sherlock Holmes. He had encountered them before, in one of the Admiralty plans.

He unlocked a drawer in the table and took out a thick folder containing a sheaf of papers entrusted to him by Sir John Fisher. These were copies of Admiralty documents. Holmes had requested them as being the most likely to attract our antagonists. Already, he had spent more than a day and a night working on these copies. Now a needle glimmered somewhere in the haystack.

We worked together. Holmes read out sequences of figures from the naval documents and I checked them silently from a list of numbers he had drawn up as he had worked on the German signals over the past few days. After more than two hours, none of the numerical sequences in the signals had matched any in the Admiralty papers. I lost count of our failures as we came to yet another paper. Still the double digits that stood for an alphabet in the German code meant nothing. Only the ancient system of counting, which Holmes had deciphered after several days' study, might help us.

He read out a sequence of almost fifty numbers from the present document. As I checked them against the list he had made from the code, I held my breath. We read again to check for errors, and, I confess, my hand holding the paper trembled. There was no mistake. Call it luck, but from first to last, every number in the coded signal matched its equivalent number in the Admiralty document. It was soon evident that this entire coded paper must be an exact copy. Having got the numbers, we could now read the adjacent code for the objects to which they referred. The weariness left the voice of Sherlock Holmes as he grasped the key that would unlock Dr. Gross's enigma.

"Six hundred and eighty-five! Three thousand, three hundred and thirty-five! Five thousand, six hundred and sixty! One hundred and twenty! . . ."

I knew, not for the first time, that my friend had done the impossible. This was Sherlock Holmes at his best and most invincible, doing something that no other man on earth could have done. He stood with his back to the fireplace as he read out the list. When we came to the end, he sat down again and spoke as if he feared it was too good to be true.

"Those numerals, Watson! Identical and in the same sequence throughout the cipher and the document! It is thousands to one against mere coincidence."

"But what is the Admiralty document you have been reading figures from?"

"The design calculations for the latest and most powerful battle cruiser of all, HMS *Renown*. By the pricking of my thumbs, I knew they would be after information such as this!"

He sat at the table for a moment and then turned to me again.

"Look at this dockyard manifest. It is a list of weights when the battle cruiser is fully loaded. All the tonnages in the right-hand column correspond to the numerals in Henschel's signal. An entire sequence of fifty! It must be the same document. Very well. If that column of figures is correct, then each of Henschel's double-digit code words on the left-hand side must describe the item whose weight appears on the right. See here. We have our decoded numerals for weight on the right. They stand opposite two unknown words in Henschel's code, the first being 46-24-47. The word in the Admiralty list at this point is 'General' in 'General Equipment.' Therefore 46-24-47 in Henschel's code surely stands for 'General,' in whichever language. You see?"

I began to see but he was not to be stopped.

"And here again. Against the entry for '3335 tons,' the word in the Admiralty document is 'Armament.' Henschel encodes this as 25-80-13-24-59. We know that the Ashmolean Museum can put sounds to Linear B syllables. In English, these five double digits must sound something like 'Ar-ma-me-n-t.' Thus five of the eighty-seven syllables of the alphabet are revealed! The syllables before '5660 tons' must match 'Machinery.' Before '120 tons' the numerical syllables, if one may call them that, must encode 'Engineer's Stores.'"

By evening, ignoring the tray that Mrs. Hudson brought, Holmes had broken what secret Admiralty files still refer to as the Linear B code. Dr. Gross had not translated his ciphers into German but simply encoded whatever he received. No doubt an elderly scholar of ancient languages may quail before engineering terminology. Holmes had deciphered every numerical sign for weights, the load calculations for HMS *Renown*. Matching the words of each item to its known tonnage, he pieced together the German code of Dr. Gross's ancient Mycenaean "alphabet." He found that 80-41-24-53 must stand for "MACHINERY," so that 24 stood for "NE." He confirmed it in the next line where 18-46-24-27 must be "ENGINEER," for 24 was "NE" in both cases. It was the same throughout the document and, indeed, in all the other coded signals. Our enemies had never varied the basic Linear B code, so sure were they that it could never be overcome.

By next morning Holmes had equivalents for seventy of the eighty-seven letters of the word code, as well as all the numerals. Whether the learned Dr. Gross exactly copied the symbols of King Minos five thousand years ago—or varied them to suit his masters' purpose—Sherlock Holmes had him by the tail as surely as Theseus ever had the Minotaur.

As if to confirm this, the next transcript to reach us from the Admiralty contained a page opening with the familiar sequence of double digits 57-09-83-62-15 || 19-80-05. I checked the pencilled note I had made at the time and found that it was identical to the opening of the cipher written on the paper that Dr. Gross had left in the stool rack of the Ashmolean Museum. This time the message had nothing to do with armaments but, rather, with the time required to gather Class A Naval reservists at Chatham and other ports of the Thames estuary, in the event of general mobilization and impending war.

7

NOT MANY MONTHS AFTER THIS, on a hot summer day in the far-off dusty Balkan town of Sarajevo, two bullets from the gun of a Bosnian student shot dead the Archduke Franz Ferdinand of Austria and his duchess. It was well said that the bullet that killed the heir to the throne of Austria-Hungary was a shot that echoed round the world. At the time, I confess, I could not have believed that this

Balkan outrage, shocking though it was, would precipitate a war unparalleled in human history. Yet there was no longer any doubt that the blindfold war that Holmes and I waged against unseen adversaries was in earnest. Our Baker Street rooms resembled more and more a battlefield. Several times that summer, during the remaining weeks of peace, Sherlock Holmes was absent for the entire day on a visit to the Admiralty. His business was with a mysterious group of people known only as Room 40.

In the wake of our Linear B discoveries came Superintendent Alfred Swain of the Special Branch. That branch was created at the time of the Fenian explosions in the 1880s and had originally been known as the Special Irish Branch. Before long it concerned itself with every kind of threat to the security of the nation. One afternoon, when Baker Street was a trench of white summer fog and the street lamps popped and sputtered at noon, was the first time that this Special Branch officer was our guest. The clatter of a barrel organ serenaded us from the opposite pavement with "Take me on the Flip-Flap, oh, dear, do," as coins rattled into the grinder's cap

The Special Branch may consist of hard, resolute men well able to take care of themselves, yet Superintendent Swain was a tall, thin figure, neatly but plainly suited. He spoke quietly and, as he sat down, he turned an intelligent equine profile and gentle eyes toward us. Inspector Lestrade had warned us scornfully what to expect from a man who read Lord Tennyson's *Idylls of the King* or Mr. Browning's translation of the *Agamemnon*—or even Tait's *Recent Advances in Physical Science* and Lyell's *On Geology*. There had been a movement among his colleagues to get rid of Alfred Swain by posting him to the Special Branch. He was thought by his CID superiors to be "too clever by half." He certainly gave the impression of a man who would rather have come to tea to discuss the novels of Mr. George Meredith—one of Sherlock Holmes's unaccountable enthusiasms. Holmes took to him from the start. As his grey eyes studied my friend intently, Swain picked his words carefully, almost fastidiously.

"Mr. Holmes, it must be said at the outset that you have lately performed a service to your country such as few men have done for many years past. Thanks to you, we now have Dr. Gross and Herr Henschel where we want them."

Holmes looked alarmed.

"Not under arrest, I hope? I have had Sir John Fisher's word on that."

Swain shook his head.

"No, sir. The First Sea Lord has kept his word. Indeed, you have given us an invaluable advantage in this. We are now reading their coded signals. But before we can take the matter further, we must identify the third member of their conspiracy, presumably at the Admiralty. When that is accomplished, we shall endeavor to turn their stratagem against them, rather than throw them into prison. Thanks to you, we have the means in our hands to save the lives of hundreds of our soldiers or sailors in the event of war, even to save our country from defeat."

"I am relieved to hear it," Holmes said, indifferent to such flattery. "And what have you done to identify the traitor in the Admiralty?"

"Both Dr. Gross and Henschel are closely watched. From their method of procedure, it seems that Henschel probably knows nothing of the spy's identity. It is possible that neither of them does. Henschel appears to be a mere technician who transmits whatever is given him. Each man works, as it were, in a watertight compartment. None of them, if he were caught, could betray any part of the conspiracy but his own."

"But you have connected their movements together?"

Swain sat back in his chair and folded his hands across his waistcoat.

"We have had Dr. Gross under observation. He uses no telephone. He has sent two wires, both of which we have read. They were directed to the librarian at the British Museum, requesting certain books to be brought up from the stacks for Dr. Gross's visit. He also receives a small amount of post, three communications in the past five weeks."

"You have opened those envelopes, Mr. Swain?"

"We are aware of their contents, sir," said Swain evasively. "Apart from Henschel and Dr. Gross, there is the man whom I will call the naval spy. There appear to be twenty-four people at the Admiralty, from senior officers to junior clerks, who might have taken the design calculations of HMS *Renown* from the building in order to copy them. We have had them all under observation for some weeks and they have made no evident contact with either Dr. Gross or Mr. Henschel. Yet during that time, in the present international tension, the coded German signals have been transmitted almost nightly. We do not believe that Henschel can be transmitting from his rooms. Yet the signals are going out from somewhere near Sheerness, no doubt to a German naval vessel or trawler in the North Sea."

At this point Swain took a notebook from his pocket and began to read a list of the information transmitted in the past few weeks.

"Particulars of Armament: *Indefatigable* Class. Particulars of Anti-Torpedo Boat Guns, 4-inch and 6-inch. HMS *Princess Royal*: replacement of nickel steel, armour diagram. Comparison of Boiler Weights and Performance in HMS *Inflexible*, boiler by Yarrows, Ltd., and HMS *Indomitable*, boiler by Babcock & Wilson. I understand, gentlemen, that Yarrow boilers are lighter and would allow *Indomitable*'s six-inch armor to be increased to seven inches without affecting her speed."

Alfred Swain paused, then added.

"That is a sample of the technical information passing to our adversaries. More recently there have also been manoeuvre reports, gunnery ranges, torpedo matters, fire control, and signals. Last week, for the first time, there were answers to questions that Henschel must have received. Which parts of the fleet have been in the Firth of Forth since the beginning of May—the First and Eighth Destroyer Flotillas or any ships else? Have there been mobilizing tests of flotillas or coastal defences? What numbers of the Royal Fleet Reserve Class A reservists are called in for the yearly exercise?" Swain paused and looked at us. "All these are details vital to the other side in any immediate preparations for war."

Holmes crossed to the window, drew aside the net curtain, and looked down into the thin summer fog. It was possible to see across the street, and no doubt, though the barrel organ was still rattling out its tunes, he satisfied himself that the movements of our visitor were not under observation by our enemies.

"Tell me about Dr. Gross, Mr. Swain."

Swain looked a little uncomfortable.

"There is little to tell, sir. He was an archaeologist as a younger man, with Schliemann at the discovery of Troy, and then deputy keeper of antiquities at the Royal Museum in Berlin. He has lived quietly as a retired gentleman in Beaumont Street for the past two years. He goes out either to the Ashmolean or to work in one of the libraries. He takes lunch at the Oxford Union Society, of which he is a member. That seems to be his only social contact. He retires early to his rooms until the next day. In the past five weeks he has visited London each Monday and stayed for one night at the Charing Cross Hotel. He leaves each morning after breakfast and walks up the Charing Cross Road to the British Museum."

"Who watches him?"

"He works all day in the North Library, Mr. Holmes, where I have kept him company—at a distance. He speaks only to the assistants and leaves at five thirty. He dines early at an Italian café in Holborn, then walks back to the hotel by eight P.M. One of my colleagues is already dining at the café when he arrives. Dr. Gross speaks only to the waiter and returns direct to the hotel. Whoever the spy in the Admiralty may be, it seems he does not write to Dr. Gross, or speak to him, or communicate by telegram or telephone. We have watched the old man every minute, so far as we can. There appears to be no dead letter box except the hollow frame of the rack of camp stools in the Ashmolean Museum. Dr. Gross uses that only to leave the encoded messages for Henschel. It is possible that Henschel does not know the code and, though a member of the conspiracy, does not know precisely what the signals contain when he transmits them."

Holmes sighed deeply.

"I ask myself, if I were Dr. Gross, how would I manage it? Easily enough, I believe. There are so many ways! I daresay I would receive a letter at the Oxford Union Society. I understand it is run like a gentlemen's club, where there is a very large green baize board next to the porter's desk, criss-crossed with wire. Any letter through the post or a message by hand may be inserted there and left until the member collects it. The place is reserved to members only and you might keep observation outside for a month of Sundays without knowing what goes on inside."

Swain looked a little embarrassed.

"One of our plain-clothes officers has walked through that corridor and scanned the letter board every morning. There is never a letter for Dr. Gross."

"He may use another name and collect the letter even so."

"Mr. Holmes," said Swain quietly, "there are dozens, scores, of letters sent there every day. We cannot open them all, under every name, without giving the game away. In any case, he might as easily receive a letter at the Charing Cross Hotel, under any name."

Holmes seemed to change tack.

"Precisely. Then it must be a matter of observation—the most tedious of occupations. Yet it seems evident that Dr. Gross receives his information in London. Communication evidently does not take place between the time he leaves the hotel and the time he returns, unless something is slipped between the pages of a book on a British Museum shelf and he obtains it from there."

"I think not," said Swain quietly.

There the matter rested until three days later. At breakfast, Holmes said cheerfully, "I trust you have no engagements this evening, Watson?"

"As it happens, I have not. Why?"

"Because it is Monday and Dr. Gross, being a creature of habit, will spend the night at the Charing Cross Hotel."

"He may not."

"He will. I took the precaution of calling there yesterday and asking if a message might be left for him. It might, though I did not leave one. What shall we say? Eight o'clock precisely."

"How long for?"

"My dear fellow, if I knew that, I should hardly need to go at all! All night if necessary, though I think that unlikely. It seems that the contacts Dr. Gross makes in London must take place during those hours at the hotel. I have also considered Swain's suggestion that something is slipped into a volume at the British Museum. The reader inserts a message between the pages, hands the book in, the book goes back to the underground stocks. It is then ordered by another reader who retrieves the paper. I confess, I think that an unlikely method. There is the risk that it might be ordered by a third reader between those two or that the message between the pages might be noticed or even lost. Moreover, any investigation would instantly identify two members of the conspiracy rather than one. The Charing Cross Hotel seems altogether more probable."

So it was that our cab carried us to the great lamplit space of Trafalgar Square and then into the Strand to the Charing Cross Hotel, next to the continental railway terminus. We made our way along soft carpets, down an avenue of gilt-columned mirrors and pillars of raspberry-coloured marble, to the First Class Lounge. The deep blue velvet arm chairs with a polished table next to each were reserved for those first-class passengers of the Southern Railway who awaited trains, at all hours of the day or night, to take them to the Channel ferries and on to Calais, Ostend, Paris, Berlin, or Milan.

Holmes selected a chair by the wall and pressed a small electric bell. A moment later it was answered by a "buttons," a youth in a page-boy's tunic and trousers with a matching forage cap in chocolate brown. The brass buttons of the tunic had been polished until they almost dazzled the sight. At a second glance, I recognised his face as one of those young rascals who formed what Holmes called his Baker Street Irregulars and who had been our eyes and ears on so many occasions. In this case, the lad had grown out of childhood by a year or two but remained on what Holmes called his "little list" of informants.

"Been and gone, sir," he said, even before Holmes could ask the question.

"Already?"

"Yessir. Your gentleman that usually comes back from reading his books at eight o'clock must have missed his dinner tonight. He was back here at seven. Calls from his room at half past and gives me half a crown to fetch his package from the station cloakroom for him. He give me the cloakroom ticket and I come back with a little attaché case. Locked. Couldn't say what was in it. Give me the other half a crown when I got back. A good night's pickings, Mr. Holmes."

"A little attaché case," Holmes repeated thoughtfully. "Well done, Billy. Well done, indeed." His hand went into his pocket and a gold half-sovereign glinted as he discharged it into the waiting palm. "That will double what the other gentleman gave you. Now you may bring us two glasses of single malt and a jug of hot water."

"Not soda, Mr. Holmes?"

"I am not accustomed to ruin a single malt with seltzer, Billy. Now, cut along." As soon as the lad was out of earshot, he turned to me.

"Watson, we have them! Or we will have them by next Monday. Monday is the clue. A man who abstracts confidential papers on Friday evening knows that they will not be called for until Monday morning. He has the entire weekend to copy them. The maximum time and the minimum risk. On Monday morning he leaves the attaché case in the station cloakroom; inside it are the copies he has made. No doubt he then enters this hotel, seals the cloakroom ticket in an envelope, and leaves it as a message to be collected by Dr. Gross, on his arrival from Oxford later that day."

"By Jove," I said, half admiring these scoundrels, "and all that Dr. Gross must do on Monday evening is to give the boy the cloakroom ticket. The case is fetched for him."

"Just so. On Tuesday morning Dr. Gross gives the boy the empty case to deposit at the station cloakroom, and the boy brings back a new cloakroom ticket. Dr. Gross then puts the ticket in an envelope and posts it in the hotel letter box, so that it reaches his man by Wednesday, in time for the attaché case to be taken by this friend to his Admiralty office on Friday. Or he may summon a page to his rooms and send the lad to post it outside. The Special Branch would see nothing out of the ordinary. And so the game goes round."

"Indeed," I said, improving on this. "And when he sends the attaché case back to the cloakroom, it may not be empty. Gross would surely leave instructions in it, as to the documents to be copied that weekend. The Admiralty spy collects them on Wednesday evening at the latest, in ample time for this."

"Admirable, Watson! No doubt you were about to add that our Admiralty spy may also find in the case an envelope of banknotes, the wages of treachery."

Billy returned with two glasses and the jug of hot water. Once he had gone, Holmes resumed.

"Dr. Gross returns to Oxford on Tuesday and encodes the information, in time for Henschel's visit to the Ashmolean on Saturday. And so the circle is closed. I should wager that none of the three men has ever seen either of the other two."

Sherlock Holmes was proved correct in almost every particular. By the following Tuesday the Admiralty spy was revealed as a young man by the name of Preston, a naval draftsman. Those who knew him called him diligent, solitary, a man of impeccable moral character and strict conscience but with few friends. He lived in a modest house in a South London street where he nursed an invalid sister.

Only a search in the Criminal Record Office files revealed that Preston's brother-in-law, an attorney's clerk married to this invalid sister, had sought her cure by plunging heavily into the stock market with money borrowed from the firm's client account. As usual, he had hoped to replace the "loan" and take the profits it had made for him. As is often the case, his desperate investments had failed him. When he went to gaol, his wife who was Preston's sister had taken poison. However, she misjudged the dose. The poison did not kill her but left the invalid now crippled and imbecile. Preston had cared for her thereafter. Whether her tragedy bred in him some hatred of his nation or of mankind in general, both of whom had turned their backs upon her and driven the husband and the brother to their respective crimes, who can say?

8

UNDER THE AUTHORITY of Superintendent Swain and the Special Branch, the railway police at Charing Cross were enlisted. With their assistance and the authority of the Home Secretary, the attaché case was removed from the cloakroom once it had been deposited on the following Tuesday morning. It contained the instructions, as Holmes had guessed, and the banknotes, as I had suggested. They were £5 notes and the banks have a habit of listing the names to whom they are issued. One had been in a German Embassy draft, while the other had circulated in Germany itself. Within an hour the case was returned to await collection.

Now the blindfold war took a new form. Every Tuesday the attaché case was opened and the list of information required by Dr. Gross or his masters was copied. For the next two days, however, in Room 40 of the Admiralty Building, two draftsmen drew up bogus inventories and plans, details of manoeuvres and gunnery, signals and mobilisation. It was these that Preston was allowed to purloin and that sowed error in the finely worked espionage of our adversaries. Ranges were understated, locations of shore batteries revised, movements and manoeuvres misreported. The armor belt diagrams of our warships were sometimes thickened or extended, sometimes diminished in extent. The High Seas Fleet of Admiral von Tirpitz, which had previously been trained to destroy a precise target, would now shoot at random—or, worse still, in error.

Sherlock Holmes was a frequent visitor to the famous Room 40 of the Admiralty cryptographers during the war that was to come. Yet his greatest service to the nation's cause was performed before a shot had been fired. Thanks to my friend's machinations, as the last glorious summer of peace darkened across the continent, Dr. Gross was no longer to be seen at the Charing Cross Hotel. The Great Northern Hotel was his lodging and the railway termini at Kings Cross and Liverpool Street became his promenade. As for his confederates, the Special Branch acted on advice it did not entirely understand and paid out still more rope for the spies to hang themselves.

At the Admiralty, a secret signal was decided upon. It was to be broadcast to all ships of the Royal Navy as soon as a state of war with the German Empire and its allies was declared. That signal was to be "England Expects." Upon receiving it, ships' captains would open their secret orders, discover their meaning, and act accordingly in the war of which they were now informed. Yet this signal was not so great a secret that Preston could not get his hands on it. During the last weeks of peace it was encoded by Dr. Gross, transmitted by Karl Henschel, and filed by the Senior Intelligence Officer of the German Ministry of Marine in the Wilhelmstrasse.

The coded signals from Henschel, received by a destroyer of the High Seas Fleet riding an oily swell somewhere off the Thames estuary, continued to carry information on Royal Navy gunnery and ship design. Increasingly these reports were supplemented by reports direct from Dr. Gross. From personal observation the elderly scholar was gathering details of mobilisation and troop movements as the prospect of war drew nearer. Trains from Liverpool Street were carrying Royal Marines to Harwich and Hull, hardly convenient for a campaign in France but essential for an attack upon the North Sea coastline of Germany. Fort Codrington, near Felixstowe and the eastern coast, had become their transit camp. The Fifth and Seventh Destroyer Flotillas were seen off the Wash, moored as if to escort troop transports.

Three weeks before the day on which that most dreadful of all wars began, Dr. Gross was able to inform his masters that the British Admiralty had placed an immediate order with the Stationery Office for 1,200 copies of charts and land maps covering the Danish west coast of Jutland from the Skagerrak at the northern tip to the Frisian Islands and the German frontier in the south. It seemed that Sir John Fisher was to get his wish to "Copenhagen" the enemy and seize the Kiel Canal, perhaps without declaration of war.

Though the landing would be on their territory, there was little doubt which side the Danes would support. They had lost their provinces of Schleswig and Holstein to Germany in the war of 1863 and smarted to recover them. If the Royal Navy put 15,000 Marines ashore on friendly Jutland, these troops would be scarcely a hundred miles from the Kiel Canal, and thus poised to sever Germany's link between her Baltic and North Sea coasts. Such a spearhead would become a dagger pointed at the heart of Prussia and even at Berlin itself. Indeed, it would be a dagger at Germany's back as she faced France and Britain on her Western Front.

On the last night of peace in August 1914, as the minutes passed and Berlin ignored each ultimatum from London and Paris to withdraw its invading army from Belgium or else face war, Holmes and I were at Scotland Yard. Neither Preston nor Dr. Gross had been arrested, though both were closely watched. Karl Henschel sat before us, for he alone had been detained and his confederates knew nothing. In the green-walled office above the Thames, with its wooden cupboards, bare table, and hat rack, Alfred Swain interviewed the young man while Holmes and I sat to one side. Henschel seemed indifferent to his fate.

"I did nothing unlawful," he said repeatedly. "I was given signals to send and I sent them. Why should I not? I could not tell what was in them. I did not know and it was never explained to me."

"Listen to me carefully," said Superintendent Swain, leaning forward across the table towards the young man like a true adviser. "By your own choice, you became a British subject. Now, it appears, it would have been far better for you to have remained a German. As an alien, you could not commit treason against the King of England."

"It was not treason! To send messages!"

"Please believe me, if war comes, you will be tried for treason as a British citizen. That you will be found guilty is a certainty upon such evidence. Three weeks later you will be taken from your cell at eight o'clock in the morning, a rope will be put round your neck, and you will hang by it until you are dead. No one will notice your death among so many, and no one will care, least of all your paymasters in Berlin. To them you are no more than their post boy."

"No one has ever been hanged in England for such a thing as I have done!"

"Quite right," said Swain encouragingly. "If you were sentenced this minute, it would be for a breach of the Official Secrets Act. You would probably go to prison for four or five years. I daresay you would be released after three."

"Well, then?"

"Once war begins, what you have done will not be regarded as a breach of Official Secrets but as treachery under the Defence of the Realm Act. For that you will be hanged. The ultimatum is running out for you, Mr. Henshaw, as surely as for your masters in Berlin."

"My true name is Henschel, not Henshaw!"

"Alas," said Swain, shaking his head, "no. You may wish it was so but it cannot be. You changed it of your own free will, as you became an Englishman of your own free will. And so you will be hanged as Charles Henshaw, the English traitor. If you nourished dreams of being a hero, you may safely forget them. You will have no memorial in your own land. If you are truly fortunate, you will be shot rather than hanged, tied into a kitchen chair on the rifle range of the Tower of London. And that, Mr. Henshaw, is all that you have to look forward to in this world."

I do not know why but this, of all things, broke his nerve. He trembled and he could not speak. He was, after all, a petty figure in the conspiracy—an impoverished teacher of languages, who now found himself terrifyingly out of his depth. Sherlock Holmes intervened, for all the world as if he were "prisoner's friend," as they call it at courts-martial.

"It will be too late once war has been declared, Herr Henschel. It is neck or nothing for you—here and now. You had best decide at once between prison and the hangman. Indeed, you may yet decide between prison and freedom, but you had best be quick about it."

Henschel could not reply until he had taken a drink from his glass of water.

"How can I choose? What is done is done."

Holmes shrugged.

"By continuing to do what you have done for several years. Transmit the signals that are given you to transmit. They will mean nothing to you, as you say, but they may save both your life and your liberty. The choice is yours. Life or death. Captivity or freedom."

The choice, of course, was nothing less than betrayal of his paymasters, and I do not know who had given Holmes the authority to suggest it—possibly Alfred Swain himself. Henschel had a certain value. I am no expert, but I have heard that those who are experienced listeners can identify the very finger of the operator on the Morse code button! How long such a deception might be kept up, I could not tell. Yet every transmission that put the Germans in error was worth its weight in gold. At that moment the great bell of Big Ben, on its parliamentary tower, began to strike eight in the evening. The tolling was close to us and the reverberations long, loud enough to interrupt conversation. It came like a funeral knell for Karl Henschel. If he was not broken already, this broke him. He looked down at his hands in his lap and said:

"Tell me what to do."

There was a sudden relief in the room and we breathed more easily, for it is a terrible thing to send a young man to his death in such a way. Holmes crossed to the window and opened it a little for air in the warm August evening.

"You may demonstrate your expertise for us," he said coolly. Though it sounded casual enough, this was what he had been working for.

That night, even before the ultimatum to Germany expired, Henschel tapped out a brief message, repeated several times. I swear that he thought it a mere demonstration and had no idea that it was transmitted through the darkness to his friends in Berlin. Though it was encoded, I read the cipher and saw "ENGLAND EXPECTS."

Six weeks earlier, among the falsehoods passed off on Preston and Dr. Gross, this had been the masterstroke of Sherlock Holmes. Admiral von Tirpitz's intelligence officers had been informed by their spies, who knew no better, that "England Expects" was the signal for launching Sir John Fisher's "Copenhagen," the attack on Kiel by way of an invasion of Jutland with 15,000 Royal Marines. Now, on the third floor of Scotland Yard, above the Thames and the street lights of the Embankment, Karl Henschel tapped out that message. Far worse for Grand Admiral Tirpitz and the Kaiser's High Seas Fleet, the same message was echoed openly in a few hours time when war was declared and it was broadcast to the entire Royal Navy. Ships' captains opened their sealed orders and read its true meaning—merely that war had begun. Yet to those who listened in Berlin, it seemed that the air was alive with immediate orders to launch or support "Copenhagen" and the seizure of the Kiel Canal.

In the circumstances, what followed is scarcely surprising. It is a matter of history that not a single Royal Marine landed on Danish soil. Most of the "Marines" reported by Dr. Gross at Liverpool Street station were mere barrack-duty veterans dressed for the part on their train journey to the East Coast ports, to give the impression of an army on the move. The destroyers seen on the horizon were ships that passed in the night. It is also a matter of history that Helmuth von Moltke kept back from the Western Front 20,000 of his best troops in Schleswig-Holstein to protect Germany's Danish flank from this mythical attack. A month later, for want of those 20,000 troops at the Battle of the Marne, the great German advance on the Western

Front was halted and beaten into retreat only twenty miles from Paris.

"Charles Henshaw" tapped out the signals given him for the rest of that great war. For how long those who listened believed him it is impossible to say. Dr. Gross was briefly interned and then allowed to live at liberty in Oxford. Outrageous though this might seem, Sherlock Holmes insisted that it was the best policy. Preston, the spy in the Admiralty, was suddenly alone and without understanding why. He knew only that the instructions and the money that had awaited him every week at Charing Cross cloakroom ceased to appear from the moment of the war's beginning. He might have inquired of Dr. Gross or Karl Henschel, but, thanks to the ingenuity of the German espionage system, he did not even know their names, let alone where they might be found. Frightened and bewildered, he went on with his work as a naval draftsman, watched by those he never saw. His disloyalty in peacetime would lie within reach of the gallows if he continued it in wartime. The temptation to be a spy had gone for ever. Once again, Holmes insisted there must be no arrests, no headlines to tell our enemies that their agents had been unmasked. Only by this means could Karl Henschel be used as the means of undermining German intelligence with his false reports.

What the full consequences were, who can say? It is certain that the diversion of 20,000 troops from the Battle of the Marne saved Paris and France, if not England. The battle cruisers of the Royal Navy suffered considerably at the Battle of Jutland in 1916. How much greater their losses would have been had the secret documents concocted by Sherlock Holmes and Jackie Fisher not found their way into the hands of Tirpitz and his staff is a matter of conjecture. Certain it is that my friend was absent for an entire afternoon at Windsor soon after the outbreak of war. He returned and would say little. After a little while he took from his pocket a fine silver cigarette case. Presently he handed it to me.

"In all the circumstances, old fellow, I should like this to be yours."

The sterling silver was engraved with a crown and a single royal name followed by "R" and "I" for "Rex" and "Imperator." In addition, as if this were intended for a recipient of exceptional merit, the case was further engraved on the back with the words "ENGLAND EXPECTS."

3

THE CASE OF THE PEASENHALL MURDER

1

Sherlock Holmes was not a man much given to holidays or to any form of travel for its own sake. I once made the mistake of assuring him that the Taj Mahal and the treasures of the Nana Sahib would merit a journey. He answered me in the words of Samuel Johnson to James Boswell, who had promised his friend that the Giant's Causeway was worth seeing.

"Worth seeing," said Holmes with a sigh, "but, alas, not worth going to see. Life is too short to allow of making mere excursions."

Apart from his professional visits, he was generally content to remain in London and, indeed, in Baker Street. The only exception he allowed was in his pursuit of archaeology and antiquity. The isles of Greece and the great sites of Troy or Mycenae were too far distant, but the Dark Ages of his own land held a fascination for him. During one of these expeditions, it was my own calling as a medical man that involved us in the strange mystery of the Peasenhall Murder.

Holmes had conceived a taste for the history of East Anglia with its flat landscapes running to the sea and its wide horizons above fields and waterways. Here the noble Saxons of Mercia had fought unavailingly against the Danish invaders twelve centuries before. It was, he said, unspoilt rural England at its best. Our visit was arranged for the first half of June. We were to make our headquarters for ten days at the Bell Hotel in Saxmundham, a grey brick structure adjoining the Town Hall. The Bell was a well-appointed hostelry, built just before the coming of steam, in the last days of horse-drawn mail coaches.

The train from Ipswich deposited us at a little station where one feels the fresh breeze from the North Sea hardly more than five miles distant. No sooner had we finished lunch than Holmes must be up and doing, as the saying goes, carrying out his inspection of the ancient parish church that stood close by. In his impatience, he was for all the world like a major-general reviewing a summer camp.

It was a bright afternoon when my friend introduced me to the ancient tower of Norman stones and flint. It rose beyond the great trees that lined a steep path from the town. Within the nave, there was a fine old hammerbeam roof and a charming mediaeval font carved with emblems of the Evangelists and supported by two dwarves carrying clubs. I noticed, however, that my friend stood longest by a grave in the churchyard that was marked with a skull and crossbones. Its inscription was carved in memory of Joel Eade, "whose soul took flight in 1720." The macabre suggestion that the poor fellow had been carried off by devils was precisely of the kind to attract Sherlock Holmes.

The rest of the day was uneventful, though the sight of the sky gave me some uneasiness. There had been rain the night before, and the dark clouds across the fields promised worse to come. As we sat down to our dinner in the comfortable hotel, the gathering winds outside assured us that a true storm was blowing up. It was an apt prelude to the horrors of the following day.

Until four o'clock next morning, the rain fell as if it never meant to stop, the wind driving against the windows of our rooms. By breakfast time, the gale had blown itself out and the rain had dwindled to a fitful drizzle. We had just risen from the table when our landlady bustled across the room; she was followed by a stranger in police uniform. It was the constable who spoke.

"Dr. Watson, sir? Police Constable Eli Nunn. May I speak with you, Doctor?"

There followed a most vexing conversation. A medical man, like any other, wishes to take his holiday leisure without interruption. However, a young woman had been found dead that morning in the nearby village of Peasenhall. She had been six months pregnant, with no father to her child, and it was believed that she might have made away with herself. It was imperative that a doctor should attend before the police could move the body to a mortuary. Dr. Lay, the regular medical practitioner, was out on an urgent call, but some convenient busybody had noticed the name of another doctor in the list of guests at the Bell Hotel, Saxmundham! If I would be so good as to attend for a few minutes, it would then be possible for the police to proceed in their business.

It promised to be a most tiresome errand, but, in the circumstances, I could scarcely refuse. Nor, I believe, would Sherlock Holmes have permitted it! A pony and trap waited outside. Constable Nunn whipped up the horse and we bowled along the little Suffolk roads in a thin sunlight, which now followed the storm. Had I known what awaited me, I believe nothing would have induced me to climb into that trap.

The distance was greater than I had expected. We went through the charming village of Sibton with its ruined abbey and cottages in pink and cream, before coming to the more remote and workaday settlement of Peasenhall. I could not help wondering whether Eli Nunn's choice had fallen on me because someone at the hotel had let slip that I was in the company of the famous Sherlock Holmes.

Presently, Constable Nunn reined in the horse outside Providence House, a well-built residence in the main street of Peasenhall, a village that seemed little more than a single long street. We were escorted to the back and entered by a rear conservatory, which in turn led into a small kitchen, about ten feet by eight. A narrow flight of stairs led upward from one corner, so that the servants might reach their attics without appearing on the main staircase. Someone had draped linen over the only window, which cast a further gloom on the scene.

The moment I stepped into the kitchen from the conservatory, I smelt a strong odour of paraffin and a nauseous taint of burnt flesh. Then I looked down and saw the body of a girl lying across the floor on her back. She was wearing her stockings and a nightdress that had been partly charred, as had one side of the body itself. The cause of her death was never in doubt, for there was a wound extending from under the angle of the right jaw across to the left jaw, completely severing the windpipe. Another wound below the angle of the right jaw ran upward underneath the chin. Either of these injuries would have been fatal, but there was also a puncture wound near the breastbone. I also noticed that the door of the little staircase had been thrown back with such violence, presumably in a struggle of some kind, that it had broken a bracket of the narrow wall shelf.

How anyone but a throughgoing village idiot could imagine that this was a case of suicide defied explanation. If the poor girl had inflicted either of the throat wounds upon herself, she would certainly not have lived long enough to carry out the second. Indeed, the blood that had spurted from the wounds had splashed the little stairway to the second step. It needed no examination to tell me that she was dead, but I satisfied myself that she was almost cold and that rigor mortis was well-nigh complete.

"She has been dead for at least four hours," I said, turning to Constable Nunn, "and possibly for much longer, since a body will cool more slowly in summer temperatures."

The worst aspect of all was that the murderer—for this was murder if ever I saw it—had apparently tried without success to set fire to the place. In the event, the body and its linen were only charred on one side. A broken paraffin lamp lay on the floor, where it had presumably fallen at the moment of her death or a little before. Perhaps the oil from this had caught fire, but it would probably not have been enough to cause such damage to the body or the clothing as we now looked upon it. Where the rest of the paraffin had come from, I could not say.

My presence at the scene made very little difference. A few minutes after our arrival, Dr. Charles Lay, the village physician, returned from his visit to Sibton, and I handed the investigation to him with considerable relief. Though one grows accustomed to the horrors of medical life, there was much about the death of this poor young girl in so brutal a manner that shook me more than I would have expected. Sherlock Holmes stood quiet as a statue and said nothing. However, he accompanied me when I stepped out into the back garden to confer with Dr. Lay. He stood apart a little as we held our conversation and then approached me.

"There are two curious pieces of evidence in this matter, Watson. I fear they may yet lead the Suffolk constabulary far from the truth. Did you not observe them?"

"I can't say that I did," I replied rather impatiently, for the whole thing seemed plain enough to me.

"There was a newspaper folded under the young woman's head and it had been charred a little in the abortive fire. It was a copy of the *East Anglian Times* for the day before yesterday. We must assume that the murderer put it there—but why? There were also fragments of a medicine bottle scattered on the floor. One of them included the neck of the bottle with the cork so well jammed into it that it appears immovable. Another fragment of the bottle had a label with writing upon it. Unless I am much mistaken, it read 'Two or three teaspoonfuls, a sixth part to be taken every four hours—For Mrs. Gardiner's children.' The ink had run a little but I believe that was the inscription. I gather the name of the owners of this house is Crisp, not Gardiner,"

"Perhaps it contained paraffin to add to the blaze," I said a little irritably. "Mrs. Gardiner may have something to answer for."

Holmes looked across the little garden towards the rear door of the house.

"Were I to commit a murder and attempt to burn the body," he said thoughtfully, "I do not think I should wedge the cork so tightly in a bottle of paraffin that I could not withdraw it quickly at the critical moment. I would, at the very least, make sure of that."

I was too much affected by what I had just witnessed to pay much attention to my friend's forensic niceties.

During the remaining ten days of our stay at the Bell Hotel the murder of Rose Harsent, as her name proved to be, at twenty-three years old seemed to pursue us. It had seemed natural to me that the little community of Peasenhall should prefer a verdict of suicide by a poor girl who was six months pregnant with no father to her child rather than that one of its own members should stand accused of both the paternity and the murder. The facts made nonsense of this, however. So, at least, the coroner's jury found.

For the next week our good landlady at the Bell Hotel lost no opportunity to bring us the latest gossip. I cannot dignify it by the name of news. What neither Holmes nor I had realised was that what the newspapers now called "The Mystery of the Peasenhall Murder" had been preceded a year earlier by "The Great Peasenhall Scandal." Our hostess described this earlier sensation with more relish than seemed quite decent.

She told us that two Peasenhall youths, George Wright and Alfonso Skinner, belonged to that unsavoury class of Peeping Toms, whose amusement it is to spy on courting couples and the like. This pair of scoundrels let it be known that on the evening of 1 May, they had witnessed grossly indecent and dishonourable conduct between Rose Harsent and William Gardiner, a married man who was father of six children and who had risen to the position of foreman at Messrs. Smyth's Seed Drill Works in the village.

The alleged incident had taken place at a building in Peasenhall that they call the Doctor's Chapel, a Congregational chapel presided over by a local worthy, Mr. Crisp of the ill-fated Providence House. Rose Harsent was a servant at the house and it was part of her duties to clean this nearby chapel. Hence she had need of the chapel key from time to time. William Gardiner and his family lived two hundred yards further down the main street, at Alma Cottage. This industrious foreman was also a leading light of the Primitive Methodist connection at the pretty village of Sibton a couple of miles to the east. Rose Harsent sang in the choir at Sibton.

Once the scandal reached his ears, William Gardiner denounced it as a disgusting falsehood. He confronted his two slanderers, as he called them, who scornfully stood their ground. Gardiner then asked the superintendent minister of his congregation, Mr. Guy, to hold a chapel inquiry into the allegations. This was done, his accusers were heard but disbelieved, and Gardiner was exonerated. The minister and his elders thought the accusation "trumped up," nothing but "a tissue of falsehood," and reinstated Gardiner, who had resigned as a matter of honour from his positions as steward, choirmaster, and Sunday school superintendent when the story first reached him.

He now went to a solicitor and began proceedings for slander. Unfortunately, he then dropped these proceedings. His explanation was that Wright and Skinner had no money, that even if he won he must bear all the costs. He had no funds for this. On reflection, he also thought Rose Harsent would not be "strong enough" to face the ordeal of the witness-box and cross-examination. Innocent or guilty of the scandal, her reputation must be indelibly tarnished.

All the same, it looked bad for William Gardiner when he withdrew the slander action. It seemed halfway to an admission of guilt. His wife Georgina never believed the charge, for she said her husband had been at home with her during the time when he was alleged to have been with Rose Harsent at the Doctor's Chapel. Rose had been the friend of Mrs. Gardiner and continued to be so after the scandal, an ally who came regularly to the house, and a co-religionist at Sibton chapel. Throughout the entire affair, however, Georgina Gardiner's evidence, true or false, was ridiculed by spiteful locals as that of a wife protecting her husband, herself, and their six children.

Naturally, Gardiner became the first suspect in the subsequent death of Rose Harsent. Worse still for him, various "evidence" or tales now emerged from the year when the gossip ran riot before the murder. I recalled that Holmes had seen the name Mrs. Gardiner written on the label of the broken medicine bottle beside the body. Yet Mrs. Gardiner explained that she had given Rose the bottle, which then contained camphorated oil for a throat complaint. No doubt it might later have held paraffin, used by the intruder in the attempt to start a fire.

A Methodist preacher, Henry Rouse, claimed to have seen Gardiner and Rose walking together between Peasenhall and the chapel some weeks after the scandal. He had written a letter to Gardiner, warning him against indiscretion. Unfortunately, for reasons he could not explain, Mr. Rouse sent the letter anonymously and in his wife's handwriting. It was subsequently proved that this old man had been the instigator of slander and author of anonymous warnings in another village, from which he had moved to Peasenhall at short notice.

Gardiner himself had to admit sending two letters to Rose during this time, although when read in public they contained only the most unobjectionable account of the measures he was taking to seek justice for them both. The most damning letter, said to be Gardiner's, was an anonymous lover's assignation note. This came to Rose Harsent by post not many hours before her death. The writer asked her to leave a candle in the window of her attic room at ten P.M. that night. If this signal told him the coast was clear, he would come to her at midnight, by way of that back kitchen, where her body was afterwards found. The great courtroom expert, Thomas Gurrin, held that this note and its envelope were in Gardiner's writing. Two humble bank examiners of suspect signatures swore that the script was not Gardiner's. It seemed to me, as they say, six of one and half a dozen of the other.

Undeniably, it was a case of the most sordid kind. Holmes and I seemed well out of it. All the same, I was not the least surprised that it made headlines in the local papers or that before the end of our visit William Gardiner had been arrested and charged with the young woman's murder. The evidence, such as it was, pointed only at him.

Holmes said little or nothing about it, contenting himself with the antiquities of Suffolk.

On the last Saturday of our visit, however, my friend suggested that we might make a railway excursion to the nearby coast and enjoy a little sea air. Great Yarmouth was the destination chosen for our day by the sea. It was a pleasant enough place, though inclining a little too much toward a resort for trippers, in my view. That need not have mattered, had Sherlock Holmes not noticed a gaudy placard on the promenade for a beach sideshow. It was a fly-by-night affair in a canvas booth, and it promised a tableau of "The Dreadful Peasenhall Murder."

Poor Rose Harsent had not been dead a week, and the man accused of her murder had been arrested only a few days ago. Already some rascal was taking his profit from their misfortune. All the same, Holmes must visit this disgraceful display. It was evident that the proprietor of the waxwork had never heard of laws relating to contempt of court or indeed the presumption of innocence. Neither the setting nor the persons of the display resembled reality, of course. Yet there before us was a make-believe Rose Harsent in the pose of having her throat cut by a make-believe William Gardiner—all in wax. The whole thing was a trap to fleece idlers and muckrakers.

Holmes said not a word as we stared at this outrage. I am pleased to say that the police had already been informed. The exhibition was closed down and the proprietor taken into custody a few hours later. It was only when we had left the booth and walked a few yards by the sea that my friend turned to me and remarked:

"Unless I am very much mistaken, Watson, we shall hear more of this wretched matter. As yet, we know far too little to judge the case. Curious, is it not, how so many ignorant people believe that creating a scandal will draw the veil from some hidden truth? In reality, scandal obscures the truth more effectively than anything else. For the present, however, William Gardiner may thank his lucky stars that the law of Judge Lynch does not yet operate in the fair county of Suffolk."

2

Why Holmes or I should hear more of this hateful business was beyond me. The trial of William Gardiner for the murder of Rose Harsent came on before Mr. Justice Grantham and a jury at Suffolk Assizes in Ipswich, and neither of us received any summons to appear as a witness for either the prosecution or the defence. I had not even been called to give medical testimony at the inquest. Dr. Lay could say all that had to be said about such matters. It was Holmes who brought up the case six months later, after breakfast in Baker Street, on a dank November morning.

"I trust, Watson, you have no pressing engagements for the next few hours. I believe we are about to have a visitor, and I should greatly appreciate your company."

"Oh, has someone made an appointment? I thought the day was free."

"No appointment has been made. Indeed, I and the gentleman in question are complete strangers."

"Then who the devil is he to come here in such a manner?"

"His name is Mr. Ernest Wild and he is the author of a successful operetta, *The Help,* and a widely praised volume of verse, *The Lamp of Destiny.*"

"My dear Holmes, perhaps you would tell me why in thunder this librettist and versifier, unmet by either of us, is to descend upon us unannounced. If he is to descend at all!"

My friend chuckled.

"Because, Watson, Mr. Ernest Wild is also a young barrister of the Inner Temple and defence counsel to William Gardiner of Peasenhall in his trial for the murder of Rose Harsent. The famous Marshall Hall should look to his laurels, for Ernest Wild has already defended thirty murder cases and saved twenty-seven clients from the gallows."

I was impressed by this and said so.

"He did not, of course, obtain acquittals in all twenty-seven cases but, at the very least, murder was reduced to manslaughter and his client lived to fight—possibly to kill—another day. Mr. Ernest Wild is what they call a coming man."

"And why should he visit us?"

"For a reason known to all the world but you, old fellow. I was up unaccustomedly early this morning and have had the advantage of reading the *Morning Post* long before you came down to your breakfast. Two trials of William Gardiner have come and gone. The result is that two juries could not agree upon a verdict and he must be tried again. The worst is that at present eleven jurors would hang him but one held out. Even that man did not think Gardiner innocent. However, he has a conscientious objection to capital punishment and has written to the paper to say so. Had I not a distaste for puns, I should say it is only thanks to that one man that Gardiner's life still hangs by a thread rather than by a rope. Ernest Wild knows very well that the likely outcome of another trial will be the hanging of his client. As a defender, he has done almost everything within his power and it has been too little. Where else should he look for assistance?"

"Yet how can you be sure he will come to us?"

"Wait and listen!" he said softly.

We did so for several minutes and heard nothing. Then, as I was thinking what nonsense the whole thing was, there came the unmistakable jangle of the Baker Street doorbell.

"Voila!" said Holmes with a smile of insufferable smugness.

It seems he had advised Mrs. Hudson of this likely visit. The door of the sitting room opened and with "Mr. Wild to see Mr. Holmes, sir!" she ushered in a dark-haired man in his earlier thirties. His wide-boned face, strong features, the firm line of his mouth, and the penetrating gaze of his pale eyes gave him a look of solemnity and determination. Yet the line of the mouth and the hard gaze of the eyes could turn in an instant into the most charming and boyish smile. At present, there was no occasion for a smile. He shook hands with us both, took his seat almost without waiting for an invitation, and came straight to the point. He nodded at the *Morning Post* which lay on the table, a little the worse for wear after Holmes's attentions.

"Gentlemen, it is good of you to receive me at such short notice. I observe you have read the morning paper. No doubt you have seen the outcome of the murder trial at Ipswich yesterday. William Gardiner has evaded the hangman briefly by virtue of a single juror's whimsy. Unfortunately, he has not escaped for long, if the Crown persists in trial after trial."

"As they will most certainly do," said Holmes, reaching for his pipe with a weary gesture. "They cannot do otherwise, if eleven jurors are already of one mind."

"Just so. All he has gained is three more months in a squalid prison cell. He eats, sleeps, and breathes next to the room where he will be hanged. The gallows remain so close to his bunk that, were it not for the wall, he might reach out and touch them. Mr. Holmes, I speak as a man and not as a lawyer. I believe William Gardiner to be innocent, upon my life I do, while most of Suffolk prefer him to be guilty. He will never be found innocent at Ipswich assize court in the face of such prejudice and insinuation as he now faces."

"Surely," said Holmes, drawing his pipe from his mouth, "surely he is fortunate in his defender."

Our visitor smiled awkwardly and shook his head.

"No, Mr. Holmes. I have taken on more than I should in a case like this. Gardiner needs more than a junior barrister; at the least his case requires a man who has taken silk and is a King's Counsel. That was why I came straight to London last night after the verdict and called upon Sir Charles Gill and Sir Edward Clarke. If either of them would lead for the defence of Gardiner at a retrial, I should be honoured to act as their junior counsel."

"And they will not?" Holmes raised his eyebrows, though scarcely in surprise. "There again, Sir Charles and Sir Edward are two of the busiest men at the bar. I see that Sir Charles is leading counsel in the Marylebone Railway inquiry and Sir Edward Clarke leads for the defence in the Dunwich by-election petition. As for Sir Edward Marshall Hall. . . ."

"Mr. Holmes, the retrial will come on in a few weeks. Such men are fully booked, as they say, for many months and cannot alter their arrangements. They say that they could not give Gardiner's defence the time and attention it deserves, nor could they get up the facts of the case as thoroughly as I have already done. Yet, as you will know, a junior counsel without a leader carries less weight with a jury and far less weight with a judge."

Holmes laid down his pipe and nodded sympathetically.

"Mr. Justice Lawrence had no business to make those interjections of his during your speech to the jury yesterday. However, I do not see how I can be called to the bar and equipped with a knighthood as a King's Counsel before the retrial of Gardiner takes place."

Wild folded and unfolded his hands.

"No, sir. Yet it remains within the power of the solicitor-general to call a halt to the prosecution of William Gardiner. In other words, to enter a writ of *nolle prosequi.*"

I saw Sherlock Holmes tighten his nostrils, one of those small gestures of skepticism.

"I cannot believe that the solicitor-general will abandon a case in which eleven men out of twelve have found the accused guilty of murder—a murder that was little less than butchery. Suppose for a moment that Gardiner was the murderer and is now set free—and murders again?"

Wild shook his head.

"My hope is that Gardiner may be judged in a tribunal quite different to that which he has faced so far. One that may persuade the solicitor-general to stay his hand. The case against this man is based entirely on a mass of circumstantial evidence and scandal. There is not a shred of direct evidence that connects the accused man with the murder of Rose Harsent. Yet circumstantial evidence has been fueled by a previous scandal. That is enough to prejudice any jury and carry the day against him. Even his own good character may destroy him."

Holmes contracted his brows sharply.

"But is not your defence based, in part, on the fact that Gardiner is a man of principle and morality, a man of religion who is assistant steward, Sunday school superintendent, and choirmaster in his Methodist congregation?"

"Precisely," said Wild, bringing his hand down on his knee. "A rogue would be easier to deal with! Among the malicious, his nickname in the village before the scandal was Holy Willie, and I can see why. When Gardiner is in the witness-box, he is almost master of the courtroom as a revivalist preacher might be. That is the problem. He believes he is master and will endure no insinuation. When I questioned him in the witness-box about Wright's story of the alleged misconduct with Rose Harsent at the Doctor's Chapel, Gardiner fairly rounded on me and told the court it was a vicious lie from beginning to end. Very well. I daresay it was. Then I asked him about the evidence of Mr. Rouse, the preacher who said that he had seen Gardiner and Rose Harsent walking quite innocently along the road to Peasenhall together. 'A downright lie!' he said. His neighbour recalled that Gardiner had lit a fire in his washhouse the morning after the murder. 'A deliberate lie!' snaps Gardiner."

He paused and then resumed.

"You see where this leads, Mr. Holmes? He will brook no contradiction. Gardiner will never say that a man or woman may be in error, that his neighbour must have mistaken the day on which the fire was lit in the washhouse, for example. The village folk are all downright or deliberate liars when they contradict his account. Small wonder if he was unpopular. But imagine the effect of all this on a jury."

Taking the pipe from his mouth, Holmes began quietly to play act a courtroom scene of cross-examination. As I listened, I thought, not for the first time, what a ferocious antagonist my friend might have been, had he chosen a career at the criminal bar.

"'I see, Mr. Gardiner,' says the cross-examiner gently. 'So all these other witnesses are liars, are they, including some who have been your friends in the past? Tell me, what reason have all these good people for telling lies about you? You cannot name a single reason—and yet they are all liars! You alone are telling the truth? And you ask my lord and the jurors to believe that?'"

Holmes put down his pipe and then continued in the voice of an imaginary prosecutor.

"'Unlike those whose evidence is against you, the truth that you alone tell has hardly a shred of corroboration? And you ask my lord and the jury to believe that?'"

He paused again, for effect, and then concluded in the same voice.

"'All these people, some of whom, like Mr. Rouse, have supported you in the past, now combine together to tell lies about you for this mysterious reason that you cannot name? And you also ask my lord and the jury to believe that, do you?'"

Mr. Wild winced and Holmes inquired sympathetically, "It goes something along those lines, I suppose, Mr. Wild?"

"It goes like that almost word for word, sir."

"Of course it does," said Holmes with a sigh.

"The facts of the case, sir, are becoming lost in slander and innuendo—and I almost fear that I may become lost with them!"

The facts of the Peasenhall murder! Such as they were, they became our constant companions in weeks to come. Indeed, there were now embellishments of the original story, all of them to William Gardiner's prejudice. Skinner had claimed he went to a hedge near the Doctor's Chapel with Wright and had listened to a couple engaged in an immoral act. He now remembered that the man and woman had jokingly discussed passages from the Book of Genesis, which may have a lewd interpretation in certain minds. He and Wright had already recalled that, as they waited, they saw quite plainly Rose Harsent come out after some time, followed by Gardiner a little while later. It was not only the voices of the guilty couple, but their appearances as well, to which these wretched youths were prepared to swear.

Whatever was believed in court, the "truth" that circulated in the neighbourhood, through the little villages, seemed to be unquestioned. The Peeping Toms were believed. Gardiner had been the girl's lover. She had conceived a child by him, and, in order to conceal his guilt and avoid a paternity summons, he had murdered her in the most brutal fashion. This also carried the comforting hope that if William Gardiner could be made to bear the guilt, the rest of the neighbourhood would breathe freely again.

I have put the facts that Mr. Wild gave us into a nutshell, for it took him a good hour and more to explain the entire case. When he had finished, he sat back in his chair and looked at each of us in turn. Sherlock Holmes got to his feet, crossed to the sideboard, and refilled his pipe from the tobacco jar.

"I sympathize entirely, Mr. Wild. I see the threat of a great injustice here, though I am not convinced of Gardiner's innocence. I do not entirely see, however, what it is that you would like me to do."

The young man looked him straight in the eyes.

"I would ask you to fight a duel, Mr. Holmes."

Despite the solemnity of the case, my friend threw back his head and laughed as he took his seat once more.

"Would you have singlestick or pistols for two?"

Ernest Wild did not smile.

"I do not believe that William Gardiner can receive justice at the assize court where he now stands, though it is heresy for me to say so. His only hope must lie in another arena."

"Of what possible use would that be?" I interposed.

The young lawyer turned to me.

"Dr. Watson, William Gardiner's last hope may lie in the Crown withdrawing the prosecution because they see that the man is innocent. It is in their power to do that, whatever local prejudice may say."

I almost gasped at the audacity of it.

"The Crown has won eleven of the twelve jurors to its side and might have got the other had he not been an eccentric! Why should they withdraw from the case?"

"One moment," said Holmes. "Tell us, if you please, Mr. Wild, a little about this other arena, where it seems I am to fight my duel."

The young advocate let out a long breath, as if he knew that he had won my friend to his side at last.

"Mr. Holmes, it is no secret that you count among your associates—if I may call them that—some of the best men at Scotland Yard."

"They would not have to be so very good to be the best of a bad bunch. No matter. Pray continue, sir."

"Let their best man be chosen. Let the two of you sift the evidence and the witnesses, free from all slander, prejudice, intimidation. Work together if you wish, fight it out if you must. When that is done, your findings shall be presented to the Director of Public Prosecutions or the solicitor-general, or the Home Secretary himself for that matter. If you can carry the day, your reputation is such that I believe a plea of *nolle prosequi* may be entered by the Crown and the agony of William Gardiner brought to an end. No less than that, the agony of his wife and children too."

"And if I do not carry the day," said Holmes nonchalantly, "my reputation and much else shall end in the mud. And I must warn you that if I investigate the evidence, you, Mr. Wild, may not get the answer you are hoping for."

"Whatever fee you may think fit shall be paid. I have undertakings as to the expenses of the case from two newspapers, the *Sun* and the *East Anglian Times*."

It seemed to me that Holmes bridled a little at this.

"A man does not take money for seeing that justice is done. Before I move a single inch in this matter, however, I must take sight of William Gardiner. Even then, I do not suppose that Scotland Yard or the solicitor-general will look favorably on what you propose."

Ernest Wild looked a little awkward.

"Sir Charles Gill and Sir Edward Clarke were unable to accept a brief in the case. However, both men sit in parliament, and they have assured me that in the circumstances they will urge Sir Edward Carson, as solicitor-general, to permit such an investigation, independent of the Suffolk constabulary. These two are men of great influence at the bar and well known to him. Sir Edward Clarke was solicitor-general before him and afterwards led for Oscar Wilde against the Marquess of Queensberry in the notorious trial. Carson led for Queensberry with Sir Charles Gill as his junior. You see? I think Carson will not lightly dismiss advice from two such learned friends. Meantime Gardiner cannot be released, of course. If you must see him first, I will obtain a visitor's warrant and you may travel down to Ipswich Gaol."

"To the ends of the earth, if necessary," Holmes said quietly. His voice was so soft, as he stood gazing at the drizzle of rain and soot falling across the roofs of Baker Street and beyond, that I was not quite sure if there was irony or resolve in his tone. Only when he turned round could I see that his eyes were bright with a strange chivalry of justice.

3

As the train carried us north from Liverpool Street to Ipswich three days later, I asked my friend how he knew that Ernest Wild would come to us so promptly.

"I have deceived you again, Watson," he said, drawing up the strap and closing the carriage window against the draft. "I have followed the events of this case in the papers. I thought it might come to such a point as this. The night before we entertained our visitor, I received a note from Sir Edward Clarke, just before dinner. He informed me he had been unable to accommodate Mr. Wild but that they had discussed such an arrangement as is now proposed. Sir Edward too had misgivings about this case. He asked me to see the young man. I replied at once and suggested an early hour next morning. After the first case at the assizes, I rather thought that the defence would get itself into a scrape. Once again you have trusted me too far in supposing that I can perform miracles."

He gazed out across the damp ploughland north of London, and added without prompting:

"I have disliked this business from the start. Gardiner may be the murderer of Rose Harsent. It seems someone in the village surely is. Yet here is a man who has raised himself by his own efforts, acquiring the arts of reading and writing on the way. He is surrounded by many who have done nothing to improve their minds or skills, some of whom are no doubt envious clodhoppers. Of course, I do not think such jealousies make him innocent of murder. He is a man of resolve and so perhaps he has the resolve for such a crime. To be sure, he is a man of religion. Primitive Methodism, as I understand it, is a faith of the poor and the simple. It has no charms for me, Watson, yet I honour those who embrace it. But too many men of religion have committed murder. Therefore I cannot suppose that a sense of self-righteousness makes him innocent either."

The train jolted to a halt at the signal for a country crossing, and we sat in a silence broken only by the long escape of steam. Then we jolted forward again, and Holmes resumed.

"Yet, Watson, what better target for the rustic voyeurs and scandal-mongers than a serious-minded man, an industrious worker who professes to be devout? People love to sniff out hypocrisy, perhaps in the hope of drawing away attention from their own, for it is a universal vice. You saw for yourself that within hours of Gardiner's arrest, his guilt was being proclaimed in a waxwork display on the sea-front at Great Yarmouth. The evidence alone must determine his fate."

Sherlock Holmes had seemed to blow this way and that until I had no idea what was in his mind.

"From all that we know so far, can you not decide whether you believe him guilty or innocent?"

He pulled a face at the trees and fields of Hertfordshire beyond the carriage window.

"As to that, my dear fellow, I will tell you when I know him a little better."

Mr. Wild and his instructing solicitor, Arthur Leighton, were waiting for us as the train pulled into Ipswich station. The horse and trap outside carried us through the streets of the country town to its prison gates. As there is a sad similarity to the fortress-like appearance of provincial gaols, so there is a common odour within them of sour humanity and despair. We were shown into a room where prisoners facing trial were permitted to consult their legal advisers. Inspector Lestrade of Scotland Yard, the burly rival of Holmes, stood beside a former military man who was now the prison governor. It was a dismal place, in reality a meanly furnished cell with a single barred window high in its opposite wall. A table and half a dozen wooden chairs were all the comforts that it contained. Even at noon, on this winter day, the white gaslight sputtered in lamp brackets along the pale green lime-washed walls.

Once the introductions had been performed, the governor addressed us.

"Gentleman, the prisoner Gardiner and whatever other witnesses you may care to see shall be brought before you. I will grant you such privacy as I may. You have Inspector Lestrade with you, so I think we may dispense with a guard in the room itself. Two prison officers will be on duty outside the door. In the circumstances, however, Gardiner must remain handcuffed while he is with you. I respect your need for confidentiality and shall withdraw as soon as the arrangements have been made."

He left the four of us—Wild, Lestrade, Holmes, and I—and went to order the escort to fetch Gardiner. The Scotland Yard man turned to my friend.

"Well now, Mr. Holmes, this is a favor I should not have done for any man except yourself."

Holmes gave him a quick and humourless smile.

"My dear Lestrade, it is I who have undertaken to pay a favour and the recipient is the English legal system. Favour or not, let it be in respect of a man who deserves to hang if he butchered that poor girl but shall not go to the gallows when he is innocent. My mind is as open as I trust yours is. I must draw such evidence from witnesses and circumstances as will convince you that Gardiner did or did not murder Rose Harsent. You will inform your superiors or the solicitor-general accordingly. That is all I ask."

"The whole thing might be far better done in a court of law," said Lestrade with a tired shrug. He drew up one of the plain wooden chairs to the table and sat down with his notes spread before him.

"I would trust this man's life to you rather than to a jury," said Holmes quietly. "That is the extent of my confidence in your love of justice."

This seemed to catch Lestrade on the hop, as they say, and he sat there without speaking a word for the next few minutes. Holmes, Wild, and I had taken our seats next to him with one chair on the far side of the table for our witnesses. Almost at once the door opened and we heard the bustle of a large man being led between two escorts. Before us, in handcuffs, stood the accused whose life was now in our hands. William Gardiner was a finely built man of thirty-four with clear eyes and hair so black that he might have been of Spanish origin. His descent was, as I soon learnt, from those hard-working Huguenots who had sought refuge in Suffolk from religious persecution in France two centuries earlier.

It had been agreed that Ernest Wild should abandon his role as examiner to Sherlock Holmes and Lestrade. My friend looked up at the tall prisoner with his raven-black beard and said quietly, "Sit down, if you please, Mr. Gardiner."

There was a pause and I saw the emotions contending behind the prisoner's quiet demeanour. It must have been many months since anyone had done him the courtesy of addressing him as "Mr." Gardiner. Though he was wearing prison handcuffs, he managed the chair easily enough. Holmes looked him directly in the eyes and Gardiner held his interrogator's gaze. His manner was not hostile, but utterly confident.

"My name is Sherlock Holmes. To my right is Inspector Lestrade and on my left is my colleague Dr. Watson. Mr. Wild is already familiar to you. You know who we are and why we are here?"

"I do, sir," said Gardiner in that strong, quiet voice that seldom wavered except under the emotion of questions respecting his wife, children, or religion. "I know all that, and my gratitude to you is unbounded."

Holmes sat back in his chair, a little brusquely as it seemed to me.

"We are not here to earn your gratitude, but to serve justice. If you are innocent, we shall do all in our power to demonstrate it. If you are guilty, that shall also appear."

"Then we are at one in our purpose, sir," said Gardiner in the same firm but quiet voice, "and if the truth shall indeed shine through all this, I have nothing to fear."

Only then did his eyes cease to search those of Sherlock Holmes and look down at the table. Sitting in that drab and tainted cell, I thought that the power of Gardiner's personality seemed at times almost to dominate Holmes and Lestrade. Either this was a man whose piety and decency were an example to us all, or one of the devil's own breed in his cunning and dissimulation. The next two or three days would tell.

Holmes took him through the course of his life, eliciting how one of nine pauper children born in the workhouse had by dint of hard work become foreman carpenter at Smyth's Seed Drill Works in Peasenhall. He had taken a loving wife from the Primitive Methodist congregation at Sibton, two miles away, and accepted salvation through its faith. He rose through the ranks of the chapel as he had done at the works. At thirty-four, this pauper child was assistant steward, Sunday school superintendent, choirmaster, and organist, though the choir was a mere dozen voices and organ-playing little more than an accompaniment of chords on the harmonium. It was in this Methodist chapel that William Gardiner, the married man, had met Rose Harsent, who was twenty years old at the time. It seemed that she had been brought to the primitive faith by her former suitor, though their courtship had now ended. Miss Rose had been a member of Gardiner's little choir and had asked him to teach her the harmonium.

Among his other accomplishments, he could read well and write passably, though his penmanship lacked a number of refinements. His reputation with his employers was such that two years earlier he had been sent to manage the firm's stand at the Paris Exhibition and had written several letters to them reporting on the event. It was said among some of his more envious neighbours that he had "done well for a workhouse brat."

"Very good then," said Holmes, when all this ground had been cleared. "Now let us come, if you please, to the night of 1 May, thirteen months before the murder. It was the evening that gave rise to so much talk about you and Miss Rose Harsent, was it not? Tell us what you did and where you were between seven and nine o'clock."

Gardiner held his gaze once more.

"That is easily done, sir. I had been driving Mr. Smyth on business that afternoon, over to Dunwich. He will vouch for it that we were late back. We came to the drill works again just after seven that evening. I rubbed down the horse, which is my job, and gave him his feed. Yet the animal would not take the bait to start him eating. I thought I should leave him a while and then, if he still would not eat, I must report the matter to Mr. Smyth. Home I went and had my tea at seven thirty, as my wife will tell you. The walk is a quarter mile or so and not more than six or seven minutes."

"At what time do you usually have your tea?" asked Holmes.

"Normally, sir, I have my tea at six. On this occasion, it was a little before eight when I finished the meal and about five minutes after that when I was ready to go out again. Then I went back to the drill works to attend to the horse, to see if he had eaten. I found that he had. I would have reached the works very soon after eight o'clock, I daresay not much more than five minutes past. I came out again about eight fifteen. It was then that I saw Miss Rose Harsent standing by the gate of what we call the Doctor's Chapel, which she cleaned every week. I did not see Wright hanging about then. If he was there, he was concealed from me. Rose was in service with Mr. and Mrs. Crisp at Providence House. That chapel was Congregational. Mr. Crisp being one of the deacons, cleaning it was part of Rose's duties."

"You went across the road to her?"

"No, sir. She called me over and said that she had finished her cleaning but could not get the chapel door to close, so that she might lock it. She had been a friend to Mrs. Gardiner and me for a few years, so naturally I went to help. The door was an old one and I found that the rain had swollen it at the bottom. I caught hold and gave it a good slam, enough to close it so that it might be locked. We came back down the path together, for the chapel stands back thirty yards from the road. That is the distance they have now measured. We walked together a little way to Providence House, a few minutes, half of my way home. We talked of chapel matters as we went, choosing hymns for the anniversary and so on. I left her at the corner, saw her go into Providence House, and walked the rest of the way home, just a couple of minutes more. And that was all there was to it, sir, no matter what they may say. My wife will tell you that I was home before half past eight."

Inspector Lestrade had been fretting to get his own question in.

"What of the young man, George Wright, who tells a different story?"

"I saw him twice, sir. When I left the Seed Drill Works and went home to my tea, just before seven thirty, he was hanging about the gate of the works. He was there, still hanging about, when I went back about half an hour or so later. I knew him, of course, for he is a labourer at the works, but I never stopped to say more than a word as I passed."

"And that is all?"

"And that is all, sir."

"Not quite," said Lestrade ominously, "for this is not a court of law and the suspicion still stands against you. What do you say to the allegations of Wright and Skinner? Please do not tell me that it is all a lie from beginning to end, for that will not do in this room. William Wright swears on his oath in court that he saw Rose Harsent enter the Doctor's Chapel about seven thirty that evening. He saw you follow her a few minutes later. Contemptible though it may be, he then went to fetch his young friend Alfonso Skinner to have some fun, as he put it, by spying on you and the young woman. At about eight o'clock these two youths crouched down behind a hedge, on a high bank near the southwest window of the chapel. They have sworn in court that they heard your voice and that of a young woman, whom they later saw to be Rose Harsent. They heard the sounds of an act of gross indecency. . . ."

Gardiner's face was tight as canvas under full sail and dark as indigo.

"It is. . . . "

"Kindly do not interrupt me," said the Scotland Yard man calmly, "and in your own best interests do not tell me again that it is a foul lie unless you can show that to be true. These two young men heard the two of you clearly enough. Your voices were plain enough for Skinner to make out the exact passage from the thirty-eighth chapter of the Book of Genesis which you and Rose Harsent used to describe your misconduct. Wright left his friend for about ten minutes during the time that you were in the chapel with the girl. He came back and stayed another fifteen minutes. He was in time to hear the rest of your conversation and to see you both leave. From where they were hidden, they were able to see the girl leave first and then to watch you following her."

Gardiner would keep silent no longer.

"It is an abominable falsehood! By all I hold sacred, it is! A libel on holy scripture as surely as on my reputation! Why should they do such a thing to me? I never in my life wished them harm."

Sherlock Holmes intervened.

"One moment, Lestrade. Is it said that Mr. Gardiner and the girl left the chapel together?"

Lestrade turned over several pages of his papers.

"According to Skinner, Rose Harsent left and Gardiner followed a few minutes later. The girl went on ahead to Providence House, he says, while Gardiner came out, tiptoed across to the other side of the road, and took the same direction. Skinner followed him in turn. I daresay, Mr. Holmes, your cases are in a superior class to this kind of thing. For your information, however, guilty parties in conduct of this kind seldom leave the scene of their amours together."

For some reason that was not plain to me at that moment, a look of relief appeared on the face of Sherlock Holmes. Before he could speak, however, Gardiner burst out again.

"Those two young men say they hid behind that hedge about twenty minutes after eight. I was on my way home from the chapel by then. Skinner says they were there about an hour, and Wright too, except for the ten minutes he was away walking about the road. I was at home before all that. He says he was there for an hour and Wright was there three-quarters of an hour. As my wife will tell you, I was with her all the time that this wickedness was supposed to be happening at the chapel. She knows it, and for that reason she never believed a single word that these slanderers spoke."

"So she has said," Lestrade remarked coldly. Gardiner stared at him.

"Will you believe these two foul-minded rascals or her? I never saw Rose Harsent at all that evening except when I came out of the works at about quarter past eight. I went to the Doctor's Chapel and slammed the door so that she could lock up. I never so much as set foot inside the building beyond that. When I heard what was said about me by those two young men, I started an action for slander."

"And withdrew it," Lestrade said quietly.

"Only because the attorney told me that those two had nothing and I must pay the costs even if I won. I had not the money to pay costs. After that, there was always two of those wretches to back each other up. I had only my wife, who is disbelieved because she is my wife, and Rose, who might have spoken for me too. But I could not put that girl through such an ordeal as an action for slander."

Holmes leant forward a little and took up the questioning.

"Mr. Gardiner, tell me this. It is a very simple question. Let us suppose it was only slander or malice on the part of Wright and Skinner, perhaps a vicious sense of fun. Why would these two youths stick to their falsehood after Rose Harsent had been murdered and your life was at stake in a murder trial?"

I quite expected Gardiner to act a dramatic part over this, but he became very quiet.

"Because, Mr. Holmes, they are evil through and through. That is the simple answer to your simple question, and I will tell you why I make it. They saw that if they told the truth and admitted their falsehoods about me after Rose died, I should certainly be acquitted on the charge of murdering her. There would be nothing to connect me with this young woman in an immoral way and their lies would be turned against them. They feared that when I was set free, I should find the money to sue them in earnest for their slanders. I would have the decision of a jury behind me. And they knew very well I should win. Worse than that, for them, they might be indicted for perjury and sent to prison for many years. What worse perjury can there be than trying to swear a man's life away? Rather than risk prison, they would see me hanged. It was the only way they could be safe. I never said any of this when I was in the witness-box, for it would be no evidence in the case. My only witness to the truth, Rose Harsent, was dead. But as you ask me, Mr. Holmes, that is the depth of their evil. Those two are a hundred times more likely to have murdered her than anyone else I can think of."

It was an argument that might have gone against him in court, when he was cross-examined. Spoken in that prison room, as he spoke them, the words carried a terrible probability to my mind, though not to the Chief Inspector's.

"It is easy enough, Gardiner, to call men evil," said Lestrade sharply, "but of little use unless you can show them to be so. These are two witnesses who submitted to the chapel inquiry, which they were not bound to do, and have never refused to cooperate with the law."

"I can show you what they are!" said Gardiner quietly, and for the first time his dark eyes glittered with malice. "Suppose, sir, you had seen filthy behaviour of the kind they allege, seen it between a young woman you knew and a married man who was also of your acquaintance. What would you have done?"

Lestrade colored a little at this.

"You are not here to ask questions, Gardiner, but to answer them!"

"All the same, Lestrade," said Holmes gently, "it may do no harm in this one instance."

Lestrade glared at him, I can use no other word. Reluctantly, he gave way.

"Very well, if I knew the fellow, I should take him on one side and speak to him."

"Just so," said Gardiner gratefully, "or, sir, if that accomplished nothing, you might speak to his wife. You would not ignore the man and his wife but spread dirty stories of him behind his back, among all those who knew him. Among his neighbours and friends. There, sir, is the difference between the good and the evil man. Whether you believe me or them, I leave you to judge of what kind these two witnesses show themselves to be. Evil tongues."

"The tongue can no man tame," said Holmes thoughtfully, "it is an unruly evil."

"Full of deadly poison," Gardiner took up the quotation. "The General Epistle of James, Mr. Holmes, sir, chapter three, verse eight."

By the time that Holmes and Lestrade had finished questioning Gardiner over the allegations of his conduct with Rose Harsent, it seemed to me that a long couple of hours had passed. So great had been the intensity of these exchanges that it was only when we stepped out into the dark prison courtyard that I looked at my watch and saw that four hours and a half had gone by.

Darkness had fallen before we stood in that yard with a winter drizzle falling. The oil light was reflected in pools on the smooth paving of the yard and on the rough stonework of its walls. The burly figure of Lestrade in his travelling cloak confronted Sherlock Holmes as we waited under the light of the stone porch for Arthur Leighton and the cab that was to take us to the White Horse hotel.

"Well, Mr. Holmes," said the Scotland Yard man rather huffily, "I don't see how all that has got us much further. I don't believe your client stands an inch further from the noose."

"He is not my client," said Holmes patiently. "Mr. Wild is my client, so far as I have one. I am prepared to find Gardiner guilty or innocent, as the evidence presents itself. Yet if you believe that what we have heard gets us no further, I shall be sadly disappointed in you."

"I say only that we have wasted our time this afternoon."

Holmes rounded on him.

"This allegation of misconduct in the Doctor's Chapel is the only sinister link between the accused and Rose Harsent prior to the murder. She was a member of the Primitive Methodist congregation, a friend of Gardiner and his wife who visited their house regularly. She continued to pay these visits after the scandal broke. That could hardly be the case if Mrs. Gardiner believed her husband to be the girl's lover. The world has seen that good lady twice in the witness-box. Is it likely that such a woman would have welcomed Gardiner's mistress under her roof—as the companion of her six children? Gardiner denies the truth of the scandal, his wife denounces it as impossible because he was at home with her at the material times. If it were not for the story told by Wright and Skinner, Gardiner's name would have no connexion with the murder nor, indeed, with the pregnancy of Rose Harsent. I do not think, Lestrade, that we have wasted our time."

"Then you had better have a look at these, Mr. Holmes."

Lestrade put his hand in his pocket and drew out an envelope, from which he took two photographs. They had been taken by a police photographer and were reproductions of two sets of handwriting. The first showed a pair of single-page letters carried to Rose Harsent by her young brother, telling her that Gardiner proposed to sue Wright and Skinner over "some scandal going round about you and me going into the Doctor's Chapel for immoral Purposes." Gardiner had signed both letters. The handwriting was firm and rounded, but the phrasing was laboured, as might befit a self-educated man. The writer also showed a tendency to use a capital 'P' and 'R' in the middle of his sentences to begin certain words, where a small, lowercase initial letter would have been usual.

"And now this," said Lestrade confidently. The second photograph showed an assignation note for the night of Rose Harsent's death, written by a lover who was surely her murderer. It was accompanied by the envelope in which it had been posted, addressed to "Miss Harsent, Providence House, Peasenhall, Saxmundham." I read the note, whose dreadful appointment the poor young woman had kept.

> *"Dear R, I will try to see you tonight at twelve o'clock at your Place if you Put a light in your window at ten o'clock for about ten minutes. Then you can take it out again. Don't have a light in your Room at twelve as I will come round the back."*

"Well now," said Holmes quietly, "it seems you have the better of us all, Lestrade. And this is the evidence on which the famous Mr. Thomas Gurrin, handwriting expert extraordinary of Holborn Viaduct, proposes to swear a man's life away? I fear, my friend, that he will have to do better than this."

"You deny the resemblance, Mr. Holmes?"

"Oh, no!" said Holmes at once, "The resemblance between the two letters is quite remarkable. Perhaps a little too remarkable. What I deny is the authorship of the murderer's note. In the first place there is the literary style, which I know is not a matter of handwriting. The first two letters to Rose Harsent, signed by Gardiner and admitted by him, are a little awkward. They are the work of a man not born to letter-writing. Look where he says 'I have broke the news' and 'she say she know it is wrong.' Then there is a sentence eleven lines long but with hardly any attempt at punctuation, which was still beyond him. By contrast, the unsigned assignation note, which we may assume was the work of her murderer, has a confidence and a precision. I do not think its author would write, as Gardiner does, 'you and me' rather the more correct form 'you and I.' A small matter, but significant."

"I don't see that," said Lestrade gruffly.

"Do you not?" Holmes now held the two photographs side by side under the light of the porch. "Then let me help you a little in the matter of the handwriting. In the unsigned note, presumably from the murderer, there is much play of using incorrectly a capital initial 'P' or an 'R' in the middle of a sentence. It occurs three times in seven lines. In the two signed letters by Gardiner, the first is eighteen lines long and the curious capital 'P' occurs only once, the 'R' not at all, though there were four opportunities. The second letter is more than thirty-six lines long and no error of the sort occurs whatever."

"Which signifies what, precisely, Mr Holmes?" There was no mistaking the skepticism in Lestrade's voice.

"Which signifies, my dear fellow, that someone has taken an occasional eccentricity of handwriting, imitated it, and turned it into a regular feature of the script. And then there is the accuracy of the script. It is Gardiner's style but more rounded and regular than Gardiner could ever be. Many a bank forger might be caught if our experts were alive to a single fact: It is very difficult for any man or woman to sign his or her name identically on every occasion. Where it appears to be identical, time after time, it has very likely been counterfeited with great care."

"Which gets us where, Mr. Holmes?"

"To the point, Lestrade, of acknowledging that the unsigned assignation note is written in Gardiner's style, but a style more polished than Gardiner ever attained. And then there is the envelope in which the unsigned note was posted."

"You don't deny that the unsigned assignation note and the envelope are written in the same hand and by the same person?"

"Not in the least." Holmes wagged the photograph a little. "Yet look at the address."

Lestrade read slowly, "Miss Harsent, Providence House, Peasenhall, Saxmundham."

"There you have it," said Holmes triumphantly, "and the postmark on the envelope is Yoxford—which is also the postmark for Peasenhall itself. This letter was surely posted in the box opposite Hurren's post office in the main street of Peasenhall and collected by the postman. It was franked at Hurren's and delivered. To add Saxmundham is superfluous. Saxmundham may be the largest village between here and Ipswich but the note would never have gone there. This is as redundant as if you were to address a letter to London, England, when you posted a letter in London to be delivered in London. A man who has lived as long in Peasenhall as William Gardiner would not address a Peasenhall letter to Saxmundham."

"Unless he wished to disguise his intent," Lestrade replied.

Holmes laughed.

"Unless he wanted to draw attention to himself. If he wished to disguise its origin, better by far for him to walk to Saxmundham and send the letter with a Saxmundham postmark on it. When we began our labours this afternoon, I was quite prepared to find that Gardiner was the murderer. You, my dear fellow, have helped to bring me to the near certainty that he can only be innocent."

This caught the inspector on the raw and he became a little snappish.

"Be that as it may, Mr. Holmes, my time grows short. At the risk of trespassing on your hospitality, I should be grateful if we could deal with Gardiner's murder alibi after dinner this evening. The facts are known and it hardly requires an inquisition or further witnesses. I cannot stay in Ipswich for ever."

"Good God, man! You have only been in the town for a few hours!"

I was not surprised that there was general silence in the cab until we drew up in the half-timbered yard of the White Hart. The old low-beamed hotel was busy that evening with barristers on circuit for the assize court at the Shire Hall. The White Hart is where the bar mess meets for dinner during these weeks, though Mr. Wild absented himself in order to keep us company. The ice was broken a little, as the saying is, when the four of us sat round our table in the panelled dining room. By an unspoken agreement, we avoided all mention of the case, which was soon to occupy us into the small hours.

4

As usual, Holmes had engaged a private sitting room adjoining our bedrooms. With Lestrade and Mr. Wild we took our ease in armchairs, a decanter of whisky and a jug of hot water with a plate of lemon on the table between us.

"Let us clear the ground," said Holmes, looking about him. "Certain facts are plain. On 31 May last, Rose Harsent received an anonymous note from her lover, asking her to put a light in her attic window at Providence House at ten P.M. and promising to come to the back door at midnight. It is disputed whether that note may or may not be in Gardiner's handwriting."

"It is his handwriting," said Lestrade hastily. "Mr. Thomas Gurrin has said so on two occasions in court. He is the greatest expert we have."

"Or the greatest charlatan," said Holmes equably. "However, let us return to the night of 31 May. Rose lit a candle in her window that remained there for ten minutes or so. Gardiner and his neighbours were standing in their doorways or in the street watching the storm. Had Gardiner stood in the middle of the road, he might have seen the candle in the window, two hundred yards away. All other evidence apart, Rose Harsent was certainly alive at ten P.M. and dead at eight A.M. next morning."

"Let us say four A.M.," I added quickly, "and quite possibly two A.M., according to postmortem evidence of rigor mortis."

"So it shall be." Holmes put down his glass and glanced at the sheet of paper before him. "Gardiner and his wife were asked by a next-door neighbour, Mrs. Rosanna Dickenson, an ironmonger's widow, to keep her company because she was afraid of the storm. Mrs. Gardiner arrived at Mrs. Dickenson's house at about eleven thirty P.M. Gardiner had said that he would look to see that the children were sleeping. He then followed his wife about fifteen minutes later, let us say eleven forty-five P.M. Gardiner was described by Mrs. Dickenson as 'calm and collected.' He was wearing carpet slippers and not dressed for going out, even in fine weather, let alone in the storm that was still in full force. The couple stayed with Mrs. Dickenson until one thirty A.M. and left together. I see that Mrs. Dickenson was not cross-examined at the trial, so I take it we may accept the truth of her evidence?"

Our Scotland Yard man took the pipe from his mouth.

"I think we may."

"Very well. Mrs. Gardiner then describes how they walked straight home and went to bed. She recalled that the first predawn light began to appear in the sky just before two o'clock. Remember that this was 1 June and almost the earliest sunrise of the year. As they got into bed at two twenty A.M., she said to her husband, "It is getting quite light." Furthermore, the walls of those cottages are thin and their neighbour, Amelia Pepper, heard Mrs. Gardiner's voice and her tread on the stairs at about two A.M. Mrs. Gardiner tells us that she had a pain in her body and did not sleep until after five A.M., when she heard the clock strike. Her husband was in bed with her all that time. If this is true, then he cannot have murdered anyone after eleven forty-five P.M., unless we disregard his wife's evidence."

"Which we should be well advised to do," said Lestrade quickly. "It is completely uncorroborated after two A.M."

Holmes looked at him without expression.

"I think, Lestrade, that a little common sense will suffice. If you check your diary or your almanac, you will find that the sun rises at that time of year at two forty-five A.M. and that it lights the sky from below the horizon somewhat before then. Were I Gardiner intent upon murdering Rose Harsent, it would be a deed of darkness. I should not walk down the main street in broad daylight where a wakeful neighbour or an early riser might see me from a window or even meet me on the way. Peasenhall is not Park Lane or Baker Street. Country people rise with the sun, not several hours after it. Added to that, the medical evidence cannot place the crime later than two or three o'clock, four o'clock if we accept Dr. Lay's unsupported guess."

"That is certainly true," I said before Lestrade could intervene again. "In any case, Miss Harsent was in the kitchen when she was murdered, and the candle in her bedroom had been put out. If her lover failed her at midnight, she would surely have gone to bed and not sat up in the kitchen for two hours and more in her nightclothes."

Lestrade turned round to us all.

"This may be very a very amusing game to you, gentlemen. To me, it is something else. The young person may have been murdered as late as four A.M., according to Dr. Lay. If that was the case, then she had indeed sat up waiting or gone to the kitchen at that hour, however unreasonable it may seem to you. Remember she was wearing night attire and may have gone downstairs in answer to a knock or signal. Let that be enough."

"Enough for suspicion and innuendo, far too little for guilt," said

Holmes quietly. "If I were you, I should place the murder at a time before the Gardiners went to Mrs. Dickenson and not afterward. That would put it before eleven forty-five P.M. on the previous evening."

"Time enough, Mr. Holmes."

Holmes stared into his glass.

"Is it, indeed? Rose Harsent was seen alive by Mrs. Crisp who said goodnight to the girl at ten P.M. It was ten fifteen when Mrs. Crisp went to bed and to sleep. She woke somewhen during the night and heard a thud, followed shortly after by a scream. She said at first it was at midnight; now she is not sure of the time, but it was dark. No matter. We have a period between ten fifteen and eleven forty-five, less than that if Gardiner was the murderer. He had to be at Mrs. Dickenson's in his carpet slippers at eleven forty-five, so let us say between ten fifteen and eleven thirty."

"Long enough," said the inspector decisively.

"What about the blood with which he was covered when he arrived at Mrs. Dickenson's?"

"What blood?"

"Precisely, my friend. There was none. Gardiner is said to have cut the throat of this young woman during a struggle in the kitchen. There was a struggle, of course, since Mrs. Crisp heard first of all a thud and then a cry soon afterwards. The thud, no doubt, was the staircase door banging back against the wall and the cry was the poor girl's last utterance."

"I don't entirely follow you, Mr. Holmes."

"I quite see that, Lestrade. The kitchen of Providence House is a small one, some ten feet by eight. The blood had spurted to the second step of the staircase. A man who grappled with his victim while he cut her throat, in a space as small as that kitchen, would have been covered by it. His shoes would have trampled it all over the kitchen floor. Forensic examination shows that there was not a speck of blood on Gardiner's shoes or clothing, neither the clothing that had been washed nor that which was waiting to be washed. All his clothing was examined by Dr. Stevenson of the Home Office, a man who can not only detect blood on clothing that has not been washed but the remains of blood on clothes that have been washed. There was not a drop."

Lestrade said nothing, for Sherlock Holmes now held the floor.

"What there was, however," my friend continued, "was a copy of the *East Anglian Times* under the girl's head. Why? Is it likely that Gardiner would bring a paper to which he subscribed and the Crisps did not in order to leave it under her head? Then again, there was a medicine bottle with a label 'For Mrs. Gardiner's children.' Is not that the first thing he would have taken away? Might it not be the first thing that another man would leave there to incriminate Gardiner? In which case the crime was committed by someone known to him, well enough known to be informed that the Gardiners of Alma Cottage subscribed to the *East Anglian Times*, rather than the *Chronicle*, which was taken in by the Crisps at Providence House."

"You tell me nothing I have not heard already."

"Then how can you hear it and still believe that Gardiner was the murderer of Rose Harsent? It can only be because no case has been built against any other man. That is not a good enough reason to deliver any poor devil to the hangman's mercies."

Lestrade hung on like a plucky terrier to a thief's coattails.

"Gardiner had ample time to burn a bloodstained shirt before his clothes were taken for examination three days later. If murder was his purpose, he might have gone barefoot into that kitchen and wiped away any prints as he left. Mammal's blood, possibly human, was found in a crevice of his pocketknife. . . ."

"Rabbits!" said Holmes furiously. "Have you never heard of hulling rabbits? There is not a countryman who does not use his knife regularly to prepare them for the pot. I should find it far more incriminating if his knife was perfectly clean."

But Lestrade would not be stopped.

"He has no alibi but for the time spent with Mrs. Dickenson. The Gardiners' neighbour, Amelia Pepper, swears only that she heard the voice and step of Mrs. Gardiner after two A.M., not her husband. Rose Harsent may have met her death as late as four A.M. If she died the evening before, Gardiner had time to kill her at eleven P.M. and be back in Mrs. Dickenson's sitting room forty-five minutes later."

"Then his wife is necessarily a liar."

"Not necessarily, Mr. Holmes, but she is his wife. There is not an insurance company that would take a wife as sole witness in a husband's claim! If Gardiner killed that girl, he killed that girl. Not all your clever theories, Mr. Sherlock Holmes, can alter that!"

"Very well. Then if he killed her, he must have had good reasons."

"He had good reasons, indeed," said Lestrade triumphantly. "He had such reasons as being the father of her unborn child and being determined to protect himself, his family, and his reputation by putting an end to it!"

"Which brings us back to the Doctor's Chapel and the scandal again," said Sherlock Holmes thoughtfully.

"So it does."

"Well then, Lestrade? Had we not better have an understanding between us? We have done enough sitting about in chairs. Let us take this matter of the chapel *au serieux* and fight the battle there, at the scene of the scandal. Shall we do that as soon as the principals can be gathered? I believe we shall have you back in London in no time at all."

"We might do that, Mr. Holmes. I will go this far. If you can disprove absolutely the scandal of the Doctor's Chapel, you shall have your way. For then the motive of the murder falls to the ground. I do not see how you can do it, but I will go that far to meet you."

"There must be sound tests of what, if anything, can be heard behind the hedge."

"They have been tried."

"They must be tried again. And there must be an examination of the two youths who claim to be witnesses of immoral conduct between Gardiner and Miss Harsent."

"That has been done. Wright and Skinner have said all that there is for them to say."

"Nonetheless, Lestrade, I shall require George Wright, Alfonso Skinner, and Mr. Crisp, who was deacon of the chapel and who with his wife employed Rose Harsent."

"Mr. and Mrs. Crisp? What have they to do with it now?"

Holmes let out a long sigh, which may have been of satisfaction or relief.

"You see, my dear fellow? It seems they have not said all they have to say. I believe, Lestrade, this is another of our cases in which you and Scotland Yard will live to thank me for my assistance."

5

The rain had cleared before midnight, and by dawn the clear sky had laid down a frost to accompany our visit to the Doctor's Chapel at Peasenhall. For the number of us who were to gather there, we might have hired a char-a-banc. Peasenhall consists of the main road, which they call the Street, and a road running south from it at the mid-point, which is Church Street. The Doctor's Chapel is two hundred yards down Church Street, reached through a narrow iron gate on the south side. Beyond this lies the equally narrow path that runs along by the building, overlooked on the other side by a tall bank topped with a hedge and a hurdle fence.

The chapel itself is a small structure with the appearance of a single-storey thatched cottage. It has three square windows and a plain door on this southern side. I doubt if its pews would accommodate fifty worshippers. It is surrounded and overhung by trees which give way to open fields a little distance beyond. Such was the scene of the scandal, upon whose proof or disproof the fate of William Gardiner must now depend.

Waiting for us by the door were PC Nunn, with a face of the severe but thoughtful type, Mr. Crisp, with an ear trumpet and walking stick, and his wife, who was, as they say, a stout body of fifty or so. We were introduced to them. The other two witnesses present were the Peeping Toms of the scandal, merely indicated to us as they stood apart sullenly. William Wright and Alfonso Skinner now wore their Sunday best.

I confess that I did not like the look of these two from the start. Wright was a sallow, even swarthy young man who looked entirely out of place in a suit and cravat. His heavy jaw and the morose stare of his dark eyes gave him a mingled look of malice and Neanderthal stupidity. Skinner was quite the contrary, a more dangerous antagonist. He had a sharp, impatient manner, hair closely cropped, and narrowed eyes that stared without emotion. I swear that those eyes would watch suffering with indifference, would look on without either anger or compassion. In all my experience with Sherlock Holmes, I had seldom had the sense so strongly of men who would crush their victim as a matter of habit, hardly caring whether they did so or not. If it was necessary for William Gardiner to be hanged in order that they should be safe from prosecution over their perjury, I wager they would send him to the gallows as readily as they would order a chicken to be slaughtered for Christmas.

If Gardiner's life was in the hands of Sherlock Holmes, I was never so grateful for my friend's reputation. It seemed plain from the two scowling figures that PC Eli Nunn had given Wright and Skinner little choice as to whether they attended this interrogation or not. A request from Holmes had been as good as a bench warrant from a High Court judge.

I stood with Nunn and Holmes a little apart from the others, while we discussed how the experiment was to be carried out.

"I must tell you, sir," said Nunn apologetically, "that we have already carried out a test of our own. On 28 July last, I stood behind the hedge up there, where these two young men claimed they were hiding on the evening of the alleged incident in the chapel. For the purposes of the test, Wright and Skinner went into the chapel, the door was closed, and, as I had instructed them, each in turn read out the first ten verses of the thirty-eighth chapter of the Book of Genesis, the story of Onan."

"Thank you," said Holmes, interrupting him. "I am familiar with his story."

"Then I must tell you, sir," said Nunn reluctantly, "I could hear every word."

My friend was remarkably unruffled by this.

"You do not surprise me in the least. Which other officer was in the chapel with these two when they read from the Book of Genesis?"

"None, sir. There was no need. I saw fair play by making sure the door and every window was shut."

"But not by having an official witness in the chapel, where these two scoundrels could read or shout as loudly as was necessary to make their voices carry to you? Nor by choosing some other passage with which you might be unfamiliar but one whose words you expected to hear?"

Nunn was a decent fellow, I felt sure, and I was sad to see him cut down like this. I would have preferred him as an ally rather than an antagonist, for I cannot believe he liked Wright and Skinner any better than we did.

"No matter," said Holmes reassuringly, "we will return to these things later. For the moment, let us carry out an examination of the *locus in quo*."

He handed me his travelling-cape and walked once round the outside of the little building. Then he began to inspect the door, windows, and ventilation. The white-painted door was unlocked and opened easily as he knelt down and studied the lower edge, where Gardiner swore it had stuck fast on the night when Rose asked him to slam it for her.

"You see, Watson?"

"I see nothing."

"Precisely. You see nothing because this door has been repainted. It is now eighteen months since the night of the alleged scandal, and the state of the paint suggests to me that it has yet to see a single winter before this one. In other words, it has only been painted after the murder. No doubt that was done to conceal something else that had been done to it before. Now, if you will be good enough to run your hand down the edge of the door where it meets the frame, you will feel that the upper stretch is smooth because the new paint is built upon a previous coat. Down here, however, you can feel the grain of the wood quite easily. In other words, at the bottom of the door someone had planed away the swollen surface so that it would close and lock more easily. After the murder, someone else painted the door, concealing what had been done. It may have been by chance, but it made a liar out of William Gardiner when he first told the story of slamming the swollen door because it had stuck—told it when his only witness was now dead and buried."

"Those two wastrels have something to answer for!" I said angrily. Sherlock Holmes straightened up from his inspection.

"Let us not jump to conclusions. On its own, this does not mean that Gardiner has told the truth in every respect. However, in his story of the swollen chapel door, it seems he has spoken the entire truth and that someone has tried to make him appear a liar."

"Of course! Skinner described himself in court as an odd-job man for Mr. and Mrs. Crisp. Surely that would make him the odd-job man for the chapel as well, would it not? He planed the door to make Gardiner seem a liar and then painted it to conceal what he had done."

"No doubt, if it can be proved."

My friend was busy with the three square windows, each made up of small leaded panes.

"You will recall the words of Skinner at the trial, 'We heard rustling about and the window shook.'" Holmes turned to me. "Be so good as to shake that window, if you please."

I was not sure quite what he had in mind, but there was no way of causing any vibration, except by vigorous contact with the glass or the glazing bars. The window frame was set solidly in the wall and nothing else would do. Holmes looked through it into the interior of the little building.

"The only way to shake the window from inside would be to strike directly at the glass, preferably at about the level of the windowsill. Yet there is a fixed seat running just beneath it on the inside. That would make it almost impossible to hit the window accidentally while standing up. Sitting down, one would almost have to hit it with the back of one's head. Tell me, what else would produce such an effect?"

I lost his drift for a moment and he laughed.

"Come, Watson! Surely, a servant girl doing her duty, cleaning the chapel with vim and vigor—including its windows! That is something they may have heard and adopted it for their story. If anything moved that window, it was Rose Harsent and her duster!"

He had not done with the small leaded panes.

"Consider these little panes of glass. Seven up and five across. There are thirty-five of them in a space the quarter of our sitting-room window in Baker Street. They do not suit a chapel, where all should be light and airy and delicate. Where else would you find such things as these? I will tell you where, my dear fellow. In the grim walls of lunatic asylums and prisons. In those unhappy places from which it is judged best that no sound of grief or frenzy shall be heard. What, then, of the lowered voices of a man and woman in intimate conversation?"

He turned from the window and looked at a small and narrow flap of metal, angled downward from the wall, level with the middle of the window and a few feet from it. For the first time since our arrival, I heard him chuckle and guessed that all might yet be well.

"See here, Watson. This is an old friend. The ventilator system. How extraordinary that a few months ago the mysterious death of the great novelist Emile Zola from charcoal poisoning should have taken us to France to examine just such forms of apparatus as this! Because there could be no proper intake of air through their windows, the good Congregationalists of Peasenhall installed a form of tube. I know it well. Devised by Mr. Tobin of Leeds. This model made by a rival is known as the Hopper."

He pressed the metal flap that projected downward from the wall and I heard it click, as though it was now shut. Taking the lip of metal, he then opened it again.

"A small catch inside does the trick. Within this flap is a draft-proof boxed-in ventilator. Imagine it as a square drainpipe on a larger scale. It is made of perforated zinc but lined with wood. The air passes from the outer world though this inlet and so through the wall. It then turns a corner downward, drawn by the warmer air within the building, which naturally rises upward in the room. At floor level the incoming air turns again and is released into the interior. It may be assisted by a fan of some kind, though I think not in this case."

He closed the outside flap again with the same click.

"Now, my dear fellow, with the ventilator closed, the door shut, and with windows that cannot be opened, no conversation in a normal voice could be heard distinctly—if at all—even where we are standing. Those two louts were six feet above us and nine feet further away, crouching behind a hedge. Even an exclamation or a casual cry would be so indistinct that its location would not be certain at such a distance. With the ventilator open, it might be possible to hear voices without being able to detect what they were saying. I doubt even that, since the sound would have to enter the tube low down on the inside wall. It must then pass along deadening wooden surfaces, against the flow of air, and round two corners before it reached anyone outside. Even if it was audible when it did so, the flap outside would direct it downward, not upward to the bank and the fence."

"Then we have them!" I said exultantly.

He shook his head.

"Not as securely as we need to or as surely as I mean to have them when they are brought in to be questioned."

6

Once again it was Holmes and I who sat with Lestrade and Mr. Wild at a table, this time inside the Doctor's Chapel. Its interior suggested the plain and humble devotion practised there. The walls were merely whitewashed over, and it was evident that they had been built of simple cob, as country folk call their mixture of clay, gravel, and straw. Sherlock Holmes sat at the center of our "inquisition." If he had been the patient inquirer at Ipswich gaol, he was now the avenger, seeking justice for William Gardiner. He knew the truth, but it was another matter to prove it.

Mr. and Mrs. Crisp came in first. Conversation through the ear trumpet of old "Tailor" Crisp, as they called him, was almost impossible. It was his wife who submitted to the courteous but direct questioning of Sherlock Holmes.

"Tell me, Mrs. Crisp, I presume you do not leave the chapel unlocked at all hours?"

"No, sir. It is always locked when not in use."

"And you—that is to say you and your husband—have the key?"

"We do, sir."

"How many copies of the key are there?"

"Two copies, sir. We hold them both. The one in use is with other keys in a drawer of the desk, kept locked, and a spare key is kept in the safe. That is in case the first should be lost."

"Rose Harsent would be given the key from the drawer when she went to clean the chapel on Tuesday evening and would hand it back it to you when she had finished?"

"Exactly so, Mr. Holmes."

"Always on the same night?"

"As soon as she got home from the chapel or a very little later."

"Why was the chapel cleaned on a Tuesday, Mrs. Crisp? I should have thought it might have been more likely to be cleaned on a Saturday, ready for Sunday service."

"Saturday is a busy day, sir, and the chapel deacons hold their meeting on Wednesday. I like to have it cleaned on Tuesday, for the deacons next day, though the work is not always done as late as the evening. First thing on Wednesday morning, about half past eight, Mr. Crisp and I go down Church Lane and satisfy ourselves that everything is in order and the place properly cleaned for the evening meeting and prayers. By going early, it gives time to have anything put right that needs putting right."

"And when you went to the chapel first thing on the morning after the alleged scandal, everything was as you expected? The chapel had been cleaned?"

"It had, sir. Even the numbers on the hymn board had been changed as usual and the hymn books put in order."

"And you are quite sure that you entered by using the key that was in the desk drawer?"

"It was the only one we had ever used, sir. The other had never left the safe. Naturally, it was where I put it the night before, when the girl handed it back. I can't say exactly what time that was, for I had no reason to remember until the murder. It might have been as late as nine o'clock that she gave it me, because she was sometimes back and busy in the kitchen before I came in. Not later than nine, though. If it had been later than about nine, I should have wondered where she was. She was a good girl and dependable, except for whatever put her in the family way."

"Very well," said Holmes. "The time of her return is of great importance, Mrs. Crisp. However, you must not let us persuade you to say anything that you do not accurately remember. There is one thing more. When she returned that evening, was her dress as it normally might have been?"

"Indeed it was, sir. By the time I saw her, she had put away her shawl, and of course she would not wear a bonnet to go so short a distance."

After Mr. and Mrs. Crisp had withdrawn, Wright and Skinner entered together. Whether Eli Nunn had sent them both at once or whether they had insisted upon this, in case one might contradict the other in his absence, I could not tell. A meaner-looking pair of bullies I had never seen. I do not say they would lie in wait to garrotte a man for his purse, but, I thought as I looked at them then, they would blast the reputation of man or woman without a second's thought. Skinner, I think, was the worse of the two.

One by one they told their stories again. Wright, who was loitering in Church Street, had seen Rose Harsent go up the path to the chapel at seven thirty that evening, and Gardiner had followed her at about seven forty-five. Wright had gone to Skinner's lodgings about eight o'clock and urged him to come and watch some fun. They arrived outside the chapel at eight fifteen or eight twenty and crept up along the raised bank until they might crouch behind the hedge. From there they could look down at the southwest window of the chapel. Skinner had remained in position for about an hour. Wright had been absent for about ten minutes during this time, but they had both been there when the couple in the chapel went their separate ways home.

Skinner gave the more complete version of what he alleged had happened in the chapel, though both agreed that it was getting too dark to see distinctly through the window. Skinner heard a woman's voice, which he could not recognize, say "Oh! Oh!" At that point Wright went away for about ten moments. Skinner heard the woman say, "Did you notice me reading my Bible last Sunday?" The man, whose voice was allegedly that of Gardiner, said, "What were you reading about?" "I was reading about like what we have been doing here tonight. Chapter thirty-eight of Genesis. It won't be noticed."

"You may save yourself the trouble of being coy with us, Skinner," said Lestrade. "Onan spilling his seed upon the ground, you mean?"

To my astonishment, Skinner blushed.

"That is correct," he said. "'And Judah said unto Onan, Go in unto thy brother's wife and marry her and raise up seed to thy brother.'"

"You are to be congratulated on your knowledge of Holy Writ"—the voice of Sherlock Holmes had an edge like a freshly honed razor—"especially since you say you are not a church-going man. And was that all you heard?"

"Later on the female said, 'I shall be out tomorrow night at nine o'clock but you must let me go now.' George Wright had returned by then and was with me when that was said."

Wright nodded his head but without looking up at us.

"And that was all?" Holmes inquired gently.

"All that I remember, sir."

"You had known this young woman for years, had you not, Skinner? By your account, you did what you call odd jobs at Providence House. You tell us that you heard her talk of Bible-reading in chapel on the previous Sunday. Since you heard everything so plainly, how is it possible you could not know her voice after an hour of listening to it, but only recognized her when you say she came out of the door?"

"She talked low."

"And yet you heard her so plainly?"

Skinner scowled at his shoes and said nothing. My friend exchanged a glance with Lestrade, as if it was time for some prearranged ceremony to take place. Then he turned to the two young men again.

"Wright and Skinner, you will please go outside with Dr. Watson and Constable Nunn to the fence behind which you say that you crouched. You will crouch there again. I shall stay here and Chief Inspector Lestrade will see fair play. This time, I shall be the one who recites the thirty-eighth chapter of Genesis. You will be able to demonstrate to Dr. Watson and Constable Nunn that you are able to hear the words."

"It is not a fair test!" said Wright scornfully.

"Fairer by far than the test to which you have put William Gardiner!" Holmes snapped. "The ventilators will be open, which they may not have been that evening. You will have as good or better chance than then of hearing what is said."

They would have wriggled out of this, I swear they would, but for the presence of PC Nunn and a Scotland Yard man. With Nunn and the two youths I went up to the bank and crouched behind the fence. At a signal, Holmes began to read. With the ventilators open, I could just hear the murmur of a man's voice but not the words. The ventilator flap was at least twelve feet away from us and the sound would have had to travel round two corners in a muffled tube. It was impossible, of course, to say that a younger witness with exceptionally acute hearing might not pick up something. With the ventilators closed, I could hear nothing. All the same, there was nothing to prevent Skinner with a young man's sharp ears telling the court of what he alleged had taken place. We returned to the little chapel and I took my place at the table again. Eli Nunn stood behind the two witnesses.

"Well, now," said Holmes to the two young men, "let us decide whether you have been truthful witnesses or willful perjurers before the King's justices. How much did you hear?"

"Some of it," said Wright sullenly. "It was in the evening then, not the afternoon with the drill works going."

"Same here," said Skinner.

The eyes of Sherlock Holmes glinted very slightly with triumph.

"It is a quiet afternoon. If you can hear any sound of the road at present, please tell us. As for the machinery at the seed drill works, that is silent at my request."

Skinner glared at him, but Sherlock Holmes had got him on the run. Before long, this malevolent lout would be fighting for his life.

"You tell us that you heard some but not all of that passage from Genesis," said Holmes courteously. "Let me tell you, gentlemen, that I would not profane this little chapel or dignify you by using Scripture for such a purpose. Inspector Lestrade will read out the words I used and to which he was a witness."

Lestrade glanced down at a small sheet of paper before him and looked more self-conscious than I had ever known him before. He read slowly and solemnly.

"Hey! diddle-diddle, the cat and the fiddle, the cow jumped over the moon, the little dog laughed to see such craft while the dish ran after the spoon."

"Quite." Holmes looked again at the two witnesses. "I repeated the verse twice to give it sufficient length."

"It is nothing but a filthy trick!" said Wright angrily, while Skinner's eyes narrowed with fury.

"Oh, no"—Holmes shook his head slowly—"the trick was yours. A trick that may yet have William Gardiner, who has never done you the slightest harm, dangling at the end of the hangman's rope. Constable Nunn, be good enough to lock the door and oblige me by arresting these two and charging them if they should try to leave before they have answered fully."

He stared at the two witnesses.

"Let us come to certain questions that you have never been asked in court and for which you may be less prepared. You have both sworn that you saw Rose Harsent leave the chapel, followed a little later by William Gardiner. How did you see them?"

Skinner hesitated, but Wright had the answer.

"We were above them looking down. The hedge is about ten feet from the chapel and perhaps we were six or seven feet further along it. Not more. Easy enough to see anyone in the dusk."

"How did you see them?" Holmes repeated. "In your evidence, you told the court that when you reached the chapel it was eight fifteen and getting dark, so that you could not see clearly what was happening inside. If you are to be believed, the man and woman did not leave until nine fifteen or nine twenty. When you verify the fact in your diary, you will see that the sun had set at seven fifteen. It may still have been getting dark, as you swore was the case, when you both reached the chapel at eight fifteen. By nine fifteen it was not dusk but pitch dark and had been so for up to half an hour."

There was silence in the little chapel for a moment before Holmes continued in the same level voice.

"Anyone coming from the chapel into the path that runs beside it would be in a canyon below the hedge. That path is unlit, the road beyond has no street lighting, the seed drill works would long ago have been in darkness. Further along, the road might be illuminated by the reflection from the windows of the houses, but near the chapel there are no houses. Even had there been a glimmer of light, every man that I have seen in Peasenhall—and in numerous photographs of Peasenhall—wears a similar cap, large and round. Every woman wears either a hat or a shawl—she wears the shawl over her head after dark. Identification might not have been easy in full daylight, yet you ask us to believe that it was simple, through a hedge, in complete darkness. I may have some say in what happens to you both as a result of the evidence you have given. Do not try my patience."

"They might have had oil lamps," said Wright desperately, "I do not recall."

Holmes nodded as if he accepted this, but Skinner could hardly restrain himself from glaring at his companion for the stupidity of the suggestion.

"I see. You do not recall it but they might have had oil lamps, might they? You have given evidence at the coroner's court, the magistrates' court, and twice at the assizes. Neither of you has mentioned a single oil lamp until now. Let that pass. They had oil lamps, did they? Yet rather than light them, they spent an hour in the chapel in total darkness, did they? They must have done so, for you took your Bible oath four times that it was too dark for you to see inside the building. Mrs. Crisp tells us that, next day, the chapel had been cleaned and even the hymn books put in the correct order and the numbers of the hymn board changed. A remarkable accomplishment in total darkness. Indeed, if you are correct, Rose Harsent had a lamp. Rather than light it, she did all this in darkness."

Neither of them answered him. Sherlock Holmes sat back in his chair and continued without mercy.

"If they had lamps, when did they light them?"

"I don't recall they did," said Skinner grimly.

"That is something else you do not recall." He was the quiet assassin now. "But they would have lit them before they left the chapel, surely. Why else carry them?"

"I suppose so." Skinner gave up the struggle.

"If you have spoken a word of truth between you, those lamps must have been lit long before. If your story is to be believed, Rose Harsent said of some mishap that might have stained or disfigured a surface, 'It won't be noticed.' How could she tell what would be noticed and what would not if she could not see it?"

"I don't know."

"If they lit lamps, you could have seen what was happening. You swear you could not. Therefore they did not have lamps and you could not have seen who it was that came out through the door."

Wright had given up and was staring at his feet. Skinner struggled in the net. I do not think, in all my experience of Sherlock Holmes, I had ever seen such a mixture of fear and anger as in the eyes of this young rustic. He was not done for yet.

"You do think yourself clever, Mr. Holmes, the Baker Street detective! Perhaps if you'd spent a little less time in London and a little more in the country, you might have learnt a good deal."

"I am always ready to learn," said Holmes humbly.

"Well then, look at the sky at night! You talk about it being pitch dark. That sky ain't pitch dark all the time. Moonlight and starlight show a good deal."

"I hardly think starlight would have illuminated the sunken path, hemmed in by shadow as it is."

"I daresay not, but moonlight would. With a clear sky and the moon almost at the full, as it was."

"You say the moon had risen?"

Skinner relaxed, as if he had sprung a trap on his victim.

"Of course it had risen, or we wouldn't have seen Rose and Mr. Gardiner, would we?"

"Dear me," said Holmes, "a perfect example of *petitio principii*, better known as begging the question. Do go on."

Skinner went on.

"Three nights before, on the Saturday, a dozen of us went rabbit-catching. We do that when the moon is full sometimes. I can give you the names of witnesses enough. We went off early, about seven or eight, seeing that was when the moon come up and crossed the southern sky, as it generally does. That night, the moon would have shone almost directly onto that chapel door, the path, the gate, and the road beyond. It rises always a few minutes later every night, don't it? We all know that. But not so much later as to make much odds only three nights after, when we saw what we saw at the chapel. Don't tell me what we could and couldn't have seen, Mr. Holmes. We were the ones that were there."

"Very well," said Holmes meekly, "then let me ask you one more thing and we shall have done."

My heart sank. Was this all? It seemed as if these two wretches might be almost safe in their tale of "seeing" Rose and her lover together at the chapel. Safe enough to hang William Gardiner. Skinner squared his shoulders confidently for the one more question. He truly seemed to think that he had beaten Sherlock Holmes at last.

"All right," he said magnanimously, "what do you want to know?"

"Who locked the chapel door?" asked Holmes in the same meek voice. "Mrs. Crisp and her husband found it locked as usual when they went there at half past eight on the following morning. You have both sworn that a woman left first on the evening before, Rose Harsent, if it was she. You did not follow her but waited for the man, William Gardiner, if it was he. You understand?"

"Well enough, I should say."

"Who locked the door that evening, for locked it was and locked it was found the next morning?"

Wright joined in.

"Gardiner must have done that. He was the last to leave. It can't have been anyone else, can it?"

"It cannot," said Holmes in the same subdued voice. "And you followed Gardiner, did you not? According to your evidence, Skinner caught up with him almost at once. Let me see. Here we are: 'I walked level with him for about twenty yards.' You then stood at the crossing and watched him continue home down the main street of Peasenhall, which is simply called the Street? Is that correct?"

"Of course it is," said Skinner with a slight laugh at the absurdity of it all. Sherlock Holmes changed his manner in a split second. He came in, as they say, for the kill.

"Kindly do not laugh, Skinner; a man's life depends on our conversation this afternoon. So does your liberty for the next seven years and that of your foolish friend. All this was at nine twenty, you say?"

"I have said so in court. It was nine twenty or perhaps by then nine thirty."

"Mrs. Crisp was able to tell us this afternoon that long before nine twenty, let alone nine thirty, the key to the chapel was safely locked in a drawer of her desk. Gardiner could not have used it to lock the chapel door."

"Then he did not lock it!"

"Mr. and Mrs. Crisp found it securely locked the next morning. According to your sworn testimony, you watched Gardiner walk home from the Doctor's Chapel. Rose Harsent was nowhere around. You did not follow her when she left and had gone on ahead. Gardiner, also according to your evidence, did not approach the door of Providence House. To use your own words in court, he walked straight past it."

"Then. . . ."

"I am there before you, Skinner. Then, perhaps, Gardiner returned in the middle of the night, burgled Providence House, ransacked the desk, forced open the drawer, took the key to the chapel, and locked it? Or Rose Harsent got up in the middle of the night, broke open the desk, and took the key for the same purpose. By a fairy's magic wand, all trace of breaking and entering vanished before Mrs. Crisp went to her desk the next morning. And all this happened at a time when neither the man nor the woman in your story had any idea that they had been watched—and therefore they had no reason for doing it. In any case, they would have thought that early next morning would do just as well for locking the chapel."

"It must have. . . ."

"Do not tell me what must have happened, Skinner. Had you been a little more skilled in falsehood, you would have invented a story in which Gardiner caught up with Rose and handed her the key before he went home. If there were a word of truth in anything you have sworn to, Gardiner could not have given the unlocked chapel door a second thought and it would have been still unlocked next day—which it was not. Had he been uneasy, he would have hurried after Rose Harsent, got the key, and gone back to lock it then and there, which you swear he did not. My only regret in all this is that public flogging has been abolished for willful perjury."

It was a masterly cross-examination. He had them by the throat as perhaps only Sir Edward Marshall Hall might have done in a court of law. Neither of these surly young fellows could muster an answer, for they had expected only a repetition of the more kindly questions asked at the assize court. But still he had not quite done with them.

"Before we are rid of you this afternoon, I will add one brief lesson in astronomy. The moon's orbit is somewhat more eccentric than that of the earth round the sun, where sunset and sunrise have a more regular principle. In the autumn, the time of the moon's rising will scarcely vary from one night to the next. Therefore, when it rises just after dusk, it is good moonlight to make hay by, the so-called Harvest Moon. In October it is Hunter's Moon. Unfortunately for you, the springtime month of which you speak is one when the differences in the moon's rising are far greater from day to day, sometimes more than an hour and often fifty minutes between one night and the next. The fact that the moon rose conveniently for you at seven thirty P.M. on Saturday means that it would not rise three days later until after ten o'clock. At nine twenty, in the darkness of that alley below the hedge, you could not have seen a single thing by moonlight to which you have sworn in court, even had those things taken place."

They hung their heads, but still he had not done with them.

"Every item of your evidence taken together is now exposed for what it always was—a tissue of vindictive lies. At first you told these falsehoods for motives of malice, to ruin the lives of an innocent man and woman, a man whom you despised as 'Holy Willie.' Then murder was done, and you dared not confess your slanders."

In the matter of his reputation, William Gardiner was triumphant. Sherlock Holmes had fought the two bullies to a standstill, and they stood silent before him.

He spoke once more before Eli Nunn led them out.

"Repeat your vicious allegations in court once more and you will find that you have gone to sea in a sieve. I will myself lay an information against you with Inspector Lestrade as my witness. I will seek a warrant for your indictment on charges of willful perjury, for which you may be sent to penal servitude upon conviction for a term of seven years. Think on that."

There was a silence in the chapel as the door closed upon them. Even Lestrade and Ernest Wild sat in awe. Presently Wild turned to the Chief Inspector.

"I cannot anticipate what you will say to the solicitor-general, Mr. Lestrade, but I must tell you this. If there is a third attempt to try William Gardiner for murder, after all that you have heard and he has suffered, I do not think the Crown will offer those two scoundrels as witnesses on its behalf. However, I promise you that I shall subpoena them for the defense, as hostile witnesses, and treat them as Mr. Holmes has treated them this afternoon."

Lestrade got to his feet and shuffled his papers together. His bulldog gruffness had softened and he almost smiled.

"It is not in my gift to decide such matters, Mr. Wild, only to make my recommendations. However, after what we have seen and heard this afternoon, I do not think you will be called upon to do anything of the kind."

7

WHATEVER LESTRADE'S FAILINGS as a detective, the inspector was a man of honour. He had given his word that his recommendation to the Metropolitan commissioner of police, and thence to the Director of Public Prosecutions, should be based upon the evidence. He was not to be influenced by the local prejudice that had brought William Gardiner so close to the gallows trap and the unmarked grave by the prison wall. My own part has been to reveal, for the first time, the role played in the famous Peasenhall case by Sherlock Holmes.

The world knew in a day or two that William Gardiner would not be called upon for a third time to stand trial for the murder of Rose Harsent. Yet innocent though he was, he and his family were punished by public opinion. He was forced to leave his home in Alma Cottage and take his wife and children to London, where their future lives were hidden in its twenty thousand streets.

At dusk on the day when the end of the prosecution was announced, as a soft January snowfall began to cover the stretches of Baker Street beyond the window, Holmes stood looking out at the smoky sky, from which the large flakes were falling slowly through the first yellow flush of lamplight.

"*Fiat justitia, ruat coelum*," he said thoughtfully, drawing the velvet curtains and turning to the firelight. "'Let justice be done, though the heavens fall.' The heavens are certainly falling at the moment, rather pleasantly, and justice has been done to William Gardiner in ample measure."

He sat down and began to fill his pipe with the black shag tobacco that he habitually kept in a Persian slipper, a souvenir of some long-forgotten adventure.

"Tell me," I said, "did you ever believe the man to be guilty? Was your promise to Lestrade of being willing to find him innocent or not anything but a blind, as they say?"

He looked into the crackling logs of the fire and sighed.

"You see, Watson? You are too quick for me, as usual. I decided at the outset that I could not appear to be a counsel for the defence, for that would have turned Lestrade into the prosecutor as well as the judge. It was obvious from the start that the slanders that Wright and Skinner spread about the poor fellow were false. They were demonstrably false upon common sense and deduction. It really mattered nothing whether one believed Gardiner and his wife. The importance attached to her evidence and his was the red herring in the case. It was the one crucial error committed by Ernest Wild that he made so much seem to depend upon it."

"It was not thought beside the point in court."

He waved this aside like the smoke of his pipe.

"It was why the jury nearly convicted him, all but one man. The whole thing was settled in my mind by the impossibilities in the slanderers' stories. Such people can rarely spread lies without giving themselves away. Mr. Wild did not quite appreciate the extent of this. He is good and we shall hear more of him, but after all he is not Sir Edward Marshall Hall and never will be. He never even suggested, I think, that Gardiner could not have left the chapel last and yet the door was found locked next morning. He did not point out that two hours after sunset it was pitch dark and yet Skinner claimed to identify two people, seen in total darkness through a hedge, on a path below him and a little distance away."

"It has been pointed out now," I said quietly.

"When they were cornered, of course, they said there must have been a lantern and that was when I knew we had them! The whole story was an impossibility."

"And they were wrong about the moon."

He paused a moment.

"There, Watson, I must confess a small subterfuge. I do not know when the moon rose that night, though the nightly intervals of its rising are certainly far longer at that time of year, more than an hour sometimes between one night and the next. I did not know that it was pitch dark rather than moonlight at the time they claimed to have seen such goings-on. Yet, faced with the challenge, nor did they. For me, that was the final proof of their malice, dishonesty, and stupidity."

"You used a trick?"

"A trick if you care to call it that. What is in a name? Our friend Professor Jowett used to say much the same of logic. Logic, he said, is neither an art nor a science. Logic is a dodge."

Having had enough of this, he reached for his violin case.

"While you were out yesterday, I made some small improvements to my prelude and fugue on the theme of 'Pop Goes the Weasel.' It is, I believe, now ready for Messrs. Augeners' attention. Ah! I see from your expression that I have played it to you before, I think?"

"Just the other evening."

"Nonetheless," he said happily, "you might care to hear it again."

4

THE CASE OF THE PHANTOM CHAMBER-MAID

1

IT WAS A COOL MIDSUMMER MORNING, during the week in which the Poisons Bill was before a House of Commons select committee. After a glimpse of early sun, a thin mist had gathered over the pale blue Baker Street sky, even while I read a summary of the previous day's proceedings from the parliamentary columns of the *Times*. I folded the paper and was about to say something to Holmes concerning the deficiencies of the new law, when he rose from his chair, stooped to the fireplace, took a cinder with the tongs, and applied it to the bowl of his cherrywood pipe. The red silk dressing gown made his tall, gaunt figure seem even taller and gaunter in the faint sunlight. Puffing at the pipe and staring down into the grate with his sharp profile, he spoke thoughtfully.

"The season is passing, Watson, and it is high time we got away. Everywhere else the sun must be shining. In London, it might as well be February. Do you not feel it? Even the footpads of the East End will have deserted us for Margate sands. Life has become commonplace, the newspapers are sterile, audacity and romance seem to have passed for ever from the criminal world."

I was well used to these periodic outbursts of self-pity.

"We might take lodgings for a week or two at one of the Atlantic resorts," I said hopefully, "Ilfracombe or Tenby, perhaps. There is also a standing invitation from the Exmoor cousins at Wiveliscombe."

He turned a tragic face to me and groaned.

"One of those unwelcome summonses that call upon a man either to be bored or to lie."

I thought it best to ignore this passing dismissal of my family. I said, rather brusquely, "Once the matter in hand is dealt with, you have no further commitments. You may travel where you please and for as long as you please."

He groaned again.

"The matter in hand! Oh, Watson, Watson! The Reverend Mr. Milner, Mrs. Deans, and her daughter Effie. A girl who was, I understand, a chambermaid at the Royal Albion Hotel in Brighton and was, I also understand, dismissed because someone saw her enter the room of a gentleman during the night. Really, Watson! Why should I care if a hundred chambermaids enter the rooms of a hundred gentlemen—or whether they are discharged from their employment or not? No one suggests that anything was stolen from this room—from any room, indeed. Merely that this young woman was seen entering during the night. That such a case should attract the least attention attests to the triumph of the banal in our society."

"You have often remarked, old fellow, that it is the banal and the commonplace that are the hallmarks of major crime."

"Well, well," he said grudgingly, "that, at any rate, is true."

He went off to his room and for several minutes I heard him banging about, making a quite unnecessary disturbance. When he returned he had changed his dressing-gown for a black velvet jacket.

"The Royal Albion Hotel." He sat down and sighed. "I smell the tawdry odour of its brown Windsor soup from sixty miles away."

It was half past ten when a cab stopped below our windows and there was a sound of voices. When the Reverend James Milner had wired to make his appointment, he informed me that he and two members of his Brighton flock would take an early train from their seaside homes and be with us by eleven o'clock. He was, I gathered, superintendent of the Wesleyan Railway Mission in the town, ministering to the workers and families in the little streets that cluster round the lofty terminus of the London Brighton and South Coast Railway.

Mrs. Deans and Effie had brought their trouble to him. In a most quixotic gesture, he had decided to announce the child's trouble to the famous Sherlock Holmes.

They were an odd trio. Mr. Milner in his black cloth suit and tall white clerical collar lacked the more exotic qualities of other clergy and could only have been a plain Methodist minister. His sleek hair was prematurely gray, but his spectacles gave him a youthfully studious look. Mrs. Deans, in a flowery summer dress, came up our Baker Street staircase like a cruiser under full sail. Her round face and porkpie bonnet gave her the air of one who could hold her own. I could imagine this doughty person with her sleeves rolled up to drub the washing in its bowl or give what-for to anyone who exchanged cross words with her. When I heard that the terrace of cramped little houses in which the Deans family lived was called Trafalgar Street, I saw her at once as one of those formidable women who had sailed on HMS *Victory* to Nelson's famous battle and had loaded the great guns for their menfolk to fire.

Effie Deans, the subject of this consultation, was probably no more than fifteen or sixteen, a chubby or cherubic girl with a cluster of fair curls under a blue straw boater. In the circumstances, it was not surprising that her prettiness was clouded by apprehension.

"Gentlemen," said Mr. Milner, once Holmes had sat us all down, "what may be a matter of sport to the rest of the world is life and death to the honor of Miss Deans and her mother."

Mrs. Deans nodded emphatically. The minister continued.

"Effie Deans has been dismissed from a post that she had held for almost two years, sent away without a reference or a character, for an offence which she cannot have committed. The gentleman in question made no complaint against her—indeed, it seems he was not even questioned. A hotel porter claims that he saw her enter the room during the night. He reported the matter and she was dismissed next day, despite her most positive denials. I have known her as a good, honest, and truthful girl, who attended the Wesleyan Mission Sunday school every week of her childhood."

Holmes had been staring at him with a curiosity that was discourteous, if not hostile.

"Unfortunately, Mr. Milner, what you know her to be is not the issue. Let us keep to the facts. If Miss Deans is as bad as Jezebel, it matters nothing so long as she was not there and did not enter that room. If she was there and did enter it, she may be as good and truthful as you like, but she was guilty of the fact and was properly dismissed. Let us have no more of Sunday school, if you please. It will not get us very far."

Holmes was in an unfortunate mood. He should never have mentioned Jezebel, to judge by the look on the face of Mrs. Deans and the flush that rose from her neck to her cheeks. No Baker Street detective was to say such a thing of her daughter. Before Milner could add a word, she let fly.

"See here, Mr. Holmes! It's not just that my Effie is a good girl and wouldn't have done it. She was at home all night and *couldn't* have done it!"

He admired her spirit.

"Excellent, madam! You have, if I may say so, an unerring grasp of the laws of evidence. Pray continue."

The Reverend Mr. Milner was out in the cold now.

"Well, sir," Mrs. Deans went on, "she come home as usual close on half past eight that evening. Don't take my word for it. We had the Todgers."

"Todgers, madam?"

"Them that live next door. Had them in for a hand or two of whist and Beat-Jack-out-of-doors, also a glass of shrub and a pipe."

I swear I saw in my mind Mrs. Deans smoking her pipe with the rest.

"I assume they were not with you until two in the morning?"

"Near midnight. They saw her all the time. Then we went to bed. She went to her little room in the attic. To get out, she comes down through the room where Alf and I sleep. I laid awake an hour and more with my stomach after the shrub. How could she come down and I not see nor hear her? How could she unbolt the downstairs door and go out without I hear her—or without Alf seeing it when he gets up at three? Which he must do to go on early turn at the railway goods yard at four. And don't tell me, Mr. Holmes, that I can't prove what I say. Do I look the sort that'd let her daughter go out on the streets at one or two in the morning and never say a word?"

"No, madam," said Holmes uncertainly, "indeed you do not. In any court proceedings, however, you will be asked the following question: Why should this porter, whoever he was, say that he saw your daughter entering a guest's room at one or two o'clock that morning, if he could not have done so?"

Her eyes narrowed as she looked at him.

"Yes, Mr. Holmes! Oh, yes! I'd like him asked that question! I'd like him asked good and proper, in such a way as he wouldn't forget being asked for a very long time!"

If ever a woman had captivated Holmes in quarter of an hour, it was Mrs. Deans. The Reverend Mr. Milner had given up. His parishioner was doing his job far better than he could have done it for himself. Holmes stretched out his long thin legs, and when he looked up, his eyes were brighter than I had seen them for a long time.

"It seems," said Mr. Milner hastily, "that the night porter said he recognized her in part by her uniform, the black dress, white apron, and white cap. Of course, that might have been worn by someone else, though it is not clear why anyone else wishing to enter the room should have bothered to put the uniform on. Whoever did so can hardly have expected to do it without disturbing the occupant."

"Quite so," said Holmes thoughtfully. "What do we know of the gentleman who occupied the room? He was alone, I take it?"

"He was talked about in the town during the weeks since he came there." Mrs. Deans had once again got in ahead of the Reverend Mr.

Milner. "A spiritual gentleman. Always seeing ghosts, he said. Something to do with the Society for Cyclical Research."

"Society for Psychic Research," Mr. Milner said quickly. She stared at him, then turned back to Holmes.

"They say he saw that many ghosts, he had to put himself to sleep at night with clara-something from a smelling bottle. My girl could still smell it next morning. And he had a rumpus with the showfolk at the Brighton Aquarium. Professor Chamberlain and Madame Elvira that do tricks with ghosts and guessing. He thought he was superior to all that tommyrot. The Brighton papers wouldn't print his letters nor theirs for fear of being took to court."

I looked at Holmes. An extraordinary change had gradually come over his face during these exchanges with their hints of ghosts and fraud. His eyes were shining like two stars with a hint of enthusiasm ill-contained. His hands gripped the arms of the chair and I almost thought he might spring from it. The Reverend Mr. Milner got in his twopenny-worth at last.

"The gentleman in question is a spiritualist," he said quickly. "Mr. Edmund Gurney is a scholar and a gentleman who resents the cheapening of his beliefs by the mind-reading entertainments, mesmerism, and trances at the Aquarium, as do all those who take a sincere interest in such matters. His own work for the Psychical Research Society is at a far superior level. He is, I understand, a classical scholar of Trinity College, Cambridge, a friend of Dr. Frederick Myers and his circle. He is certainly a musicologist and has written upon the theories of sound. His particular interest appears to be in what are called phantasms of the living. That is to say, the possibility that we may have a vision of those we know or love at a crisis in their lives, not infrequently at the moment of their deaths. It is the case of a man who sees at the end of his garden path the figure of a friend whom he had believed to be still in India. He then hears that the friend was, indeed, still in India and that he had died at the moment of the apparition."

Holmes had listened to this last revelation with eyes closed and fingertips pressed together. He now looked up.

"Mr. Edmund Gurney sounds an admirable gentleman. I cannot believe that it is any of his doing that Effie has been dismissed. Indeed, if what you say is true, Mrs. Deans, it seems that he sleeps with the aid of a soporific and may well not have known anything of this incident. This is a curious and, indeed, intriguing inconsistency. My dear Mr. Milner! My dear Mrs. Deans! My dear Miss Effie, if I may so address you. You may count upon this difficulty of yours receiving my fullest and most immediate attention. This enigma is almost more than I had deserved!"

"You will take the case?" Milner asked nervously.

"Mr. Milner, I could not do otherwise. Indeed, you may depend upon Dr. Watson and myself being in Brighton by this evening. You yourselves must return there forthwith. I shall ask Mrs. Hudson to summon the boy. A wire must go to the post office at once engaging rooms for us."

Milner eased his starched clerical collar with a forefinger.

"In the matter of your fee, sir. My friends are scarcely in a position. . . ."

"We will not talk of a fee, if you please. Some things, my dear Milner, are more than money to me."

"Then where shall we find you? Where will you stay?"

Holmes, mystified by the question, looked at him.

"Where else should we put up but at the *locus in quo*?"

This stumped all three of them.

"Why," said Holmes blithely, "at the Royal Albion Hotel, Mr. Milner. We may even learn to relish its cuisine."

The change that had overtaken Sherlock Holmes since his sullen mood after breakfast would hardly have been believed by those who did not know him well. He had pined for adventure and challenge. Now that this had presented itself, if only in the form of a dismissed chambermaid, he was transformed by an excess of energy. Though he sometimes used to talk of retiring to the Sussex downs and keeping bees, I swear he could not have endured it for more than a fortnight.

That afternoon we took tea in the Pullman car of the express that whirled us to Brighton, the sunlit fields and downs of Sussex spinning away from us, the sun glittering on the sea ahead. The light was in his eyes again. He hummed or sang quietly some battle hymn of his own throughout the journey until our train drew into Brighton and we felt a light ocean breeze on our faces.

2

So it was, upon my friend's impulse, that we had left the comforts of our quarters in Baker Street for an indefinite spell of indifferent cooking and the sound of breakers on shingle carrying to our ears at the Royal Albion Hotel. Within two hours of leaving London, we had moved into our suite, a spacious sitting-room with our bedrooms to either side. Its windows enjoyed a view across the busy esplanade to a broad expanse of waves that stretched between us and the coast of France sixty miles way. At this time of year, the edge of the sea was a promenade for mothers in full skirts, blouses, and straw boaters, fathers in their best suits and hats. Children gathered excitedly before the puppet booth of the Punch and Judy show on the beach when its little trumpet announced each performance.

We soon accustomed ourselves to the daily round. Each morning, several ponies drew the wheeled cabins of the ladies' bathing machines down to the water's edge and pulled them back up at sunset. The regimental band of the Coldstream Guards played briskly every afternoon at two P.M. on the far end of the old Chain Pier, while bearded fishermen mended their nets on the lower esplanade. Fishing boats and yachts lay drawn up on the shingle, except for a few jolly little craft like the *Honeymoon* and the *Dolly Varden*, which bobbed and twisted in the swell with their apprehensive passengers.

Within an hour of our arrival, we were sitting down to an early "theatre" dinner provided by these seaside hotels for patrons who have booked seats at some theatrical performance. Holmes, in one of those infuriating moods which took him from time to time, would say nothing beyond remarking, "There is not a moment to be lost." On the contrary, I thought, we seemed to have all the time in the world. He withdrew behind the *Evening Globe* while the waiter attempted to serve us *turbot a la mayonnaise*. The Royal Albion was a large, solid building, now past its best, which qualities were reflected in its menu. Holmes ate rapidly but in silence, evidently turning over possibilities in his mind. Even before the coffee was served, he pushed back his chair and stood up.

"Come, Watson. I think it is time we were on our way."

As we came out into the evening sunlight of the esplanade, I was about to ask him what our way might be. Before I could do so, he very pointedly drew a deep breath, swelled out his chest, tapped his cane sharply on the paving of the esplanade and said, "How good it is to breathe sea air again after a winter of London fogs. What was it that they called this town in the days of the good King George III? They nicknamed it Doctor Brighton, I recall. And not without reason."

"I daresay I should breathe a lot more clearly if I knew where the blazes we were going."

He looked at me in astonishment. "But you must have known, my dear friend. You heard the tale told this morning, of second sight and phantasms of the living. Where should we go for entertainment on our very first evening in Brighton but to the lecture-room of the

Aquarium, apparently disapproved of by Mr. Gurney, for a display of Professor Chamberlain's magical accomplishments with the talented Miss Elvira. Their names are on the bill over there."

So that was it. Why such vulgar entertainment should be of the least use to our defence of Effie Deans was quite beyond me.

If you have ever visited Brighton, you will know that the Aquarium has less to do with sea creatures than with popular entertainment. It stands under its famous clock tower just at the landward end of the Chain Pier with its strings of colored lanterns. We paid our sixpences and passed through the turnstiles to a land of fairy lights and fireworks. Among the shows and exhibitions advertised, its theatre offered Madame Alice Barth's Operetta Company in the Garden Scene from *Faust* and "Dr. Miracle," a one-act piece never performed before. Holmes led the way to the plainer fare offered by the lecture theater which was placarded by "Professor Chamberlain's Experiments in Mesmerism and Thought-Reading."

At the door, a newspaper review was displayed under glass. It was a cutting from the *Brighton Herald*, praising the excitement of last Saturday's performance, when "Dr. Mesmer" had hypnotised a youth and a girl. The youth was subjected to kickings and prickings, the girl to abuse and mockery. When brought back to consciousness, each of the dupes smilingly acknowledged the applause and confessed to having no memory of the ordeal. A heckler in the front row who had denounced the display loudly as a "put-up job" was thrown out of the hall by several members of the large and excited audience. I cannot pretend that this was the entertainment I should have chosen for my first night in Brighton.

Across a bill advertising the show was a more recent banner still damp with paste. It announced that Professor Chamberlain and his medium, Madame Elvira, had been retained by other managements to provide "select high-class seances for the popularizing of phenomenal science." In consequence, this week must be the last of their present season in Brighton. It seemed that they had been in residence at the Aquarium during most of the summer so far.

We paid a further shilling and were ushered to seats near the front of what was not so much a lecture hall as a music hall or a palace of varieties. It seemed less crowded than on a Saturday night, but the buzz of excitement was still unmistakable. Professor Chamberlain, playing the role of Dr. Mesmer with an electrical magnet, first invited several victims onto his platform and made some magic passes over them. They then submitted to a few blows without apparent resentment. Among roars of approval from the onlookers, they also performed as though they believed themselves to be dogs or cockerels, infants at feeding time, or soldiers at drill. They finally woke up at the snap of their master's fingers, remembering nothing. For half an hour we endured this sort of thing. Nothing would have been easier to counterfeit.

Chamberlain was a broad-shouldered young man with a flop of pale gold hair aslant his forehead and penetrating blue eyes. He was, I suppose, the type who might be handsome to a shopgirl or a maidservant, perhaps because there was a common look to him that brought him within every female's grasp. Yet the more one looked at him, the more his youthfulness came into question. He was like a modern French painting, best seen from a distance, since cracks and crevices appear on closer inspection. As I studied him during his performance, I thought that after all he was not so much a young man as the ideal of what an indulgent old woman might think a young man should be. In this, at least, I was to be proved right. Quite probably he would never see forty again and must have spent some time each day concealing the fact. Perhaps his appearance alone would not have mattered quite so much had it not been for his voice, or rather its confident twang. It was not so much an accent as a distortion of his speech, which might equally well have been acquired in the stockyards of Chicago or the dockside of Liverpool. It seemed to me that he had no real voice at all, merely a self-confident nasal bray.

Presently the audience fell silent, as if it knew that we had come to the serious business of the evening. Whatever flippancy had been evident in Chamberlain until now, he became as solemn and as insinuating as the Reverend Mr. Milner could ever have been in the pulpit of his Wesleyan Railway Mission.

We were introduced to Madame Elvira, a shrewish little person with ginger hair. She was wearing a dress of electric blue with white ruffs. It seems that she was blessed with gifts of many kinds, including "second sight," which may have been the least of her accomplishments, if Professor Chamberlain were to be believed.

"Madame Elvira was born in the Middle West, where her ancestry included Indian blood from the tribes who fought at Fort Duquesne a century and more ago. She lived many years of her childhood as a friend of those tribes with the most happy results. By long practice and sympathetic attention she has attuned her spirit to those of the dead warriors and chiefs by whom messages from the beyond are so often brought to us."

"Which is to say," remarked Holmes softly, "that Madame Elvira has very probably never been further west than the terminus of the Hammersmith railway."

The professor explained that a man whom Madame Elvira had never seen nor heard of might write his name upon a card. The card would then be handed to the professor, who would stare at it long enough and hard enough to fix the image of the signature in his mind. Twenty feet or more away from him, Madame Elvira would sit at a typewriter with her back to him. She would be blindfolded by volunteers from the audience. The image in the mind of the professor would then be transmitted to that of his protegée, before our eyes. She would type it correctly on a sheet of paper without removing her blindfold. Rarely in the past had she been mistaken and even then only in a syllable or so.

The professor called for several more volunteers to do the blindfolding and see fair play. He was down among the audience now, handing out several dozen blank cards to those of us in the front rows. On these we were to write our names and individual seat numbers. When the cards had been gathered in, he invited a woman in the first row to stand upon the stage and shuffle them like playing cards so that there could be no question of any prearranged order. Then he sprang back behind the footlights. Madame Elvira sat patiently at her table before the typewriter. Her back was toward Professor Chamberlain and the audience as she clenched and stretched her fingers, no doubt in preparation for her task. Two other women were still blindfolding her to their satisfaction.

The professor in his swallowtail evening coat addressed his public in his confident twang.

"Thank you very much, ladies and gentlemen. In a moment we shall come to the highlight of our evening and our seance will begin, as soon as the two good ladies who have volunteered to ensure that my partner cannot by any means see me or any clue I might give her have completed their task. We have all heard of cheats in the thought-reading profession who signal to one another, haven't we? Eyes right for hearts, left for diamonds, up for clubs, and down for spades. One wink for an ace, two for a court card. We know all about that, don't we? Of course we do! And we aren't having it here, are we? Of course we aren't! What you see before you now is genuine second sight, authentic mind-reading. It may succeed, it may fail. One thing you may depend upon, ladies and gentlemen, is that it is entirely genuine."

He had all the panache of a man who sends you a dishonored bill with a note to say that payment is guaranteed.

"I have here fifty cards, ladies and gentlemen, each with the number of a seat and the name of a customer. I shall look at each in turn because, you understand, in order that second sight may operate it is necessary that another person should first see them and transmit them. But I shall do more than that. It is when thoughts are transferred in this way that the mind is most open to messages from the spirit world. For that reason, I shall also repeat to you whatever messages come to my mind as I hold the card before me. I cannot promise you there will be such messages, of course. I am in the hands of those beyond the veil who transmit them. What vulgar people call ghosts. However, whatever messages I have for those who have written these cards shall be relayed to them."

Beside me I heard Holmes emit a despairing sigh. Professor Chamberlain had not finished.

"Blindfolded though she be, Madame Elvira has a magic touch with a typewriter. On that machine she will print out the name from each card as it appears in her mind. A copy shall be given to the lady or gentleman whose name and seat number appears upon it, thus putting her performance beyond any suspicion of trickery."

He was staring at the first card, as if to fix it in his mind. He closed his eyes.

"I address the gentleman who wrote this card—for it is a gentleman in this case. Now, sir, while Madame Elvira sees in her own mind the very image that has just left mine, my thoughts are wandering, open to whatever message may be waiting for you in the world of the spirits. That world is infinite and we, in our finiteness, may not easily interpret its signals. . . . I have something. I do not say I understand it, but the letters of the message begin to form in my mind. I see the word 'Death.' What follows? Now it comes to me. *Death is but some means of reawakening. . . .* Wait, there is more! *Think nothing joyful unless innocent. . . .*"

"Intolerable rubbish!" said Holmes *sotto voce.*

Chamberlain opened his eyes. It was possible to hear the brief rattle of the typewriter keys, the ting of its bell, and the whiz of the paper being drawn clear. A volunteer from the audience who had helped to blindfold the girl brought the writing to him. Chamberlain came forward to the footlights.

"The number of the seat is twenty-four and the gentleman sitting in it is Mr. Charles Smith. The messages from another world are also typewritten upon the card."

There was a murmur of expectation. Chamberlain stabbed a finger dramatically through the limelight, towards seat twenty-four.

"Am I right, sir?"

I could just catch a murmur and a nod.

"Have I ever met you before, air? Are we known to one another?"

Another murmur and a shaking of the head.

"Do you understand how the message applies to you?"

A briefer, less certain nod. An assistant or runner carried the piece of typed paper to the man who had been named, as if it were a prize. This seaside entertainment began to intrigue me. Holmes affected boredom. We went through a dozen names, each embellished by strange "messages" from the hereafter that combined the impenetrably obscure and the blindingly self-evident. If it was a trick, I could not make out how the devil it was done. The girl could see nothing and yet she was never wrong.

The minutes passed and now he had taken another card at which he was staring. I heard him say, "A message is coming clearly to me but from very far off. I beg you will keep silence, ladies and gentlemen. . . . Perhaps it is directed to a professional gentleman, a man of learning. It is in two parts . . . or even three. . . . I hear the first one. *Knowledge protects its opposite*. . . . And then, *Experience brings understanding*. . . . Wait, there is one more! *Time precedes oblivion*. . . . Ladies and gentlemen, the meaning of much of this is hidden from me, but I have faith that it will be clear in some way to the recipient."

"That experience brings understanding is clear enough to a baboon!" said Holmes quietly beside me. "And unless I am much mistaken, my dear Watson, you are about to win a prize in a monkey show."

The typewriter rattled and the paper was brought back.

"The number of the seat is thirty-one and the customer is Mr. John Watson! Am I right, sir?"

"Yes!" I called back abruptly. "And I have never met you before."

"Congratulations," said Holmes acidly. "Why is it that I am the only one to see how the trick is done?"

This rigmarole continued on the stage. Then, without warning, Holmes began to mutter each correct name even before Madame Elvira could begin to type it. I was alarmed that he might be overheard and that we might be identified as spies. Presently, however, we received another instruction from the hereafter. *Triumph in false strife makes power destroy itself.* This was followed at once and even more dramatically by *I pledge my name for truth.*

"The seat is number thirty-two and the occupant is Mr. Sherlock Holmes."

His name meant nothing to the performers or their audience, I think, though I believe I heard a laugh from someone who perhaps thought him to be a wag playing a joke on the professor.

"Am I right, sir?"

"Indeed you are," said Holmes in his most charming manner, "and, of course, I have never had the pleasure of your acquaintance until now."

The scrap of typing was brought and he thrust it into his pocket.

The rest of the performance was a variant of this game. Cards were drawn from a pack and correctly guessed at. Once or twice Madame Elvira even pronounced in advance which card a volunteer would draw. Yet in all this there was nothing much beyond the manipulation of a deck of cards as a skilled poker cheat might have done it. The deck was torn from a manufacturer's wrapper each time, but that would not prevent it being tampered with. The whole thing reeked of the gaming saloon.

All the same, the audience seemed well pleased. Yet the second-sight act had soon become what they call "dead lead" to them. A moment later they were noisily applauding the return of the mesmerized when young men stooped, were kicked, and turned round to thank their assailant, as "Dr. Mesmer" had commanded them in advance, or young women barked like dogs and scuffled on all fours. This was far superior to messages from "the beyond" that sounded as if they might have a profound meaning and yet tortured the brain unendurably in any attempt to draw common sense from them.

I was ready to leave long before the end of the show, but Holmes seemed determined to see it through to the finish. Afterwards we took a final stroll along the deck of the Chain Pier while a crescent moon formed a thin path of pale glittering light all the way to Boulogne. I took the scrap of paper with my name typed upon it, screwed it up, and was about to throw it over the rail into the water.

"No!" said Holmes sharply. "That is our first trophy of the battle."

"A trophy of a wasted evening!"

He chuckled at this.

"A trophy of time well spent. You really could not see how it was done?"

"I suppose there was a trick," I said grudgingly. "All I saw was the fellow staring at a card, mumbling so-called philosophical remarks about knowledge, power, and staking one's soul for truth. Then the girl typed out the answer—the name on the card and the messages. Professor Chamberlain cannot have been a muscle-twitcher, that much is evident, for she could not see him. As for those spoken messages, how could there be a meaning in all that foolish babble?"

"Very easily, my dear fellow. In the first place, he talked a great deal, but only the messages from the spirit world were important."

"Did you hear mine? Knowledge protects its opposite. Experience brings understanding. Time precedes oblivion."

"Quite so. The kind of gibberish that seems to the simple-minded to be the wisdom of the ages. It quite occupies one in trying to decipher it while the real trick is pulled. Our Professor Chamberlain is a clever fellow, make no mistake of that. A clever fellow, although a ruffian and a fraud."

"Then there is a message in the gibberish?"

He threw back his head and laughed.

"Oh, there is, Watson! Indeed there is. Try the first letter of each word in your own message. Knowledge protects its own. Experience breeds understanding. Time precedes oblivion."

"K-I-P-O. E-B-U. T-P-O. It makes worse gibberish than ever."

"I confess that it took me until the third attempt to work it out. All the same it is a commonplace device. Now, replace each letter with the one in the alphabet which precedes it."

"J-O-H-N. W-A-T-S-O-N."

"Just so. John Watson. She could not see him, therefore it had to be a spoken code. Even then, the girl could not possibly have deciphered his endless verbiage; therefore, the clue must be contained in a few of the words. What else could provide it but those messages from the beyond? She is, I imagine, a simple soul, therefore the method must be consistent. The first letter of each word seemed likely. As I listened, I realized that it was not the first letter but that the number of words in the spirit messages exactly matched the number of letters in the customer's name. Ten in your case. Chamberlain did not, you observe, choose long names. I believe mine was the longest. Interesting, by the way, that it appeared to mean nothing to him. I daresay he has been abroad or in the colonies."

"And then?" I inquired.

"Quite. I deduced that it could not be the first letters of the words after all. That would have been too obvious to anyone in the audience with an ounce of sense. However, it would not be difficult for the girl to transpose each letter in the alphabet by one place. That would do it. Most of those people would give up after finding the initial letters did not work. For the rest, Chamberlain could alter the system a little each week during the weeks of their engagement. To be sure, he and the girl would probably be caught out in the end if they remained in one place long enough. That, however, they did not propose to do."

"He called me a man of learning."

"And so you are. We will not go into the matter of the way in which the brushing of your medical stethoscope wears away the nap of your waistcoat as it dangles there. Chamberlain is not clever enough to observe that. However, look at you against a sea of cockneys and yokels in such a place. Why, Mrs. Hudson's cat would appear a figure of learning in such company."

"With whom we have wasted an entire evening!"

He stopped and lowered his voice.

"Watson, our time has not been wasted. It is plain to me that our two pigeons are about to take wing. I should give a great deal to know why."

"Indeed?"

"You will have observed that there was scarcely an empty seat in that auditorium. They cannot be taking flight for lack of custom. Had they arranged another engagement, they would have known long before now and there would be no need to paste an urgent sticker across their advertisements. They have every reason to remain here. Moreover, why such haste to be gone? Today is Tuesday and it now seems they are obliged to close on Saturday."

"They must close somewhen and must announce it."

"Precisely but why was the paste on the closure stripper across their bill still wet? They are leaving a successful run with a minimum of notice. If you ask me, that has the mark of two people doing a bunk."

We reached the pier turnstile again and crossed the esplanade toward the hotel. In the lobby, Holmes went to the desk and began negotiations with the night porter. A large cream envelope embossed with a post office stamp was produced. A few coins changed hands. Holmes, dipping the pen in the white china inkwell, wrote a brief message on hotel notepaper and addressed the envelope. The night porter beckoned an infant pageboy who took the envelope, received a further coin, and disappeared into the night at a run.

When Holmes came back across the lobby, I noticed that he no longer carried the theatre program for Professor Chamberlain's antics, prefaced by photographs of the performer and his medium, the "professor" looking a good deal younger than he appeared in reality.

"Where has it gone?" I asked. He knew exactly what I was talking about.

"Little Billy, or whatever his name may be, is running for the midnight post from the railway station. I have every hope that by tomorrow morning those two most interesting faces will be on the desk of Inspector Tobias Gregson at Scotland Yard."

We withdrew to our quarters where we settled ourselves with whisky and tobacco. Holmes still kept up an irritating pretence that I had been taken in by Chamberlain's performance, merely because I had not at first seen how the tricks were done.

"Surely, my dear fellow, you did not believe that a common young fellow and girl like that were capable of reading one another's minds."

"I had not given the matter much thought," I said a little irritably. "It seemed scarcely worth it."

"Let us be thankful that it is not," he said, yawning. "If men and women up and down the land became capable of reading the thoughts in one another's minds, murders would be as common and disregarded as sixpenny coins. We, my dear fellow, might be looking for some other means of livelihood."

"And what of Miss Deans in all this? That poor child has lost her employment."

"You may be sure that I have not forgotten the plight of our young Miss Effie Deans. If I am to help her, however, I now require what out legal friends call further and better particulars. Let us turn our attention next to the mysterious Mr. Edmund Gurney to whom she is said to have made advances. A man whose life is devoted to phantasms of the living rather than voices of the dead and who seems to be that most interesting person—a chloroform addict who is either an eater or an inhaler. It is said that the girl was seen trying to enter his room at an unseemly hour. I should greatly like to know why the accusation was made, and, I daresay, the answer lies within that room. I believe that our next task must therefore be to search Mr. Gurney's room and his possessions quite thoroughly but without his knowledge. We should lose no time in doing so."

3

"THE THING IS QUITE IMPOSSIBLE," I said, for the fourth or fifth time. "There is no suggestion that Gurney has done anything criminal or improper. You cannot simply burgle a fellow guest in a respectable hotel! Even if a chambermaid entered his room during the night, that is the affair of the management. For its part, the management appears to feel that the question is settled. You may be sure that they will not let you in there."

"Burglary by night and housebreaking by day," he said, his eyebrows drawn down as if in deep thought. "It would, I suppose, be termed breaking and entering on premises such as these—were it not for the fact that you, my dear Watson, are the man to do it."

You may imagine that I was appalled by the suggestion.

"I shall do no such thing. Whatever you think we might find in there. . . ."

"I have no precise idea what we might find. However, let us drop the matter of burglary and consider the peculiar self-anaesthesia of Edmund Gurney."

I made no immediate answer to this, but the matter remained fixed in his thoughts. Presently he tried to revive the topic.

"It is a matter to interest a medical man, Watson. Mr. Gurney appears to be an habitué of chloroform, very probably an addict by this time. Oh, very well, let us put it more kindly and say that the poor fellow suffers from neuralgia. The anaesthetic dulls his pain sufficiently for him to enjoy a night's rest."

"What then?"

"The practice may nonetheless be lethal," Holmes insisted.

"It is foolish in the extreme but also difficult to prevent. Once a man is habituated to sleeping under the influence of chloroform, he may find it impossible to do without it."

"Precisely. If memory serves correctly, anything over two fluid ounces swallowed or inhaled is liable to prove fatal. The quantities are very small—so is the difference between life and death. In the hands of a layman, it must be a threat to life under any circumstances."

I began to see what was coming as he leant back in his chair.

"If someone approached you, Watson, and told you that there was a very strong smell of chloroform coming from a room where a man was sleeping, you would be prepared to investigate, as you would if there were an odor of escaping gas or a smell of smoke."

"I daresay. But who is going to tell me that?"

"The hotel manager, once I have had a word with him. You may be sure that he will not risk having one of his guests found dead in the morning. He is, after all, not the owner of the hotel and I fancy he would not keep his job long after an incident of that sort. Mr. Gurney, I have no doubt, lies sedated by fumes. He will be your patient for a few hours, if that seems reasonable. We shall both keep him company and I shall look around me."

I confess that I was filled with curiosity. What Holmes had first proposed now began to sound less heinous. Any medical man must thoroughly disapprove of these amateur experiments with anaesthetics, however great the discomforts of neuralgia. Such misuse will lead to addiction and the victim will never break himself of it. I might still have jibbed at what Holmes suggested. However, it would certainly give me the authority to have a straight talk with Gurney over the folly of these practices and a chance to put him on the proper path for treatment. That at least was in keeping with a doctor's Hippocratic oath. Moreover, Holmes's intention of merely looking around him seemed to fall far short of burglary.

So it was that on the following night, just after eleven o'clock, Holmes went to the hotel desk and alerted the manager to a strong smell of chloroform in the corridor outside Gurney's room. He voiced his fears of a tragedy but added that a doctor of considerable experience was his companion on this visit. Unless he was a complete fool, the Italian restaurateur who had been appointed by the owners to manage the hotel must have realized that his guest practised something like self-anaesthesia. Five minutes later the three of us stood in that corridor and I allowed myself to be persuaded that I could detect a sickly sweetish whiff of chloroform in the enclosed air, sufficient to suggest that a man breathing the enclosed air of the room was in danger.

The manager tapped lightly at the door, but Holmes had watched Gurney go up to his room after dinner and had timed his report accordingly. By now, I suspected, the foolish fellow was in the arms of Morpheus. Of course he was not anaesthetized as deeply as a patient would be for a surgical operation, but nor would he be easily roused within the next hour or two. I was not surprised when there was no response to the knock. We both looked at the manager, a Milanese of lean and cadaverous appearance, as if to imply that should there be a mishap, he was bound to be held accountable. To me, he looked more than ever like some mournful bird of prey.

He motioned us back, then slid his passkey into the lock and pushed open the sitting room door. In truth, there was an odour but it was suggestive of operating theaters generally and not overwhelmingly evident as chloroform. We waited. As many of my readers will be aware, Brighton was the first town in England to have a supply of electricity under the Electric Lighting Act of 1882, so that the manager had only to turn a switch in order to illuminate the sitting-room. It was furnished with a pair of armchairs, a table with two upright seats at it, and a bureau. To one side was the bedroom door, which had been closed but not locked. Within that was a further division with separate doors for bedroom and bathroom.

When the first inner door was opened, there was a definite odour of chloroform, so strong that I opened the bedroom door in fear of what I might find. The dose had been potent enough for Edmund Gurney to succumb to sleep even before he could turn off the light. Yet nothing had prepared me for the grotesque spectacle that I now saw. He lay on the bed in the stark electric glare, wearing his nightshirt, the upper part of his body propped against the headboard. His body had slumped at an angle and his head was almost entirely encased in a rubber sponge bag, which he had drawn down far enough to cover his nostrils and mouth. His practice was evidently to soak the rubber bag in a measure of chloroform and then draw it over his head as he lay down to sleep. It was dangerous and foolish in the extreme, for he had no means of controlling the amount he ingested. He was a perfect subject for "The Hypochondriac's Tragedy."

First of all the sponge bag must come off. As I pulled it clear, he hardly stirred and I prayed that, this time, he had not gone beyond recall. His face was deathly pale, the countenance of a tall, lanky, big-boned fellow, perhaps forty years old. His blue eyes were a fraction open, but I am sure he saw nothing. The moustache was lank and the hair combed like thatch down either side of his head. I took his wrist and felt a pulse, which was stronger and steadier than I had feared. Perhaps, like so many habitués, his constant use had hardened him to the effects of the fumes. Holmes meanwhile had opened the window and fresh air began to drift into the room. I turned to the manager, who was hovering over us. There was no need to use deceit, for what I told him was the perfect truth.

"You had better leave him to me for an hour or so. His life is not in immediate danger from the chloroform, which will pass off slowly. However, it may sometimes act as an emetic. If that were to happen when he is deeply asleep, there is a risk that he might choke on his own vomit without waking."

I did not add that it was a remote risk. All the same, had such a thing happened after I had abandoned him to return to my room, matters would certainly not have gone well for me at an inquest. The manager's relief was tinged with apprehension.

"You do not ask for an ambulance or a doctor from the hospital? There will be no police?"

"It would serve no purpose. He must be watched for an hour or two. That is all."

In his gratitude, I thought he might seize my hand and kiss it. He had, of course, dreaded the publicity that hospitals and ambulances—let alone the police—bring to an establishment like his. Holmes and I did not appear to him as the types who would tell the story round the streets of Brighton.

"Mr. Holmes has some experience in medical matters," I said to him reassuringly. "He can watch for me if I should be out of the room at any time."

I did not add that my friend's experience in medical matters, such as it was, usually concerned those who were already dead. Indeed, the manager with his thin, stooping gait and black clothes might have graced an undertaker's parlour. He now withdrew in a fusillade of thanks and assurances while promising to be at beck and call if he were needed.

Holmes closed the door as the man left and came into the bedroom.

"Well done, Watson! A first-rate performance!"

I looked at Gurney; I was convinced that I could have fired my revolver into the ceiling without waking him.

"It was no act, I assure you, Holmes. His pulse is a little above normal. In the case of poisoning by chloroform, the rate may rise to one hundred forty or more, at which it is fatal. If it should increase now, I shall indeed summon whatever assistance is needed. He has taken a dose sufficient to put him to sleep. At least he is not one of those chloroform-eaters who prove to be suicides."

"Or victims of murder," said Holmes casually. "You will find at least three recent cases in Caspar-Liman's *Handbook of Medicine*. Let us hope we can prevent anything of that kind. If someone were able to enter this room, think how easily they could pour a further thimble or two of chloroform over that sponge bag with the poor fellow already unconscious and knowing nothing further. You know how little coroners and coroners' juries are to be depended upon. The whole thing would be put down to the dead man's folly."

He withdrew to the sitting room and I could hear him moving about. I left Gurney for a moment and went into the bathroom to find the chloroform. It was necessary to calculate, if possible, what dose he might have taken. I opened the cabinet and undid the top of a dark green bottle to smell the sweet and colourless contents. A fatal dose would probably have been between four and six ounces. Not more than an ounce or two had been used from this bottle altogether, some of it perhaps on a previous night. That, at least, was a welcome discovery.

From what little I knew of the man, I was not surprised that the rest of the cabinet contained an array of patent medicines and quack remedies. Carter's Little Liver Pills, Beecham's Powders, and the respectable potions of their kind rubbed shoulders with the Patent Carbolic Smoke Ball Inhaler, guaranteed to prevent influenza, Kaolin-and-Opium for the dysenteric, Propter's Nicodemus Pills or "The Old Man Young Again," Klein's Opening Medicine by Royal Appointment, Chocolate Iron Tonic, and goodness knows what. Holmes appeared in the doorway.

"What have you found?"

"Only that the poor wretch has turned his digestive tract into a druggist's waste pipe," I told him. "At least he has not taken anything like enough chloroform to kill himself."

"Come in here," he said peremptorily. "I believe we are a little closer to knowing a useful fact or two about Professor Chamberlain. The hotel bureau was absurdly easy to open. Not least because Gurney had simply left the key to the top flap under a sheet of paper in the drawer beneath. I have always maintained that those who lock away their papers and valuables are far less fearful of thieves who may find the key than that they themselves will lose it or, more often, forget where they have put it. In this case there were no valuables in the upper section but a correspondence file and a series of letters."

The flap of the bureau was down, supported on the two runners that Holmes had pulled out. On the table at the centre of the room was a long cedar-wood letter box in which a series of papers had been filed in order of date. It was characteristic of Gurney's punctilious and scholarly mind that the letters sent to him had not only been filed in order but had their envelopes pinned to them with the date of receipt written in pencil upon them. Holmes took one letter from the file, put the cedar-wood box back in the top of the bureau, and closed the flap without yet locking it again.

I was still uneasy at the manner in which he had made free with Gurney's possessions, but my friend had anticipated this.

"It had to be done, Watson. There is a dark plot in these papers, unless I am much mistaken. What a fastidious fellow he is! Every letter kept and filed. These relate to his residence here and go back only a few weeks. When I think of my own unanswered correspondence, transfixed by a jackknife to the center of the mantelpiece in Baker Street, I become aware of deficiencies in my way of life. Look at this!"

He laid before me a type-written envelope addressed to "Edmund Gurney, Esq., The Royal Albion Hotel, Brighton." It was postmarked with a date several days earlier and was one of the most recent to be received. Gurney had noted its receipt in pencil with a date one day later than the postmark.

"What of it?"

"Now look at this."

It was another typewritten letter also bearing the date of the postmark and a pencil date of receipt by Gurney a day later. It bore the address of "Marine Parade, Brighton," and was signed "Professor Joshua D. Chamberlain." I read it without waiting for any invitation from Holmes.

My dear Mr. Gurney, I write to thank you for your generous letter and to express my delight that all differences between us have been resolved. I now see that they were never more than misunderstandings, for which I must hold myself entirely responsible. I should have made it plain that my performances, however much they may overlap your own more serious interests, were never meant to be more than entertainments of the kind offered by Jasper Maskelyne or the Davenport Brothers at the Egyptian Hall in London and elsewhere. You, for your part, are a well-respected investigator of second-sight phenomena and apparitions of the living. Though I maintain that Madame Elvira has remarkable abilities in respect of the former of these, I see that I must have caused you offence and for this I am truly sorry.

I am gratified that we may now be partners rather than adversaries. It would give me great pleasure if, as you suggest, we were able to undertake a tour together in the eastern cities of the United States. Whether we should appear under the same billing, or myself as entertainer and you as the true scholar and investigator, is a matter we might discuss. The interest in your book Phantasms of the Living *would be intense and I believe you would find yourself acclaimed there as perhaps you have never been in your own country. As you know, the work of Madame Elvira and myself in popularizing psychic inquiry has been nominated for an award by the Psychic Research Society of Philadelphia, though without our prior knowledge or consent. We would be honoured if it were possible for us to withdraw that nomination and to put your name forward in our place.*

My partner joins me in sending our sincere and cordial greetings.

I looked up at Holmes.

"A quite extraordinary letter. The fellow was still claiming his psychic powers last night."

"Yes, yes," he said impatiently. "But I did not ask you to read it, Watson. Look at it! Do not read it! And look at the envelope."

I could see nothing. The date on the letter and the postmark were the same. Both bore a pencil date a day later, when Gurney had noted them, a few days ago.

"The typing, Watson!"

Those who have followed our adventures will recall that Sherlock Holmes quickly developed an interest in the new invention of the type-writer. "I think of writing another monograph some of these days," he had said, "on the type-writer and its relation to crime. It is a subject to which I have devoted some little attention." He believed, as he said, that "a type-writer has really quite as much individuality as a man's hand-writing."

In the present case, he took a magnifying lens from his pocket and handed it to me as I studied the black carbon lettering.

"Had this correspondence been set in type by a printer, Watson, the level of the printed letters would be straight as the edge of a rule can make them. However, one can see immediately that this note was typed by bar-end letters. That is to say, capital and lowercase of each letter are at the top of a thin bar. The bars stand in a semicircle above the ribbon of the machine. When a key is pressed, the chosen bar comes down, hits the ribbon, and imprints the letter on the paper."

"There is no doubt, I assume, that this letter and the envelope were typed upon the same machine that Madame Elvira used in her performance?"

"None whatever, though that is not the most significant feature. If you consult the paper that you were about to throw into the sea, you will observe certain similarities between it and these two items. Place a ruler under this line of type, the letters *e*, *s*, *a*, and *t* drop slightly below. Whereas *h*, *n*, and *m* rise slightly above. The letter *c* drops when it is in lowercase but rises when it is a capital. That is caused by a minute variation in the metal casting of each bar that carries the capital and lowercase characters. So many parts are produced by machinery alone that any bar arm will vary minutely from the average setting. It is also evident that letters that drop are on the left-hand side of the keyboard and those that rise are on the right. That is not uncommon."

He looked up at me quickly, lips lightly compressed in a pantomime of calculation.

"Forty bar arms carrying two characters each, each arm subject to slight variation. A further variation in casting eighty characters. The odds are easily half a million to one against two machines of the same make being identical. Add to this the wear caused to the machine by the individual user. A criminal who disguises his own handwriting has a better chance of escape."

It seemed to me a good deal of fuss about nothing very much.

"Since Chamberlain signs the letter, it is presumably his machine. For the life of me, Holmes, I do not see what the dispute is about."

He stared at me.

"When this matter comes before the Central Criminal Court, as I have no doubt that it will, there may be a good deal of dispute. It will not do to say that the machine is presumably his. It must be his without question. By then it may have vanished. The piece of paper that you so nearly threw into the sea may be all that will tie Professor Chamberlain to this letter and, therefore, perhaps tie him ready for the gallows."

"The gallows?"

"Unless we look about us very smartly indeed. Do you not observe something psychopathic about his manner of speech? There is a man who would smile and smile—and be a villain. Now will you look at that letter and that envelope. Do not read—look!"

I looked and still thought only that the letter and envelope seemed to have been typed on the same machine. I said so, but this was not what he wanted. At last I made the only comment that seemed warranted.

"The letter is clearer than the envelope."

"Clearer? How?"

"The letters are more distinct, blacker I suppose."

"Well done, Watson! The ribbon that typed the envelope is well worn. The ribbon that typed the letter is significantly less worn, though not new. It would seem that the letter and the envelope, though bearing the same date, were typed days apart—or more probably a week or two apart."

"Gurney has penciled the same date of receipt upon them."

"Such a jotting would be easy enough to imitate."

"The letter and the envelope may have been typed on the same day. The envelope was typed first, then a new ribbon was used to give the letter a smarter appearance."

"My dear Watson, I will wager you a small sum that not more than one in a hundred people usually type the envelope before the letter. Moreover, they would change the ribbon for both the envelope and letter—or for neither. In any case, this letter was not written with a new ribbon, merely a ribbon that was much less worn than when it was used for the envelope. You may depend upon it, this letter was written well in advance of the date now typed upon it. Indeed, if you will take the glass and look closely, you will see that the date, as it is typed, has a somewhat blurred appearance compared with the rest of the letter. I recognize the machine as a product of E. Remington & Sons of Ilion, New York. It is an admirable make of machine on which one may move backwards by one space and type a character again, if it has been rubbed out for correction. The date on this letter has been typed over two or three times on a worn cotton ribbon to give it superficially the same appearance as the rest of the writing done with a newer ribbon."

"Why should he write an undated letter admitting his fault to Gurney, withhold it for a week or two, then date it and send it?"

Holmes returned it to its envelope and placed the envelope in the bureau again.

"Because this letter was never sent."

"And the envelope with its stamp and postmark?"

"The envelope originally contained a quite different communication, something innocuous and not ostensibly from Chamberlain. Why, then, the substitution?"

"Why could Chamberlain not simply have sent the letter we have found?"

"My dear Watson! This letter is utter nonsense! With our own eyes we saw Chamberlain practicing his old frauds some days after it was sent. This message of reconciliation was not intended to be read by Gurney. It was to be found by others when Gurney could no longer contradict it."

"Found by whom and when, if not by Gurney?"

"His executors, no doubt, or perhaps the police authorities. This whole scheme depends upon the near certainty that once Gurney has filed away his post bag he is unlikely to consult this item again in the next few days or hours merely to reread—what shall we say?—some innocuous and dreary cutting from last Saturday's paper."

"And then?"

"And then it will not matter, Watson. In this scheme of things, the next few days are all that Edmund Gurney has left to him."

I could not see murder in all this and, for the moment, dismissed it as melodrama. We looked again at the drugged and unconscious figure on the bed. He was in no danger now, but I was reluctant to leave him just yet. Holmes had opened the medicine cupboard and was going through the contents. Inspecting the pills and powders, he called out names from time to time and asked me to identify the ingredients. We went through the list, from the Carbolic Smoke Ball remedy to Propter's Nicodemus Pills. Holmes gave a short sardonic laugh at the promise by the latter to make "The Old Man Young Again."

"And by what means is that to be accomplished?"

"Chicanery and imposture," I said, coming into the bedroom for fear of waking Gurney. "I have had patients who take these and many other cure-alls. They are ineffective but usually harmless. You will see that Propter's Nicodemus capsules contain a tonic dose of arsenic, but you could eat an entire box of them and not suffer the least harm. They have a pinch of aphrodisiac cantharides, but not enough to make the old man any younger than he was before."

Holmes drew an envelope from beside the bottles. It contained slips and receipts from the firms that had supplied Gurney through the post with the nostrums of the hypochondriac. He had no doubt kept these scraps of paper so that the addresses were to hand for his next order. "The Carbolic Smoke Ball Company begs to assure its clients that £100 has been deposited with the City and Suburban Bank to be paid out to any who shall suffer influenza for six months after using the smoke ball three times daily before breakfast during four weeks." "Learmount's Patent Chocolate Iron Tonic is best taken in warm water upon rising. A further tablespoonful may be administered before retiring. It is entirely safe for children at five years of age."

Kaolin-and-Opium of Hackney Downs and Propter's Nicodemus Pills of Fortess Road, Kentish Town, both contained a leaflet of praise from various invalids throughout the country whose health, if not their lives, had been saved by resorting to these concoctions. Propter's added a circular to long-established clients, accompanying a complimentary box of twenty "improved" capsules, "designed to prevent the nighttime restlessness that may previously have been consequent upon their use. To obtain this effect, it is of the utmost importance that the capsules should be taken in the order indicated, twice daily."

"At any rate," I said, looking into the box, "he can come to no harm from these, for he has taken eighteen of the twenty already and there is another box unopened."

We went back to the sitting room and occupied the two armchairs. It was close to the hour when Gurney might safely be left to sleep off the remaining effects of the chloroform. I proposed to read a lecture to him in the morning on the folly of meddling with anaesthetics.

"As for that last letter of Chamberlain's," I said to Holmes, "we can hardly discuss it with Gurney, unless you choose to confess to having broken open his bureau."

"There was no breaking," he said indifferently. "However, as you say, it is not a matter for discussion. I think we must take the fight to the enemy. Tomorrow morning we shall have Chamberlain's lodgings at the Marine Parade apartments in our sights and we shall not lose him from that moment on. I require to know everything about him—where he goes, what he does, who keeps him company. For that, I shall need your assistance. It is too easy for a man to give the slip to a single pursuer. Chamberlain is a most dangerous, I would almost say pathological, villain. I do not believe that he would stop at murder, if it truly suited his purposes. Do not tell me, Watson, that I am neglecting Miss Effie Deans. I swear that the solution to that poor girl's difficulties lies somewhere in all this."

It was almost two o'clock in the morning before we summoned the manager to assure him that Edmund Gurney was in no danger and might safely be left. The courteous Italian was effusive in his thanks and assured me that whatever was in his power by way of obliging me for my help should be done. Prompted by Sherlock Holmes, I said there was one thing. On no account must Mr. Gurney be asked to leave the hotel until I had had the chance of a serious discussion with him. I undertook that I would settle the matter before the following night and would, I trusted, put paid to his pernicious habit of self-anaesthesia. I think the gaunt *maitre d'hotel*, with his pale features and black suiting, was a little uneasy at this, but he assured me that everything should be done as I instructed.

4

HOLMES AND I RETURNED to our suite at the Royal Albion a little after two in the morning. I had earned a night's rest and wanted no assistance in dropping off into a profound sleep as soon as my head touched the pillow. It seemed to me that this had lasted for no more than an hour or so when I was roused by a sudden tugging at my shoulder. I woke to find the electric light full on and Holmes standing over me, his face shining with energy. Before I could ask him whether Gurney had taken a turn for the worse, he said:

"Come, Watson! It is gone six o'clock and we must be up and doing! If the game is being played as I suspect, our birds will have flown before long."

He was talking about Professor Chamberlain and Madame Elvira, of course. Despite the ungodly hour, he had already been downstairs, roused the night porter, and sent a further telegram to Inspector Gregson at Scotland Yard, to follow his letter as soon as the post offices should open.

"We ourselves cannot wait for such offices to open, my dear fellow. We must be on the Chain Pier as soon as its gates are unlocked for the seven o'clock steamer to Boulogne."

"They surely cannot be going to Boulogne. Their last performance is tonight."

"I have just taken the precaution of walking a little distance down to the theatre billboard. Another flyer was pasted across it late last night or early this morning. There is to be no more mesmerism nor mind-reading. The Aquarium management regrets that tonight's performance is cancelled in consequence of the indisposition of Madame Elvira. If they attempt to take the steamer, we shall catch them. More to the point, the deck of the pier looks diagonally across to those apartments on the Marine Parade. They cannot leave without our seeing them."

I was wide awake now and soon ready for the pursuit of our suspects. A little before seven o'clock, we were at the pier, where the steamer for Boulogne was alongside and the first passengers were filing aboard over her paddle-box. It was a fine cool morning, the mist still clinging over the sea and a band of pale sun along the eastern horizon. None of the passengers was recognizable as Chamberlain or Madame Elvira. Presently the ropes were thrown off, the gangway was pulled aboard, and the paddles of the *Sea Breeze* churned the green channel water to a hissing froth as she went astern and swung round towards the French coast.

Holmes and I were the first to take deck chairs on the pier that morning. I had with me my neat Barr & Stroud precision field-glasses in their military leather case, with which he could almost have read a newspaper headline on the promenade. We waited, under the pretext of reading our copies of the *Times* and the *Morning Post*, as the sunlight grew warmer and the first promenaders appeared on the esplanade. I was about to say pessimistically that we might sit there all day and see nothing, when Holmes exclaimed quietly,

"There he is! And so is she! I would say that she looks worried but not indisposed."

He handed me the glasses. I saw that Chamberlain and the girl had come out of the doorway of the apartments and were standing on the pavement in earnest conversation. Holmes snatched the glasses back and adjusted the focus a little.

"He is going, I think, and she is staying. Let us be thankful there are two of us. She is giving him a pair of books."

"I daresay he will find a chair in the sun and spend the day reading."

"No, Watson, no! One book might be for reading. If he has two, the odds are that he is taking them somewhere."

"At this hour of the day? The libraries will not be open, nor will the bookshops."

"Then his destination is evidently a place where such institutions will be open by the time of his arrival. There is, I think, a label pasted on the cover of one book. An orange oval with black writing. We have him!"

I was intrigued by this, but still far from understanding how we had him!

"The St. James's Street Library, in the shadow of the great palace, founded by John Stuart Mill and his friends for the public good almost fifty years ago. A treasure house of learning and the arcane, a scholar's paradise. For many years I have been a member. So it seems has friend Chamberlain, though I imagine he has only temporary privileges there. You may depend upon it, Watson, he is going to London—and so are we."

It was hard to realise that we had only left London two days before. Yet every instinct told me that Holmes was right. Chamberlain was opening a Gladstone bag and adding the two books to whatever else it might contain. Then he swung round, striding toward West Street and the long climb that leads to the railway station at the top.

"Watson! Quick as you can! Cut through the little streets to the side, past the Royal Pavilion! Book two first-class returns to London before he can get to the railway ticket office and see you. I doubt whether he will recognise us among so many of his audience, but we must not take the chance. I shall follow him, in case he should have other plans, but I swear that Gladstone bag has the look of the London and Brighton railway about it."

I did as he asked, Holmes following the fugitive westward while I strode at my best pace past the lawns and Georgian houses of the Steyne, the oriental onion domes of the Prince Regent's palace by the sea. My years of playing rugby for Blackheath have served my constitution well. I cut through quickly by way of the little streets where our client Mrs. Deans and her family lived. I came out at the lower level of the station, the smoky air leaving a gritty deposit of soot between the teeth. The booking hall was empty when I arrived and took our tickets for London. I had beaten Chamberlain to it! I saw him approach up the long slope of Queens Road, and by loitering I overheard him take one single ticket for London. Holmes was right. Professor Chamberlain had no intention of coming back to Brighton. What of Madame Elvira?

There was no sign anywhere of Holmes as the pursuer. Only when I walked toward the departure platform did I hear a quiet voice behind me.

"The ticket, if you please, Watson. We shall travel as strangers and meet at the far end in an hour's time."

And so it was. I chose a compartment on one side of Chamberlain with Holmes on the other. He could not leave the train without being seen by us both. As our train crossed the Thames below Chelsea Bridge and began drawing into Victoria Station, our quarry was on his feet, the bag in his hand, ready to be one of the first to alight.

Then the chase began, though it was one in which we must not allow our fugitive to suspect that he was followed. Chamberlain had commandeered the only hansom cab just then upon the station rank. By the time that another had arrived and we swung ourselves aboard, his had turned away down Victoria Street and taken the corner into the long curve of Grosvenor Place. Holmes lifted the little trap in the roof and shouted to our driver, "Follow that fare in front! As hard as you can go down Grosvenor Place! Five sovereigns for you if you still have him in sight when he reaches his destination!"

Happily for us, we had a sportsman on the driver's perch. Wrenching the horse's head round, he drove it at a hand-gallop after the receding hansom. He slowed briefly as the observant eye of a policeman glanced in our direction, then picked up speed as we turned the corner. We were nearly done for at the next junction, as a lumbering railway van pulled out in front, but we carried on round the stern of it. Then we were bumping and bouncing over the cobbles towards Hyde Park Corner. Unless Chamberlain looked back, for which there was no occasion, he would have no idea of our cab swaying and lurching in his wake.

We seemed to be in a mad stampede, in and out of the vehicles as we careered round the busy crossing of Hyde Park Corner with the grand park trees and handsome terraces to either side. Once or twice in our zigzag course the horse's hooves slipped on the greasy cobbles, but we came to no harm. Once a man, taking the horse for a runaway, tried to grab its bridle. Then a bread delivery van came out of a side street. But now we were in Piccadilly. If we were blocked in among the traffic, so was our quarry. For a moment I thought we had lost him, but our driver shot through a gap, almost grazing the pole of an omnibus. As Chamberlain turned into the Haymarket, we were very nearly on his tail. His cab stopped at the bottom, opposite the Duke of York's Place, and I went after him on foot while Holmes emptied seven golden sovereigns into the cabman's palm and I heard the cry of, "You're a toff, sir, you are! A real gent!"

Unaware of all this, Chamberlain had entered the offices of the Messageries Maritimes, whose vessels link metropolitan France with North Africa, Indo-China, Southampton, and New York. Holmes gestured to me to enter, while he remained outside. Under the pretext of consulting the company's timetable, I was able to hear Chamberlain claiming the ticket that he had booked for the next day's sailing from Southampton to Cherbourg and New York.

As he emerged, Holmes and I observed our usual routine for keeping a fugitive in sight without alerting him. I do not think I had been recognised by Chamberlain but, in any case, I now hung back, and it was Holmes who kept pace at a steady distance behind him as we moved westward down the handsome avenue of Pall Mall towards the ancient brickwork of St. James's Palace at the far end. Chamberlain still carried his Gladstone bag.

Our little procession went the entire length of Pall Mall and then turned into St. James's Street. About halfway up, Chamberlain stopped, looked about him, and then went up the steps of the St. James's Street Library. Holmes followed him discreetly. Through the window, I saw Chamberlain standing in the vaulted entrance hall, which might have graced one of our larger banks, and handing a clerk the two volumes from his leather bag.

He came out and walked away down the street. What was Holmes doing? Why were we not in pursuit? Presently he appeared on the steps and looked at the disappearing figure.

"We can find him when we need to," he said quietly. "Our first task must be to save Edmund Gurney."

I then noticed that he had, under his arm, a volume borrowed from the library on whose steps we stood. It was a slim book in royal blue cloth stamped with gold, which Chamberlain had handed to the library clerk a few minutes before. The author's name meant nothing to me at first. Comte Henri-Gratien Bertrand. Then I remembered dimly that he had been an aide-de-camp of some kind to the Emperor

Napoleon. Even in the labyrinthine world of Sherlock Holmes's scholarship, this seemed far removed from the matter in hand. I saw the title: *Journal Intime: Recueil de pieces authentiques sur le captif de Ste.-Helene*. I was none the wiser, beyond gathering that Bertrand had kept a private journal as a companion of the emperor in his last years of exile on St. Helena. Abstruse works of this kind were meat and drink to Holmes. Among other readers, I doubt if one in ten thousand had heard of the Comte Bertrand.

Then he opened the pages and I saw a slip of paper with writing on it. It appeared to have been left there inadvertently by a previous reader of the book and so, presumably, was Professor Chamberlain's. "Pages 464 & 468. The whole worth reading twice. 19A + 1C. 19th to the 28th June." The pages referred to were toward the end of the book and presumably described the emperor's last days. The 28th of June was today's date.

"19A + 1C. 19th to the 28th of June," Holmes murmured. "To obtain this effect, it is of the utmost importance that the capsules should be taken in the order indicated, twice daily. Watson, we must go at once! Let us pray we are not too late."

"Back to Brighton?"

He looked at me as if I had lost my senses and hailed another cab as it came sailing down from Piccadilly.

"To Brighton? By no means! To Kentish Town, driver! Fortess Road! As fast as you can go!"

If the race to follow Chamberlain had been a madcap drive, this was worse. We flew down Dover Street, across Oxford Street to the Euston Road, up the Hampstead Road, through Camden Town, and presently drew up in Fortess Road. Throughout the journey Holmes had been muttering to himself, as if for fear that he might forget, "It is of the utmost importance that the capsules should be taken in the order indicated, twice daily."

We had stopped outside the North London Manufactory of Propter's

Nicodemus Pills. It was a drab red-brick building whose signboard was visible through a veil of soot. Holmes led the way, demanding to see the proprietor upon a matter of life and death and uttering threats of prosecution before the fact upon a charge of attempted murder.

The proprietor was not there, or if he was he had taken shelter. We were shown into the office of the manager, a room that had a good deal to do with ledgers and invoices but little with the healing of the sick. It was just the accommodation I had supposed that vendors of quack medicine would inhabit.

Holmes ignored the invitation to take a chair. He stood before the manager, the aquiline profile now hawk-like and the eyes burning, as it were, into those of his adversary. He did not even inquire the man's name.

"Listen to me," he said quietly, "and think very carefully before you reply. Unless I have the truth now, it is very probable that you may face a charge of attempted murder and not impossible that you may be tried for murder outright. This is my colleague, Dr. Watson of St. Bartholomew's Hospital. He will recognize any attempt at evasion or imposture, and in that event you will be in very serious trouble."

The manager looked at first as though he thought Holmes was an escaped lunatic of some kind. After the brief introduction of my name, however, he began to appear gratifyingly frightened.

"I am Jobson and I have done nothing!" he said.

"Very well, Jobson who has done nothing, listen to me. Have you at any time in the past few months sent to your regular customers a complimentary sample of an improved version of Nicodemus Pills?"

Jobson looked as if this might be a joke or a trick.

"No," he said at length, "of course not. We don't send out complimentaries."

"Let me give you the wording. The box of twenty improved capsules is 'designed to prevent the nighttime restlessness that may previously have been consequent upon their use. To obtain this effect, it is of the utmost importance that the capsules should be taken in the order indicated, twice daily.'"

"I never heard of such a thing." To look at Mr. Jobson was to believe that he spoke the truth.

"What are the principal ingredients of your Nicodemus Pills?"

"The largest is milk sugar, then liver salts, cream of tartar, liquorice, arsenic in homeoepathic dose, cantharis similarly, coffee, sarsaparilla. . . ."

"Calomel?"

It was evident from Jobson's eyes that he had not the least idea what this was.

"A substance derived from mercury," I said quickly, "used as a rule for laxative purposes."

"Never," he said earnestly. "That would never do."

"Nor do you use gelatine capsules for your potions?"

"The price," he said, "would be too high. Our powders are compressed into tablet form."

Holmes looked at me. His eyes were gleaming with triumph.

"Very well," he said, "our cab is waiting for us. You may expect, Mr. Jobson, to hear from Scotland Yard. I daresay Inspector Tobias Gregson will want a word with you in the course of his investigations."

Holmes stopped the cab at the first post office and wired again to Gregson, instructing him to meet us at all costs upon our return at the Royal Albion Hotel, Brighton. If that was impossible, he was to send the "most competent" of his men on a matter of life and death.

We cabbed it direct to Victoria and then caught the Pullman to Brighton. Even so, it was six o'clock by the time of our arrival and the summer sun was already declining across the tract of sea beyond the canyon of Queens Road and West Street below us. We reached the Royal Albion as the early dinner guests were sitting down to their meal. Among them was the sad, dishevelled figure of Edmund Gurney who, presumably, still knew nothing of my ministrations to him during the previous night.

Holmes watched him like a falcon through the open door of the dining room, though what he was waiting for was not yet plain. If there was such danger, why did he not go and speak to the man? We took armchairs in a corner of the lobby, by a dwarf palm growing in a copper tub. Gurney was coming to the end of his dinner. He poured a glass of water from the carafe, opened a little tin on the table beside him, and took out a gelatine capsule, which was the last of the complimentary set of Propter's Nicodemus Pills. My own view remained that if the others had done him no harm, there was no reason why this one should.

Holmes sprang from the chair beside me, crossed the dining room in a few swift strides, and with a blow of his arm knocked the tin and the capsule from Gurney's hand. The invalid Gurney sat ashen and quivering with shock at the sudden attack. Other guests were motionless and silent, all staring in one direction. It was a complete study of still life, the lean and menacing figure of Holmes included, as he leant forward towards his victim. The shock was broken by a voice from the hallway behind me.

"Mr. Holmes, sir! Mr. Holmes!"

I turned and saw Inspector Tobias Gregson in his three-quarter topcoat and carrying his hat in his hand.

5

As the three of us sat together in our room later that evening, Inspector Gregson put his glass down and said, with a further shake of his head, "It was an assault, Mr. Holmes. It was as surely an assault upon the man as any that I have ever witnessed."

"Gurney held death in his hand, Gregson, as surely as if he held a bomb that was about to explode."

"And how can you say that, when you do not know what might be in the capsule?"

Holmes held a flame to his pipe.

"I have no doubt, my dear fellow, as to what is in that capsule, none whatever. When it is analyzed it will be found to contain calomel. At a guess, I would say about ten grains of calomel."

"Well, ten grains of calomel would not kill him," I said reluctantly. "At the worst, it would upset his digestion."

Holmes ignored this, refusing to rise to the bait. In the silence that followed, it was Gregson who began to tell a story that at first seemed to have little to do with the events we had witnessed.

"As to Professor Chamberlain and Madame Elvira, Mr. Holmes. Upon receiving your wire and the theatrical program with the photographs of the two performers, I made one or two inquiries. Forewarned is forearmed, gentlemen. Madame Elvira's photograph meant nothing to me, I must confess. Professor Chamberlain, however, I recognized. Indeed, we have our own photograph of him in the Criminal Record Office. Nothing to do with second sight, I assure you, but everything to do with forging two letters of credit on the Midland Counties Bank. He served six months for that, but he almost escaped us before the trial by taking passage for North America. He was brought back from Quebec at our request."

"Then I trust your men will also be in Southampton early tomorrow morning," said Holmes quietly. "It would not do for Chamberlain to elude you a second time in that manner."

"Two of my men will be watching the liner *Bretagne* from the moment she docks until the moment she sails again for Cherbourg and New York. He will not get far on this occasion."

"Then you had better watch out for his accomplice," my friend interposed. "His partner in crime may already be aboard the *Bretagne*. I have no doubt that Madame Elvira slipped across the Channel to France today and that she travelled by train to Cherbourg. She is either waiting for him there or possibly has boarded the *Bretagne* already for the outward crossing to Southampton."

By little more than a flicker, Gregson's eyes betrayed that he had taken no precautions as to Madame Elvira. He sipped his whisky again and then resumed.

"Yesterday afternoon, gentlemen, I also spent an hour at the Pinkerton bureau in London inquiring as to the American antecedents of Joshua D. Chamberlain. Though he is an Englishman born and bred, he has spent a considerable amount of time in the United States. I was told a most interesting story. While there, a year or so ago, he made a profound impression on Mrs. Marguerite Lesieur of Philadelphia, the middle-aged widow of the railroad builder. He persuaded her of his powers of communicating with the dead when assisted by a medium. This was Madame Elvira, who proved to be his sister. Mrs. Lesieur was generous in return and promised greater rewards to come. Chamberlain is clever. He demurred at first and returned to England, pursued by her letters at every post. In the end, Mrs. Lesieur set up the Psychic Research Society of Philadelphia and made it the means of offering him a handsome reward."

"And then he was unmasked in England?" I asked.

It was Holmes who now took up the tale, looking at me and shaking his head.

"Not quite, I think. It is evident that he and his sister took to the stage. They were ignored at first by those like Gurney and Myers whose interests in psychic phenomena were sincere. When Gurney came to Brighton for a month's convalescence, the performances of Professor Chamberlain were drawing crowds of holidaymakers for the fun of the thing. Gurney, however, at once saw the man as a charlatan and all he stood for as a mockery of true interest in unexplained psychic phenomena. We know that there was a bitter and probably libelous exchange of letters sent to the local newspapers. Chamberlain dared not sue, of course. He would have been proved a liar, and news of that must sooner or later have reached Philadelphia. Rumours of his quarrel with Gurney would inevitably reach occult circles in London. From there, they might easily cross the Atlantic in letters to like-minded spiritualists in Philadelphia and elsewhere. As a result of his cheap and demeaning vaudeville acts in Brighton, Chamberlain stood to lose everything that Mrs. Lesieur had promised him."

Holmes paused, reached for the whisky decanter, and refilled Inspector Gregson's glass.

"Matters had gone almost too far for Chamberlain to retrieve his position, unless. . . . "

"Unless, Mr. Holmes?" Gregson asked.

"Unless Edmund Gurney were to recant and confess his belief in these frauds. Chamberlain might say that Gurney had recanted. He might announce it all over Philadelphia, but of course Gurney would deny it and reveal him as a liar as well as a charlatan. It was necessary for Chamberlain that Gurney should recant and then be in no position to deny it."

"Because he had taken calomel?" I asked skeptically.

"No, my dear Watson. Trickery is Chamberlain's trade and he was more diabolical in planning Gurney's death than in contriving any of his stage effects. Whether he learnt this art of murder from the Comte Bertrand's account of Napoleon or whether that merely refreshed his memory, I cannot tell you. Certain it is that he had that nobleman's account of the St. Helena poisoning with him for the past six weeks—borrowed from the St. James's Library. The dates are stamped in the two volumes."

"I have lost you, Mr. Holmes," said Gregson, "with the Comte Bertrand and Napoleon."

"Very simply, inspector, if the Comte Bertrand is to be believed, the Emperor Napoleon was murdered on St. Helena. Probably it was done at a distance by the command of his enemies in Paris. He was given arsenic in his medication over a period of time. It was not enough to kill him, indeed it may have stimulated his system a little. Yet arsenic in such doses very often produces both restlessness, as in Gurney's case, and constipation. One night the Emperor Napoleon was prescribed a remedy for these afflictions. Ten grains of calomel to be taken with a glass of wine and a biscuit. After a night of severe sickness, he was dead the next day. None of these facts is in dispute."

"But he did not die from calomel, surely?" I persisted.

"No, Watson, indeed he did not. The secret that our modern judges at murder trials have so far prevented the press from reporting is this. The effects of arsenic, given in moderate doses over a period of time, are of questionable benefit but not fatal. Let us suppose, at the end of a few weeks, the victim is then given a single but sufficient dose of calomel—ten grains would be ample. The chemical reaction with arsenic in the stomach will create mercury cyanide, which kills quickly. Not only does it kill quickly, it also removes the traces of arsenic and is almost impossible to detect on postmortem examination by methods at present known to us. Hence the continuing debate as to the proximate cause of the Emperor Napoleon's death."

Gregson and I looked at him in silence. Holmes drove his argument home.

"This devil Chamberlain worked it to a nicety. From London he sent the complimentary box of Propter's Nicodemus Pills in capsule form. He had, of course, bought a box of the pills and substituted gelatine capsules, nineteen filled with a moderate dose of arsenic and the last with a heavy dose of calomel. They were to be taken in order, so that the calomel would be swallowed last. To take capsules in a prescribed order is so common nowadays that the victim would think nothing of it. Chamberlain had also ordered a printed slip from a jobbing printer, who would not think twice about an apparently innocent prescription of this sort. The empty capsules themselves were readily available from any pharmacy, as was the calomel. Even the arsenic will present little difficulty until the new Poisons Bill becomes law. No alarm would be raised until tonight, when Gurney took the last capsule with its calomel—or rather until tomorrow morning when his body was found. By then Chamberlain and his sister would be far away. Moreover, the overwhelming probability is that death in his case was likely to be attributed to an overdose of chloroform. Such a pernicious habit was the perfect cover."

So that was it! The last piece of the puzzle which Holmes's conduct had presented to me in the past few days had now fallen into place.

When we were alone together, my friend added an explanation which was not for Inspector Gregson's ears.

"As for the letter of apparent reconciliation from Chamberlain to Gurney," he remarked, "it required only a girl dressed as a chambermaid to enter the room while Gurney slept or was elsewhere. Whether she or Chamberlain himself carried out the exchange of papers, it was simple to take the key from the bureau drawer—the first place that any thief would look. It was then only necessary to replace whatever document was in that envelope with the letter that we found the other night. It required only the commonest black dress and white apron, purloined from an unlocked servants' cupboard on the landing, for Elvira Chamberlain to impersonate a hotel servant if she was challenged. In the dim light of an internal corridor, at midnight, the night porter saw a chambermaid, or rather a girl in a chambermaid's livery. The only girl who served these rooms was Effie Deans. Therefore, the fellow easily persuaded himself that he must have seen what Mr. Gurney might call a phantasm of the living—in the shape of Miss Deans."

"They appear to have found entering such rooms and opening bureau drawers rather too easy," I said with a trace of skepticism.

Holmes laughed.

"We may never know how, or when, one of them purloined the key to Gurney's room and made a wax impression. I swear that Chamberlain the burglar reconnoitered his victim's rooms at the start, saw the Nicodemus Pills and the way to be rid of his antagonist. Perhaps Elvira was able to do everything else with a passkey. However, I may tell you that with my burglar's kit at hand, I could open any of these old bedroom locks in a twinkling. At some point, I have no doubt, the sister replaced some ephemeral piece of correspondence by the effusive thanks that is in Gurney's correspondence box now and that Chamberlain marked with whatever date of receipt he pleased. In consequence, the world, including Mrs. Marguerite Lesieur, was intended to hear that the two men had made up their quarrel and that Chamberlain's reputation was restored. Had the villain's scheme worked, his benefactress would also have heard that the psychic investigator Edmund Gurney had, tragically, been found dead in a Brighton hotel bedroom from misuse of chloroform."

"Does all this make Madame Elvira a murderess?" I asked.

"I suspect she is no more than her brother's dupe in the matter of the letter and that she knew nothing of the poison. That will be for a court to decide when the pair of them are tried for attempted murder. I have no doubt that if Chamberlain also entered Gurney's room at some point, which on the face of it seems almost certain, his principal intention was not to exchange the two letters but to inspect that counterfeit tin of Propter's Nicodemus Pills and to satisfy himself that Gurney was taking his prescribed doses of the capsules."

Not all of this was revealed at the Central Criminal Court a few months later. Chamberlain was proved to have been previously convicted of a number of petty offences of dishonesty before the forgery of two letters of credit from the Midland Counties Bank, which had sent him to Pentonville prison for six months a few years earlier. The jury in the present case found him guilty of attempted murder by "arsenical poisoning," but all mention of calomel was omitted. He went to penal servitude for seven years. Madame Elvira was not proved to have known of his intention and was found guilty of no more than breaking and entering the hotel room. She went to Millbank prison for six months.

As for our client, Effie Deans was taken back by the manager of the Royal Albion Hotel on the positive insistence of Sherlock Holmes. To be sure, the manager had reason to be grateful to us. However, the matter did not rest there. The owners of the establishment undertook that upon her seventeenth birthday, not that many months away, Miss Deans was to be promoted to the position of assistant housekeeper. This, in itself, was the first rung of a ladder to higher things than she or her parents had dreamt of.

Needless to say, we never saw the remote delights of Ilfracombe or Tenby with their respectable families building sand castles or riding the local donkeys. We were, as Sherlock Holmes was soon reminding me, far too busy for that and much too occupied to visit the Wiveliscombe cousins.

Yet for the man I believed we had saved, the drama did not end happily after all. A year or so later I picked up the *Times* one morning after breakfast, as wheels and harness rattled up and down the length of Baker Street. I was turning the pages of the newspaper when my eye was caught by a brief obituary column.

> We regret to announce the sudden death, by misadventure, of Mr. Edmund Gurney, Joint Secretary of the Psychical Society, author of *The Power of Sound* and other works. Mr. Gurney, who was born about 1847, was the son of the Rev.

> Hampden Gurney, late Rector of Marylebone. He received his education at Trinity College, Cambridge, of which he became a Fellow after taking his degree as Fourth Classic in 1871. Mr. Gurney was the author of *Phantasms of the Living* and had published two volumes of essays. He suffered from obstinate sleeplessness and painful neuralgia, and succumbed to an overdose of chloroform, incautiously taken last Friday evening when alone at the Royal Albion Hotel, Brighton, whither he had gone for a night on business.

I passed the paper without comment to Sherlock Holmes. He was sitting in his black velvet jacket while very precisely dividing the leaves of a cigar butt in the butter dish with the aid of a small surgical knife, in pursuit of a case of robbery with violence. He made no immediate reply as he read the newspaper notice.

Presently I said, "My warnings about chloroform, such as they were, seem to have done him little good."

He put the newspaper down, picked up the scalpel, and resumed his inspection of the cigar butt. Without looking up, he said, "Had it not been that Chamberlain is still serving seven years in Pentonville, I should have been haunted by the spectre of the professor crossing the threshold of that hotel room and dripping chloroform remorselessly onto the face of the sleeping victim until respiration ceased. I hold no very high opinion of coroners and their juries, as you know. You might murder half of London and they would bring in a verdict of natural causes. In Gurney's case, I assure you, they would have called it misadventure. Not suicide, you observe, and certainly not murder. The poor fellow's weakness was the centre of all that passed. Without that, Chamberlain would have got nowhere."

"I fear my advice to him was ill judged, for all the good it did," I said quietly.

Holmes frowned at the work upon which he was engaged.

"Then make amends now, my dear fellow, by warning the world against such pernicious habits. When you come to write up this little adventure of ours, which I fear will probably happen, play up the dangers of the practice and give it some such title as 'The Mystery of the Brighton Chloroform-Eater.'"

As the reader will observe, I declined Holmes's advice in the matter of the title.

5

THE QUEEN OF THE NIGHT

1

IT WAS NOT OFTEN that Holmes and I had a client whom we served twice, in quite different matters. Yet such was the case with Lord Holder. The events of this second inquiry followed at some little distance the Newgate Adventure, as my friend described it, early in 1902. More than once they hinted at the great criminal enterprise, frustrated by Sherlock Holmes on that occasion, which had involved the great but deserted prison as a command post of the underworld.

It was on a morning not long before the coronation of Edward VII that Holmes first mentioned Lord Holder. I confess I did not recognize the name of our intended visitor and said so. Holmes folded his newspaper and said,

"You would know him better as Mr. Alexander Holder, of Holder & Stevenson, bankers of Threadneedle Street. He is now both a peer of the realm and an alderman of the City of London."

At once my mind went back to the Case of the Beryl Coronet, one of our earlier investigations. Mr. Holder had been approached by an illustrious client whose name was of the noblest and most exalted. As security for a short-term loan, this client deposited a coronet of thirty-nine fine beryl stones, pale green shading into yellow and blue. It was one of the most precious public possessions of the Empire.

The sequel requires few words. While the coronet was in Mr. Holder's possession, there was a robbery—three jewels were broken from their settings and stolen. Suspicion fell on his son. Holmes proved the boy innocent, a youth of generous instincts, one of whom any father should be proud. Since then, the banker had been ennobled for his services to the nation, not least to patrician families who raised money in difficult times by pledging jewels and works of art.

When he entered our sitting room, I still recognised Lord Holder as our client in the former case. Though now about sixty, he remained a man of striking appearance. His figure was tall, portly, and imposing with a massive, strongly marked face and commanding figure. He was dressed in a somber yet rich style: black frock coat, neat brown gaiters, and well-cut pearl-grey trousers.

After we had talked a little of his son, who had risen to become private secretary to Lord Milner in Cape Colony, he came to the purpose of his appointment.

"Gentlemen, the matter at issue is a delicate one. May I ask what you know of the imitating or, indeed, counterfeiting of sapphires and Brazilian diamonds?"

Holmes took the pipe from his mouth and frowned.

"They are two very different things. my lord. A good reproduction of sapphires may be obtained by using cobalt oxide. The process is similar to the imitation of rubies and often more successful. A Brazilian diamond of the first water would be impossible to imitate with any success. Even a close examination by a retail jeweller would reveal the fraud at once. A casual glance need not betray, certainly not in some lights. However, the deception could not be kept up for more than a short period of time and certainly could not be depended upon."

I turned to our visitor.

"Why do you ask, my lord?"

Our visitor looked distinctly uncomfortable.

"Since I know that everything said here will remain in confidence, I shall try to explain my unease. You are, I imagine, aware of the Earls of Longstaffe?"

I laughed at this.

"Anyone who reads the racing papers or the gossip columns could not be unaware of them."

"Our firm has for many years been bankers to the family, most recently to the present Lord Adolphus Longstaffe, as we were to his father, Lord Alfred, before him. There has frequently been occasion to advance money against security until such time as funds could be raised by the sale or mortgage of a further portion of the Longstaffe estate."

"A sale more often than a mortgage, I fear," said Holmes, gazing at his pipe.

"The Longstaffe family suffered greatly from the depredations of the late Lord Alfred. It is common knowledge that his way of life in the German spa towns, not to mention Paris and Biarritz, left the estate crippled by debts and claims against him in the courts. He died in Baden-Baden, I believe, at the gaming tables with a hock and seltzer in one hand and not a single lucky card in the other. I fear that his successor, Lord Adolphus Longstaffe, has continued in much the same way," he continued.

"I fear so, Mr. Holmes. We customarily hold certain family jewels for safekeeping and, when necessary, as security until the value of land can be realized. Among these is a splendid royal clasp, the so-called Queen of the Night, bequeathed by William IV to his favorite, the young Lady Adeline Longstaffe, seventy years ago."

"I am aware of the Queen of the Night," said Holmes in a quiet voice. "When the clasp was shown in the Paris Exhibition, the catalogue gave a specification of its extreme dimensions as three inches laterally and vertically."

His long, slender fingers drummed on the arm of his chair absent-mindedly.

"I fear I am a stranger to this treasure," I said frankly. Lord Holder turned to me.

"Lord Adolphus Longstaffe as the senior member of his family is herald to the Prince of Wales, or to any heir-apparent to the throne. It is a ceremonial rank only. The neck of the robe covering his lordship's tunic on great occasions bears this clasp, the Queen of the Night, whose value is perhaps greater than most state jewels. As with so many priceless ornaments, even the Koh-i-Noor diamond in the royal crown, the gem is not large. You might hold it on the palm of your hand, but not quite in it."

"I am still not entirely clear what it is, other than a clasp at the neck of his cloak."

"A fine Brazilian diamond, Doctor," said Lord Holder patiently, "a twelve-sided rhombic dodecahedron, set among sapphires of the deepest blue. There is also a small silver clip. This enables the diamond to be detached and worn alone, if so desired. The great Koh-i-Noor—the River of Light in the royal crown—is said to weigh one hundred eighty-six carats, though there has been some dispute of late. Estimates of the Queen of the Night may also vary, but it cannot be less than one hundred forty carats. The entire clasp is a work of art, a brilliant star among midnight blue, as well as a jewel. Like any treasure of that nature, the workmanship makes it almost impossible to put a realistic value on it. It is, quite simply, beyond price."

"From where did it come?"

Holmes intervened.

"You may believe if you choose, Watson, that the star came from the looting of the Portuguese vice-regal palace by European mercenaries during Brazil's wars of independence. It is said to be the ransom paid for the viceroy's life and the vicereine's honour. I prefer the tale of it, being wagered and lost against a woman's affections, during a game of faro played between a royal brother and a future prime minister in the presence of the Prince Regent at Carlton House."

"You are admirably informed, Mr. Holmes," said Lord Holder with a faint smile.

"However, why should it be the cause of trouble now?"

His lordship shook his head.

"It is not yet the cause, but I fear it may be. In a matter of weeks, we shall begin the ceremonies attendant on the coronation of His Majesty Edward VII. Lord Adolphus Longstaffe must play his part as herald to the Prince of Wales, and the Queen of the Night will be the clasp at the neck of his robe."

"Where is it at present?"

"Just so, Dr. Watson. At present it lies in a velvet-lined box, within a safe of two-inch steel, inside the strong-room of our bank. That is where it is usually kept, except on ceremonial occasions or when securely on display."

"Why should it be at risk on this occasion if not on others?"

Lord Holder folded his hands uneasily.

"The Queen of the Night has appeared in many places. It has been photographed, exhibited here and in Paris, and is well enough known to jewellers and connoisseurs. There is hardly a book on *bijouterie* in which it does not make its appearance."

"I see no harm in that."

"Nor I, Dr. Watson. Yet such photographs and displays give ample scope to counterfeiters. I have it on good authority that in the past three months, since the date of the coronation was announced, a jeweller in Brussels has been commissioned to produce a passable imitation of the Queen of the Night. It is such a commission as a thief might offer, particularly at a time like this."

"Raoul Grenier et fils is the firm in question," said Holmes calmly.

Lord Holder sat suddenly upright in his chair.

"Mr. Holmes! There are only two or three men in the City of London who know that! It has been held in the strictest confidence! How can you possibly know?"

"Because," said Holmes thoughtfully, "it was I who gave the order."

The silence in the room had the quality of the stillness that follows the explosion of a shell or a grenade.

"You, sir? The thing is impossible!"

"It is not only possible, Lord Holder, it is the truth. I must ask you to trust me. It is plain that I should not have done this with dishonest intent, for if that were the case, I should not have told you now."

"But if an imitation is produced, you make the task of a thief all the more easy!"

"On the contrary, my lord. In my opinion, what I have done is the sole means of saving the precious clasp from being lost for ever. I need hardly remind you of your own words just now. Much of the value lies in the workmanship. Moreover, this is not the Koh-i-Noor diamond, which stands alone. The Queen of the Night might be broken up and its recut stones sold for a small fortune."

"But why should you care about the Queen of the Night? You are not commissioned to guard it, surely?"

Holmes shook his head.

"I care nothing for it, sir. It is a matter of no importance to me whether it is stolen or not. I play a larger game. In that game, the diamond and its sapphires are no more than pawns. Beyond that, you may summon Inspectors Lestrade or Gregson from Scotland Yard so that I may be handed over to them. Or you may trust me and say not a word to anyone of what has passed between us this morning."

"And that is all?"

"That, I fear, is all, my lord. There is no other course."

It was hard to say whether our guest, who made his way down the stairs half an hour later, was more shaken or shattered. Had it not been for the service Holmes had done him in proving his son's innocence all those years ago, I really believe that Lord Holder would have summoned Lestrade and Gregson, and told them to do their duty

2

HOLMES! What the devil was all that about?"

He raised his hand to silence me and went off to his room. When he came back, he was holding a large buff-colored envelope. He sat at the dining table, laid the envelope before him, and looked up.

"What was it about? It was about matters that I cannot reveal to anyone but you, my dear fellow, not even to a loyal and impeccable servant of the Crown like Lord Holder."

"Has this something to do with the matter of your disappearance some months ago?"

He smiled.

"Dear old Watson! There is no pulling the wool over your perceptive eyes, is there?"

"I should hope not!"

"Then you will recall the proceedings of the criminal tribunal that condemned me to death in Newgate. I described to you how hyoscine wiped many of the details from my mind. With some effort, fragments of them came to me in sleep. I recall a remark of the late Henry Caius Milverton about Colonel James Moriarty, the surviving younger brother of my ancient enemy, the late professor. Milverton apologized for the fact that Colonel Moriarty had been temporarily detained over a dispute relating to a family heirloom. You will recall my saying that the colonel had been looking forward to my rope-dance, as they called it, having cut me to pieces beforehand."

"I should not have thought the finances of such a family as the Moriartys would run to an heirloom to dispute about!"

He smiled again at this.

"It was not their heirloom, I assure you. The Moriartys are consummate thieves, Watson, and I concluded at once that the heirloom in question belonged to somebody else. Then, quite lately, I was invited to the Grosvenor Hotel, Victoria Station, at the behest of Monsieur Raoul Grenier."

"The jeweller from Brussels?"

"The same. He had come over by ferry from Ostend to Dover and so to London, for no other reason than to consult me. The matter was so delicate that it was confided to me on condition that I divulge it at that time to no one, not even to your good self."

"Nor Lord Holder?"

"Lord Holder and the entire world were suspects, to Monsieur Grenier. He knew of the forthcoming coronation, of course, and he well knew that it is a time when the jewels on display are at their most vulnerable. Even the crown jewels of England must leave the Tower of London, where at all other times they are guarded day and night by a regiment of the Foot Guards. I concluded that was assuredly the thought behind the Newgate conspiracy. Grenier himself, incidentally, has been retained by two crowned heads of Europe to alter the ceremonial headgear to fit the skulls of a new generation. It is sixty-four years since our late queen was crowned."

"This Monsieur Grenier sounds to me like a very fortunate and prosperous fellow."

"Scarcely. He told me that he had been visited by a certain Count Fosco. The count had commissioned him to make a glass replica of the Queen of the Night. My mind went back to that remark of Henry Milverton's about an heirloom. My nostrils scented a Moriarty."

"But surely Count Fosco was a name in a novel, assumed to disguise a member of an Italian secret society."

"It was that which brought Grenier to me. He guessed that the name was a mere cloak, and yet he dreaded to turn away the man, for fear that a secret society lurked behind him. He could not believe the imitation was required for any honest purpose. It is not uncommon for the owners of such treasures to have high-class copies made so that they may be worn on less important occasions, while the originals are held safely in a bank vault. There are also foolish people who cannot afford such originals but whose vanity is satisfied by an artificial resemblance. Grenier's visitor was neither of these. To use the poor fellow's own words, the man who came to him reeked of dishonesty. Our jeweller knew very well that the original of the clasp belonged to the Longstaffe family—and feared the worst. Either the so-called count proposed to steal the original and substitute the imitation—or the last of the Longstaffes planned to perpetrate a trick of some kind upon his creditors."

"Surely not!"

"I think not. Yet it must be conceded that Adolphus Longstaffe, like his father, has a rackety reputation. Much of the Caversham estate in Suffolk has been sold and the great house at Pickering Park in Sussex with all its lands has been at risk."

"Not to mention Portman Square in London and most of Marylebone!"

"Exactly so."

"Mind you, if Lord Adolphus Longstaffe were to go smash, the whole world would hear it."

"Quite correct, Watson, and when a man of that sort faces ruin, there is no knowing what he may do. It might seem a mere peccadillo to place the imitation as surety with a bank, while breaking up the original and selling its stones."

"But what of Grenier?"

"I asked him as a great favor to me, for he once received a favor *from* me, to make a cheap imitation of the clasp. Such an insult to his professional reputation! He was to tell no one. At the same time, he must wait until it was too late for our friend Count Fosco to have one made elsewhere before the coronation. Then he would regretfully inform this bogus nobleman that, under such pressure of work as the coronation demanded, he could not fulfil Fosco's commission for several more months."

"Then you put Grenier in danger!"

"I think not."

He opened the envelope and drew out a number of photographic prints.

"Count Fosco is a made-up name. There are Italian secret societies to be sure, but not in this case. That part of the trick was a bogey to frighten the dupe. But Grenier is no dupe."

"What are these?"

He spread the photographs before him.

"You will recall our friend Colonel Piquart, to whom we were able to render a service during the deplorable Dreyfus affair in Paris.* He became thereafter Minister of Defence in the government of Georges Clemenceau and director of military intelligence. It was the work of a day for him to establish that the address given by Count Fosco in the Boulevard Saint Germain was merely an office where letters had been collected for several months on behalf of Colonel Jacques Moriarty of the Rue des Charbonniers in the slums of Montmartre. Inquire in Montmartre and you will probably find that this domicile is as elusive as the first one. The more accurate Christian name of its lessee is, of course, James, rather than Jacques. See for yourself. I do not think Monsieur Grenier need greatly fear the threats of Count Fosco and the assassins of the Red Circle. This is single and single-minded fraud."

The photographs showed a man in outdoor clothes striding towards, or from, an ill-painted door in a dark courtyard of some kind. It was plain that these were images obtained secretly, perhaps from a passing vehicle, of a man who had no idea that he was the object of in-

*"The Case of the Unseen Hand" in Donald Thomas, *The Secret Cases of Sherlock Holmes,* New York: Carroll & Graf, 1998.

terest. The quality of the prints suffered a little from the conditions under which they were taken.

Several of them gave a clear view of a man who was dark-haired and a little stooped, though with something of a military bearing. He had a withered look to him, beyond his years. In my own medical practice I often connect this last symptom with foreign or colonial service. There had been a good deal of that as France acquired her colonies along the Mediterranean coast of North Africa. From what I could see of him, he looked little enough like a count or, indeed, an Italian assassin.

"It is incredible!" I said as I stared at the monochrome portraits.

"Not in the least. Even after all my captors were accounted for, I thought we might hear from one or two of their friends. For me, this is not a matter of jewels and baubles, Watson. Let us call it a contest to see whether Colonel Moriarty shall live in peace and safety. It is plain that neither he nor I can do so while the other remains alive. That is what will bring him to London. Once in London, of course, he will not resist the Queen of the Night, even without a counterfeit to switch for the real clasp."

"Can you be so sure?"

He looked at me thoughtfully.

"You will recall, Watson, the matter of the tie-pin."

"I cannot say that I do. Which tie-pin is that?"

"It is a green emerald tie-pin, in the form of a serpent of Aesculapius. Professor Moriarty was wearing it on that late afternoon in the mist at the falls of Reichenbach. When at last he fell to his death, for one of us must fall to end that long struggle, the weight of his body as he went backwards ripped it from his shirt and it came off in my grasp. Even before he hit the rocks in the torrent, so many hundreds of feet below, I had slipped it in my pocket."

"Where is it now?"

"That is the point, my dear fellow."

He pushed towards me another item from the envelope, a cutting from a newspaper, *Paris Soir*, dated some weeks ago. The column carried a small announcement in English that if Colonel James Moriarty of the Rue des Charbonniers would call at the Banque de l'Orient in the Avenue de l'Opera, he would find something to his advantage.

"He has it now?" I asked.

"For some weeks past. I asked to be informed when it was collected. You may depend upon it, he will recognize what it is. I admit the device is less picturesque than throwing down one's gauntlet in the days of chivalry. Yet he has determined to exact vengeance from me and I can do no more than offer myself. You may depend upon it, he will be in London when the new king is crowned. I would go so far as to say that he will put up at the Dashwood Club in Curzon Street."

"Named after Sir Francis Dashwood of the Hellfire Club in the 1760s!"

"That tells one of its reputation, does it not?"

3

By the evening, I was in a solemn mood. The thought of Colonel James Moriarty evoked all the old fears and perils from which we had so lately escaped. After supper, however, my friend pushed back his chair, got up from the table, and crossed to the fireplace, where he stood with his back to it, hands clasped behind him.

"My dear fellow, there really is no cause for such gloom. The game will be won by he who has knowledge on his side. I have devoted a little time to repairing the gaps in our acquaintance with a man who must now be our prime adversary. Colonel Moriarty, as his name suggests, was once a military man and a member of the gentry. To this day he is curiously but legitimately the lord of the manor of Copyhold Barton in the county of Dorset. Unfortunately, behind this grand hereditary title he owns not a square inch of land in Copyhold Barton or elsewhere. He has fallen so low that he haunts the worst districts of Paris. His habitation is among the apache street robbers of Montmartre and the ladies of the twilight in the Avenue de Clichy or the Parc de Monceau. That is his true manor and in it he is lord, under the law of the fist and the razor."

He scraped at the bowl of his pipe for a moment, then he looked up.

"The world knows little of him. Therefore, he is a man of presumed good character in the county of Dorset. His grandfather was obliged to sell the estate—but not the title—and nothing is known to the grandson's discredit. His grandfather had acquired that title for a mere fifty pounds to add respectability to a dubious business of promoting foreign railway shares."

"But surely the present Moriarty is a proven criminal and something can be done about him?"

He shook his head.

"There is not a single criminal conviction against him. He is not, as they say, known to the police. Were I to associate him with my captors and make accusations of attempted murder a few months ago, he could take me to court and recover punitive damages. I have nothing but my unsupported word against his."

"Then who were his family, other than the late professor?"

Holmes sighed, sat down, and stared at the fireplace, unused just then and covered by a silk Chinese screen in the summer warmth.

"The lordship of the manor is not worth a penny piece, but it confers certain ancient ceremonial privileges. For five hundred years its owners have enjoyed burgage tenure. That is to say, they had the right of a mediaeval burgess to represent that part of Dorset at coronations, the opening of parliament, the trooping of the color, and other royal ceremonies.

Two of them are grooms of the chamber to the Earl of Dorset. To be sure, they are mere servants of a greater servant of kings, but they have bought a place in a greater man's retinue on these occasions."

"And that is all we know? Why, the scoundrel may be present at the coronation!"

Holmes smiled and leaned back in his chair.

"While enjoying the hospitality of Mr. Jabez Wilson, I made use of Somerset House, the census returns, registers of births, marriages, and deaths for the past forty or fifty years. I consulted the annual Army Lists. The name of Moriarty is not common and the entries were few. It surprises me that my enemies had not gone to greater lengths to conceal their secrets."

"They imagined you would be dead by now."

"True. The titular father of the professor and the colonel was Major Robert Moriarty. According to the Army Lists, he served in India and died there of a fever. His wife, Henrietta Jane, was a creature of too delicate health for the Indian climate. She is listed in the 1851 census as living throughout his absence in rooms near Hyde Park Gate. The land registers show a lease purchased by Lord Alfred Longstaffe just before her arrival."

"A kept woman!"

"You have such an ear for the bourgeois cliche, Watson. A kept woman, if we must call her that. The reason for her sudden removal to Hyde Park Gate, where she was previously unknown, became evident when I put the census of births and the Army List together. When Professor Moriarty was born, Major Robert Moriarty had been serving in the China Wars for at least eight months. When a still younger child, a blameless station master now deceased, first saw the light of day, the major had left for India a year earlier and had now been dead two months. You may recall from the Roman history lessons of your schooldays a sardonic comment by the historian Suetonius on such misalliances."

"'How fortunate those parents are for whom their child is only three months in the womb.'"

"Precisely." Holmes lit his pipe and shook out the flame. "Only the elder boy, the colonel, was his father's son. Imagine the scene when the unmarried Lord Alfred Longstaffe refused Henrietta Jane's demand that he should accept the two natural sons as his own. If the census of 1861 is to be believed, she was obliged to settle for a small allowance and genteel poverty in the charming cathedral city of Wells."

"The future Colonel Moriarty, as the eldest son, would inherit the title of lord of the manor."

Holmes nodded.

"In the Army Lists, that eldest son was also a junior captain in South Africa and the Transvaal during the 1870s. If he has a genuine title to his colonelcy, it is by purchase of some kind in a frontier force. Diamond-mining in Kimberley was in its first buccaneering phase. Fortunes were made in the mines and lost at the card tables. So the military Moriarty came back richer than he went out."

"What of his criminal conspiracy with Milverton and Calhoun?"

"Captain Calhoun and Henry Caius Milverton had a common interest in the sea. Calhoun was a mere pirate. Milverton was a partner in the London-to-Antwerp line that bears his name, among others. Their signboard still faces the Thames, above the dock gates at Shadwell. Yet this Milverton was quite as vicious as his brother. He escaped notice in the 1885 exposure of what the penny-a-liners call 'the white slave trade.' Yet the public denunciations by the Salvation Army and the *Pall Mall Gazette* put an end to those activities for a time. His part was to transport young women from this country to France and Belgium, while bringing those from France and Belgium to the streets of our own cities. By such means, in whatever country they found themselves, they were far from home, having only so-called protectors to depend upon."

"Had you encountered Colonel Moriarty before you and I met?"

"Only by reputation. I was able to assist the father of a young girl and in so doing to secure the conviction of Mrs. Mary Jeffries, a keeper of houses of ill repute in Chelsea and the West End. After the 1885 newspaper outcry over the protection of young girls, London became too warm for Colonel Moriarty, and he made his way to Paris. We may assume that his income still derived from the trade in female misery practised in partnership with Henry Milverton."

He smoked in silence for a moment and then resumed.

"To tell you the truth, Watson, I never believed that Milverton and Calhoun had gone to such trouble over the ruins of Newgate Gaol merely to murder me. They would have murdered me with great relish, of course, but a barrowload of bricks tipped from a rooftop onto my head in Welbeck Street would have done the job. Yet there was more to it. My death was to be a bonus, a mere entertainment. There was a greater coup with a well-organized criminal conspiracy behind it. You know how at the time of a coronation there is loose talk about the crown jewels?"

"You cannot believe that!"

"I do not disbelieve it. Newgate Gaol is at the heart of the City of London and secure as the Bank of England. Yet there could be no better bolt-hole in the aftermath of robbery, which is when even the most ingenious villains are liable to be caught. Who would dream of searching a prison—not the likes of Lestrade or Gregson, you may be sure! I believe that with a network of foreign accomplices and a team of bullies, the thing could have been done. With such resources, I know I could certainly do it."

"I still say the whole thing is a fantasy! In any case, with Calhoun and Milverton dead, there is an end. Colonel Moriarty alone would not attempt it."

He looked at me patiently.

"That is why he will confine his interest to the one treasure that was his goal from the beginning. Of course he cannot walk off with the crown or with the royal orb and scepter. I doubt if he ever wanted them. He could not sell such treasures for profit, least of all among the apache gangs and the throat-slitters of Batignolles or Belleville. He is a dedicated maniac, prepared to take a man off the streets of London and strangle him privately in the execution shed of Newgate Gaol purely for pleasure."

"And what is his mania now?"

Holmes leant towards the fireplace and concluded his history.

"By the time they grew to manhood, the two elder Moriarty brothers were plainly fired by resentment. Yet they lacked the opportunity to revenge themselves on the Longstaffe family, most of all upon the Longstaffe father who had disowned two natural sons and consigned them to beggary, and upon the half brother, Lord Adolphus, who had usurped them. When the mind of a Moriarty is warped into criminality, a single gem will suffice."

"And that is the reason behind today's playing at fox-and-geese with Lord Holder?"

My friend was unmoved by skepticism.

"The loss of the Queen of the Night would disgrace the Longstaffe family utterly. It would bring criminal suspicion and rumours of complicity upon such a spendthrift and prodigal as Lord Adolphus himself. To lose the appointment as royal herald after several hundred years would be ruin to family honour. Such is the vengeance that I believe Colonel Moriarty seeks, in addition to a handsome souvenir."

Among the coronation postcards and placards for sale in the shop windows of Baker Street, I had noticed one which showed the Prince of Wales with his retinue. Royal blue was their colour, their robes lined with white satin. I had noticed one of them whose blue velvet cloak was fastened at the throat by a clasp of night-blue jewels set round a blazing white star. Such postcards are mere caricature exaggerations, but the design was plain enough. The memory of this determined me.

"We must see what Lestrade has to say tomorrow."

Holmes got up and began to interest himself in his chemical table.

"We will leave Lestrade out of this, if you please, and Brother Mycroft too. I have a more important matter to settle with Colonel Moriarty, and no man shall come between us. If either he or I would live in safety, a duel to the death must decide which of us it shall be. The same thought has surely crossed his mind, for he will know by now that I survived the Newgate blast. Besides, if you truly wish to see the last of the Queen of the Night and the rest of the crown jewels, to bring in Scotland Yard is quite the best way to accomplish it."

Then he slipped into silence and stood over his chemical table in deep thought until he straightened up to withdraw for the night. As he went, he turned to me.

"You may rest easily, Watson. I have deduced everything about this robbery—where it will happen and when, as well as the name of the man who will carry it out. It is only his method that still eludes me."

"I call that a pretty large exception!"

"Not at all. If Colonel Moriarty proposes to steal the Queen of the Night, it is of the first importance that we should dictate the method to him."

Naturally, he did not explain to me how that could be done.

4

It was most unfortunate that at this juncture Mycroft Holmes should have muddied the waters by certain conversations with Inspector Lestrade, whom he was apt to regard as his luggage porter or bootblack, and whom he was also apt to chivvy or bully as though it were a sport. From his lofty perch as the government's chief accountant and interdepartmental adviser, Brother Mycroft now raised the matter with Lestrade of security at the coronation festivities, as it affected the crown jewels and those of visiting royalty. He then suggested to the Scotland Yard man that Sherlock Holmes might be retained to supervise or implement whatever security seemed advisable.

Inspector Lestrade, who hoped one day to be Superintendent Lestrade or even Commander Lestrade, was aware of the considerable influence exercised in such promotions by Mycroft Holmes. So the inspector spoke to his superintendent, who spoke to his commander, who spoke to the Commissioner of Metropolitan Police, who spoke to the Home Secretary, who, in his turn, spoke to his interdepartmental adviser, Mycroft Holmes, who commended it as a capital idea—and so the message was relayed all the way back down again.

As a result, Mycroft Holmes and Lestrade paid us a visit soon afterward, on an otherwise sunlit afternoon, to inform us of the decision that had been taken. The inspector was already briefed and prepared to discuss the particular arrangements for Coronation Day, 2 August. In what manner did my friend think he might best protect the jewels of the state at Westminster?

"By sitting here in my chair with my pipe and reading the death-chamber memoirs of some criminal of rare distinction, I daresay," Holmes replied without a glimmer of humour. "A French Bluebeard would promise something more in the way of style than our own marital assassins."

Lestrade went red in the face, but Brother Mycroft was not to be denied.

"This will not do!" he boomed at his fractious sibling. "On the subject of your protection of the regalia, I have given my word!"

"But not mine," said Sherlock Holmes humbly.

"Why, for heaven's sake? Why will you not do it?"

"Because I should dance attendance to no purpose and that is something I decline to do. There is a great and most interesting robbery in prospect. The papers will be full of nothing else if it happens. Yet it has nothing to do with Coronation Day. I have seen that for myself."

"What have you seen?"

"Only what you or anyone else might have noted, with a little care and a modicum of common sense. I know that there will be an attempt. I know the item to be stolen and I know the name of the man who will steal it. That is nothing. Any fool might guess at it. Unlike any fool, however, I now know how it is to be done and where. I know the time of the theft to within five minutes."

"Five minutes!"

"Oh, very well, let us be generous and say within ten minutes. There remains merely the question of whether the thief can screw his courage to the sticking point when it comes to the moment. I cannot be answerable for his nerve. However, I think you and Lestrade had far better leave the whole thing to me."

"Then at least tell me where, when, how, and by whom!"

"No."

I knew he was talking about the Queen of the Night but did not dare to say a word. Mycroft Homes seemed to swell beyond his normal size.

"Then, I am to take it, you do not trust your own brother!"

How I wished I had been somewhere else just then. I had a vivid impression of their nursery tantrums in days long gone by

"I trust my own brother implicitly," said Sherlock Holmes evenly.

"But you do not trust him sufficiently to prevent this criminal outrage, whatever it may be."

Sherlock Holmes stared at him and then spoke very quietly.

"You have understood nothing, Mycroft, if you believe that. I do not wish to prevent what you call an outrage. In fact, I would encourage it, if I could. There is a personal affair that must be settled and this theft is the occasion of it but no more. It cannot be resolved in any other way."

Mycroft had evidently heard something from Lestrade about his brother's subversive political outbursts, for now he asked, "This is not some trumpery, I hope, which involves stealing the crown jewels and giving them back to the princes of India?"

Sherlock Holmes shook his head.

"No. If it were merely that, I should tell you everything and invite you to join me in the venture. I have already pledged my word to Lord Holder in the matter of securing the Lord Mayor of London and the Mansion House during the festivities. What you propose would create the most flagrant conflict of interests."

This was news to me. I did not know that he had seen Lord Holder again.

"I cannot see it, Sherlock," said Mycroft Holmes ominously.

"I daresay not."

It was, as they say, the last straw that broke the camel's back. Mycroft Holmes swept from the room without another word, Lestrade at his heels, and was driven away into the summer dusk. That was as far as anyone could get with my friend.

After they had gone, I tried to soothe Holmes by reverting to the Queen of the Night, in whose safety he had a real interest. I thought this might please him. In the course of conversation, I said:

"It seems extraordinary, does it not, that all this magnificence was created just to button the neck of a man's cloak?"

He had just picked up the evening paper and glanced at it. Now he threw it down again and got to his feet, striding restlessly across to the window and turning back.

"Just so, Watson. Magnificence and flummery. Whether flummery is the price one must pay for magnificence or whether magnificence is the cost of flummery, I should not care to say. Let it suffice for the moment that I swear Colonel Moriarty means to have the Queen of the Night and I care for nothing else. To be sure, he has money enough, the reward of human bondage. To him, I daresay, theft is a way of vengeance against those who have wronged him and his martyred brother ever since birth. I am one of the guilty. You might call it a matter of justice by his own perverted lights, against the Longstaffe family and society as a whole."

"He will be caught."

Holmes sat down again and shook his head.

"Not by Lestrade and his kind. Colonel Moriarty is that most dangerous type, a criminal who is not known to be one and who works alone. Curiously, it is a species encountered often in what Professor von Krafft-Ebing calls lust murders. Because he works alone, there is no one to betray him, which is far the commonest method of detection. He works in utter secrecy, deep in the bomb-proof shelter of his skull."

One of my most uncomfortable evenings drew to an end at this point. For the next few weeks, however, during his visits to us Lestrade became slyly witty in a manner that was most provoking. He would refer, with a wink at me over the rim of his glass, to the value of the jewels on display at the ceremony in Westminster Abbey and the dangers they must be exposed to. Then he would add that the humble efforts of Scotland Yard might prove sufficient to keep them safe without the assistance of a higher intelligence. It was galling in the extreme, and I feared there must be an explosion.

Holmes kept himself in check for longer than I had expected. However, when these pleasantries were repeated for the fourth or fifth time, he remarked casually, "I do not imagine that the disappearance of the royal jewels would be regarded as theft by those Indian princes from whom they were looted by British power in the first place. Indeed, if I could be quite sure that they were stolen only to be returned to their rightful owners, I daresay I should be ready to put my meagre talents at the disposal of those who perpetrated such a robbery."

Lestrade's bluff laughter in response to this had a false note about it. I believe that he had been truly shocked by the utterance of these subversive comments, whatever their intent. The anarchic and radical element in Holmes's character was one with which our visitor could never get to grips. We heard no more from him on the subject of the royal regalia. However, when the inspector left us that night, Holmes burst out in anger.

"It is quite obvious now, if it never was before, that Lestrade and his crew are utterly unsuited to dealing with a threat of this kind. I lose all patience with such people! Thank God I have never mentioned Colonel Moriarty to Lestrade. One might as well hand over the Queen of the Night to the robber and be done with it!"

A day or two later, he was absent from morning until evening. On his return, he revealed that he had spent the day with Lord Holder. Despite his outburst to Mycroft Holmes and Lestrade, my friend so far relented as to permit his lordship to conduct him upon a tour of the coronation routes and to introduce him to those buildings where the great jewels of state and their wearers might be gathered. Apart from the royal apartments of Buckingham Palace, which neither Colonel Moriarty not any other thief would get near, these consisted of the ceremonial area in Westminster Abbey, as well as its antechambers, and the robing-rooms of the House of Lords. As a chamber-groom to the Earl of Dorset, our adversary would have brief and limited access to these. In company with Lord Holder, Holmes had examined these rooms and their adjacent reception areas. Here, if anywhere, a surreptitious theft might be possible or a sudden attack might take place on Lord Adolphus Longstaffe as the Prince of Wales's herald. But Holmes came home disgruntled and sat in his chair biting a thumbnail with vexation.

"Contrary to the urgings of Brother Mycroft and Lestrade, it is out of the question that there will be an attempt to steal the Queen of the Night during the Coronation."

"Then the treasure is safe?"

In the frustration of the moment, he cried out:

"Good God, Watson! This scoundrel was prepared to murder me to gain his ends! Do you not understand that if there is no attempt at robbery during the coronation, it will be made in some other manner? That is our certain hope!"

"Or perhaps the entire story of the theft is a fairy tale."

He looked at me more calmly but sadly, as if I had failed to listen to a word.

Next morning he went again to Lord Holder, who had been created an alderman of the City of London the previous year and had now been accommodated by the Lord Mayor with a room at the Mansion House for the course of the celebrations. The coronation itself was only the first of several occasions at which the royal regalia and state jewels were to be worn. A monarch who is crowned in the City of Westminster must also take possession of the City of London a few days later. The second processional route would lie through the districts of law and finance. At noon a grand luncheon was to be held in the great Egyptian Hall of the Mansion House, where the Lord Mayor of London would play host to His Majesty and where Lord Holder would have much to do with the arrangements and the custody of the jewels.

"Since you are already acquainted with Lord Holder," said Holmes to me next morning, "you may find it instructive to see for yourself the areas of the Mansion House that must be guarded."

An hour or so later we stood in his lordship's room, which looked through a round-arched window towards the river and London Bridge. Our host then indicated a slightly built man who had just come in, an individual in a brown suit that was almost a match in color for his luxuriant mustache and eyes.

"It would have given me great pleasure, gentlemen, to show you the banqueting hall and the anterooms myself. Unfortunately, I am sitting in the Lord Mayor's court this morning. Therefore I must leave you in the capable hands of Inspector Jago of the City of London Police."

"Inspector Jago and I are old friends," said Holmes graciously. "I am sure we shall get along admirably."

The inspector extended his hand to each of us in turn,

"It is a year or two since then, Mr. Holmes. A matter of the Bank of England, as I recollect, robbed handsomely by three enterprising young American gentlemen."

He took us straight to the Egyptian Hall, lofty as a cathedral nave, whose plan had been based upon an Egyptian chamber of the ancient world. Inspector Jago opened the double doors and waved us in, as if he were the owner of the place. Two tables, each a hundred dinner places long, ran down either side with a high table across the far end. Side screens of lofty Corinthian columns supported a vaulted roof and framed the great classical arch of the west window. I was quite unprepared for such magnificence as this. The niches between the columns at either side were filled by sculptured groups or single figures in the manner of Grecian antiquity. Royal banners and shaded flambeaux hung before each alcove. Gilt chandeliers on triple chains were suspended at intervals from the roof down the entire length of the hall. Here the newly crowned King Edward would take lunch.

"Four hundred guests at a time, gentleman," said Inspector Jago quietly, for all the world as if we were in church. "Even this will be too little for His Majesty's visit. We shall be using the Venetian Parlour, Wilkes's Parlour, and every hole and corner. In short, we shall hardly know what to do with everyone."

I glanced at Holmes, hoping he was not about to denounce flummery again. He merely inquired, with a little impatience, "And what of the other offices appointed for the day?"

Inspector Jago touched his forehead briefly, as if to indicate a lapse of memory.

"Quite right, Mr. Holmes. Follow me and you shall see what we have by way of robing-rooms and the like. With space so tight, it would never do for our guests to be seated at luncheon in their robes!

We have provided the most secure accommodation for cloaks, robes, and insignia. This way, if you please."

We followed him up a broad flight of marble stairs and a little distance along a wide passageway. He stopped outside a double door of stout oak panels furnished with an impressive selection of locks and bolts.

"Here, gentlemen, are the rooms always set aside by the Lord Mayor as robing apartments for ceremonial occasions. Royalty and majesty, of course, have apartments of their own. At other times we use these as aldermen's committee rooms of the Common Council. They run along this side of the building and look down into the courtyard at its center. This door is the only way in. On the day of the royal visit, it will have a guard of two sergeants and two reserves from the Provost Marshal's Corps under the command of a senior captain. Once the rooms are locked after disrobing and the guests have gone down to lunch, no person will be permitted to enter until the function is over and the robing begins again."

He took out a key, unlocked the oak doors, and led us into a spacious oblong room. This was the area where each courtier in turn removed his robe with the assistance of his attendants and put it on again after the luncheon. Three tall sash windows along the left-hand side looked down into the courtyard. A large table at the centre, equipped with upright chairs padded by black horsehair, certainly had the air of a committee room. At the far end a second locked door led into the room where the robes were to be kept after they had been taken from their wearers. All furniture had been cleared from this second room and it was now occupied by three ranks of tailor's dummies in pale brown canvas set out as precisely as soldiers on parade.

"Here we have a second room almost identical to the first," said Jago reassuringly, "occupied at other times by the filing staff of the Clerk to the Common Council. There is no access but by the way we have just come. A mouse could not get in or out on the great day without authority."

"It is not a mouse that concerns me," said Holmes mildly. "A rat, perhaps, but a rat bearing such authority as you and your men might defer to without a second thought."

Jago laughed as uproariously as he could manage.

"Well and good, Mr. Holmes, if you say so. I am sure we must all be guided by you in this matter. In this second room, the cloaks will be mounted on these dummies; they will be safe as in the Bank of England. It is divided from the first room and the room beyond by doors securely locked."

"In the light of the case upon which you and I were engaged so many years ago," said Holmes coolly, "'safe as the Bank of England' appears to me an unfortunate choice of simile."

The thirty or forty tailors' dummies consisted of stuffed canvas bodies, from neck to hips, mounted on black-painted iron poles. Inspector Jago had bounced back from Holmes's rebuke with the aplomb of a rubber ball. He brushed his moustache confidently on the edge of his hand and beamed proudly.

"This, gentlemen, is what our frog-eating friends on the far side of the English Channel would call the *garde-robe*. Because, indeed, it is where the robes are guarded." He spread his empty hands like a conjurer performing an impossible trick. "Once again, there is no access except by the way we have come, which will be guarded as tight as the Tower of London. Safe as the Tower itself!"

"Do you really think so?"

"I think so, Mr. Holmes. I believe I am entitled to think so."

"And what of the third room beyond this?"

"You may see that, if you please, sir. Of course you shall. It is not in commission just now—quite *hors de combat* and locked up, in fact. For it is the post-room. Not much to the purpose, except when the clerks are here. But you wish to see it, sir, and so you shall. Not much to the purpose on the great day, we may safely say, but you shall see it indeed."

"I doubt very much," Holmes replied caustically, "if you may safely say anything."

Jago slipped his key into the Yale lock and opened the door. Here was a room about half the size of the first two, a dead-end with no entrance or exit but by the way we had come, as Inspector Jago hastened to assure us. There was only a single sash window. The further wall, an exterior wall of the building, was filled by cupboards floor to ceiling. For further security, these were built some way into the wall itself. The cupboards appeared to be locked, perhaps by a single key that fitted the entire suite. Holmes surveyed them in a long single glance.

"I think we have seen enough," he said, "except for the matter of the windows."

"The windows?" For the first time, Jago lost a little of his bounce.

"The windows," Holmes repeated. "You have done so thorough a job, Inspector, creating a strong room from these three offices, ensuring that the only access—and, indeed, the only exit—is by way of a heavily guarded exterior door. Come now, you have surely seen that the only remaining weakness can be the windows. You were teasing us—or testing us—by not mentioning them, were you not? Putting us to the proof!""

This caught Mr. Jago nicely, on one leg, as it were. It was plain he had never given a thought to the danger of attack at such a height by way of the windows which were on view to the courtyard. However, to admit that now would demolish him.

"I have had the windows in mind, Mr. Holmes," he said uneasily.

"To be sure you have," replied Holmes consolingly.

"I did not, however, consider them the most likely approach."

"Did you not? Surely they are the only approach, once your guards are in place."

"I was about to mention them, however."

"To be sure you were. I did not suggest the possibility of an attack down through the ceiling or up through the floor, for I was quite certain that you must have taken precautions against that too."

"Indeed so," said Jago hastily. "Police constables are to be posted in rooms above and below."

"Excellent! In that case you can have no objection to assisting me in a small experiment with the windows. Would it be possible for one of us to go down into the courtyard and maneuver a small weight attached to a piece of string?"

He drew from his pocket a ball of thin cord, to the end of which a one-pound scale weight with a hook had been attached.

"It would be possible, Mr. Holmes, only. . . ."

"Only your instructions are to trust no one, not even Dr. Watson and myself. You must not leave us alone up here to wander about at will. Equally, you could not send one of us alone to roam the building on our way down to the yard. You are quite right, you have thought of everything, and you have passed the first test—loyalty to those in command of you. I should not dream of compromising you. Indeed, I insist that if you would be so good as to go down and manipulate the weight as I shall instruct you, you must lock us both in here and, if possible, one of your constables should keep surveillance upon us. However, it is imperative that I should have this assistance with my little experiment, and I would prefer not to involve anyone but the three of us."

In the end, as Holmes had foreseen and contrived, Jago went down to the courtyard after locking us in, with a pantomime of reluctance. As soon as he was gone, my friend said:

"Quick about it, Watson. That wretched fellow is worse than Lestrade. If we leave it to them, there will not be a jewel left in the entire royal collection. I must make a survey of the rooms. Open the window over there and lower the little weight on the cord—as slowly as you can. That will occupy him for a moment."

I pushed up the window and began to pay out the cord. While doing this, it was not easy to watch what Holmes was up to, but he was striding about the anteroom, the garde-robe, and the post-room while pausing briefly from time to time. Once or twice I heard a tiny rasping sound of metal on metal. Then he appeared at the window beside me and began to shout instructions at Jago, thirty feet below. I cannot bear to repeat them all, for some were so idiotic, but at last he called down:

"Take the weight! See how far it will swing side to side, along the wall. If our man comes down over the roof, he may gain a window ledge by descending to one side and swinging across. We must take measurements of that possibility."

"But the windows can be locked, Mr. Holmes."

"With a small steel jimmy, he can wrench them from their frames."

"In the City of London and in broad daylight, Mr. Holmes?"

"He may carry a cloth and pail and masquerade as a window-cleaner."

"During His Majesty's visit?"

"Or he may enter by night."

However low Jago's opinion of my friend's detective skill, it was lower still by the time the inspector returned to what he called facetiously his garde-robe. He must surely have suspected something from this farce but he could not see, let alone prove, anything amiss. I had been a little put out when Holmes made his tour of Westminster Abbey and the House of Lords without me. Now I wished that I had also spent the day of the Mansion House visit at home.

4

THE WORLD KNOWS that Coronation Day came and went without the loss of a single jewel. This enabled Lestrade to be still more witty at our expense, ruminating over his evening whisky and water at the manner in which the bumbledom of the Scotland Yard force had triumphed without the assistance of a detective genius. Sherlock Holmes remained unruffled, favouring him only with a quick humourless smile that was more than anything a grimace of impatience.

My thoughts still turned from time to time to Colonel Moriarty. Though Holmes and I knew of his criminal intent, he had surely missed the boat now that the main coronation ceremony was over. Even Holmes himself, when he sent a final refusal to stand guard at the coronation itself, remarked, "The whole alarm over the coronation and the jewels is a fuss about nothing."

"You cannot know that," I said. "No one can."

"You will recall my reply to the wretched thief in the Case of the Blue Carbuncle, as you chose to call it. 'My name is Sherlock Holmes. It is my business to know what other people don't know.'"

So it came to the week of the Lord Mayor's luncheon. The street banners and loyal flags that had decorated the West End on Coronation Day now appeared in the great commercial streets of the City of London, around St. Paul's cathedral, on banks and insurance offices, at commodity brokers' and stock dealers'. Little rows of bunting also adorned the close-packed houses of the adjacent East End, as well as the docks of Wapping and Limehouse.

The behavior of Sherlock Holmes had created a dilemma for me. He would say nothing more, yet he appeared sure of everything. He had long ago left Lestrade and Brother Mycroft high and dry. Even my loyalty was put to the test. Had he got the wrong end of the stick, as the saying goes? All men are mortal, even Sherlock Holmes. It was not beyond possibility that he was in error over some vital detail. He had admitted errors in certain past cases.

How could Holmes know from the start that it was not the coronation but the Lord Mayor's luncheon that would be the occasion of a sensational theft? Unless the colonel was to knock down the wearer of the Queen of the Night in full public view, the only opportunity must be while the robes, cloaks, and their insignia were locked away in the garde-robe during the official luncheon.

Unless our opponent had a team of labourers with pick-axes to break through a twelve-inch stone wall, the only approach to that room was by double doors securely locked and bolted, guarded by armed sergeants of the Provost Marshal's Corps. Within the anteroom, the communicating door, which led into the garde-robe with its rows of tailor's dummies, was also locked. There were the windows down one side, overlooking the courtyard thirty feet below. However, since Holmes had made such play of these to Inspector Jago, police guards in the courtyard were to keep constant surveillance to frustrate any attempt at the casements. The smaller post-room at the end would also be locked but its own cupboards, large enough for a cat but not for a man.

The integrity of the Provost Marshal's Corps was unquestioned. Even if an intruder could hide himself in these rooms during the royal luncheon, any theft would be discovered once the minor courtiers and their attendants returned to assume their robes for the rest of the ceremonies—while the thief must still be there. The disappearance of the Queen of the Night would cause any suspect to be stripped to the skin—however discreetly. Then, if nothing was found, he must be free to go. Yet he would go without his trophy. Every room or cupboard would be taken to pieces, floorboards taken up. No one would be permitted to return, certainly not a thief who might have hidden his booty there.

Suspicion must fall primarily on the two unfortunate sergeants at the door of the garde-robe, who entered it alone when they collected and handed out the robes after lunch. Or perhaps it might fall upon a chamber-groom who assisted his master to disrobe and robe again. Holmes had calculated how such a crime might be carried out. If he could calculate it, so might someone else.

If ever there was a mystery in a locked room, this must be it, and I am not a great believer in such riddles. Colonel Moriarty would take one look at the provost sergeants and abandon his plan—if he ever had one. This would not suit Holmes, who intended a final encounter with his adversary, but Colonel Moriarty was not there to suit Holmes.

That evening after dinner I watched Holmes cautiously from behind my newspaper as he sat at his work-table. He unwrapped a chamois leather and took out what might have been the Queen of the Night, had the famous ornament been nothing but a Christmas-tree decoration or a glass fancy-dress trinket. Perhaps he hoped to trick Colonel Moriarty into stealing a mere gewgaw rather than a Brazilian diamond set among indigo sapphires. In the heat of the moment the colonel might be deceived, though I doubted it. In any case, a counterfeit may be of use to the thief. I could not see what help it would be to those who hunted him. I opened my evening paper, certain that this trumpery, as Mycroft would call it, seemed unlikely to warrant the duel to the death that Sherlock Holmes had set his heart on. I was wrong—but I could not know it then.

5

The sunshine on the Lord Mayor's day of glory showed that first mellowing that comes with the turn of summer into autumn. Holmes and I were at the Mansion House by early morning. Lord Holder and Inspector Jago left us much to ourselves, his lordship believing we knew best and the inspector regarding our presence as unnecessary. We both wore formal court dress of black frock coat and white tie, striped trousers, and silk top-hat.

Four hundred of the noblest were to sit with King Edward, Queen Alexandra, the Prince and Princess of Wales, the Lord Mayor, and Aldermen of the City of London in the grandeur of the Egyptian Hall. Lesser chamberlains, heralds, and those who could not be accommodated in such splendour were to take lunch either in the Venetian Parlour or Wilkes's Parlour. Lower still were those officers and officials who would be accommodated with little more than a buffet.

"You would do me the greatest service," said Holmes as we made our itinerary of the upper floor, "if you were to take up your position in Lord Holder's room. From there, you will have a direct view across the courtyard into the windows of the garde-robe and a room to right and left. That is to say, the anteroom on the left, the garde-robe, and the post-room on its right, as we saw them on our tour of inspection. On Lord Holder's desk you will find a pair of field-glasses with Zeiss precision lenses. Train these on the opposite windows. Leave nothing unobserved."

As an afterthought, he added, "No matter what you see, remain there until the appointed time. You may observe what looks like a crime in progress, but it may be nothing of consequence."

"It would help a good deal if I knew what I am supposed to see."

"I anticipate there will be a crush in the anteroom when the royal procession from Buckingham Palace breaks up in the courtyard and the minor nobility enter to disrobe for lunch. That will dwindle, everyone will leave to go down to the Egyptian Hall, and the doors will be locked and secured by the provost guard. The rooms will remain quiet for an hour or more during the royal lunch. The two armed sergeants and the captain of the Provost Marshal's Corps will stand guard on the only door giving access, with two more sergeants in reserve. Jago and several of his men will be in the courtyard. A bluebottle fly, I suggest, will not get in or out during that time."

"And you, Holmes?"

He shrugged. "I shall await events and keep my eye on Colonel Moriarty throughout lunch. He with his co-chamberlain will attend in the robing-room as grooms of the chamber to Lord Dorset. Then he will be seated in the Egyptian Parlour. Lord Holder has placed me there as well, with a convenient pillar between us. When the meal is over, you will make your way to the doors where the provost sentries stand. The keys are guarded by the Lord Mayor's chamberlain. He will hand them to the guard commander, who will open the doors and stand back for the minor courtiers to enter. The two sergeants will unlock the garderobe, enter, and hand out the robes to the attendants in a strict order."

"And you?"

"I shall be there. You have your revolver with you and it is loaded?"

"Of course. All the same, I cannot see that there is the least opportunity for Colonel Moriarty to lay hands on the Queen of the Night!"

"That is precisely how he would wish it to seem. You understand your instructions."

"Such as they are."

"Capital! We may have every confidence that this will end well."

I had not the least confidence of any such thing. I had no clear idea of what Colonel Moriarty looked like except from shadowy photographs of a tall black-coated man coming and going in a dingy courtyard. As one of the grooms of the chamber to the Earl of Dorset, he would be dressed in a scarlet tunic with a little gold piping, but almost every man in the building would be wearing one of those. He would have no robe of his own, being merely a servant of the earl.

I calculated that the distance across the courtyard was about eighty or ninety feet. My field-glasses were rather of the Barr & Stroud pattern with precision-ground lenses. They brought the opposite windows sharply into view and gave me a clear enough image beyond them for the canvas texture of the naked tailor's dummies to be plainly visible. As yet there was nothing to observe. I remained in position until I heard the deep bell of St. Paul's in the distance, striking noon. Presently the buzz of conversation from Inspector Jago's men in the courtyard gave way to the first rumble of carriage wheels.

Briefly, I trained my glasses on the arrivals below: King Edward and Queen Alexandra in an open brougham, she graceful and he majestic; the Prince and Princess of Wales, he in royal blue as befitted the occasion; Lord Longstaffe behind him with the Queen of the Night—the cause of all the trouble!—at his throat. I brought it into focus. There was no mistaking this as the genuine article when the August sun flashed upon it. Surrounded by its cluster of twelve sapphires, the twelve planes of the great stone glittered and dazzled alternately. A sapphire may vary from pale blue to indigo, and generally the lighter cornflower blue fetches the highest prices. In this case, the effect of stones of the deepest blue was far more dramatic. As Lord Holder had remarked, what might be lost in price was made up for by the value of the clasp as a work of the jeweller's art. Behind the stout figure of Lord Longstaffe, I made out princes and princesses, several crowned heads, the shah of Persia, ambassadors and diplomats. Though less grand than the coronation ceremony, it was in some ways more lavish.

Turning the field-glasses to the windows opposite, I saw the locked double doors of the anteroom swing open. The royal party and its distinguished guests were disrobed elsewhere. In the anteroom, as Jago called it, the lesser aristocracy—heralds and chamberlains—presented themselves to the dressers who drew off each robe and entrusted it to a uniformed provost sergeant at the doorway of the garde-robe. It was carried through and arranged on its allotted tailor's dummy. There was an air of slow ceremony and none of that rush, disorder, or confusion that enables a thief to snatch a treasure and run.

After fifteen minutes at the most, the last of the lords and ladies-in-waiting had left and the three rooms opposite me were quiet, as Holmes had prophesied. The garde-robe itself had undergone a transformation. Its forty or so canvas dummies were now a glittering parade, robes of scarlet and gold, blue and gold, green and silver, adorned with clusters of brilliants. Black cocked hats, some gold-braided and some not, sat upon the round canvas polls of the heads, uniformly tilted forward to secure their balance. Yet these canvas figures reminded me not so much of court splendour as of carcasses strung up for dissection in an anatomy theatre.

For half an hour I scanned the three rooms through my glasses with little idea of what I might expect to see. Once I fancied that I caught a movement. It startled me almost as much as if a corpse had winked at me during an anatomy class. There was nothing more. Surely a thief would not choose to be trapped with two burly provost sergeants guarding the only door and police under the windows.

I settled down for a moment and then—there it was again! Just a fleeting sight of red moving among the rows of dummy torsos which obscured most of the view. One thing was certain: if anyone was in the garde-robe, he would be in full view the moment he came out into the antechamber. But how would he have a key to let himself out? Perhaps I was only seeing what I feared to see. Possibly a provost sergeant had been left to patrol the room. Holmes had told me the garde-robe would be quiet. He did say it would be empty or unoccupied. Who knows what last-minute instructions had been issued?

I had taken up my position so as to have a full view of the garde-robe, a three-quarter view of the anteroom to the left, and perhaps a quarter view of the post-room to the right, which contained only drawers for stationery and was not involved in the present arrangements. In any case, that was also locked. I tried to locate the royal-blue cloak of Lord Longstaffe, the Prince of Wales's herald, among the files of those mounted on the dummies. In the spaces between the first ranks I caught glimpses of dark blue, scarlet, emerald-green, and gold on the figures behind. Of the rear two ranks I could see little or nothing. Through one gap there was the left shoulder and lapel of a dark, blue cloak. It might have been one of a dozen, but beyond question the blue nap of the velvet was bare of any ornament. Either it was not the Lord Longstaffe's cloak, or else the Queen of the Night had been removed.

For what seemed like an age but was probably no more then thirty seconds, I was torn between unease and the fear of making a monumental fool of myself by getting into a panic over a cloak that never carried an insignia in the first place! Through the field-glasses, I studied as much of the gold braid on the epaulette as I could see. It was no great help, because all these robes and cloaks had gold-braided epaulettes of some pattern. Even if this was Lord Longstaffe's cloak, perhaps the diamond and its sapphire cluster had been laid in a locked drawer for further security.

I could see three or four inches of the upright collar and a gold-embroidered frieze upon it. I looked again. Just within my range of vision and no more than an inch high, the gold embroidery formed a motif of three feathers—beneath, in letters so tiny that I could not be sure of them, I swear were the two words "*Ich dien.*" You may believe that this is the "I serve" motto of the King of Bohemia, slain by the Black Prince at Crecy in 1346, or the Welsh "*Eich dyn*"—"Behold the man"—with which Edward I presented his son to the people at Carnarvon. In either case, it was the Prince of Wales's motto and his emblem of three feathers on the tunic of its herald! And where the Queen of the Night should have sparkled and glittered, there was only bare blue velvet! My heart and entrails sank with panic.

Still dreading that I had somehow made an utter fool of myself, I bolted out of Lord Holder's room and raced for the main doors of the garde-robe where the two sergeants and captain of the Provost Marshal's Corps were on duty. In one of Holmes's famous exhortations, there was not a moment to be lost. But what was I to do? The provos would not open the oaken double door at my mere request. Almost certainly they would not have been entrusted with the key to do so. To denounce Colonel Moriarty as a thief who was ransacking the rooms would expose us to him completely, if the figure I thought I had seen proved to be somebody else.

I had the sudden thought that I must flush him out—whoever he was—and as I came within sight of the provost guard I thought I knew how to do it. I now see that I had little time to consider the wisdom of my action. Yet one thing was certain. If Colonel Moriarty was in the garde-robe he could not be simultaneously eating lunch in the Venetian Parlour or any other venue. I confronted the young provost captain.

"It is imperative that I should speak at once to Colonel Moriarty, chamber groom to the Earl of Dorset. He is at lunch, I believe, in the Venetian Parlour."

If he was in the garde-robe, this would betray him. The young captain coloured a little.

"If Colonel Moriarty is at luncheon, it is impossible for him to be called away."

"I am Dr. John Watson, surgeon-major of the Northumberland Fusiliers. It is imperative that I should speak to the colonel at once! The matter cannot wait!"

The truth was I had been regimental surgeon-major fifteen years ago in Afghanistan. I was so no longer. The white lie seemed a forlorn hope, but I had the most prodigious stroke of luck. As a medical man, I am used to reading from their facial expressions the thoughts of those who learn what my calling is. The young captain plainly sensed a medical emergency. He inquired no further.

Striding to the corner of the passageway, he barked out a name. A young trooper came to attention before him, received his command, and doubled away. As I followed the captain, I saw in a shadowy alcove to one side three Martini-Henry rifles stacked wigwam-style. The defenders of the realm and the monarch were taking no chances!

For a minute or two I paced the marble balcony above the broad staircase until I heard the sound of distant footsteps. My heart sank. It seemed plain that Colonel Moriarty had the unshakeable alibi of having been at lunch in the Venetian Parlour during every minute of the time that I had been telling myself stories about the Queen of the Night.

I drew back. He came up the first flight of the staircase, the rear view of his scarlet tunic and dark trousers marking him out as what he was. The plain cocked hat, left off in the Venetian Parlour, was now on his head again. I knew not what to expect as he came up the second flight to the level of the balcony, his head bowed. As he turned towards me, I strode forward, displaying far more confidence than I felt. He looked up and my heart almost stopped dead. I found myself staring into the face of Sherlock Holmes!

6

"Congratulations, my dear fellow," he said sardonically. "Your inability to follow the simplest instructions is, happily, something I might have depended upon. You have very nearly ruined everything."

"Where is Colonel Moriarty and why are you wearing that uniform?"

"This is not a uniform, merely an ordinary military tunic, borrowed for the occasion. Colonel Moriarty is, I trust, in the process of robbing the nation of the Queen of the Night. Indeed, I imagine that by now the gem must be on its way to its destination."

"On its way? The outer door is still locked and guarded by the provost sergeants. The door between the anteroom and the garde-robe is still locked, so for that matter is the last one between the garde-robe and the post-room. Anyone in there is still there—trapped."

Then I saw the certain answer.

"Is our man in his place at the luncheon-table?"

"There is no doubt of it. Indeed, he has not been out of my sight since before the garde-robe was closed and locked."

"Then what the devil is going on?"

My friend merely chuckled.

"Poor old Watson. I fear you would never make an international jewel thief—let alone catch one. I have not the least doubt that Colonel Moriarty has somehow had the run of the garde-robe and the rooms either side of it at some time in the recent past. Perhaps long before the coronation, when no one was paying attention to them. Indeed I have been counting on this, and I have kept his secret for him. As to the diamond and sapphires, I imagine they are on their way to Paris."

How this was possible, or why Holmes made light of it, was beyond me.

"Why are you in that tunic?"

"Despite the pillar between us in the Venetian Parlor, it is best to be inconspicuous. The best way is to dress as most people here are dressed. Lord Holder was kind enough to arrange it."

"Then who is at lunch?"

"With Colonel Piquart's assistance, I went to some trouble over the photographs he was kind enough to send me. I observed that each was marked with the date on which it was taken. One of those dates was no other than the day on which Colonel Moriarty paid his call upon our jeweller, Raoul Grenier, in Brussels. Therefore the man in the photographs could not be he. I had doubts about it from the first. On Colonel Piquart's recommendation I applied to that most useful organisation in Paris, the Deuxieme Bureau. They were able to identify the man in the photographs as an accomplished swindler and fluent linguist, known in their records as Colonel Lemonnier. In his line of business, he naturally has a number of pseudonyms. Perhaps he sometimes calls himself Colonel Moriarty—I doubt it. Perhaps Colonel Moriarty sometimes calls himself Colonel Lemonnier, I doubt that too."

"And Lemonnier, no doubt, was one of the lesser breeds for whom a champagne buffet was provided and where no one would notice if a man was missing or not!"

"Excellent, Watson. As for appearances, Colonel Moriarty has seldom been in England for the past seventeen years, since the so-called white-slave scandals. Few people would have much recollection of what he looked like. Fewer still would care to be his friends."

"But the theft has not been prevented. That seems the long and the short of it."

Holmes sighed and leant back against the marble balustrade.

"I have said, until I am weary of saying so, that I have no wish to prevent it. If it is prevented, Colonel Moriarty goes to prison for a short term. If it is committed, he and I may settle matters in our own way."

He now drew out his notebook and laid upon it three tiny wafers of steel, unfolded from tissue paper. The metal was dark and pliable, speckled by bright dust.

"The other day, while you assisted our friend Jago by swinging a weight from his garde-robe window, I made a quick but meticulous survey of that room, the anteroom, and the post-room, whose doors were conveniently open. These wafers are magnetized steel. The powder is metallic dust, easily attracted when a delicate magnetized probe is inserted into a keyway. I obtained it by using one still wafer in the Yale lock on the door that passes from the anteroom to the garde-robe, a second on the door between the garde-robe and the post-room, a third in the locks on the post-room cupboards until I found one which produced a similar result. It was the work of a minute."

"What is the dust?"

"Bright steel with a low carbon content. The low content makes it easier to work in the construction of Yale-pattern locks. This is the residue from an attack on the mechanism of the three locks. The weapon was almost certainly a very fine diamond-head drill. The brightness of the dust confirms that the attacks were recent, no doubt while the rooms were still being used as offices and without a special guard. Even today, the post-room has no part in the ceremonial."

He folded the metal wafers into his notecase again.

"The Yale works on a novel principle. Other locks open by the key lifting the levers that hold the bolt in place. Unless the outline of the key matches the position and shape of the levers, it will not lift them. In a Yale, the entire lock turns, provided the contours of the key match those of the interior. Otherwise the key may not even thread the lock. With other locks a burglar may use two or three picks simultaneously. In the narrow Yale keyway a thief can only insert one pick, which makes the method almost impossible."

"You presume that Colonel Moriarty prepared these locks in advance?"

"There would have been no metal dust in the keyways otherwise. The interior of a Yale is a series of steel pins. Drill them all and there is no obstruction to a key of that make. It will turn the lock. For every pin you drill, the more likely that any other Yale key will turn it. Drill them all and there is no resistance to your key, but the lack of resistance would betray you. The trick is to drill two or three pins and work a fourth with a single pick. The two pins remaining provide to make it seem the lock is in order, moving easily as if freshly oiled."

"Every lock, surely, is different."

"Very few keys and locks are unique. Each firm has quite a small number of patterns. The odds that your door key will open another particular one are many thousands to one. You would not know which to try. That is of no use to a criminal. Yet every pin removed shortens those odds. When three have been removed and a fourth can be manipulated with a needle-probe, a man with a hundred keys of general stock pattern could probably open a lock. Indeed, the latchkey of 221b Baker Street came within an ace of moving the lock that separates the anteroom from the garde-robe."

Behind us, on the stairs rose a hubbub of voices as the minor courtiers returned to be robed. The Lord Mayor's chamberlain in black breeches and buckles, lace cuffs and collar, passed us with Inspector Jago in uniform and a City of London police superintendent. The chamberlain presented a key to the captain of the provost guard. The captain unlocked the oak double doors, than pushed them inward and wide to either side. The first dozen dignitaries whose cloaks or robes were mounted on the tailor's dummies made their way into the anteroom, among them the tall and dignified Lord Holder and the stout gray-mopped figure of Lord Adolphus Longstaffe. The two provost sergeants who were to unlock the garde-robe at the far end and hand out the garments followed them respectfully.

Holmes motioned me onward, while he hung back. I kept to one side, in a corner of the anteroom by the window. The sergeants had unlocked the next door and now brought forward the robes, one at a time, and handed them to the chamber-grooms who would assist their patrons to put them on.

There were still fifteen or twenty minor courtiers in tunics and breeches, awaiting their cloaks or robes. To one side stood a belted earl and two attendants in scarlet with black braid. One of them caught my attention, as I watched from a little behind him and out of his present range of vision. He was tall, thin, no more than fifty, but with a dry look to him and the skin-texture of a wrinkled prune. It was not this that held my gaze, but rather the way his reddened forehead seemed to curve outwards, the look of his sunken eyes, and his manner of letting his head turn slowly from side to side, as if in time to some inner music or the demands of a deep intellectual problem. I had seen such movements before and knew that they betrayed concealed agitation. They had been a compulsion of the late Professor Moriarty, whose bulging forehead and sunken eyes I seemed to see before me now. There was only one man in that room who could be Colonel Moriarty.

How easy it would be for Colonel Lemonnier, whom nobody knew, to masquerade at lunch as Colonel Moriarty, whom nobody knew either, while there was one guest fewer, unnoticed, in the crush of the champagne buffet. I turned away, sure that he had not noticed me, and went to find Holmes, who was standing next to Jago. I noticed that the inspector's color was rather high, his moustache appeared to bristle, and he had withdrawn into a dignified silence.

"Thanks to official incompetence," said Holmes to me behind his hand, "Lemonnier left the Venetian Parlour unobserved, before luncheon was over, and has disappeared. Nonetheless we will wait here, if you please, and be ready to move quickly. If you wish to witness my *pièce de resistance*, keep your eyes on Lord Holder."

Lord Holder stood an inch or two taller than anyone in his immediate vicinity. He was walking towards us, smiling contentedly, and the little crowd of courtiers drew back a little before his regal person. He was escorting the bowed figure of Lord Adolphus Longstaffe. The whole appeared to have been staged so that among the front rank of onlookers was Colonel Moriarty. As if by instinct, my fingers closed on the cold metal of the revolver butt in the pocket of my black morning coat. What followed took only a few seconds and seemed like a lifetime.

Lord Holder and his protégé came on, their heads and necks visible above the others. As they drew closer, their epaulettes and then their lapels came into view. When I stared at Lord Longstaffe, I felt the wonder of a small child witnessing the first miracle of a birthday conjurer. There, on his left lapel, blazed a white diamond fire and a deep indigo of surrounding sapphire. The outline of the Queen of the Night, an irreplaceable treasure that Holmes had assured me was on its way to Paris, shone brilliantly among us.

My gaze swung to the gaunt but inflamed face of Colonel Moriarty, whom I quite expected to draw a gun and tear the gem from Lord Longstaffe's breast. But if my face reflected utter astonishment and disbelief, the colonel's betrayed only the deepest horror. He did not reach forward to snatch the jewel but recoiled at the sight of it.

At that moment Sherlock Holmes beside me doffed the black cocked hat of the uniform that he had borrowed and made an exaggerated and eye-catching gesture. Colonel Moriarty, with a stony fear still flooding his sunken eyes, for all the world as if Don Giovanni's devils were dragging him down to hell, turned his heavy head and saw us. He knew well enough who we were. Beside us he saw the unmistakable figure of Inspector Jago in his ceremonial uniform, flanked by a superintendent of the City of London Police. My revolver was halfway out of my pocket before our adversary could reach for his. I did not doubt that he was carrying a gun, but, to my surprise, he made no attempt to reach for it. Instead, he turned and ran, pushing aside those behind him, and disappeared down the marble corridor with Jago and the superintendent in pursuit.

"Jago!" Holmes's voice rang out like a parade-ground command. "Let him go but lay a trail for us!"

My friend now pushed through the crowd of astonished onlookers. In a few strides he was through the anteroom and the garde-robe, swooping into the post-room, opening a cupboard with a key that Lord Holder had given him. The cupboard contained a machine of some kind, a cast-iron box with a brass-framed, airtight lid, inset with a glass panel. To one side of this rose a white porcelain handle, like a small beer pump. Inside the box I saw through the glass a three-inch bell-mouthed opening at one end, an incoming air pipe at the other. Lightweight envelopes of black rubbery gutta-percha in felt covers lay to hand, ensuring that each exactly fitted the tube.

Thought I had never seen such a thing before, I knew what this apparatus must be. This was a house tube connecting the office in the Mansion House with the pneumatic dispatch system—the system that carries telegrams and small post through forty miles of London's underground postal system. The pipe at one end of the box would exert a pressure of some ten pounds to the square inch on sending, or a vacuum of six pounds on receiving. It could transport bundles of seventy-five telegrams in a gutta-percha envelope, and would cover a mile through a three-inch tube in about two minutes. The diamond and the surrounding sapphires, unclipped, would be light enough to fit into two envelopes.

Sherlock Holmes checked the list of possible destinations framed on the inside of the cupboard door.

"I hardly think he will have communicated with the Houses of Parliament, Buckingham Palace, or Scotland Yard. I prefer Charing Cross Station! That is quite another matter. I will bet a pound to a penny on the next ferry train to Paris."

He scrawled a message on a dispatch form, inserted it into a fold of gutta-percha, and addressed it. Over his shoulder, I saw the words, "Lestrade. Scotland Yard." All this, which takes so long to tell, occupied less than a minute in reality!

"I have had my doubts," I gasped as we raced down the stairs to the courtyard, "but I confess them ill-founded. The manner in which you have duped this last Moriarty rivals the best you have done. I shall never forget his face when he stared at Lord Longstaffe's lapel and knew he had stolen the fake that you planted for him!"

He stopped dead at the turning of the staircase and looked at me.

"Have you understood nothing? That bauble on Longstaffe's lapel was the fake! The Moriarty family knows a counterfeit when it sees one plainly. However, in the half-light of the passageway, he could not tell. He thought he saw the very thing he had stolen half an hour before, as a murderer sees a ghost. It shook him! By God, you saw how it shook him! Then he turned his head to find the two of us and two policemen staring at him. After that, it mattered nothing whether the bauble was a fake or not. Your revolver was half out of your pocket and he knew he was almost caught."

We flew through the doorway into the courtyard and Holmes shouted at a constable for a closed brougham to follow Inspector Jago. As we clattered out of the courtyard, he turned to me more calmly.

"I will borrow your revolver, old fellow, if I may."

I handed him the cold butt of the gun.

"Charing Cross?" I said.

"Think of it. Moriarty easily contrived to be locked in the anteroom or garde-robe, and quite possibly hid himself in the post-room, when everyone else had left. Colonel Lemonnier represented him in the Venetian Parlour. Within five minutes, the colonel came out of hiding and removed the Queen of the Night from the lapel of Lord Longstaffe's cloak, unclipped the diamond center from the sapphires, and dispatched two small envelopes in the pneumatic tube. When the minor courtiers returned, what was easier than for the thief to stand back against the wall behind the open doors or step out from the concealment of a long curtain when the coast was clear and mingle with them. Up to that time, there was no cause for alarm. When that alarm was raised, there would not be a shred of evidence against him."

"The hunt would be up as soon as the theft was discovered."

"Those cloaks were brought out one by one. Half the people there would have drifted away. Colonel Moriarty would have ample time to slip away before Lord Longstaffe noticed his loss. He might prefer to stay. The Queen of the Night would not be found on him, whereas any one of the twenty or thirty people who had left might have it. Colonel Lemonnier would be the first to reach Charing Cross. Have no fear, his freedom is important to our plans."

"And our colonel?"

"He must bolt for home, among the apaches of the Place Pigalle and the street women of the Avenue de Clichy. You may be sure that his rooms at the Hellfire Club are deserted—and the bill unpaid! The next ferry train for Folkestone and Boulogne, I think, Watson. He need only collect two small and unremarkable packages from the telegraph office, assume the style of a boulevardier, and dine tonight beyond the reach of the English law, while Jago and Lestrade are still searching the Mansion House!"

We were pelting downhill toward Ludgate Circus, the great dome of St. Paul's and its pillared portico at our backs.

"The game is altered for him," Holmes said grimly. "He believes he has seen the very jewel he stole and dispatched half an hour before. It could not by any means be where he saw it now unless he was betrayed. In his place, how would you respond to that?"

"I should go straight to wherever I expected it to be—to see what trick had been played upon me."

"Exactly."

Our driver, a uniformed constable, saw ahead of him a barrier across Fleet Street and the Strand, routes reserved that afternoon for the royal procession.

"With any luck," said Holmes softly, "our fugitive will have been delayed by that."

We swung right towards Blackfriars Bridge. In a moment we were racing along the Embankment towards Westminster, the river sparkling on our left, penny steamers trailing banners of black smoke; on our right, the trees and lawyers' chambers of the Temple. We swung again, up the narrow canyon of Villiers Street, Charing Cross Station on a vast undercroft of sooty brick rising massively above us.

Holmes was out of the carriage first, racing for the departure platforms. We found Inspector Jago, still in black uniform with gold piping, pacing the concourse, studying the passengers who filed past the ticket-collectors. I saw Holmes signal to him and they drew back cautiously behind a corner of the bookstall, where they could keep watch on the post and telegraph office.

As I joined them, Holmes was saying earnestly, "Twenty past two. There is a ferry train at three and calculate the packages were collected from the office half an hour ago. You may be sure the name on them will not be Moriarty. It may be Lemonnier. It may be anyone."

He strode across the busy concourse in full view and entered the office while Jago and I watched. I saw him at the counter, confronting the manager, a man of middle age, no doubt accustomed to dealing with postal fraud. Their conversation continued until I saw Sherlock Holmes shout something at the unfortunate guardian.

There was a pause during which the man may have replied. Then he very slowly raised his hands in the air. I guessed that Holmes had drawn—or threatened to draw—my revolver from his pocket. There were moments of passionate anger in him when he might certainly be capable of shooting a postal official who obstructed his investigation.

Fortunately, Inspector Jago was looking in the other direction just then, watching the crowds who pressed homewards from their day of celebration along the royal route. The postal manager stepped to one side. Holmes had him covered with the gun in one hand and was rifling the rows of wooden pigeonholes in which messages and small packages awaited collection. He drew them out by handfuls, glanced at them, and threw them on the floor. Finally he shouted at the terrified postal official, received a reply, threw open the door, and strode in our direction again.

"For God's sake, Holmes!"

"I am told that I have seen every telegram or package that is awaiting collection. Not one! Not one item here that is bulky enough to be what we seek. Someone has got them!"

"Not Colonel Moriarty," I said reassuringly. "He could hardly have been here long enough before we arrived to enter the office and leave again. Lemonnier, under whatever name they have agreed, is another matter."

Inspector Jago had evidently paid little attention to what Holmes was saying. He now spoke without turning to us.

"Well now," he said quietly, "there's a thing!"

The minute-hand on the large four-sided clock on the girders above us approached the half hour. We followed his gaze.

"Now there is a curious thing," he said. "That grizzled man wearing a livery cape coming towards the steps down to the washrooms—he has a Robert Heath livery cape, just as a cabman might. No harm in that. But where it hangs open, see if that isn't a silk surplice shirt underneath, such as only a gentleman would wear. He doesn't try to look a gentleman, to be sure, and yet he happens to be carrying a Jenner & Knewstub leather travelling-bag. A most expensive item with compartments for clothing, shaving brushes, and all else that a real toff might require."

"One thing certain," said Holmes peremptorily, "he is too short and too well-set to be Colonel Moriarty. Meantime, we must keep watch here. For the moment you have your curious acquaintance bottled up, if you need him."

The minute-hand on the large clock above us touched the next Roman numeral. Half past two. We were within sight of the ticket-barrier for that platform which served the ferry train. None of the passengers who had filed through showed the least resemblance to our prey.

"And behold!" said Inspector Jago presently. "Our man has come up again with his livery cape still on, his surplice shirt, but without his expensive travelling-bag. Unless I am mistaken, he is making for the cab rank. I think, however, he is not a cabdriver but a passenger in a hurry."

Jago turned and looked hard at two men reading newspapers on a passengers' waiting bench. I had not noticed them there when we arrived, nor had I noticed them arrive since, so unobtrusive were their movements. Now they rose separately and set off in the wake of the livery cape.

Holmes, Jago, and I watched the iron-railed space within which the steps led down to the steam and marble of the washrooms. There was a cloakroom for the deposit of luggage down there, and the explanation of Jago's curiosity might be as simple as that. I waited for the first sign of a red tunic, but I waited in vain. It was Holmes who moved first. His target was a man in black city coat and trousers with a silk hat and silver-knobbed ebony stick. It was only at a second glance that I saw that he carried a Jenner & Knewstub overnight bag in his left hand.

I should not have known him as Colonel Moriarty, though he was of the same height. The silk hat disguised something of the bulging forehead; a pair of heavily rimmed spectacles gave him a studious air that somehow brought forward the deep-set eyes. He had a dark moustache and was walking in a curiously determined manner.

At the top of the steps from the underground cloakrooms, he swung away from us rapidly and approached the revolving door of the Charing Cross Hotel. We took up the pursuit, striding at a little distance behind him. As the door turned slowly, we were just in time to see him enter the ground-floor lift. The lift-boy pressed a button. Holmes sprang up the stairs, striving to keep level with our fugitive, while I stood guard at the ground-floor entrance. Jago was to take the second lift to the top of the building so that our man should be cut off from above. Then, to my consternation, the first lift, which had been ascending, began abruptly to come down from no higher than the second floor. The man must still be in it. The result was that my two companions had overshot the mark without knowing it and I must face this maniac alone. My hand went to my pocket. Then I stopped and recalled that Holmes had my revolver.

I braced myself for the struggle, grateful that I had not forgotten all my tactics from years of playing rugger for Blackheath. As I watched and listened, the lift rumbled to ground-floor level and then, without a pause, continued to descend. We had completely misjudged our levels for it was now dropping to the lower side entrance of the hotel, coming out into Villiers Street. Our man had stranded the three of us. Yet I was still sure he had not seen us. This charade was a final precaution in order to throw off the scent anyone who might be tracking him unobserved.

The next point where he might be caught was at the entrance to the platform for the three o'clock ferry train to Folkestone. The race began once more. It was now twenty minutes to three and the three o'clock ferry train must be preparing for departure.

"Leave all this!" Holmes shouted to me, as he came back down the stairs, gesturing at the cream and raspberry decor of the grand hotel.

As we came out into the station concourse, I said, "We shall catch him at the platform for the Continental Ferry Train."

"No! That is what he will expect us to do!"

"What then?"

"Every train from here crosses the short distance across the river bridge to Waterloo Station and stops before it goes on elsewhere. He still has time to catch a suburban stopping train in five or ten minutes, alighting a few minutes later at Waterloo, while we are left guarding the platform here. Then he may take the ferry train from Waterloo— or any other train that will carry him to Folkestone or Dover. We should still be waiting here. Or at Waterloo when it is too late. We must catch him now."

"But there will be police at all the stations."

"Good God, man! From Waterloo, he can get to any station in London or the rest of the country."

"There will be police everywhere by now, surely."

He heaved a sigh, drawing breath.

"At this moment, there are perhaps half a dozen people in London who know the Queen of the Night is missing—and three of them are here. The entire Metropolitan police force is probably still guarding His Majesty's ceremonial route."

By now Jago had come up with us. Far away, at the shabbiest platform of Charing Cross Station, stood the shabbiest train, a collection of ancient carriages destined for a modest suburban itinerary that would wind slowly to New Cross, Lewisham, Blackheath, and the stations of Southeast London. Passing the ticket-collector at the barrier, I noticed a tall athletic man in a brown tweed overcoat, carrying a leather Jenner *&* Knewstub bag.

How easily a reversible coat can change from City black to the brown tweed of a racing man on his way home! Holmes took off at a sprint, Jago and I a little behind him. The iron gate was closed now and a whistle had blown. Jago shouted a command at the ticket-collector as the train began to move forward slowly across Hungerford Bridge, the brown tide of the river turning silver in the afternoon sun. Holmes hurdled the gate and raced ahead of us, but it seemed we had lost sight of our man. Then I heard a crack, rather like the detonation of a lifeboat maroon. The revolver, whatever type it might be, was a heavier gun than mine. I calculated that it had been fired at us from the forward carriage of the slowly moving suburban train.

There was no time to run back and communicate an urgent message to the railway police at Waterloo, for the train would arrive there and leave again before the signal was received. If we lost him now, Colonel Moriarty might alight at any station among the homeward crowds, drop down to the track far from anywhere, and be in London, in England, in Europe—for that matter, in Timbuctoo.

Holmes had jumped from the platform and was running along the track at the rear of the train. He was sheltered at this angle from the aim of the marksman, but then, as the wheels gathered speed, he was exposed once more to two further bullets from Colonel Moriarty's revolver. The sound of the shots was hardly audible above the iron rumbling of the wheels, but one passed close to Jago. If I heard correctly, three shots had been fired so far and three more live rounds would probably remain in the chambers of the gun. If the colonel could kill, maim, or even drive us back, he had the world before him and a racing start.

The several carriages of the train, with a fussy-sounding little engine at their head, rolled forward across the ironwork and planking of the river bridge. In the sunlight, Waterloo Bridge to our left was heavy with road traffic; Westminster Bridge to the right was still decked with red, white, and blue bunting for the royal occasion. I knew we should never find Colonel Moriarty in such crowds as besieged the platforms at Waterloo by this hour. If we failed, I thought, no one else was even looking for him.

Just then a metal signal arm on a tall gantry, which had so far been pointing earthward, rose to the horizontal with a heavy clang, and its light changed from green to red. The train slowed down with a jangling of buffers and a squeal of iron wheels on steel. It halted almost in the center of the long bridge in a long silence. Whether it was waiting for an empty platform at Waterloo or whether the signalman in his box had noticed three of us on the line, I had no idea.

With Sherlock Holmes in the lead, my revolver in his hand, we moved forward, our backs almost pressed against the coachwork to give the smallest angle of fire to our adversary. There was a shout from the engine driver.

"Get off the track!"

It was not directed at us, but at someone on the far side of the train. From ahead of us, though out of sight, came a sound of feet on gravel.

"He's making a run for it!" Jago called out.

"Not with a fully loaded travelling-bag in his hand," said Holmes quietly.

We skirted round the rear coach to take our enemy from behind. As we came out from cover, I was prepared to throw myself down to avoid a bullet from Colonel Moriarty. Yet there was no sound of gunfire or even of a voice. The summer afternoon was as quiet as if we had been on some remote beach or mountainside. No train came in either direction, and for the first time I realised that someone must have seen us and ordered all traffic across the bridge to be stopped. I now saw a most extraordinary sight. The tall figure in the brown tweed coat was standing at the parapet of the bridge, facing downstream. The black leather travelling-bag was in his hands. Or rather, he was holding it open and turning it upside down. I had a brief glimpse of shaving brushes and soap-stick, clothes-brush and razor, a pajama case and a tight wad of clothing tumbling helter-skelter into the current of the river below.

It might have been an act or surrender or probably the quickest way of discarding the bag that weighed him down. He took the gun from his pocket. As he raised it, I jumped for cover of the stationary carriages. But he had turned toward the far end of the bridge ahead of us and fired. Why had he not fired at us?

I need not have worried. He swung round almost at once and there was another crack. A bullet chipped the woodwork of the carriage door about two feet from my head. Then I saw the reason for the previous shot. From the far end of the bridge, where the track ran into Waterloo station, a dozen men were working their way slowly in our direction, keeping their heads down and ready to throw themselves flat. All but two of them wore blue serge tunics and trousers with the tall helmet and silver star marking them out as officers of the Metropolitan Police. In the lead, a man in grey sidled along the parapet. In front of him, wearing a short summer-weight overcoat and a bowler hat, walked the cautious figure of Inspector Lestrade.

It was impossible to see whether any of these men carried guns. I could see none. Whether they did or not, Colonel Moriarty would hardly have bullets enough to kill them all. In any case, he would surely be overpowered while he tried to reload. He now looked at them and then threw the black leather bag after its contents. Had the Queen of the Night gone the same way? If it had, there was an end of the evidence that might prove a charge of theft!

His way back was as securely blocked as his way forward so long as Holmes had my revolver in his hand. If I was correct, Colonel Moriarty had one live round in his gun and Holmes had all six. On both sides, the colonel's captors moved forward, hemming him in. What followed was the work of a few seconds. He jumped onto the wide iron ledge of the balustrade and looked downstream toward Waterloo Bridge. His gun was in his hand. No one could have said what use he might make of the final bullet.

Lestrade and the men behind him stopped. Much as they wanted their man, they wanted the contents of his pockets still more, if these should include the splendid Brazilian diamond and its clusters of sapphires. Sherlock Holmes paced slowly forward, the gravel of the track shifting and grating under his steps, his aquiline features calm in the presence of a glare of pure hatred from the last Moriarty. He held the borrowed revolver at his side, pointing at the ground from his right hand as he walked. Deliberately and slowly he strode into the range of the colonel, the last of those men who had planned his ritual murder in the execution shed of Newgate Gaol.

The tall figure of the colonel was motionless. He was surely judging the moment when his antagonist would be close enough for the remaining bullet to find its mark. No one else moved. Holmes had wished for a final settling of accounts and it seemed that his wish had been granted. If Moriarty should miss him, the bullet that was fired back would settle the matter. Standing against the sky, the colonel presented the clearest possible target.

Holmes was about thirty feet away when his antagonist raised his arm. My friend took one more step, the revolver still pointing at the ground, and then our hearts jumped with a sense of sickness as Moriarty fired. Holmes swayed, not as if he had been hit but as though he had heard the bullet coming and had moved out of its way. Then he took another step and moved slowly on. I do not know what the phrase "mad with terror" customarily implies, but to me it described the expression of Colonel Moriarty's features to the last detail.

The only sound now in the warm afternoon was the distant hiss of escaping steam from the boiler of the little engine and the measured sound of gravel at every stride that Sherlock Holmes took. At about ten feet he raised the gun. Moriarty spat out some curse or expletive that I could not distinguish at the distance separating us. At the same moment, the revolver in Holmes's hand jerked briefly. Colonel Moriarty went forward at full length, toppling and then cartwheeling through the air into the current below.

Even so, I could not tell whether the last of Sherlock Holmes's would-be executioners fell with a bullet in his brain or threw himself to his death in defiance of those who had cornered him at last, casting the Queen of the Night into the oblivion of the deep river mud. His body was never found—or rather, if it was found, it was never identified. Among the poor wretches found drowned in the following weeks, two or three had been terribly mutilated by the steel paddles of passing river steamers or other accidents. Some had been carried far down the broad estuary and been given to the sea. I choose to believe that the colonel was one of them.

Even after that, fate had been crueller to him than any contrivance of our own. While Holmes faced this final duel, two of Jago's men had arrested Colonel Lemonnier in his cabman's cape as he left Charing

Cross. Lemonnier protested his innocence of any crime, beyond having changed places at the Mansion House lunch at the request of an acquaintance he had known for only a few days. He had never heard of the Queen of the Night, and offered no resistance. In his pocket, however, lay two small packages containing the two portions of the famous jewel, the unclipped diamond and the sapphire clusters. By what means he had robbed Colonel Moriarty of these in the final exchange of the traveling bag was never revealed. Lemonnier insisted that the colonel had given him the packages as a parting gift and that he understood them to be mere paste, intended as a *pourboire* for an obliging street girl in Piccadilly.

On the evening of that memorable day, Inspector Lestrade was our guest in the Baker Street sitting-room.

"You see, Mr. Holmes?" he said genially. "We're always there when we're needed. Why, now, if I hadn't used a bit of policeman's plain common sense, we wouldn't have had that bridge cordoned off as it was. And in that case, gentlemen, I needn't remind you that the late Colonel Moriarty would have reached Waterloo Station on the far bank of the river. Once he was there, he might have been on a train to anywhere in a few minutes. By now—who knows?—he might have been sitting in Paris, admiring his trinket—as Lemonnier insists it is."

Holmes muttered something but kept his peace.

Lestrade leant forward in his chair.

"And you'll both recall that case, gentlemen, when you were both walking through the park a little while back and happened to see a man get his head cut off by a galloping soldier. Well, do you know what?"

"I have not the least idea what, Lestrade, but you are no doubt about to enlighten us. You were not fortunate enough to identify the assassin, I suppose?""

The inspector sipped his whisky and water, then leant forward again.

"No, Mr. Holmes. I was fortunate enough to identify the owner of the head, despite his efforts to remain anonymous by having nothing in his pockets."

"My felicitations," Holmes closed his eyes. "Pray continue."

"Alker was his name. A former petty officer of the Royal Navy provos, identified almost by chance during a visit to the pathological laboratory where the head rests in a jar of formaldehyde. On several melancholy but necessary occasions of overseas service, the records tell us, Alker acted as a military and even a civil hangman. What do you say to that, now?"

"At least, Lestrade, you may be certain that he was not murdered in revenge by someone he had hanged. Beyond that, I do not think I can assist you."

Lestrade puffed himself up a little at our lack of appreciation.

"I may say that I have sent a few criminals to the gallows," he said portentously, "but I can't say I've ever met a hangman at work."

"No," said Holmes dryly. "No more have I. With or without his head."

NOTES

p. 33 E. Harris Ruddock, *The Homoeopathic Vade Mecum*, Roericke & Tafel, 1889, discusses the treatment of Egyptian ophthalmia at page 373.

p. 62 "The Resolution of Enclitic δε" was a problem in classical Greek grammar to which the subject of Robert Browning's poem "The Grammarian's Funeral," like Mycroft Holmes, had devoted his energies.

p. 63 "The Five Orange Pips" appeared in *The Strand Magazine* for November 1893.

p. 73 Examples of those who rivaled Sherlock Holmes in building fugues upon popular themes and nursery rhymes include Alec Templeton in the Benny Goodman number "Mr. Bach Goes to Town" and Sidney M. Lawton, Music Master of Queen's College, Taunton, England, in his ingenious fugue upon "Twinkle, Twinkle, Little Star."

p. 74 "The Red-Headed League" appeared in *The Strand Magazine* for August 1891.

p. 81 The phenomenon of the body remaining upright after decapitation was witnessed by hundreds of onlookers when Captain Nolan remained upright in the saddle for some time after his head was taken off by a Russian shell, before the ill-fated "Charge of the Light Brigade" at Balaclava on 25 October 1854.

p. 84 "*Homo sum, humani nihil a me alienum puto.*" Sherlock Holmes was, as always, correct when he ascribed this to the Roman playwright Terence in *Heauton Timorumenos* I, i, 25.

p. 86 "The Naval Treaty" appeared in *The Strand Magazine* for October and November 1893.

p. 86 Nelson's attack on the "armed neutrality" of Copenhagen, on 2 April 1801, was the occasion on which he put his telescope to his blind eye and refused his commanding officer's signal to withdraw, saying to his subordinate, "You know, Foley, I have only one eye—I have a right to be blind sometimes. . . . I really do not see the signal."

p. 90 The case of Irene Adler was the first story in *The Adventures of Sherlock Holmes*, "A Scandal in Bohemia," which originally appeared in *The Strand Magazine* for July 1891. "The Bruce-Partington Submarine Plans" appeared in the same magazine for December 1908.

p. 128 "Cold fowl and cigars, Pickled onions in jars" was the midnight feast offered by a London tavern known as the Magpie and Stump. The poet recalled by Watson is by R. H. Barham, whose verses, "The Execution: A Sporting Anecdote," appeared in *The Ingoldsby Legends* (1840).

p. 142 By the Peace of Vienna in 1864, after the British and French failure to support Denmark against Prussia, Christian IX renounced his claim to Schleswig and Holstein, first occupied and then annexed by the Prussians.

p. 202 "*Fiat justitia ruat coelum*" was pronounced by William Murray, 1st Earl Mansfield (1705–93), Chief Justice of the King's Bench, in overturning the sentence imposed on John Wilkes in 1768 for publishing an antigovernment newspaper. Four years later, in a momentous judgment, Mansfield freed a slave, James Somersett, who had set foot on English soil during his master's visit to London. "Every man who comes to England is entitled to the protection of the English law, whatever oppression he may heretofore have suffered, and whatever may be the colour of his skin, whether it is black or whether it is white."

p. 228 In his comment on murder by chloroform, Holmes is evidently thinking of Carl Liman's 1876 edition of *Practishes Handbuch der gerichtlichen Medicin* by Johann Ludwig Casper (1796-1864), a pioneer in forensic medicine.

p. 231 John Nevil Maskelyne (1839–1917), born in Cheltenham, England. A stage conjurer at sixteen, he was lessee of St. George's Hall, London, and exposed the stage magic of the Davenport Brothers' so-called Cabinet and Dark Seance. He appeared at the Egyptian Hall, Piccadilly, 1873–1904. His techniques were employed to great effect in the art of camouflage during both world wars.

p. 236 Propter's Nicodemus Pills were made famous by Edward Lear in his poem for children, "Incidents in the Life of My Uncle Arly."

> *Like the Ancient Medes and Persians.*
> *Always by his own exertions*
> *He subsisted on those hills;—*
> *Whiles,—by teaching children spelling,—*
> *Or at times by merely yelling,—*
> *Or at intervals by selling*
> *"Propter's Nicodemus Pills."*

p. 264 "The Final Problem" appeared in *The Strand Magazine* for December 1893.

p. 265 Sir Francis Dashwood (1708–81), politician and rake, Chancellor of the Exchequer and Postmaster General. As organizer of the Hellfire Club from 1755, he was reputed to have staged orgies with other "monks," including John Wilkes and the poet Charles Churchill, first among the pastoral ruins of Medmenham Abbey on the bank of the Thames and then nearby in caves on the estate of his fine Palladian mansion at West Wycombe.

p. 283 "The Adventure of the Blue Carbuncle" appeared in *The Strand Magazine* for January 1892.

JAICO PUBLISHING HOUSE

Elevate Your Life. Transform Your World.

ESTABLISHED IN 1946, Jaico Publishing House is home to world-transforming authors such as Sri Sri Paramahansa Yogananda, Osho, The Dalai Lama, Sri Sri Ravi Shankar, Sadhguru, Robin Sharma, Deepak Chopra, Jack Canfield, Eknath Easwaran, Devdutt Pattanaik, Khushwant Singh, John Maxwell, Brian Tracy and Stephen Hawking.

Our late founder Mr. Jaman Shah first established Jaico as a book distribution company. Sensing that independence was around the corner, he aptly named his company Jaico ('Jai' means victory in Hindi). In order to service the significant demand for affordable books in a developing nation, Mr. Shah initiated Jaico's own publications. Jaico was India's first publisher of paperback books in the English language.

While self-help, religion and philosophy, mind/body/spirit, and business titles form the cornerstone of our non-fiction list, we publish an exciting range of travel, current affairs, biography, and popular science books as well. Our renewed focus on popular fiction is evident in our new titles by a host of fresh young talent from India and abroad. Jaico's recently established Translations Division translates selected English content into nine regional languages.

In addition to being a publisher and distributor of its own titles, Jaico is a major national distributor of books of leading international and Indian publishers. With its headquarters in Mumbai, Jaico has branches and sales offices in Ahmedabad, Bangalore, Bhopal, Chennai, Delhi, Hyderabad, Kolkata and Lucknow.

SINCE 1946